Forget Me Knots

Owen Brookes

Forget Me Knots

Henry Holt and Company / New York

Published by Henry Holt and Company, Inc.,
521 Fifth Avenue, New York, New York 10175.
Published simultaneously in Canada.

Library of Congress Cataloging in Publication Data
Brookes, Owen.
Forget me knots.
I. Title.
PR6052.R5815F67   1986   823'.914   85-27356
ISBN: 0-03-002702-0

First Edition
Designed by Susan Hood
Printed in the United States of America
1 3 5 7 9 10 8 6 4 2

ISBN 0-03-002702-0

For Bobbi Mark,
my former editor, with gratitude

Forget Me Knots

One

The aptly and, Margaret thought, charmingly named Elinor Tidy collected the mail each working morning from the wire basket fixed to the inside of the white-painted front door and carried it through to the small breakfast room at the back of the house. This was a self-imposed task, one that had begun with her tenure as housekeeper five years ago when, singlehandedly, she had rescued Margaret Wells from the impending domestic chaos left by a string of transient au pairs and unsuitable married couples. Before taking the letters through, Miss Tidy sorted them into two piles, slipping the regular weekly missives from her widowed sister-in-law and a lifelong friend in Clacton-on-Sea into the capacious pocket of one of her many cheerful aprons. She sorted the letters not because she was curious about the mail of others, but to save Mrs. Wells the trouble of having to hand over her own scant but regular post.

The sun streamed through the conservatory-like south wall of the breakfast room, really an extension of the large kitchen/dining room, which gave onto the small walled garden. Margaret Wells glanced up from the arts page of the *Times,* smiled, and took the slim bundle of envelopes from Miss Tidy.

"Shall I take these up to . . . Julie, or leave them here?" she asked, tapping three other envelopes—two of which were conspicuously large, white, and square—against the pine table. The hesitation in

1

her voice indicated that it still required conscious effort not to preface Julie's name with the formal "Miss" her instinct and training dictated. It had taken months to break her, at least superficially, of this habit, and that of calling Margaret "ma'am."

"No. I'll take them up in a moment, Elinor, thank you," Margaret said, setting two bills aside. She anchored a long blue envelope to the table with her awkward left arm and tore it open with her right hand. "You know she's not working today?" Margaret added as an afterthought, struggling to get the letter from the mutilated envelope. She knew that Miss Tidy—mentally the housekeeper remained "Miss Tidy" to her, even though, in the interests of democracy, she was addressed as Elinor—itched to help her and knew better. Margaret glanced at the contents of the letter, then at her watch. "God, is that the time? I must go." She gulped down the last of her coffee while Miss Tidy frowned at the blasphemous exclamation. She had spent her adult life in the service of a rector, first in her native East Anglia and then in Crawley, where the rector had died suddenly, leaving Miss Tidy homeless and without employment. "I'm sorry," Margaret said. "I do try to remember." She knew that the taking of the Lord's name in vain was offensive to Miss Tidy, and she tried to curb her natural tongue, with little success. She sometimes feared that this bad habit alone might drive Miss Tidy from the house, for in every other respect they suited each other to perfection.

"Shall you be in to dinner?" the housekeeper asked, not ignoring the apology but accepting it as her own and God's due.

"Yes. Just me. A salad will do."

"You'll need more than that," Miss Tidy announced firmly. "I'll grill you a nice chop with some of them sautéed potatoes you like so much." She pronounced the word "sortied," leaning to clear away Margaret's frugal breakfast dishes as she did so.

"Which I like too much," Margaret replied, making for the door, "to the detriment of my figure."

"Go on with you," Miss Tidy responded, then continued to the empty room, "You'd be as thin as a lath if you had your own way." In fact Margaret Wells's figure remained trim and firm, though it was true that she had gained a little weight since Miss Tidy had joined the household. Quite tall and certainly large-boned, Margaret looked better if those bones were well covered; she was intended to be a rounded woman, not an angular one. Dressed that morning in a plain camel sweater over an ankle-length rust tweed skirt that fell in soft folds around her booted legs, she looked fit and well and handsome. Only her left arm, which hung stiff and mostly immobile at her side, marred the pleasing symmetry and energy of her appearance. Margaret no longer thought about the arm, though she was frequently reminded of it by the reactions of other people.

Certainly nothing was further from her thoughts that morning as she went up to the second floor of the tall, narrow house. In fact her mind already ran, as it so often did, on the day's work ahead. It was an important day for her, or could be. Menuhin had succeeded, where many others had failed, in persuading the sensational new young virtuoso violinist, Igo Japp, to make his London debut, and Margaret, using all her charm, leavened with a little judicious blackmail, had secured a meeting with him before he was to fly back to East Germany. Thus far Japp had refused to sign a recording contract; Margaret hoped to change that, if only for a one- or two-record deal.

She tapped perfunctorily at her daughter's bedroom door and opened it at once. The moment she stepped into the room, all thoughts of work dropped from her so completely that she had to pause and mentally catch her breath. It was a lovely room. It and its occupant always caused Margaret to pause and soften. It was still in many ways a little girl's room, a soft and feminine bower. Margaret knew that if she voiced such thoughts, she would leave herself open to a charge of possessiveness, of seeking to keep her daughter in a childhood state. Margaret trod lightly across the smoke-blue carpet and stood looking down at her daughter as she slept on her back, one arm flung up beside her head. She looked with a mixture of wonder and deep pleasure at this young woman, finding it difficult to believe that she had brought her into the world. In a strange way, Margaret felt that she was reunited with her daughter every time she saw her. How she enjoyed looking at her! In sleep her face lost some of its piquancy, which was currently accentuated by having her hair cut in a neat cap and clipped to a false widow's peak on her forehead. The sun caught the red highlights the hairdresser had put in its natural brown, dazzled on its healthy sheen.

"Julie," Margaret whispered, as though loath to disturb her, then repeated her name again, louder. "Wake up, darling."

Julie stirred and opened her eyes, which, though basically hazel like her mother's, lacked the many gold flecks that, in the right light and circumstances, made Margaret's seem catlike. Julie smiled and stretched. "Good morning."

Margaret bent and kissed her daughter's brow. Julie encircled her neck with her arms, cuddling her.

"Oh, it's bliss not to have to go to work," she said. "Poor you."

"I enjoy it," Margaret said, straightening up. "Mail for you."

She was still a child, Margaret thought as she watched pleasure flood into and enliven her daughter's sleepy face. She almost bounced upright in the bed, her small hands reaching greedily for the three envelopes, which she examined eagerly.

"I must rush," Margaret said, the thought of Japp intruding and nagging. "Have a nice day. What time is Barry collecting you?"

"Seven," she answered automatically, turning the envelopes in her fingers. "You know what today is, don't you? Do you think these are Valentines?" she asked, wide-eyed, almost anxious for reassurance.

"Darling, of course they are. Even I can recognize Barry's writing. Look, I'll be back in time to see you off and inspect the new dress, okay?"

"I don't recognize this one," Julie said, holding an envelope away from her, inspecting it cautiously.

"A secret admirer, no doubt," Margaret said, laughing. "So don't be too quick to tell Barry about it. 'Bye, darling."

"Oh, 'bye, Ma. And good luck with Igo . . ." she called, but Margaret had already gone, busy as ever. Julie leaned back against her pillow, drew up her knees, and contentedly arranged the envelopes side by side. A letter from her oldest and best school-friend, Sybil, and the expected, longed-for card from Barry—she wondered if he had opened hers yet and if he liked it—and the unrecognized third, with its clumsy block letters. She would save that till last, she decided, because there was something almost dangerously exciting about a complete surprise.

Sybil's letter was long and chatty, almost completely concerned with riding and the progress of her new mare, Saucy. Only at the close did she ask for news of Julie's "romance with the dishy Barry." Which reminded her of the Valentine. Tossing the letter aside so that its lined blue pages fluttered separately to the floor, she carefully unsealed the second envelope, drew out a square card that, in the soft tones of a Victorian reproduction, showed roses and cupids entwined around two dusky pink hearts. Inside he had written, *Marry me and be my love XXX.* She hugged it to her, then quickly held it away from her again for fear of crushing or creasing it. It was something to be treasured forever, gloated over, shown to her grandchildren when she was old, old. . . . Smiling, she set it carefully on the nightstand beside her bed and stared at it contentedly. It was the best, the most beautiful card she had ever received.

Although she loved Barry—loved him deeply—the flattery of receiving a second, unexpected Valentine was not lost on her. Whoever had sent it, it was thrilling and fun. Eagerly she opened the coarse, off-white envelope and exposed a cheap, gaudy card. There was a lot of shiny gilt lettering enjoining fidelity and true love forever, forget-me-nots and love-in-a-mist held together with a raised and bumpy golden heart. The sort of card she thought she would have chosen when a child, and giggled over for hours with Sybil before deciding to whom she would send it.

LOVE
EVER
JO-JO

It did not make sense. It was a joke. You weren't supposed to sign a Valentine anyway. It spoiled the mystery. Her eyes filled with sudden, frightened tears. She felt her whole body turn cold, as though the door and window had suddenly burst open to admit a ferocious Siberian wind. Even the sunlight seemed dimmer, as though the day were already dying, spoiled.

Of course it was a joke.

But nobody knew, nobody except dear old Great-Gran, and she was dead, long dead. Julie examined the card again. Perhaps her eyes had played a trick on her, she had imagined . . .

In a sloping pattern, the letters linked unevenly, clumsily, the message remained unchanged.

Love Ever Jo-Jo.

Jo-Jo?

"No," she said in a small whisper. "No, it's not, not . . ."

Then, obeying some instinct she did not understand or want to examine, she jumped out of bed, opened the nearest drawer, and thrust the card, creasing it badly, under a pile of sweaters. She slammed the drawer shut and leaned for a moment against the chest of drawers, her breathing labored, her lungs feeling clogged and tight. A thought occurred to her and she whirled back to the bed, not noticing that the brusqueness of her movements made a little wind that caused Barry's card to fall over and lie facedown on the nightstand, forgotten. From the rumpled bedclothes she snatched up the envelope, held it tight between her trembling, clenched hands. There was neither stamp nor postmark. Therefore, she thought, letting her arms drop, it must have been delivered by hand.

Miss Tidy was adamant as only Miss Tidy could be. She had collected that envelope from the box along with the rest, and if Julie thought she had either the time or the inclination to stand and check on everyone who came to the front door, then she had another think coming.

"I'm sorry," Julie said. "I just thought you might have—"

"It seems to me a certain young lady standing not a mile away from me is making altogether too much fuss about a soppy Valentine anyway. 'Words is cheap,' the Rector—God rest his soul—always used to say, 'and bought words is cheaper.' You think about it. Just look at you, all pale and shaky, like you were sickening for something. You go and put your dressing gown on and I'll get your breakfast. That sun's treacherous," she said, bustling stiffly to the other end of the kitchen. "That's not a real sun. It's got no warmth in it."

The woman's reaction forced a kind of calm on Julie. To upset Miss Tidy was a cardinal sin in her mother's book and, worse, she feared alerting the housekeeper to the depth of her shock and sneaking alarm. She made herself smile and apologize again.

"Just some toast, Elli," she said, deliberately using the pet name that usually acted like balm on Miss Tidy's ruffled dignity. "And I'll get dressed first. I've got so many things to do."

"You'll need more than toast if you're going out," Miss Tidy announced over her shoulder. "Breakfast is the most important meal of the day . . ."

. . . *as the Rector—God bless him—always used to say,* Julie finished, in her head. The very familiarity of Elinor Tidy's reactions and speech *was* calming. She felt better, she even felt a little bit silly as she went back upstairs and into the bathroom. It was only a joke, not a very pleasant one, certainly not funny, but there was nothing intrinsically alarming about it. It had just taken her by surprise, for a moment.

As she brushed her teeth and washed her face, Julie tried to recall anyone to whom she might have mentioned Jo-Jo. Great-Gran, of course. All the many nannies who had stalked her childhood. None of them had stayed in touch. None of them had liked her enough to want to tease her now that she was grown up. Yet she felt there was a certain inevitability about the card, as though she had always been expecting it, or fearing it. She told herself this was nonsense. The only way to deal with it was to ignore it, pretend it had never arrived. That way it might go away, *he* might. . . . She caught sudden sight of herself in the mirror over the washbasin. She must not go to pieces. If she ignored it, never breathed a word to anyone, then it would be all right. It would be safe again. This thought prompted her to hurry back into her bedroom and pick up the white telephone. She dialed Barry's number, listened to it ring, her smile fading. He must have left for work already, and she did not like to ring him at the office—or, rather, Barry preferred her not to ring him at the office. Personal calls, especially those from what his bosses and colleagues apparently referred to as "females," were frowned upon. Julie could not imagine Barry's office. Secretly she thought it must be incredibly boring, although she always tried to show an intelligent interest when Barry talked about the financial muddle or wizardry of one or another of the firm's clients. What mattered was that he liked being an accountant, was brilliant at it, and was determined to become a partner by the time he was thirty-five. He would be rich and successful and that would make them both very happy, would enable them to have the home and life-style and children they wanted.

Immersed in these vague and pleasant fantasies, Julie dressed, choosing a simple woolen shift that unzipped at the front; it would be easy to remove when she wanted to try on various dresses before she found the special one. Originally, Barry had wanted to go to some Valentine's Day party given by a friend of his, but Julie had persuaded him to settle for a private, romantic dinner *a deux*. She wanted him all to herself on this most romantic of nights. She wanted him all to herself when she told him that she had almost definitely made up her mind to settle for a June wedding. She would tell him that night. She really would. And he would be so pleased.

Sometimes Julie wished they could somehow, magically, just be transported to the married state, without all the fuss and palaver. All the decisions about clothes and guests and food and flowers daunted her. And really, Ma didn't have the time, and of course Barry wanted everything done properly, a big splash when sometimes Julie found the prospect of a secret Registry Office ceremony almost more romantic. Ma said Julie was perfectly capable of organizing her own wedding, that she would do it better than her mother ever could. It was true, Julie admitted, she was good at things like that. Lately she'd organized all of Ma's little dinner parties and they'd been a great—

"Julie? Your eggs are on the table, so if you don't want them stone cold . . ."

"Coming, Elli."

Suddenly she was *very* hungry.

Margaret Wells got out of the extravagant cab she had taken in part-celebration and stood for a quiet moment or two, looking around her. The deceptive sun had set more than an hour ago, but there was still a red glow in the sky, and by this and the light from the elegant, old-fashioned street lamps, Margaret was able to inspect Broom Square. She had hesitated a long time before buying the house because of its location and setting. The house itself was perfect for her needs and full of so many fine and unexpected features that she had known even when it was a dilapidated semi-slum that she could bring it back to beautiful life. But it was well south of the river and in a very unfashionable and therefore not very accessible part of London: Even cabdrivers demanded complicated instructions on how to get there. As she stood looking around her, Margaret felt, as she always did, that she had discovered a unique haven of peace. There was no through traffic, only the muffled roar of the distant main road, and even airplanes passed well to the south and west of them. The square, her house, and her family consoled her and took the edge off her slight disappointment at the compromised success of her day.

Igo Japp hadn't said yes and he hadn't said no. He was definitely interested. His agent kept reassuring Margaret that Japp liked her, but she had a gnawing sense that the agent, whom she liked and respected, was powerless to influence the violinist, who, she felt increasingly sure, was exploiting the power of his success. No matter how genuine his reservations about recordings and commitment, there was a part of young Mr. Japp, Margaret was prepared to bet, that enjoyed playing hard-to-get. The upshot was that Margaret had to fly to Düsseldorf in three weeks, a prospect she did not anticipate with pleasure, to hear Japp play Sibelius. And they would talk further. In the meantime Japp would think, would consider, would consult the *I Ching*. But, as his agent pointed out, no other recording company had gotten as close as KLB, and that was entirely due to Margaret's tact and charm. Fortunately her colleagues had endorsed the agent's view and called for a semi-celebration: sparkling Italian wine and mushroom pizza instead of champagne and smoked salmon.

Margaret put the prospect of Düsseldorf behind her as she mounted the steps and let herself into the warm and brightly lit house. She never wore her heavy fob watch on wool, and so her first act was to look at the time on the grandmother clock—which had, in fact, belonged to her grandmother—in the hall. She saw that she had a scant half hour before Barry Irving was due to collect her daughter, and she could rely on that. Barry was never late. Even traffic jams seemed powerless to delay him. She called out to Miss Tidy, checked that all was well, and ran up to the second floor. This time she did not knock and enter Julie's room, but asked if she could come in.

"Not yet. I want to surprise you," Julie shouted back. Margaret smiled.

"I take it you found something suitable, then?" she said, meaning the new dress.

"Wait and see. Are you going to have a bath?"

"Later. I'll be in the sitting room when you're ready."

Margaret walked through into her own north-facing bedroom, shrugged her bag from her shoulder with an awkward movement of her left arm, and took off her camel's-hair coat. Miss Tidy had already pulled the long brocade curtains, shutting out the undeniably chilly night. Spring was still reluctant, uncertain. Margaret touched switches, creating a warm glow of light. She inspected her light makeup, added a little more pale lipstick, ran the brush through her thick, loose, honey-colored hair, and decided that she would do. After all, Barry would only stay ten minutes, long enough to have one drink, be polite. Then she would bathe, get into her pajamas, and have a thoroughly lazy evening, trying to dream up some new angle with which to lure Mr. Japp, she reminded herself, pulling a face.

The long sitting room took up the whole of the first floor. It was painted in a soft dull blue, details picked out in a warm cream. Julie's choice and idea. There were fresh spring flowers in two plain vases, courtesy of Barry Irving, she had no doubt. She poured herself a neat whiskey, one-handed, added ice cubes, and carried it, humming absently, over to her favorite wing-back chair. It was covered in old rose velvet and the nap of the material was threadbare in places, but Margaret had refused to have it re-covered. It was her chair and it fitted her. Besides, she had argued with Julie, who had fought with all the ruthlessness of the tyro interior decorator, a room needed something worn and warm and a little shabby to prevent it from looking like a furniture display or a cold magazine photograph. She sat in the chair gratefully and looked at the second delivery of mail, which Elinor Tidy had placed on the little circular table beside her.

Putting down her drink, Margaret sifted through the envelopes without lifting them from the table. Circulars and bills. No Valentines for her. She sipped her drink, closed her eyes.

"Well?"

Julie stood shyly just inside the door, her head bowed slightly. The dress was cut low, with vast puffed sleeves and a full flowing skirt. It was a sort of dark ruby-maroon watered taffeta, or some modern simulation. Against it her skin looked very pale, and Margaret, who knew her daughter almost too well, saw tension and nervousness behind her bright smile.

"It's gorgeous, darling. You look absolutely wonderful."

Julie twirled around, held out the full skirt as though preparing to make a neat, low curtsy.

"You really think so?"

"You know so. Come here."

The material of the dress rustled softly as she moved across the room and bent to kiss Margaret's offered cheek.

10

"It was very expensive," she confessed.

"I don't doubt it," Margaret answered dryly.

"But it will do for lots of things. Anna's party and—"

"It's all right. Stand back. Let me see."

With the rich-looking dress, Julie wore plain black shoes, a black velvet band around her throat. The only jewelry was her charm bracelet, a memento of her childhood, and the milky moonstone ring Barry had given her.

"Nervous?" Margaret asked.

"No. Well, maybe, a bit."

"Darling . . ." Julie's face tightened. She knew that tone of voice. Margaret pursed her lips. "I was only going to say don't let Barry rush you into anything. You do what *you* want, please?"

"I know. But it's so silly. I want to marry him. I really do. But I just can't . . . oh, I don't know. I just don't want everything to be final."

"And that's fine," Margaret said. "You've got time, bags of it. There's no need to rush. Barry loves you. Barry will wait."

"He's going to want to announce the engagement at the very least," Julie said, sounding thoroughly miserable.

"Not much point, is there, without a wedding date?" Margaret said, trying to sound noncommittal. She really didn't want to influence Julie against the marriage, but she was unable to stand by and let Barry Irving do all the persuading.

"Well, that's what I think, but Barry says . . . I mean he'll just say let's go ahead and fix the date, then." She paused, walked toward a settee, then turned back to her mother's chair. "I thought June, maybe."

"Whenever you want, darling."

"You don't think that's too soon, to make all the arrangements and everything?"

"Not if that's what you really want."

"I think I do, but—"

"Julie, listen to me. I can only say it again. Take your time. Wait until the idea feels comfortable. There's a lot at stake here. Don't spoil it by being rushed."

"Perhaps," Julie said, trying hard to lighten the tone, "he'll be so stunned by the dress he won't think to mention it."

"Perhaps," Margaret agreed quietly.

11

"Aren't they lovely?" Julie asked, gesturing toward the two vases of flowers.

Margaret nodded. Indeed they were. Barry had good taste and an apparently easy instinct for the right gesture.

"And the most gorgeous card," Julie hurried on. "I must show it to you." She started toward the door.

"What about the other one? Who's your secret admirer?"

Julie stopped. Her shoulders seemed to stiffen and then slump a little. Slowly she turned back into the room, avoiding her mother's eyes.

"I'll show it to you later on," she said. There was a tense and almost desperate attempt at brightness as she went on, "It's nearly seven and I don't want Barry to see me gloating over it. That would never do, would it?"

Margaret stood up. Although she knew it was probably nothing serious, she felt uneasy.

"Julie, what's wrong? What's bothering you?"

"Nothing. I'm a bit overexcited."

"You're as white as a sheet," Margaret told her firmly.

"It's just nerves, Ma. Honestly." She made herself look at her mother, willing her, if not to believe her, at least to let it drop. Margaret considered this. "Please, Ma. Don't go on now."

"All right. As long as you . . ." She closed her mouth firmly, and moved away to freshen her drink.

In the excitement of finding and buying the dress, Jo-Jo's card had been pushed far to the back of her mind. Now, with it brought back to her full consciousness by her mother's light, teasing inquiry, she felt it like an ominous presence, a floor above her, in her drawer. She wished she had thrown it away. She would. She went quickly to the door.

"Where are you going?" Margaret asked anxiously.

The front doorbell sounded, one long sharp ring.

"That'll be Barry," Julie said quickly. "I'll go and bring him up."

"Yes," Margaret said quietly. But something was definitely wrong, something more than indecision, something she did not understand. And what she did not understand frightened her, especially where her daughter was concerned.

Barry Irving was twenty-seven, nine years older than Julie, and already well established in his career with a large and respected firm of City accountants. His career was progressing according to the Plan he had drawn up when he was almost sixteen, and the next steps and maneuvers already had, in his mind at least, the logic of inevitability. The Plan included many other aspects of his life as well. For example, he had already passed his Advanced Driving Test and hoped one day to start racing in a semiprofessional way. Most important of all, he had found the girl who was going to be his wife.

He first met Julie Wells when she was seventeen, and immediately promoted her to the top of his list of possible future Mrs. Irvings. Three months later he decided that she definitely fitted the bill and set about deflowering her, believing that sex was important and best sorted out before the knot was tied. Only one random element entered his calculations and almost succeeded in throwing them out of balance. He fell in love with Julie Wells, becoming privately and temporarily a modern approximation of the lovesick swains of English poetry whom he had always despised and dismissed as unrealistic. He learned vulnerability, and found himself, as Julie avoided any definite, public commitment to him, considering compromises.

At the height of this emotional turmoil, which bewildered and excited him in roughly equal measure, he tore up the Plan, which he had regularly updated and kept neatly written down. Almost immediately, though she was ignorant of both the Plan's existence and its destruction, Julie had agreed that on her eighteenth birthday they would become privately engaged. It had seemed an omen to Barry Irving, who vowed to be more flexible henceforth, and to make his first domestic consideration the creation and maintenance of Julie's happiness.

To this end he had willingly passed up the invitation to Sophy Leonard's Valentine fancy-dress party, even though he might have made several useful contacts there, and had booked a discreet table in the loggia of Julie's favorite restaurant, Chez Jacquot. The engagement, the verbal promise, and the indisputable fact of his ring on her small finger, had done much to restore Barry's confidence in himself and in the controllable direction of his life.

He was now impatient, and felt that he had a right to insist that Julie permit him to insert the necessary announcements in the *Times* and the *Daily Telegraph*, and that she choose the church and name the day. He had already picked out his best man, Reggie Collis, and it was of him that he spoke to Julie as Monsieur Bernard, the headwaiter, conducted them to their candlelit table with its pink tablecloth.

The loggia was at the back of the restaurant, a restored, wrought-iron Victorian conservatory that, in summer, opened onto a riverside terrace. Only six tables were accommodated there, and these were usually reserved for very special, regular customers. A comparatively young but pleasantly gnarled vine grew there, snaking across the roof. On this night, pots of pink and white camellias stood in full bloom about the tiled floor. Julie thought it the most romantic place in the world, and her face—which Barry, like her mother, had noticed was unusually pale beneath her makeup—lit up with pleasure as Monsieur Bernard held her golden wicker chair and she saw, as a centerpiece on the pink table, a shallow heart-shaped dish filled with the velvety heads of pansies, white and purple and deep ruby.

"Oh, they're absolutely beautiful, Bernard," she said, smiling up at him. "Thank you so much."

"Compliments of Monsieur Jacquot," Bernard said, bowing slightly and moving the branched white candelabra a centimeter or two to the left.

"Tell Monsieur Jacquot we are most grateful," Barry said, "and very touched."

Monsieur Bernard nodded and withdrew.

"I was telling you about Reggie Collis," Barry said, resuming the conversation.

Julie had no objections to Reggie Collis as best man. But her instinctive reluctance to discuss the almost hypothetical wedding, to be pinned down, made her anxious to change the subject.

"It's all right," Barry said quickly, interrupting her and reaching across the table to lay a gentle, warm hand over her surprisingly chilly and damp one. "I'm not going to nag you about that. At least not yet," he admitted with a smile that was entirely charming and gave his strong, handsome features a softer, more boyish cast. "I wanted to tell you that I'm thinking of going into business with him."

"But I thought—"

"Oh, not immediately," he said. "Certainly not until we're married." Self-consciously, he allowed a little of his native Yorkshire accent to creep into his voice on the phrase, to isolate it. Julie quickly withdrew her hand and looked down. "That's why I wanted to ask you what you thought of the idea."

"Well, I don't know. I don't really understand. I thought you were set on a partnership at Rowson's."

"Well, so I was—still am, perhaps—but I never actually ruled out the possibility of setting up on my own."

"But isn't that risky?"

"Clever girl." Barry smiled. "Without the right backing, certainly. But the risk is spread if you've got a good, reliable partner. That's the crux of the matter. And I think Reggie would be ideal."

"You get on well with him, I know."

"Right. The point is"—he lowered his voice as though he were revealing a confidence—"it looks as though Reggie could get the right sort of backing. He's got an uncle in merchant banking who's very fond of him. And with my contacts . . ."

"It sounds exciting," Julie said, picking up the hint from his tone of voice and his almost glowing eyes.

"It is. It is. Of course, we're not going to rush into anything. It's just an idea at the moment, which is why I thought, if you wouldn't mind too much . . . well, the thing is, Reggie's got a skiing holiday booked, only a week, in Val-d'Isère. I thought I might go with him so we can really chew it over. What do you think?"

Julie felt cold suddenly, and could not suppress a shiver. It was as though the very idea of Barry going away—away from her—made her cold. This thought or feeling floated into her mind and caused a physical reaction that she saw at once conflicted oddly with her reluctance to agree to the wedding arrangements, to tie herself to him properly.

"No, of course I don't . . . It sounds very sensible. When would you be going?"

"Sometime in March. Darling, are you really all right?"

"Yes, perfectly."

The sudden chill vanished as quickly as it had come.

"Just the thought of all that snow made me shiver," she said quickly, taking his hand. "Of course you must go. Make a proper plan. Discuss it thoroughly. After all . . ." she began, almost coquettishly, then stopped, flushing as the waiter approached and asked if they were ready to order. Barry sent him away.

"I hope," he said, leaning toward her, "you were going to say that after all, your future is at stake, too."

"I was," Julie said, fiddling with her menu. "Something like that, anyway."

"Then does that mean—?"

"Oh, let's order first. Do you think they've got that lovely crab thing I had last time? I can't find it."

Monsieur Bernard moved the candelabra a little closer to the center of the table and placed the heart-shaped flower arrangement between them after he had personally served coffee and Barry's snifter of Armagnac.

The meal had been delicious, the wine relaxing, and Barry had made her laugh a lot. Julie, sipping her coffee, felt capable of anything, warm and safe and happy.

"That dress really is stunning," Barry said, lifting his glass and openly admiring her.

"It cost the earth."

"You'll be a very expensive wife, then," he said, challenging her.

"I suppose I will."

"Suppose which? That you'll be expensive or—"

"Your wife. You know I will. Only I don't . . ." Oh, God, she thought, this is spoiling everything. She felt that chill again, could have sworn that a cold breath moved over her bare back.

"It's all right," Barry said, putting his hand out toward her. "I only meant to . . ."

Something happened then, something that Julie could neither comprehend nor control. It was as if time slipped into another gear or stopped altogether. She heard Barry's voice fade as though it were coming through amplifiers and loudspeakers and someone had slowly turned the volume down. There was a rushing sound in her ears, as of wind or static—wind in tall, leafy trees. She reached out her hand to his, but her eyes were distracted by the three leaping flames of the candles. They flickered, shot up, and then, as though bent by a steady, impossibly even breath, bent and grew toward Barry's extended wrist. She watched, fascinated, as the harmless, pretty flames grew, became liquid, almost solid. She tried to cry out, but her voice was overpowered by the rushing wind-noise that continued steadily in her ears. It seemed to whine her name.

Ju - lie.

She tried to grasp his fingers and pull his hand away, but her muscles were locked. Even as she watched the flames grow and curl, lap through the air as though feeding off it rather than the wax of the pink candles, they began to flick like yellow tongues at his wrist and hand. The flames grew brighter. She saw them seize and fasten on Barry's flesh. One, greedy, ran across the bones of his thick wrist, encircling it like a bracelet. It coiled there, singeing hair, embracing flesh, burning. She snatched her own hand back as, with Barry's sudden yell of pain, time began to flow again. Aghast, leaping up to save her dress, she saw the candelabra topple, spattering hot, molten wax toward her. Barry seized his wrist in his right hand and stared helplessly at the fallen candles, moaning, as two waiters, followed by Monsieur Bernard, ran toward their table.

His hand and wrist loosely wrapped in a clean white handkerchief, Barry sat beside her, grumpily criticizing her driving, barking orders that made her grind his precious, expensive gears nervously.

"Please let me take you to St. Stephen's," Julie beseeched for the third time.

"No. I've got some stuff at home. Do watch out for that cab, Julie. I don't want the car wrecked on top of everything else."

"What stuff?" she asked, slowing and dropping back, giving the cab a wide berth.

"I don't know. Some sort of stuff you paint on. It's in the medicine cabinet."

"I'll do it for you, poor darling. I'm sorry."

"It completely ruined a wonderful evening. Apart from anything else, what a fire risk that place must be running. I've a damned good mind to have a word with their insurance brokers."

Barry was at odds with himself. He felt that he should have made light of the whole incident, but the throbbing pain, the feeling that his whole hand was on fire, made that impossible. The truth was that he had never been very good with pain. He would feel better if he could only place the blame somewhere. Above all, he hated being driven by a woman, especially in his own beloved car.

"Come. I'll help you," she said as they drew up outside his flat.

"I can walk perfectly well, thank you," he snapped, but he could not manage the doors, had to let Julie rummage in his trouser pocket

17

for his keys, aware of her delicate fingers on his hard thigh, and he thought, with an inner groan, that there would probably be no point in her staying the night now. He doubted that he would be able to perform with this raging pain in his hand.

Julie went ahead, opening doors, switching on lights. She poured him, unasked, a stiff brandy and carried it to him where he had slumped on the untidy, none-too-clean leather sofa. Barry shared the flat with two other men, one of whom had something to do with the futures market; the other worked on the Baltic Exchange. Julie had dubbed them Futures Fred and Baltic Bill. They employed a Portuguese lady—the Portugoose, they called her—who came in once a week but could not, unaided, keep on top of their messiness. Once every six months or so, usually prompted by a determined girlfriend or the threat of a visiting relative, they had a collective blitz on the flat, and for a few days it was sparkling clean. Blitz-time was overdue, Julie thought as she picked her way through last Sunday's *Observer*, spread haphazardly on the floor. In the bathroom, which was festooned with soggy socks and multicolored underpants, and where an open tube of shaving cream dribbled wormlike into the hair-spattered basin, she found a bottle of Burn-Eeze, a pink antiseptic liquid, which she took back into the dingy but spacious living room.

"I'm sorry I've been such a grump," Barry said as she took his hand gently into her lap and began to paint his blisters with quiet concentration.

"I only wish you'd let me take you to the hospital. They could do this properly. Does that feel any better?"

"Mm. Cooler. Come here." With his left arm, Barry embraced her slim shoulders. "I couldn't have had you snuggle up to me in the hospital," he said, grinning.

Julie did not respond to his embrace but knotted the handkerchief, soaked in a little of the liquid, loosely around his hand.

"Where are Fred and Bill?"

"Out. I don't know. Don't worry about them. We can sneak away to my room and . . ."

Julie felt herself stiffen, felt herself grow cold and sexless, like hard, dry marble. And she saw from Barry's expression that he sensed it too, her involuntary but definite withdrawal. It was ridiculous. She had slept with him before, wanted to sleep with him again.

18

True, she could never completely relax in the flat, always afraid that Baltic Bill or Futures Fred would stumble in on them, but never before had she felt this cold, closed physical dread. Barry let his arm slip from her shoulders. It struck her as a gesture of defeat, but there was nothing she could do about it, no way she could move to comfort him.

"I don't suppose I'd be much good anyway," he said miserably. "Not with this." He waved his hand under her nose, and the smell of antiseptic made her feel ever so slightly sick. "What's wrong, pet? Something's been bothering you all evening. You can't fool me."

"I don't know." Julie said, looking down at the bottle that lay in her lap. "I had a lovely evening, really I did. That is, until . . ."

"Bloody stupid," he said, feeling the effects of the brandy, regarding his injured hand. "I don't know how I could have been so bloody clumsy."

"It wasn't you," she said quickly.

"No, right," he agreed, waving his hand back and forth in the air like an unsteady metronome. He rolled his head toward her, his eyes a little swimmy. "I wish you'd stay. You could cuddle me, anyway."

She saw what he suggested. His dim room, the lumpy, uncomfortable bed. The two of them naked, side by side. Her arms were around his naked torso, his long legs intertwined with hers, and she sensed that his flesh was cold and stickily moist, like that of a dead person in a grave-sweat.

"No. I can't." Julie jumped to her feet, almost dropping the bottle. She set it down gently, afraid that her trembling hands would drop or smash it.

"You're just upset," he said, fondling her hand where it hung loosely at her side. "It must have been a hell of a shock for you, too, especially when I yelled like that."

"Yes," she said, turning away from him to hide the sudden, helpless tears that rose to her eyes. Dead flesh, she thought with disgust. It was no accident. A bracelet of flame around dead flesh, burning . . .

"It's not very gallant, I know, love," Barry said, his words thick and slightly slurred, "but I feel bushed. Call yourself a cab, will you? I want to make sure you get home safely."

His words seemed to unfreeze her, set her free. She felt almost light with relief. The flesh was warm and living again, the candle flames small, erect, and harmless.

"You stay there," she said, and lifted the telephone receiver to call a taxi.

The cab idled, caught in the after-theater traffic. The lights of the West End, the bustling crowds, the crawling vehicles were scarcely seen and noted, even less by Julie, who stared out the window, her mind elsewhere. She was not impatient with the tie-up; in fact she welcomed the anonymity and lack of responsibility that went with sitting in the back seat of a cab, going home. She welcomed time to think. The feeling of relief had faded, but its vehemence continued to disturb her. This dread of being physically intimate with Barry was something new and altogether wrong. She had been apprehensive the first time, of course, and had always been a bit on edge about the proximity of his roommates, but this inner hardening and outward freezing of the flesh, this feeling of imminent and terrible danger, was unlike anything she could recall feeling before, in any circumstances. As though there were something wrong and bad about it, she was having thoughts she did not want to think.

A person raised in the shadow of belief in carnal sin might feel this way. But her upbringing had been normal, relaxed about such matters, and if the feeling was endemic, then surely she should have experienced it most keenly that first time. In fact, excitement and a sense of adventure had mingled with a fear that she could only perceive as normal, to be expected. Barry had been gentle and painstaking, and any innate violence in the act had been negated by his tenderness and loving concern. Afterwards he had shyly confessed that he was not exactly vastly experienced. But even the recollection of what until then had been a precious and pleasurable memory made her feel cold and awkward, uncomfortable in her bones. Could she possibly be "frigid" suddenly? The thought alarmed her. *Frigid* was one of those semi-technical words, gleaned from women's magazines and radio counseling programs, that she imperfectly understood and instinctively feared. She assuredly had not been before. Could it, like a virus, strike a person down suddenly and unexpectedly?

The cab swung violently, its horn honking. Roused from the frightened contemplation of the inexplicable, Julie saw that the

20

driver was trying to beat the traffic by making a detour. They passed through darker, less populated streets, turning and winding, only to meet the traffic again at Trafalgar Square. The driver shouted something, indicated there was nothing more he could do. Julie murmured that it did not matter, then made herself small in the far corner of the seat, to discourage conversation.

At least Barry did not know the strength and depth of her reaction to his touch and words. She remembered the look of surprise and puzzlement on his face when he put his arm around her and felt her tense up. But he would forget that, with the aid of the brandy and the pain of his hand. His poor hand. And yet now, without meaning to be, she was almost glad that the accident had happened. She hated herself for thinking that, for thinking that it had saved her from—

She brought her two small, clenched fists up to her face, pressed them against her temples. The cab began to move slowly forward, toward the Strand. She pressed her knuckles hard against her head as though to quiet or squeeze out these unpleasant, uncharacteristic thoughts.

It had not been an accident. She saw it again, so clearly, saw the candle flames become emboldened, possessed of a life of their own. She saw them reach and stretch like ectoplasm, saw them lap and fasten on Barry's extended hand. She flinched back against the seat for fear of burning herself, and let her hands drop into her lap, pressed against her thighs. She saw other flames dancing in the crisp winter air. Almost dark. The sharp and lovely smell of burning wood hanging in the still, cold air. She shook her head and turned back to the window. The cab nosed its way into the Strand, where the traffic flowed more freely. For a moment she was able to blot out the flames, to name and perceive the familiar landmarks she passed. Then the flames obliterated the window and she saw . . .

. . . *a small figure huddled in a duffel coat, dark golden hair in bunches. Mittened hands and booted feet. The black and turd-like embers of burned wood. She saw them stirred with a stick to expose blisters of glowing red. Smelled the smoke and heard the crackle. Crackle of wood catching, bursting into flame, or of steps approaching through the undergrowth. Phoenix-like, the flames rising up and dancing. The little figure, bulky with clothing, surprised by the sudden appearance of fresh flame, by the unexpected heat, moving back. Flames made almost transparent*

21

by the last daylight, the setting sun. Smoke curling from their tips, wavering and spiraling upward. The flames becoming thinner and thinner, clear yellow, transparent, and the slight yet strong figure standing beyond them.

Julie closed her eyes and did not notice that, as the taxi sped like an animal set free across Waterloo Bridge, below which reflected lights danced in the black river water like eerie flames, a low moan of misery escaped her.

She saw him reach through those flames, put his hand right into them. Saw them become thicker, coagulate around his thin, bony wrist. As though the thrust of his open, welcoming hand had made a physical hole in the tissue of the flames. She stared at the outstretched hand, at the shining face on the other side of the flames, which smiled at and beseeched her. And saw the other figure, reassured, draw closer, take that hand and feel its tight, hot grasp. Holding hands, the figure on the other side of the pale flames walked into them, passed right through them to stand beside the awed but laughing child. Friends, such close friends . . .

"No," Julie said aloud. "No."

The window glass was cold against her forehead. She opened her eyes and saw that they were traveling south, and fast. She had not thought about that for years. Indeed, she had forgotten it altogether. It had no relevance, of course, to what had happened—what she must have imagined happened—in the restaurant. And then it all became clear to her. She knew why she had fancied the candle flames behaving so oddly and why they had released this old, forgotten illusion.

Her mind was playing banal tricks on her. It was much like a scary dream that, when you really thought about it, crumbled into a hodgepodge of surreally juxtaposed events from the preceding day: the ordinary made terrible by misalignment, distortion.

That stupid, ugly, vicious Valentine had startled her mind into fantasies. She had allowed it to work on her, for it had no power of its own. Sitting upright, she vowed with a certain relish that as soon as she reached home she would pull the card from its hiding place and tear it into confetti. Better still, she would burn it, watch the flames lick and rise and blacken it to wispy ash.

There was someone sitting beside her.

She caught her breath and held it, unable to exhale.

Tear it into confetti for your wedding?

22

Someone sitting at the far end of the seat. Someone sitting there quietly, no, silently, mocking her, sure of itself, himself.

She turned her head sharply to the right, her pent-up breath leaving her lungs with an audible hissing rush. There was no one, nothing there; the streetlights showed her that in rhythmic streaks of bright but pallid light that crossed her own knees, turned her dress to sickly red, to flame. But in the moment before she quite faced the empty seat, she had seen, with half an eye perhaps, a figure melting. A figure made from smoke or carved from ice. She felt a scream of panic tighten and die in her throat.

She was overwrought. As long as she kept staring at the space, nothing could fill it except the light, reality.

The cabdriver, twisting, slid the connecting glass panel aside.

"Somewhere along here, is it?"

Julie tore her gaze from the empty seat and looked ahead, recognizing familiar, everyday sights.

"Yes. Third turn along on the right. Just before Wesson's."

The big neon sign on the south side of the packaging plant glowed, a beacon of home. As the taxi turned into the dark tunnel of Broom Road, Julie searched for her purse.

"You can drop me here and drive around the Square to get out," she said as the cab's headlights swept across the road to her own gleaming front door. A light shone in the fanlight above it. The cab slowed and stopped, its engine ticking reassuringly. Julie climbed out on the left-hand side, avoiding the seat that remained empty but had appeared occupied.

"Have to go right round, do I?" the driver asked.

"Unless you want to back up, yes. How much?"

"Three-fifty," he said, staring straight ahead of him.

Julie opened her wallet and twisted a little toward the back of the cab to catch the light from one of the ornamental streetlights. The driver whistled through his teeth, tapping on the steering wheel in time to his tune. Mesmerized, Julie watched the rear door on the other side of the cab swing slowly and silently open. A shadowy form melted into the night.

"Problems?" the driver asked suspiciously.

"No." Julie, startled, pulled a five-pound note from her wallet and thrust it at the man. "Your other door's open," she told him, her eyes

23

fixed on his face. She prayed or willed him to tell her that she was seeing things, that she was mad . . .

"Bloody hell. Did you touch it?"

Julie shook her head. The man got out of the cab, grasped the handle of the door, and bent from the waist to inspect the catch. He slammed it, opened it, tested the catch with his fingers, slammed the door again. Then he opened it once more and snicked the lock down, slamming the door a third time, hard.

"I'll get it checked," he said. "Could be nasty, that. You hear it rattling or anything?"

Again, Julie could only shake her head dumbly. The man offered her change. She took the single note, left the shining fifty-pence piece in his hand.

"Thanks," he said. "Night."

" 'Night."

She stepped back and let the cab flow away from her, bear left, circle the square. She was afraid to walk to her door. The approach of the cab, its headlights playing on her, made her scurry onto the pavement, move toward the steps that led to her door. He was behind her somewhere, concealed by the shadows of the square. The sound of the cab faded. She glanced back and saw only its red taillights, growing smaller. Her fingers clasped the keys. She turned then, and made herself face the steps squarely and look up to the white door, to safety.

He was there, to her left, standing at the top of the basement steps, a silhouette against the tightly drawn but lighted curtains of Miss Tidy's flat. She heard the muffled drone of Miss Tidy's television set and knew that he was standing there, close by, waiting for her.

She ran up the steps, refusing to look at him and fell, panting, almost sobbing against the door, fumbled her key in the lock, turned it, and stumbled inside. She closed the door by leaning her back against it, knowing that he had moved, that he stood now at the foot of the steps, waiting for her to ask him in.

The house, at least, was safe.

Two

"Citycomm Radio, can I help you?"

"I'm putting you through to Russell after the next commercial break. Hang on, Kathy."

Low, behind the answering voices of the telephone operators, Russell Dunn's voice could be heard, relayed direct from the studio next door.

"Do you think you'll be able to try that for me, Daria? Do you think you'll be able to manage that?"

A small voice on a poor telephone line said, "Yes. Thank you very much."

"Thank *you*, Daria," the bright tones of Bernice O'Hara, the program presenter, cut in. "And Russell will be talking to Kathy from Heston right after the break."

A commercial jingle chattered softly. The producer, Tom Padston, pressed a key and spoke directly to the two dimly lit people in the studio. Russell Dunn slipped his headphones off, stretched, and answered, bending over the microphone. Todd Roy, with two calls on hold, answered the next, keeping his voice low and solicitous.

"Citycomm Radio. You're through to the Russell Dunn 'Help Line.' What can we do for you?" The silent pause was common, almost expected. Todd tapped twice with his pen on the desk. The line crackled. He could hear tense breathing. "Hello? My name is Todd. You need only give me your first name and a rough idea of the problem you—"

"I want to speak to Russell Dunn."

"Okay, fine. Can I have your name, please?"

"Er . . . Hilary."

"Fine. Hello, Hilary. And where are you calling from?"

"Southwark."

"And what do you want to talk to Russell about?"

The young woman did not answer. Todd heard the jingle end, followed by three bars of the station's identifying music, and then Russell Dunn's warm, gentle voice. Todd tried again.

"Hello? Can you just give me a rough idea of—"

"I'm being haunted," she said, loud suddenly, her voice breaking. Todd's eyebrows rose as he made a note on the scratchpad in front of him.

"Okay, Hilary. Hold just a moment, please." He threw a switch and swiveled around in his chair, calling to Tom Padston.

"What?"

"Got a bird here, Hilary of Southwark, says she's being haunted."

"What?"

"Says she's being—"

"Christ! That's just what we need. How many calls have we got?" Todd glanced at his colleague, who held up three fingers.

"Five and ringing," he answered.

"No way. Refer her," Tom snapped.

"Okay, boss." Todd turned back to the switchboard. "Hello, Hilary?"

"Yes?" She sounded breathless now, almost excited.

"I'm sorry, Hilary, but we've got calls stacked up here and we can't fit you in tonight." He hurried on before the caller could protest, as so many did. "So here's what I'm going to do. I'm going to give you another number. Can you get a pen and a piece of paper? I want you to take down this number, this is Russell's office number. If you call that in the morning, I'm sure—"

"Wait."

He heard a rustling noise, the receiver clicking against something solid.

"All right."

26

As he gave the number, at slow dictation speed, Russell Dunn was saying, "And these moods always follow some incident, do they, Kathy, when your boyfriend thinks you've been flirting with some other bloke?"

"Yes. It can be anyone, you know? Just some bloke in a pub, anyone."

"Do you flirt at all, Kathy?"

"No. Never."

"You don't even speak to these guys?"

"No. I only have to look at them, you know, like just looking around a room or the pub."

"I see. So your boyfriend feels pretty insecure about you. Have you any idea why that should be?"

Todd took the next call. "Hello. Citycomm Radio. You're through to the Russell Dunn 'Help Line.' "

It was past midnight when Russell Dunn got home. After the broadcast he had called two people for whom there had been too little time on the air: a woman in urgent need of emergency shelter from a violent husband, and a teenaged boy threatening suicide because he thought he was gay. As always, Russell felt drained, vaguely dispirited. He had a cup of strong black coffee in the hospitality room with Bernice and Tom, pocketed the list of callers and referrals, and discussed the program with them. He had a reputation for calm unflappability. His warm, measured voice was kindly and reassuring, a good "radio voice," and he had a remarkable trick of being able to tune into and take on the vocabulary of each caller, which made him an instant and successful communicator. He did this naturally, unconsciously—he had described broadcasting in a recent interview as "switching over to automatic pilot"—but it took a toll on his nerves and energy. He invariably had a slight headache after the program and always had to fight a sense of panic because he could not recall what he had said, or to whom.

But he knew he was good at his job: a good psychiatrist, a good therapist, and a highly successful popularizer. This latter aspect of his work had made him a minor celebrity; in addition to the weekly phone-in programs, he wrote regularly for one daily paper and various magazines. His success pleased him, and as a result of his own analysis, he knew that this had something to do with vanity and much to do with insecurity.

27

He had his critics, of course. Sometimes that hurt, but Russell always maintained, publicly at least, that it was good publicity. The criticisms of his peers and colleagues he took seriously; he fought back, argued his case.

It was difficult to argue that one was doing good—who could ever really be certain of that?—but he was convinced he did no harm. Sometimes he despised himself for defending himself so. He knew this much: The need was there. He had the expertise, an excellent backup team, one of the most comprehensive referral services in the city. That very night he had succeeded in finding a refuge willing to accept the endangered woman. That was what it was all about, but the pressures and demands of the "Help Line" program made it impossible for him to remember and work with what he had said on the air. He would have liked to spend the time immediately after the show making notes, drawing conclusions, considering further avenues of exploration, but dealing with eight or nine individuals in the space of less than an hour made this impossible.

The chasm of doubt left by his temporary amnesia—he knew that details, voices, even whole conversations would return to him later —demanded to be filled by something. Sometimes his mental blankness lasted well into the early hours of Wednesday mornings, keeping sleep at bay. But heaven help the man who does not question his own motives and achievements, he thought as he turned the car into the mews where he lived.

When his marriage broke up, Russell had been determined to keep the house in Putney. Denise had moved into a sensible flat and urged him to do the same. Eventually, though, he had seen the folly of one man living in a house with four bedrooms and half an acre of garden. Besides, it was a family house and he was no longer a family man, only a trainee "Sunday father." His share of the profits from the sale of the house had barely covered the deposit on the mews cottage in Knightsbridge, and the alterations he had made had swallowed up most of his personal savings. A tall man, a bit over six feet four, he felt cramped in small spaces, and without turning the garage into a large living room, there would have been no "perfect" space in the cottage. Once that was done, he had set about decorating it with a total disregard of anyone's taste but his own. He had chosen a heavily flocked, dark pink wallpaper and had had all the woodwork painted with a thick black gloss. The effect was not unlike a lacquered box and was entirely intentional. Into this room he could at last fit the japanned tables, boxes, cupboards, and cabinets that his late father had bequeathed him and that Denise had consigned to a storeroom and spare bedrooms. To Russell the room looked like an exotic Oriental cave, and he loved it. It was to this room that he went as soon as he entered the house that night, shaking rainspots from his gray suede jacket.

The room, like the rest of the house, was scrupulously tidy because Russell Dunn was tidy by nature. When he shut himself in his pink and black cave he could not relax unless it was as neat as the proverbial new pin. The stereo, which poured out Cesar Franck at the touch of a button, was predominantly black, as was the jarringly modern wine rack in which he kept a dozen bottles of his favorite Côtes du Rhône and Margaux.

He selected the Margaux that night, uncorked it with practiced ease, and left it to breathe a moment while he removed his jacket and hung it in the hall. His height was accentuated by the leanness of his body. Every sinew and muscle seemed to show beneath his pale, lightly freckled skin, while the more prominent bones seemed always about to burst through. No matter how much he ate or how little he exercised, no flesh or fat ever thickened that skeleton. Lately he had noted that his hair had begun to turn gray. It was basically red and he wore it short, combed forward into a neat but unfashionable fringe. A colleague, commenting on the flecks of gray, had likened him to a lean and grizzled fox. On reflection, Russell found that rather flattering.

In sweatshirt and jeans, he poured himself a goblet of the dark red wine and sipped with closed eyes. The Franck exploded into a carefully prepared melodic climax, the full orchestra sounding almost too large for the machine that reproduced its sound. He waited for it to die away, his momentary exhilaration fading with it. He put the glass down and applied himself to the evening's routine. From his pocket he pulled the notes Tom Padston had given him. These notes recorded the names of all the people who had telephoned the program, including those who had not been put through to him. He glanced through them, his memory beginning to flicker as he recognized some—Tony, Karen, Kathy, Daria. He glanced with cursory curiosity at those who, at the producer's discretion, had not reached him.

Bill. Bill rang every week. Bill was, in Tom's phrase, their "resident nut." Here was Jack, who had wanted to discuss sodomy as an acceptable marital practice, a subject too feisty even for a relatively late-night program; Ferdy had been barred because he either did not know or would not use the correct names for sexual intercourse and the genitalia; Hilary, beside whose name was scrawled, "Says she's being haunted," and Rose, "Too drunk." He smiled at these and placed the notes under a black stone paperweight on the large table he sometimes used as a temporary desk. Next, the answering machine. He finished the glass of wine, refilled it, and waited, quite still, for the Franck to finish and the record player to click off quietly. He wondered idly about Hilary.

There were not many calls, he was glad to note as he rewound the tape and set the machine to "play," and three of these, spaced equally through the day, were from Denise, all informing him that he was not, repeat *not*, to give Rupert the expensive computer game he had absentmindedly promised him for his birthday. He was to ring her back and confirm that he had gotten the message, in both senses of the phrase. His secretary had called to say that Mrs. de Bok had canceled her three-fifteen appointment for tomorrow. A message from Dillon's told him the consignment of books he had ordered from America had arrived. . . . And finally there were two calls, the sort Russell hated most, that must have been recently made. He listened to the breathing, tense and nervous, the crackle of the open but verbally silent line. He swore silently to himself, and replayed them just in case he had missed something. One never knew. A hoaxer or a patient desperate but unable to speak to an impersonal machine, an obscene caller who had lost his or her nerve, somebody reaching out from the dark loneliness of the city. He reset the machine, the good wine tasting slightly sour in his mouth. And what about the boy, he thought inevitably, the one who had threatened suicide? He felt empty suddenly, and cold. Slipping the Franck back into its sleeve, he saw that it was too late to call Denise. He should go to bed but knew he would not sleep.

Russell Dunn employed three assistants. Lise maintained his nonpersonal files, his contacts with the many helping agencies, and all of his extra-practice activities, booking him for lectures and public appearances, and dealing with the connected correspondence.

Annie transcribed all his case notes, kept the patients' files, and acted as his prompter and conscience as well as seeing patients of her own, as a psychotherapist in training under his supervision. Valerie was his general secretary and receptionist. Val, working in close conjunction with Annie, was empowered to book in new patients for an assessment session or in an emergency, and Russell sometimes thought that these three super-efficient, self-contained women could run the practice successfully without him. But that Wednesday morning, when Valerie informed him that she, with Annie's approval, had booked a new patient into the slot vacated by Mrs. de Bok, he came close to revising his opinion of them. Val stood on the far side of his large, spare desk while he unpacked and checked his briefcase. The name Hilary rang an immediate bell, a faintly uncomfortable one. He asked Valerie to repeat the name.

"Hilary Smyth," she said, "with a 'y.' She's a Citycomm referral."

"And why does she wish to see me?"

"She says . . ." Val had the grace, under his steady, hurt gaze, to hesitate and even color a little. She kept her eyes on her pad. "She says she's being haunted."

Patients, Russell well knew, pressed a number of unlikely euphemisms into service when making a first appointment, many of them bizarre, but he had never, in all his years of practice, met anyone who claimed to be haunted. Because he blamed Val, in the first instance, and was annoyed, he asked levelly, "By whom? Or should I say *what?*"

"She wouldn't say. She said"—she tilted the notebook a little, the better to catch the light—"it is badly affecting her relationship with her fiancé. She feels under intolerable stress. 'I definitely need help quickly,'" Valerie concluded, quoting.

"You spoke to Annie about this, of course?" It was just possible that Annie had been unavailable, that Val had exceeded her authority.

Dryly she replied, "Of course," and snapped the notepad shut.

"The girl, in your opinion," Russell said without special expression, "sounded desperate?"

"Yes. She could hardly breathe. She sounded . . . terrified."

"I see." He clicked his briefcase shut, stood it neatly beside his desk. "Anything else?"

31

"Mr. Potter called. He has a meeting. He may be a few minutes late. And Lise has a few things for you."

"Later," he said, sitting in his comfortable leather chair. "Send her in in ten minutes. With some coffee, if you please." Valerie hesitated. He noticed this and guessed that she wanted to return to the subject of Hilary Smyth. After all, he did not overlook the fact that Val knew him well enough to be fully aware of his anger, even though he had deliberately not expressed it openly. He stared at her. She smiled and bobbed her head, making the dark red hair move softly, sensually against her creamy jaw, and went out without saying what was on her mind.

Soon after Denise's decampment with their son, Russell had enjoyed a brief, passionate affair with Valerie. He had been lonely, angry, scared, and these emotions had made him see Valerie as an attractive, desirable woman with a life and identity quite separate from her coolly efficient role in the office. The affair, he liked to think, had simply *happened*, not been engineered, sought, or planned. It had flared and burned itself out. Miraculously, Val, without being asked, again assumed her cool, professional persona. When, confused and for form's sake giving way to his tidy streak, Russell had asked her out to dinner even though the affair was patently dead, she had shaken her head gently.

"I don't think that would be a very good idea, do you? We've so much work to do."

He did not deserve to be let off so lightly, he knew. Part of him was nostalgic for those few hectic weeks, her calm presence and passionate body. Part of him occasionally wondered if she had taken a new lover, and if so, what he was like.

He buzzed Annie.

"Yes?"

"Hilary Smyth," he said, making the fingers of his left hand move crabwise across the desk in a manner he fancied resembled that of an accomplished pianist playing an arpeggio.

"Yes."

"Would you mind telling me why you advised Valerie to book her in?"

"I thought you'd be amused," Annie said, and he thought he sensed in her gruff, confident voice a hint of suppressed laughter.

"The possibility of exorcism, you mean?"

"Whatever," Annie said offhandedly.

"Wrong business, I'm afraid."

"Oh, come off it, Russell. You know she doesn't mean it literally. It's probably something completely straightforward. I thought you'd enjoy someone with a bit of imagination, that's all."

"Nothing," he said coldly, "is completely straightforward, as you very well know."

"I'll have Lise check out a few priests for you," Annie replied, openly teasing now. "There's bound to be someone local who's into exorcism."

"May I remind you, Annie, that we are the new priests?"

He cut her off and leaned back slowly and deliberately in his chair, making a lopsided pyramid of his fingers. If his colleagues saw fit to send him up a little, that was all to the good. After all, he had nothing to lose. He was committed only to an assessment. He doubted strongly that he would take Ms. Smyth on.

But why had his staff become skittish now? he wondered, and looked at the window where, through the opened, vertical venetian blind, he could see the rain falling, a few flakes of pale sleet mixed in with it. Despite this evidence, it was technically springtime. Biorhythms, he thought. There was, perhaps, an article there: the effects of seasonal change on the female psyche. The menstrual cycle would have to be taken fully into account, of course. He pulled a pad toward him, prepared to make notes. The door opened and Lise came in, bearing coffee, a notebook, and several matching gray folders.

She came into the room and paused, looking around. It was only on the underground from Covent Garden that she had wondered what a psychiatrist's office would look like. Her fancy had veered between something forbiddingly clinical—an operating room for the mind—and something dark, cluttered, and shadow-lit. This room was functional but quietly welcoming, as Russell Dunn had intended that it should be. The anonymous colors beloved of hotels and airports had been banished altogether. The carpet was a warm fern green, the walls primrose. There were books on shelves, a lot of light wood, and, she thought, a bewildering number of places to sit, but no obvious psychiatrist's couch.

Russell Dunn watched her keenly. First impressions were precious to him. Often, when a case had become bogged down, recollecting his first good look at a person—stance, expression, manner —had given him insight on which way to proceed. This girl's appearance spoke directly to him in a way that it was surprisingly easy to pin down. She looked as he would like his daughter to look at her age, if he had one. She had left her coat in the reception room and stood before him in a severe, almost Victorian dark red velvet dress. Its plainness was sumptuous because of the cloth, and relieved —almost coquettishly, he thought—by a collar and cuffs of creamy beige lace. She was small, no more than five feet three or four, and perfectly proportioned. Her hands, feet, and head were all *neat.* In the latter case, the neatness was accentuated by the short cut of her hair in which red highlights glimmered subtly. The face would, in a work of fiction, almost inevitably have been described as "pixie- ish," and in those first intense moments, when there was so much to take in and store, Russell could not think of a better word. He suspected dimples hidden in the lightly made-up cheeks, a generous smile. The dull yet startled eyes masked, he guessed, a lively but not intellectual intelligence. She looked at him at last and he, standing politely behind his desk, gestured to the rest of the room.

"Where would you like to sit?"

There was, deliberately, no chair immediately before his desk, although one stood at its side, turned slightly away from him.

"Might I . . . could that chair be brought around here?"

"Certainly." He picked up the chair beside his desk and carried it to the front.

"Thank you," she said, and swept her hand under her velvet skirt as she sat, so that it fell loose and full around her. There was something prim and circumspect about the way she sat, he thought, hands in her lap, one of them clutching the chain of a frivolous little purse.

"My assistant has explained my terms to you?"

She nodded quickly.

"And you understand that this is only an exploratory meeting? At the end of it, or shortly afterwards, we will decide whether we should continue."

"I'm sure that I shall . . ."

"Yes?"

"That I shall want to go on."

"Ms. . . . er . . . Smyth, I may not be able to help you. You may not feel that I am the right person to help you. In that case, there must be no embarrassment on your side. If you still consider that you need help, I will, of course, do my best to recommend someone else."

"But I've heard you on the radio and I'm sure you can help me."

He inclined his head a little to acknowledge her appreciation of the broadcasts, but said, "Then how can I help you?"

"Ah . . . well . . . that's really very difficult to say. I mean . . . if I knew that . . . well, I wouldn't really need to be here, would I?"

"Would you not?"

She looked almost panic-stricken, the first sign of unnatural nervousness she had shown. Her eyes scanned the room, her head turning jerkily on her neck.

"You don't have a couch. I thought . . ."

"It's perfectly possible and comfortable to lie down on that one," he said, indicating a long, low, blue-covered settee. "Would you prefer to lie down?"

"Oh, no. No. Thank you."

"Tell me a little about yourself," he suggested, picking up a newly sharpened pencil and holding it lightly, a little like a conductor's baton.

"Oh . . . well . . . my name . . . er . . . Hilary. Hilary Smyth. I'm eighteen, almost nineteen. I live at home, here in London. I work in a little jewelry shop in Covent Garden. It's a designer shop, run by a friend. She designs and makes jewelry. I just . . . help out. And I'm sort of . . . well, I mean unofficially . . . I'm engaged to be married." Russell would have thought her older, twenty-two at least. Her youth surprised him. He waited and then chose her last statement as a beginning.

"*Unofficially* engaged?"

"Well, yes . . ." Slipping the chain of her purse up onto her wrist, she touched and then twisted the moonstone ring on her left-hand ring finger. "I mean we are, but we haven't quite fixed the date yet, and until then, well, there doesn't seem much point in making a formal announcement. In the papers, if you see what I mean."

Russell indicated that he did with a slow nod.

"And is your problem in any way connected with this engagement? With your fiancé, perhaps?"

"Oh, no. No. He's a wonderful man and I . . . I really want to get married. Only . . ." She paused, a thoughtful and yet slightly surprised expression creeping across her face. "And yet, come to think of it, yes. In some ways, yes, it is . . . connected with that. Yes."

"In what way?"

"Well, I . . . he . . . I mean, there is something . . . someone who is connected with my engagement."

"Another man, perhaps?"

"Yes."

"A young man?"

"Oh, yes."

"Who is perhaps fond of you himself?"

"I think," she said, her voice hardening suddenly, "he would say that, yes."

"And you—how do you feel about him?"

"I don't feel anything. I mean, not in the way you mean. I can't feel anything for him, not like that, because, well, because it's just not . . . not possible."

"What isn't possible?"

"To love someone who . . ." She could not go on. She opened the clasp of the little purse and pulled out a small, neatly folded and ironed handkerchief, and held it to her nose. "It was very silly of me to come," she said. "I see that now. I'm sorry to have wasted your time. I'll pay, of course. You can't help me, you see. It isn't your sort of . . . thing at all."

Russell Dunn waited and waited, watching her patiently. She cried a little, quietly, blotted the tears away with the handkerchief, then put it away, snapping the clasp of her bag with a certain finality as though, in the long silence, she had told herself to pull herself together. She looked at him, a little smile on her face, the expected dimples just showing for the first time.

"What would you like me to call you?" Russell said, almost returning the smile.

"Julie. Oh. I mean . . ."

"Well then, Julie, you may of course be right. If it is a matter of another man bothering you, trying to persuade you to break off your engagement, perhaps, then there is little I can do. If it's a matter of harassment, then I would have to advise you to go to the police, if you can't deal with the matter yourself, that is."

36

"I can't," she said. "I can't deal with it because . . . because I am causing it."

"How?"

"Well, I . . . I'm not quite sure."

"You mean you have encouraged this young man?"

She nodded, swallowed, began to play with the chain of her purse. "I . . . once we were close, very, very close. Closer than I've ever been to anyone, really. Like we were one person, you know? Knew exactly what the other thought and felt, like one person in two bodies, if you see what I mean."

"Yes."

"But that was a long time ago." She wound the purse chain around the fingers of her left hand, unwound it, looped it once around her extended ring finger, unconsciously adding, Russell thought, a wedding band to the engagement ring. "And now he's come back," she said, seeming almost to choke on the phrase. She coughed.

"And he's pestering you?"

She nodded.

"He wants you to do . . . what?"

She glanced up at Russell Dunn, her expression suddenly confident.

"To marry him, of course." She made it sound as though this were a self-evident fact. "If I don't, I think he means to harm Barry. Can't you see I'm afraid? Afraid that he'll do something?"

"Barry is your fiancé?"

"Yes. I told you."

"And what does Barry say about this?"

"I haven't told him. How can I?"

"What makes it so difficult?"

"Because Jo-Jo . . ." She broke then. The purse slipped from her lap. She bent forward, almost as though in pain, and covered her face with her small hands. Silently, Russell Dunn pushed a box of tissues to the edge of the desk. "None of it's true," she wailed through her tears. "I know that . . . sometimes . . . but I can't stop it. I can't. I have tried. Truly, I have tried. And then, when I know I must be . . . making it all up . . . I think I'm . . . going mad. I must be. I know I'm . . . so afraid . . . that's why I rang you, had to ring you. Please, can you . . . stop me being . . . mad?"

37

"Hilary rang," he said, chancing a step forward that he did not feel sure about, but which he felt he had to take.

"What?" She looked at him, red-eyed, face streaked. She sounded and looked impatient. He nodded at the tissues and she took a handful.

"I said, 'Hilary rang.' Hilary, not Julie."

"What does that matter? It's just a name."

"Whose name?"

"Nobody's. One I made up."

"So you are Julie?"

"Of course I'm . . . I didn't want anyone to recognize me . . . on the radio. What does it matter what I call myself? The problem's still the same."

"True, but Hilary might see it or experience it differently from Julie."

"I don't understand," she said, still impatient. "My name is Julie Wells. I made up Hilary. Hilary Smyth. On the spur of the moment."

"Yes, but Hilary Smyth said—twice, in fact—that she was being haunted. You, Julie, haven't." He thought she looked embarrassed.

"Well, I . . . didn't know what else to call it. They don't give you much time. . . ."

"You didn't, or Hilary?"

"There is no Hilary. I told you. I just . . . made up the name."

"So, are *you* being haunted?"

"Yes. No. I don't know." She began to shred the damp tissues in her lap, looking sulky now, still close to tears.

"I don't know much about such . . . phenomena," Russell said levelly, "but the word 'haunted' would suggest to me that the . . . other man . . . is dead."

He could not tell for sure whether she was considering this or whether it had failed to sink in. She began to bundle the tissues together, to knead them into a sort of ball. Some fragments, he saw, clung to the velvet nap of her dress.

"I don't know what else to call it," she said quietly. "Don't think I don't know that it sounds crazy. But I feel . . . I *am* crazy." She looked at him, a genuine, desperate appeal in her eyes.

"Tell me," he said, "about . . . Jo-Jo, is it?"

"Yes." She nodded, then shook her head vehemently, lips trembling. "No. You wouldn't believe me."

"Is Jo-Jo dead? Is that it?"

"Dead . . ." She laughed a little. It was an unpleasant, self-mocking sound. "He never existed. Not really." Russell watched her, almost holding his breath, feeling something coming closer, closer. "I made him up," she said, with just a hint of pride, her chin lifting a little. "When I was small. He was my imaginary friend. Do you see?"

"Yes," he said quietly, then repeated, "Yes."

"And now . . . now he's come back." There was a moment when she fought against her tears, the crack in her voice, then she made herself look at him, angrily. "Yes. To *haunt* me. There. What do you think of that?"

"I think," he said slowly, "that you should come to see me again next week, as soon as we can possibly arrange it. Will you do that, Julie?" She did not answer, but leaned down to pick up her purse. "Shall I ask my assistant to make another appointment?" he prompted.

"Do you think you can help me?" She said this with her head bowed; the purse was still on the floor but she held its chain in her hand.

"I can try. You're asking me for first aid, Julie. In these matters there is only treatment. I hope you will feel able to come and see me next week."

After a moment she nodded and stood up quickly. Russell pressed a button on the intercom and spoke to Valerie.

Julie left Dunn's office, feeling like a miserable drunk. There was relief that she had blurted out to someone the truth of what was happening to her, as well as desolation that he had said and promised nothing. As she walked in a broken diagonal across central London to her bus stop at the top of Whitehall, she gradually began to realize the enormity of what she had *not* said. She never would be able to say it; she feared that if she did, Russell Dunn would . . . what? Dismiss her? Have her instantly committed? Look at her with loathing, as something evil, perverted? She had not even scratched the surface of her haunting, his strange, unpredictable presence, her feelings. She felt an almost physical pain, a sharp contraction of the stomach as her mind, off-guard, approached these feelings. She must bury them. No one could help her to do that. These feelings were not real, not apt, not likely or suitable. She thought desperately of

39

Barry, knowing that he *must* be able to help her. His solidity, his physical presence, the fact that he loved her—these things alone could exorcise Jo-Jo. She believed that, and yet doubted, even despaired of her own strength to subdue and control what she felt about Jo-Jo, what, perhaps, he made her feel. For that to be possible, the seesaw of her mind insisted, she needed Russell Dunn, someone older, more practiced, a doctor. And there her mind seemed to become numb, poised between hope and hopelessness, between fear and a dreadful, itching kind of excitement.

She stood in a bedraggled queue at the bus stop, under an umbrella. The rain fell with undramatic relentlessness. The traffic was slow, wearing dipped headlights that reflected eerily on the wet streets. The queue grew longer as the rush hour began in earnest. Jostled and buffeted, Julie was carried onto a bus where she stood cramped between two other passengers, one of whom insisted on reading a soggy evening paper, to the greater discomfort of his neighbors. Her life had become a stream of contradictions. She felt both lonely and safe in this crowd. Lonely because her fear set her apart; if she were to tell any of these strangers what she had not even dared to tell Dunn, they would flinch away from her, fearing contamination. But safe because, on the whole, he avoided crowds, did not reach out to her when there were many people around. His voice did not call to her so persistently above the roar of traffic and the chatter of crowds, causing that strange, tingling feeling. Not unless she listened for him, invited . . .

"Scuse, please."

A woman, loaded with shopping bags, a damp scarf plastered to her skull, elbowed Julie aside, causing her to lean awkwardly over a seated passenger who glared at her and shifted in her seat as though she sensed or smelled something wrong, something bad in Julie. She straightened up, made a little more space for herself, tried not to think at all. She was nearly home, and that, too, was a thought fretted with contradictions. She dreaded its loneliness. Her mother was still away. The trip to Düsseldorf had turned into a mini-tour of Europe. Being in Düsseldorf made it expedient for her to go to Hamburg to hear a new mezzo-soprano, and on to Vienna to discuss some hitch with Schott's. . . . All of this Julie learned in hurried phone calls. She was no longer sure where her mother was. She only knew that her mother would not be home when she got there.

About Barry's being away in Val-d'Isère with Reggie Collis, she felt even more ambivalent. Since the night the candles had burned him, she had felt an electric sense of danger whenever she was with him. She was profoundly glad of a respite from that, but his absence also made her feel vulnerable, a prey to those feelings.

She responded to a shove from behind and began moving to the back of the bus. A youth in wet jeans and soaked sneakers rang the bell ahead of her and the bus swerved toward the pavement, its wheels sending up a drenching spray from a puddle. Julie got off the bus, put up her umbrella, and waited at the crosswalk opposite Wesson's. Her heart began to thump as she turned into the dripping, comparative darkness of Broom Road. This physical reaction had become a part of her daily life, but she had not yet gotten used to it. Sometimes Jo-Jo was just visible under the trees, waiting. She hurried, head still down, not looking. There was a crumb of comfort in the lit windows of the terraced houses, in the glowing lamps of the square ahead. So far the house was safe, but again she sensed, rather than knew from any evidence, that her mother's absence made it, too, vulnerable. She broke into an awkward, trotting little run at the end of the street, her eyes fixed firmly on her front door. The house was safe. There was no need to look behind her, and she had become adept at avoiding the basement area. As she stood on the steps, awkwardly balancing her umbrella, juggling with her purse to find her key, the door opened inward and she snatched a breath, almost slipped.

"Oh!" said Miss Tidy, also startled. "I was just checking on the weather. Come in, dear, come in." Julie closed her umbrella and went into the hall. Miss Tidy leaned out into the night. "You're early, dear, aren't you?"

Julie wanted to shout at her to shut the door and bolt it. She also caught herself on the verge of another lie to Miss Tidy. She was, of course, early because Belle had told her, when she asked for time off to keep her appointment with Russell Dunn, to take the rest of the day off.

"It's the weather," Julie said vaguely, standing her dripping umbrella on the sheet of newspaper that Miss Tidy had put down for that purpose. Her nerves were jumping, but they calmed a little as she heard the door close softly behind her.

"No, well, I don't expect people have much call for jewelry on a day like this," she said. She had a lively curiosity about Julie's workplace; she had once, at Julie's instigation, visited it and been given the grand tour of the new Covent Garden complex. She had not been impressed, but had approved of the cleanliness and tidiness of "Julie's shop." She pronounced it a decent enough place for a girl to work. "Are you all right, dear?" Miss Tidy asked, and Julie turned to stare at her, white-faced.

Without one of her brightly colored, vivaciously patterned aprons, which she made herself on a small electric sewing machine —her one visible self-indulgence—Miss Tidy looked unfamiliar and, just then, gaunt. She wore a long, straight gray coat, with gray stockings and black galoshes over her shoes. She seemed taller, colorless, almost forbidding. With a lurch of the stomach, Julie remembered that it was Wednesday, Miss Tidy's night off, and the panic began to jangle in her. On the wide shelf above the hall radiator, and beneath a pretty oval mirror, she saw the familiar gray hat, which, as though prompted by her look, Miss Tidy picked up and, bending a little at the knees, adjusted squarely on her head.

"You're surely not going out in this?" Julie asked, her voice too loud and too high.

Slightly altering the set of her hat, Miss Tidy said, apparently to her own reflection, "It's my Bible class tonight. I've never missed a Bible class since I've been here, and I don't believe God or the Reverend Watkins would regard a drop of rain as an excuse for backsliding."

"You did," Julie burst out, sounding, even to her own astonished ears, like a spoiled child. "You did miss one. When you had the 'flu that time. You're likely to catch it again if you go out in this. It's sleeting, in with the rain."

"You get out of that wet coat and don't bother about me," Miss Tidy said firmly. "I shall be well wrapped up." To demonstrate the truth of this, she began to pull on a milky gray plastic raincoat. It hung, shapeless, almost to her sturdy ankles. From its pocket she took a folded square of transparent plastic, opened it, and, turning back to the mirror, tied it over her hat.

"And I've got my brolly," she said triumphantly, reaching for a stout black umbrella she had placed beside the front door. "Now, there's a nice casserole in the oven, peeled potatoes on the hob, and plenty of fresh fruit for afters. I won't be late," she added, turning to the door. "I daresay Miss Devlin will offer me a lift home and I daresay I shall accept. Nighty-night, dear."

A rush of cold, damp air entered the hall and persisted as Miss Tidy struggled to open her umbrella. Julie thought she heard herself cry out, beg the woman to stay, but all she really said was "Good night," as Miss Tidy drew the door closed behind her.

The house was safe, she reminded herself. It was very likely that Barry would telephone her that night. He had said he would. She wandered into the warm kitchen, looked into the unlit breakfast room beyond. The rain beat against the glass. The casserole smelled rich and spicy, but she had no appetite. She could phone Sybil, have a nice long chat. Perhaps her mother would call, perhaps to say that she was coming home. She should not have accepted Belle's offer; she would have been better off at the shop, and might have gone to a wine bar afterwards with Rik and Gloria, Belle's trainee assistants. But she had been unable to guess how she would feel after seeing Mr. Dunn. She went up to the first floor and into the big sitting room, turning on the wall lights. Without the warm glow of the lamps, the room looked cold, and her imagination made it more so. There were no flowers, none of her mother's usual clutter of books, scores, papers. Miss Tidy had tidied. She looked at the table where the liquor was kept on an old brass tray that Great-Gran had brought back from India, but did not want anything.

She put out the lights and went up the next flight of stairs. Her mother's bedroom door was closed. Her own room felt warm and familiar, safe. She put on all the lights and went to the window, reaching both hands up automatically to grasp the blue and white curtains.

Her own shadow stretched across the shining flagstones of the little walled garden below her, framed by the looped outline of the frothy curtains. Her shadow was enormous, flat and black. The outline of her head disappeared into deeper, natural shadows where no light fell. And she sensed him there, saw just a slight movement, then the white blob of his face uplifted to look at her, his pale hands.

She caught her breath with a sound like a sob, and pulled the curtains together. She was too afraid to turn around; she backed away from the window, and saw that in her haste she had not closed them fully and went back, tweaking at them until their folds met and shut her in completely.

43

The house was safe. She made herself listen, concentrate on the silence, the muffled roar of the boiler. What had she seen? What words would she use if she were to describe it to Mr. Dunn, for example? The mere idea of doing so invoked the image again, and she thrust it away from her. The phrase "the way to lay ghosts" floated into her mind, but she did not hang on to it. Julie wanted to avoid this problem. She did not feel brave enough to face and analyze her fears to dry dust. This thought made her feel helpless. What was the point of going back to Mr. Dunn? Even with his help, she would never be able to . . .

She sat at the small table she used as a desk and clasped her trembling hands together upon it. A little blue-glass-shaded lamp stood on one corner of it, reminiscent of a bluebell. Its light fell on the shelves above and behind the table. A few paperbacks—she was not a great reader—pebbles from the many beaches she had visited, a curious silver-and-enamel pillbox that Great-Gran had given her when she was little, because she coveted it so much, a framed photograph of herself and Sybil, dressed in shorts with hair in bunches. . . .

She gasped and gripped her hands more tightly together. She could not release the breath she had noisily inhaled. Her temples began to throb, her face to burn. She felt as though she were suffocating. The figure beside her in the old and so-familiar photograph was changed, was not Sybil, was a boy perhaps two inches taller than she, dressed in loose shorts, a T-shirt, barefoot. The image was pale, softly out of focus, as though only half of the photograph had been fully and properly developed.

She yanked her hands apart, reached for the photograph. Her breath left her body in a rush, and as her fingers brushed against the frame, shifting it so that lamplight dazzled on the shiny glass, she saw the boy fade and disappear, and Sybil smiled at her from her proper place, cheeky, cheerful, as she had always done.

The telephone rang. She snatched her hand away from the photograph and leaped up, leaving the chair askew. It was only three or four paces to the bed, but it seemed to take her an age, as though the very air had a restraining thickness, or as if the carpet tugged at her feet. She saw her right arm outstretched to the telephone, heard its persistent, urgent ring, and was certain that she could not reach it in time.

44

"Hello?"

She was sitting on the bed, breathless, holding the receiver to her ear.

"Hello?" She heard a whining noise, a distant explosion. Her eyes saw Sybil safe in the photograph, smiling at her. Then she heard a muffled chatter of French. "Hello? Hello?" Her voice sounded strained but steady. A French voice spoke to her, and every word she knew of the language fled from her memory. She heard another voice, interjecting. The line sang like a demented siren, and then a plausible English voice said:

"Hold on, caller. Trying to connect you."

For a horrible, long moment the line went dead. She imagined telephone lines tumbling in terrible storms, underground cables washed free and made useless by floods. She thought she was going to cry.

"*Parlez, s'il vous plait.*"

"Hello, darling. Can you hear me?"

"Barry?"

"It's a dreadful line."

"I can hear you."

"You're very faint."

"Is that better?" She adjusted the receiver so that it was closer to her mouth, shouted, her body tense and hunched over the instrument as though she could will it to work efficiently. "Barry?"

". . . marvelous skiing. How are you?"

"I'm fine. Missing you."

Then the line began to sing again. The note changed pitch; it was Barry's voice attenuated, like a record played too slowly. *Love you,* it growled. Then the note rose in pitch, became lighter, plaintive. *Ju-lie, Ju-lie,* it said. It was no earthly voice. From the static and the interference he borrowed a voice, called to her. *Love me. Ju-lie.* As he always called to her, his boy's treble whispering around the garden . . . *Ju-lie. Come and see. Ju-lie. Can't find me.*

"No!"

She slammed the receiver into its cradle, making the nightstand rock. A bracelet, discarded sleepily, fell onto the floor. She picked up the receiver again, heard its annoying, normal drone. She had cut Barry off, lost him. Oh, God. But they had an agreement. She remembered it. Barry had said the lines from France were invariably awful. If they got a really bad line or ever got cut off, he would call her back on her mother's number. She fancied she heard it ringing already. She ran to the door, wrenched it open, continued running down the stairs. The door to the sitting room was still open. The telephone was silent, the room in darkness. She felt it cold and empty again and went on down the stairs. There was a wall phone in the kitchen. She would take Barry's second call there, where it was warm and smelled homey. The lights were still on, as she had left them.

Hugging her arms around herself, Julie went into the kitchen. The casserole still filled the room with its tempting aroma, but the rain sounded louder, fiercer. She turned around, feeling the cold, damp air fighting the warm, and saw that the garden door was open, gently shifting in the wind. Rain spattered onto the tile floor.

She moved without thinking, closed the door with a bang, raindrops splashing onto her skirt. She bolted the door and turned the key. *The house is safe.* The breakfast room was cold and empty, rain puddled on the floor. And the kitchen beyond was also empty. The yellow telephone hung silently beside the tall white refrigerator. She made herself walk toward it. *The house is safe.*

She stood before the telephone. Barry had, of course, left her a phone number, for emergencies. But it was upstairs. He might not be at the hotel anyway. He would call. He *had* to ring back. He would call and Miss Tidy would return and . . .

Another number came into her head, unbidden, unexpected, but with a rightness that melted some of her fear. She reached for the receiver, lifted it, began to dial.

His hand closed coldly over hers, pulling it from the dial.

Don't Ju-lie. Please don't. I'll take care of you now.

His hand held hers, icily. His breath chilled her neck as, pulling against the pressure of his hold, she twisted around, mouth open, to look at him. His eyes pleaded with her. Her skin crawled. The phone slipped from her hand and hung purring, clicking rhythmically, against the side of the refrigerator. He smiled then, his mouth close and suddenly tender. There were raindrops, like stars in his dark, curly hair. She wanted, prompted by some dreadful instinct, to reach up and smooth them away.

"No," she said, cringing away from him, from some stirred and devilish part of herself that she recognized with a chilly clarity.

Ju-lie.

His eyes demanded now, burned and awoke something nameless in her.

Three

Russell was again late getting home. He had lectured to a group of American students on "Freud and Fiction." Afterwards, there had been a dinner. A taxi delivered him to the mouth of the mews shortly before midnight. His black tie and dinner jacket felt like a constricting harness, and he removed both as soon as he entered the room. He wanted a shower, certain that sleep would come without difficulty. He had enjoyed himself. He pressed a button and set himself, leaning on the table, to listen to his calls. They were routine: an invitation to dinner with friends; Tom Stopman reporting that ratings were still rising and shouldn't they seriously begin to consider an additional afternoon "Help Line"? He liked the idea, was excited by it, but he was too tired to think about it now.

Then he became aware of an open silence on the tape. He tensed. His mind focused sharply. He presumed it to be a hoax or another failure of nerve. He could not, over the lively crackle of the line, even hear breathing. Then a voice spoke, in a hoarse whisper.

Leave her alone. I'm warning you. Leave Ju-lie alone. I won't tell you again. Leave her alone. I'll take care of her. She belongs to me.

The line went dead. The tape played on, empty. He felt fear, irrational and strong, opening like a great hollow inside him and realized that he was sweating; he could smell his own frightened odor. He stopped the machine and straightened up. From one of a cluster of small, identical japanned drawers he took a pack of cigarettes, opened it, and lit one with a cheap, disposable lighter. As he drew smoke deeply, compulsively into his lungs, he reminded himself that he knew about fear, how to deal with it. Cigarette held in the corner of his mouth, he rewound the tape and played it again.

At first there was nothing particularly remarkable or idiosyncratic about the voice itself. It was neither light nor noticeably deep. The hoarseness could have been due to the poor line, the softness to deliberate muffling of the mouthpiece or the need not to be overheard. What impressed him and kept the hollow of his fear open was the lack of tonal variation. A person making a threat—something about which they must feel strongly and might even be emotionally out of control—would sound tense, angry, nervous. There was a monstrous coolness to this voice. It spoke as though stating facts, by rote. It seemed entirely certain of its right to issue orders and, perhaps, just as certain that they would be obeyed.

Russell listened again. All feeling, he thought, had been subsumed in the speaker's obsession. That obsession had motivated the call. This was the voice of someone totally convinced of the rightness of what he or she was doing, and that alone was what made it chilling and dangerous.

She belongs to me.

He rewound the tape, took the cartridge from the machine, and placed it carefully in his briefcase, which he locked. Then he reloaded and reset the answering machine and sat smoking, staring into space.

TRANSCRIPT OF FIRST TAPED INTERVIEW: Julie Wells/RD

Russell Dunn: Please sit down. You'll be comfortable there?
Julie Wells: Yes. Thank you.
R: Julie, before we begin, there are two things. . . . First, we are being tape-recorded at this moment and, with your permission, I would like to continue to tape this and all our interviews.
J: Why?
R: Convenience. I see a great many people. An instantly available, totally accurate record of our conversation saves me much time and many misunderstandings. Of course, this in no way affects

or alters the confidentiality of what is said in this room. But if you have any objections . . .

J: No. It doesn't matter. No.

R: Thank you.

J: Is that it? I thought you said we were already being recorded.

R: No. This is another tape recorder, one I use for making notes. I want you to listen to something for me, Julie. . . . I'm sorry . . . there seems to be . . . let's try again. There . . . I do apologize. If you wouldn't mind just sitting through this for a moment . . . I may have got the wrong place on the tape. . . .

J: There's a composer who does this.

R: I beg your pardon?

J: There's a composer who writes silence. Makes people listen to silence. My mother told me. She knows a lot about—

R: You haven't told me about your mother, Julie.

J: No. Is that it, then? Is there something wrong with the tape recorder?

R: I . . . suppose there must be. I'll have it checked. Let's not worry about it now.

J: What did you want me to hear?

R: A recording of a telephone call I received.

J: Oh?

R: That doesn't mean anything to you? Well, I really can't explain. We'll come back to it when I've got the, er, technical problems sorted out. Now, why don't you tell me about your mother?

J: Why? There's no point.

R: Very well. Then what do you want to talk about, Julie? How have you been?

J: All right.

R: Just all right?

J: Well, bad, really.

R: How "bad," Julie? What do you mean by—

J: It's getting worse.

R: By "it," you mean what you told me about last time? You mean Jo-Jo?

J: Can I ask you a question?

R: Please.

J: Do you believe what I told you . . . about Jo-Jo? Please . . . it's important to me. It would help.

R: I believe that what you told me is the truth of how you see what is happening to you.

J: That means . . . you do believe that I am mad?

R: I don't know what that word means, Julie. Nor do you.

J: Not normal. Crazy. What does it matter what you call it?

R: I would rather say that you are very distressed. Would you accept that as a—

J: Terrified . . .

R: And the cause of your terror is . . . ?

J: Jo-Jo. Yes. And it's getting worse. And I ask you to believe me because that would help . . . more than anything. I ask you if I'm mad because I don't believe . . . most people don't go mad . . . like me . . . and yet I'm . . . I can see Jo-Jo and talk to him.

R: It seems to me that we always come back to Jo-Jo, so we had better start with Jo-Jo, don't you agree? Will you tell me about him?

J: He's come back. I told you.

R: How? How did he come back, Julie?

J: I don't know.

R: When, then?

J: Just over a month ago. He sent me a Valentine. It was delivered by hand. Then Barry . . . Barry got burned, that night at dinner. The candles. They burned him. At Chez Jacquot. And then I saw him. He was in the taxi with me, going home, and waiting for me. He's been there ever since, off and on.

R: Off and on?

J: Sometimes I see him, just out of the corner of my eye. Or outside the shop, watching me through the window. The other night, after I came to see you, he was in the garden at home and then . . . then . . . he came into the house.

R: Does he speak to you, Julie?

J: Yes. In other sounds. I hear his voice sometimes when I can't see him. On the telephone. In other noises. I can't explain. Then, the other night, when he came into the house, he spoke quite clearly to me. He said, "Don't, Julie. Please don't. I'll take care of you now." And he touched me. I was going to ring you. I was afraid. I thought . . . I was going to tell you what was happening to me and he took the telephone from me and he said . . . he said he'd take care of me.

R: Do you believe him, Julie?

J: No. Of course not. I didn't understand . . . I don't know what he meant.

R: All right, Julie. Can you tell me what he looks like? Can you describe him to me? Julie? What does that mean? "No"?

J: Yes.

R: Can you describe his voice, then?

J: No. I don't know. It's all mixed up with other noises. Don't you listen? I told you—

R: Why are you so afraid of Jo-Jo, Julie?

J: Because . . . because . . . he doesn't exist.

R: If he did exist, would you still be afraid of him?

J: But he must exist in some way. Otherwise I'm seeing things and hearing things and I'm not. I'm not. You see, when it happens it seems like he does exist and then, at other times, like now, when I'm telling you about it, well, it seems . . . I mean, he can't exist, can he?

R: If he does not exist, Julie, where does he come from?

J: I told you. I made him up. When I was little.

R: But if you made him up, then you can unmake him, can't you?

J: I did, years ago. That's the point. He's come back.

R: You've made him again?

J: No. No. No. *He* came back.

R: How did you unmake him, Julie?

J: I . . . I just sort of . . . grew out of him. I didn't need him anymore. He just . . . went away, I suppose. That's what happens, isn't it? Lots of children . . . they have a friend they make up, don't they? And then they just . . . grow out of it.

R: Yes, Julie. Is that what happened to you?

J: Yes. Of course.

R: So why do you think Jo-Jo has come back?

J: I told you. He wants to marry me. He doesn't want me to marry Barry.

R: He's told you this?

J: Sort of.

R: How, exactly?

J: I just know it. What else could it be? He wouldn't let me call you, remember? He doesn't like me seeing you.

R: He told you that?

J: He stopped me from calling you, didn't he?

R: What does he say about Barry?

J: He doesn't *say* anything. But . . . all right, listen. That same night, last Wednesday, Barry rang me. I couldn't hear him properly. It was a bad line. Then Jo-Jo was on the line, saying my name. I could hear him but I couldn't hear Barry. And then that night—St. Valentine's night, the candles—that was Jo-Jo. Jo-Jo made the candles burn Barry. I know. I saw them.

R: Did Barry see it too?

J: No. He thought it was a draft, an accident.

R: Has anyone else seen Jo-Jo? Ever?

J: I don't know. No. But that doesn't mean he doesn't exist, does it?

R: Well, does he?

J: Yes. I've seen him. He touched me. He sent me a Valentine card. What more do you want?

R: Gently now, Julie. Here are some tissues. Better now, Julie? Julie, our time is almost up. I want you to do something for me. I want you to come and see me again. I'm afraid it won't be possible before next week, Julie, but I'm going to see if I can arrange my schedule so that I can see you more often. But in the meantime, Julie, I want you to do something for me. The next time you see Jo-Jo, I want you to be very brave. I want you to face him and say, "Go away." Just that. "Go away." Will you do that for me, Julie?

J: So you do . . . believe me?

R: I believe that you believe that Jo-Jo is bothering you, Julie. And I believe that sometimes you think you're making him up. The important question—do you see?—is why you believe these things. And that's something I'd like to talk about next time. All right, Julie? Perhaps you could think about that for me and we'll discuss it next week.

NOTES BY RD FOLLOWING FIRST TAPED SESSION: *Julie Wells*

Question: Why didn't the bloody tape work? Lise: Find someone to examine and analyze this cassette. Has it been erased? All or any part of it. Doctored? I want a full report.

Also, have my Sony TCM-737 completely overhauled. I want to know if there is any fault, especially on playback. And be sure to get them to check for intermittent faults. Get Val to help. The tape never left my briefcase since last Wednesday night. I can't see any possibility of its having been tampered with. Jo-Jo doesn't like her seeing me. Somebody phoned me and told me to leave Julie alone. Julie was trying to phone me. Julie was afraid and tried to phone me. This suggests commitment to me, first. Very early. Hypothesis: Julie was afraid, felt able to commit to me, then backed off. Believes that Jo-Jo prevented her calling me. Then called me herself, with disguised voice, to warn me off? The warning intended to make me (a) more committed to her (declare myself in some way?); (b) keep my interest.

Why has Julie never mentioned a father? Ask about this. Commitment to me as a father figure—protect her against demands (sexual/emotional) of young man (men)?

Personal note: My instinctive feelings about her as "ideal daughter." Today she was different. Jeans, loose sweatshirt. Hair looked dull, unwashed. No makeup. I had placed the chair in front of my desk, where she wanted it last time, but she ignored it. Walked straight to the green sofa and sat, hunched up small in the corner. Manner generally sulky and offhand. Reminded me that even the "ideal daughter" goes through difficult, petulant stages of rejection.

Note her explanation for Jo-Jo's "unmaking." Was she rationalizing, lying? Too pat, the explanation. She plumped for it. Received explanation. To avoid what? What really happened? Explore.

Also: Why did she need to invent Jo-Jo in the first place? Explore.

Also: Explore feelings/circumstances/doubts concerning Barry.

She loves Barry. Wants to marry Barry. Is "unofficially" engaged to Barry. What is stopping her? (Jo-Jo.) Has Jo-Jo been reinvented to prevent—no, *excuse*—her not marrying Barry? Explore.

But if that is so, then Jo-Jo should be perceived as benevolent, a protector, savior.

Has coming to me complicated that? Me versus Jo-Jo? Hypothesis: She enjoys provoking male conflict over herself; Jo-Jo reinvented as champion of her against Barry but failed in some way, became inadequate, so she sought another champion in me; and is now confused as to which of us represents her best interests?

Consider interview with Barry.

Crucial point: If she tells Jo-Jo to go away, will he? If he does, how will she feel? How will his going affect her feelings toward Barry? Toward me?

Where does the mother fit into all this? How does *she* feel about Barry/marriage?

Did Jo-Jo "fail" her in the past, as a child? Is that what she was concealing with her pat explanation of "growing out" of him? If so, she would have to be very anxious about something (Barry/marriage/commitment) in order to revive a proven inadequate protector. Desperation? A last-ditch stand?

If she commits fully to me, will Jo-Jo automatically go away? If so, am I intended to lead her toward Barry or away?

What about the multiple-personality theory (i.e., "Hilary Smyth")? Seems fainter possibility now. Unless, of course, Barry doesn't exist either.

Annie: Your comments, please.

MEMO TO RD FROM ANNIE LAMB RE ATTACHED NOTES:

Should you not be considering the possibility that you fantasized the threatening phone call? Why didn't you mention it to any of us? It would be a convenient way for you to "accept" her haunting: personal evidence and all that. I don't like this "ideal daughter" bit. Back off, Russell. The "conflicting champions" is a bit romantic, not to say sexist, no? Watch out for your stereotypes. Otherwise, I agree on basic growth points. Think it's important, though, that you choose whether to go all out for Barry or Jo-Jo. Beware confusion. Take the temperature first. Let her show a preference if she can. You should have found out about the

55

father by now. "Ideal daughters" presumably have "ideal fathers" too. Tut-tut, Russell. Shame on you.

Margaret, by her simple presence, made the house entirely safe again. This was not something Julie could explain, or properly understand. She knew it with that same part of herself that saw and heard Jo-Jo. This, for a moment, gave her a perspective on his reality, but she brushed the thought aside and clung to her mother, laughing, crying, saying over and over again how much she had missed her.

Margaret was glad to be home, too glad and too tired to see beyond her daughter's ferocious welcome to her lack of color, her nervousness, the subtle alterations that strain had made in her face. She hugged her with her right arm and presented her with gifts: chocolates, some beautiful lace-trimmed underwear, a tooled, leatherbound notebook.

"I thought," Margaret said when Julie questioned her about this last item, "you might like to use it for lists and things. You know how they always get lost. For the wedding, perhaps. Is there any news on that front, by the way?"

"No. Well, with Barry away and everything . . ."

"Is he having a good time?"

"I think so. The lines between here and France are dreadful." Julie stopped herself and smoothed the cover of the notebook, frowning. "Anyway, it's a lovely present. They're all lovely. Thank you." She kissed her mother's cheek, saw that she was tired, and said that she would leave her to unpack, rest a little. "I'm cooking you a special supper. When would you like to eat?"

"About eight?"

"Fine!"

"Thank you, darling. It's good to be home."

It seemed to Julie that her mother's homecoming completed a process begun in Dunn's office. She had carried away from that interview, like a charm, his injunction to face Jo-Jo boldly and tell him to go away. She had chanted the three simple syllables in her mind like a mantra, and the wonder of it was that she had not needed to use them. Jo-Jo had not gone. She knew that. She felt his presence, particularly in the house, but she had not seen him and had been able to resist all temptation to go in search of him. She still heard his voice at unexpected moments, but using the courage Dunn had shown her, she had been able to make the traffic roar louder or stay tuned to the background chatter of other voices.

Such incidents had given her confidence. That morning she had awakened to a different feeling in the house. Miss Tidy said it was because the sun was shining and spring was on its way at last, but she knew it was something more subtle than that. It was as though the house had been scoured from roof to basement, as though a fetid mist had been burned off by the good sun. The house was safe again; she was completely and suddenly able to look forward to Barry's return with real optimism and pleasure.

Miss Tidy did not hold with good food being all mixed up together in foreign ways, so, once she had prepared the vegetables according to Julie's instructions, she quit her kitchen. She made a fresh pot of tea, removed her apron, patted the coiled plait of iron-gray hair at the back of her head, adjusting one loose pin, and carried a tray carefully up the two flights of stairs to Margaret's room.

Her voice, in answer to Miss Tidy's quiet knock, was distant, sleepy.

"I hope I'm not disturbing you, but I thought you might fancy a cup of tea."

"How kind, Elinor. Thank you. Put it down there, will you?" She indicated a small table set by one of the windows.

"Shall I pour for you?" Miss Tidy asked, twisting her head to look at Margaret and feeling a pang of pity at her awkwardness. Lying down, she appeared helpless, clumsy. Her left arm refused to act as a lever, so that in order to sit up on the soft and yielding bed, she had to rock onto her right side and push herself up in awkward jerks. She sat on the edge of the bed, her hair tousled, and massaged her left arm absently. Margaret sank into a little chair beside the table and pulled her cup toward her.

"Is something wrong, Elinor?" she asked, sipping her tea.

"I wouldn't say *wrong*, exactly, but there is something . . ."

"Please sit down."

Miss Tidy inclined her head a little, drew out the chair tucked under Margaret's dressing table, and sat, poker-backed, her square hands planted firmly on her knees.

"You're not ill, are you, Elinor?"

"Me? No. I'm never ill. It's Julie."

"Julie? Oh don't tell me she's been upsetting you. I won't—"

"No. Leastways not by intent, but there's something not right with her, and it worries me. I can't put my finger on it. I can't say as I have any proof, but she's not herself."

"There must have been something particular," Margaret prompted gently, "or you wouldn't have mentioned it."

"Well, she looks peaked, no color. And she's living on her nerves. She's like a startled rabbit. Last week . . ." Miss Tidy hitched her chair forward and leaned closer to Margaret, dropping her voice and casting a meaningful look at the door. "My night off, it was. I left a nice casserole and everything ready for her and she never touched it. Never even turned the oven off. Now, that's not like her. And when I came in, she was sitting in the kitchen. Well, I say 'sitting,' but more sort of slumped over it was. She looked terrible. I said to her, "Why, Julie, whatever's the matter with you?" I could see straight off she'd been crying. But I couldn't get anything out of her. She shut up like a clam. And it seemed like she just didn't want to go to bed. I had to make her go in the end. And do you know, when she'd gone, I was just tidying up a bit and I found the phone was off the hook. Just dangling there, it was, right by where she'd been sitting."

Margaret did not know what to say. She cleared her throat.

"I'm sure it's something quite simple, Elinor. Perhaps she had a call from Barry and they had words. She said the lines were very bad to France. Perhaps she was just upset because she couldn't talk to him properly. You know how intense girls can be." Miss Tidy nodded gravely. "I'll definitely have a talk with her."

"There's something else."

"Yes?"

"I don't know how to put it without . . . I want you to understand, I'm not accusing Julie of anything."

"Of course not," Margaret assured her.

"The thing is, I'd say, if I didn't know better, that there had been a man in this house." Miss Tidy's lips closed and pursed as though the words, once uttered, no longer had anything to do with her.

"A man, here?"

"Of course not, but . . . well, I did wonder if perhaps, while I was out, she'd had a visitor, someone who'd upset her. But it couldn't have been Mr. Irving, not with him being abroad and everything. Besides, she'd have said."

"Of course. But what made you think . . . ?"

"It was the smell," Miss Tidy said with clipped definiteness, color mounting to her cheeks. Margaret stared at her, wide-eyed. "It sounds cranky, I know. Perhaps it's something only a woman like me, someone who's not used to men, not been around them much, would notice. But I do notice it. I was all those years with the Rector —God rest his soul—and, well, though it's not a very nice thing to say, men *do* have a different smell. I notice. I noticed the moment I came home. This is a woman's house. I know its smell. When I came back last week it was different."

"You mean like after-shave or cigarettes?" Margaret asked quickly, partly to save Miss Tidy from deeper embarrassment and partly to control her own impulse to laugh out loud.

"No. I just mean their . . . natural smell."

"I see. Were there . . . any other signs?"

Miss Tidy shook her head.

"I don't know what to think," Margaret said. "I'll talk to her. I can't think what else I can do."

"What you do is your business. I just wanted you to know. And mind, I'm not saying anything bad about Julie. She's a good girl, a proper little lady, but something is troubling her deeply and . . . well, I can't deny the evidence of my nose."

"I understand, Elinor. Thank you."

"Well, if you've finished your tea . . ."

Margaret nodded, stood up. Miss Tidy carried the tray to the door.

"I'd be obliged," she said, "if you'd treat what I told you in confidence."

Margaret remained where she was for a moment, thinking. Miss Tidy was getting old, of course, but she never complained, never carried stories about Julie or gossiped about the neighbors. It must have been important to her to mention it at all, let alone at such length. She stared at her reflection in the dressing-table mirror. Had Julie been seeing another boy? To do so behind Barry's back, not to mention her own and Miss Tidy's, seemed completely out of character. And if she had invited some boy over, knowing that Miss

Tidy would be out, so what? Only the fact that he had made her cry. How and why?

She began to brush her hair, venting on its tangles the sudden alarm she felt. But whom did Julie know, apart from Barry? There was a boy at work that she had mentioned, an assistant or trainee of Belle's. She racked her brains for others. Somebody she had just met, been smitten by? Suddenly, Margaret remembered that second Valentine card, the one she had jokingly said must be from some secret admirer. Now that she came to think of it, Julie had never shown it to her, or told her whom she supposed it to be from. A startled rabbit, Miss Tidy had said. It was easy to imagine Julie so. Whatever it was, Margaret had to get to the bottom of it. Laying down the hairbrush, she vowed that she would.

"So, how have things been while I was away?" Margaret was inclined to think that Miss Tidy had exaggerated or had based all her worries about Julie on the evidence of one particular bad day. There were signs of tension, tiredness—Margaret would not deny that— but she was tempted to attribute them to shilly-shallying about the wedding, perhaps even the long winter.

"Fine," Julie said laconically. "Are you *sure* this ratatouille is okay?"

"Absolutely. Delicious. I told you."

"Mm," Julie said doubtfully, moving her food around her plate, but not eating.

Margaret ate in silence for a while. Aware of her watchful mother, Julie ate a little.

"So," Margaret tried again, "how have you been amusing yourself in Barry's absence?"

"I haven't really."

Margaret wanted to scream. Her daughter must have more to say to her than this. "You make it sound very dull. I thought you might have seen your secret admirer," she said, aware that her teasing tone sounded forced and unconvincing.

"My—? I don't know what you're talking about." Margaret had expected a telltale blush, at least. Instead, Julie looked angry, clattered her fork onto her plate.

"The one who sent you the mysterious Valentine. About which, incidentally, you've not seen fit to tell me."

60

"Because there's nothing to tell," Julie said brusquely. "Now, if you've finished . . ."

"I haven't," Margaret said, surprised.

Julie fidgeted with her fork for a moment or two, then stood up abruptly.

"Look, if you'll excuse me—"

"No," Margaret said. "Sit down, please, darling. We must talk." She waited. Julie slowly sat down again. "I *was* prying. I'm sorry. I should just come straight out with it."

"With what?"

"I'm worried," Margaret said, raising her voice. She made herself be calm. "You don't look particularly well. More to the point, Elinor's worried."

"Elli? What's she—?"

"She wasn't tale-telling. You know her better than that. She said she came home the other night and found you'd been crying. She was worried about you. She also thought you'd had a visitor, a male visitor, which is why I was so clumsily—"

"God," Julie sighed, exasperated and shocked at the same time. She covered her face with her hands, trying to think. A male visitor? Elli? Had Elli *sensed* him?

Margaret rose quietly, walked around the table, and stood behind Julie. With her right hand she touched the girl's shoulder, and when she did not, as Margaret had half expected, shrug her off, she began to massage it gently, feeling the knots of tension beneath her fingers.

"Oh, Ma . . ." Julie twisted around and caught Margaret's hand in hers, impulsively pressing it to her cheek. "Okay, I'll tell you. I should have known Elli would make a mountain out of a molehill."

Margaret smiled and withdrew her hand. Julie looked flushed and flustered, as though finding it difficult to collect her thoughts. Margaret went slowly back to her seat.

"Rik came around, that's all. The boy from work. You know, I've told you about him. I didn't say anything to Elli because I wasn't sure he . . ." She spoke in a rush, almost without inflection. "I didn't know for certain he would come. It was just a vague arrangement, you know? Besides, it was a filthy night and Elli was so anxious to be off to her Bible class—you know how she is. But anyway, Rik turned up and we had a chat and then he pushed off. That's all there is to it, really."

Margaret nodded and did not protest when Julie, with visible relief, stood up and collected their plates.

"But that isn't quite all, is it?" Margaret had to say, staring at Julie's back. "I'm sorry to go on, but Rik really wasn't what was bothering me. Who made you cry?" Margaret waited as patiently as she knew how.

"That," Julie said with emphasis, coming back to the table for their side plates, "had nothing to do with Rik. After he left, Barry rang. Oh, it was stupid. I don't want to talk about it."

"You needn't," Margaret said quickly, relieved to have her own theory confirmed.

"It was nothing. Everything's fine now. I can't wait for him to come back. Did I tell you I'm going to meet him at the airport on Saturday?"

"No. What time does he get in?"

"Not till six," Julie said, pulling a disappointed face.

"Rik doesn't complicate things, then?"

"Rik? I don't . . . Oh . . ." She laughed. It sounded light and genuine to Margaret's sharp ears. "Heavens, no. Rik's gay. He came to tell me *his* troubles."

Margaret leaned back in her chair and closed her eyes, glad.

"What are you smiling at?" Julie asked.

"A mother's foolishness. From now on I'm not going to worry," Margaret announced, standing up.

"Please don't," Julie said softly. "Everything's going to be all right now. Really it is."

Russell Dunn stared at Valerie, uncomfortably aware of Annie's black-clad bulk looming in the doorway.

"What reason . . ." he said, his voice cracking. "Excuse me. What reason did she give?"

"None. She rang off before I could—"

"And what about the other appointments?" he asked. "The extra ones we moved heaven and earth—"

"I don't know, Russell. It was impossible to tell whether she meant just today's or all of them. I'm sorry," Val answered, un-ruffled.

"You're sorry," he said, his voice rising uncharacteristically. "I'm sure you are. I just wish you'd try to be—"

"It's not Val's fault," Annie said, moving forward with the lightness and ease that is peculiar to some fat people. She signaled with her eyes that Val should leave this to her.

"I want her file," Russell shouted after Val. He reached for the telephone. Annie's soft white hand, each pudgy finger emblazoned with hoops and swirls of silver, pressed his down onto the receiver.

"No you don't."

"But I was just beginning—"

"You never call a patient, remember? Except to cancel. You taught me that." She took her hand away. Russell reluctantly did the same. "Now," Annie went on, "what's so special about Julie Wells?"

"You've seen the notes," he said, his anger spent, leaving a feeling of weary disappointment and unspecified anxiety.

"Sure. And still I ask—"

"I was just beginning to get somewhere. You've got to admit it's frustrating."

"Well, she feels better. Or she's chickened out. Or she's scared herself off."

"Or been scared off," he said, looking at his desk.

"Either way," Annie said quietly, "there's nothing you can do about it."

"I'm frightened for her," he said, lifting his head to look into Annie's small, dark eyes, which resembled two currants pressed into the dough of her face. "Irrational, I know. Unprofessional. But there's something—"

"There's always something."

"Not like this. I've been thinking about it, Annie. The girl isn't lying."

"I never thought she was. But she's a free agent. If she doesn't want to continue . . ."

"I know. I know. I suppose I should thank you for stopping me from making a fool of myself."

"Only when you mean it. Now, I've got that tape back from the lab."

Russell did not seem to hear. Why had Julie canceled? Had the "magic" worked? Had she told Jo-Jo to go away, and had he obeyed? First aid, he thought, sneering at himself. Annie cleared her throat loudly.

"Sorry," he said. "What did you say?"

Annie put two typed sheets of paper and the cassette on his desk. "The report from the lab, about your 'threatening' phone call."

"Ah," he said, leaning forward and picking up the pages eagerly. Annie watched him as he scanned them, then went back and reread a paragraph. She saw, from his expression when he looked up at her, that he was both surprised and disappointed.

"But this amounts to nothing," he complained.

"Well, they do say that since the tape has been used many times, it's impossible to tell conclusively. It *could* have been erased."

"Except that it never left my briefcase."

"You could have done it—accidentally," Annie pointed out.

"Just that one small portion? Never."

"But that was the bit you would have replayed and rewound several times. It's quite possible."

"Are you suggesting I made a Freudian slip?"

"Either that or you imagined the whole thing."

"I did not—" He stopped himself, folded the two sheets neatly in half, and put them in a drawer. It looked as though he was meant to concede the first round to Jo-Jo, on all counts. But he wouldn't. He would not even admit the possibility. "Now, have you got your notes on Philip Potter?"

"Sure," Annie said, taking her attention from his face with reluctance. She opened the gray file she was holding.

Barry, pushing a baggage cart made awkward by skis balanced on top of his luggage, saw her at the barrier, waving, calling his name. He waved back, nearly lost control of the cart, and grinned nervously at Reggie Collis, who he knew had also spotted her. Reggie winked, returned the grin, and offered to take the cart. Then she was in his arms and everything was marvelous. She felt so completely safe, so cherished. She had forgotten, in that short time, how strong and tall he was. His body bent and seemed to enfold her. For a second he lifted her free of the ground, strong but so gentle with her, and they laughed into each other's faces.

"Oh, I love you."

"I'm so glad you're back."

"I've missed you, missed you."

"I love you, too."

"You look wonderful."

"You're so tan."

"I could eat you."

"Oh, Barry, I do love you. I do. I do."

Reggie Collis cleared his throat. Blushing, Julie shook his hand. He explained that he did not want to be a spoilsport. He had his own car. He'd be off, if that was okay. He left, waving, promising to call Barry soon.

"We had a great time," Barry told her.

"Did you manage to get that business sorted out?"

"Yes. Damn near, anyway. I'll tell you all about it later, but I definitely think we're on. There's so much to tell you. But what's been happening to you?"

"Oh, nothing. Just . . . you know." She shrugged.

In the airport car park, Barry was almost equally pleased to be reunited with his beloved car. He walked around it, inspecting the bodywork for scratches, and then, satisfied that it had suffered no damage, he unlocked the door and ushered Julie into the passenger seat.

"I've been doing a lot of thinking, too," he told her, once they were free of Heathrow and purring at a steady fifty toward London. "As well as discussing things with Reggie, I mean. There's something about the slopes that seems to clear the brain."

"All that clean mountain air," Julie put in comfortably. It was snug and warm in the car. Her happiness, the fact that she felt so comfortable with Barry, made her feel better for the first time about the lies she had told her mother, the snap decision not to go back to Mr. Dunn. She was still confused about her motives, but it was connected with her hatred of having to lie. And if she went on seeing him, sooner or later her mother would have to know. She felt a cold horror at the prospect. And Barry . . .

"Anyway, I realize that I've been forcing the pace, pushing you. It was only because I was scared of losing you. I'm one of those people who like to get things done. What I'm trying to say, pet, is that I can wait. Just as long as you're there. I don't want to push you. Not anymore. That's a promise."

She felt silly and weepy at his kindness, and could guess a little of what this speech and its preparation must have cost him.

"You are sweet," she said, "but I've been thinking, too, and . . ."

Something made her pause, some dark and shadowy fear that lurked at the back of her mind but failed to materialize. "I think the sooner the better, really."

"You mean it? Oh, darling, that's the best news I've ever had."

It would be best, she told herself. She would be crazy, really crazy to forgo the safety of his arms, his presence. Barry would protect her from . . . everything.

"But to prove that I meant what *I* said," he was saying, "I'm not even going to ask you for the date. Not now." She smiled gratefully. "I wish I could kiss you . . ."

"There'll be plenty of time for that later," she said.

"Can you stay the night? Will you?"

She hesitated, consciously examining herself for feelings that had become familiar: fear, a sense of danger, repugnance at the thought of being too close to him. There was nothing except a little excited tingle of anticipation.

"Yes," she said. "Only I'll have to ring Ma and let her know."

"Great," he said, and squeezed her hand.

At the flat, Barry presented her with a beautiful inlaid wooden box.

"That's edelweiss," he told her, pointing to a detail of the floral design. "I don't know what those are supposed to be."

"Forget-me-nots, silly. We used to have them . . ." Her mind showed her an involuntary picture of her great-grandmother's garden, and a grassy plot edged with small, delicately tinted blue flowers. "When I was a child," she finished quickly, afraid that he would notice and draw conclusions from her hesitation. He kissed her cheek.

"For me, there will always be something childlike about you," he said. "That's what makes you so sweet and adorable. But right now there is one thing I want more even than you."

"What's that?" she asked, looking into his eyes.

"A shower. I feel sticky. Airplanes always make me feel sticky." He began to pull off his clothes. Julie sat on the edge of his bed, tracing the inlaid design on the lid of the box with her finger. "Why don't you call your mother and then scout around, see if Futures and Baltic have left us anything to drink."

"All right," she said, looking at him. His skin was very pale against the deep tan of his face and hands. She looked at him greedily, without realizing that she did so. She was hungry for his strength.

"Hey," he said, pulling on an old, almost threadbare robe. "Don't look at me like that or I'll begin to think you only want me for my body."

Laughing, Julie picked up a pillow and threw it at him. He ducked and ran out. After a moment she heard him whistling. She looked at the box again, twisted it to catch the light. It was beautiful. She put it carefully on Barry's bedside table and went into the living room, to the telephone. Looking around her, hearing Barry's muffled singing, she noticed that Futures and Baltic, both of whom were away for the weekend, according to the note they had left, had made some attempt to clean up. She picked up the receiver and dialed her home number.

"Ma? It's me, Julie."

"Hello, darling. Everything all right?"

"Yes. The plane was even a little early. I'm ringing from Barry's now. He's got a wonderful tan and he's brought me such a pretty box. . . ."

"And I don't expect I'll see you until late tomorrow."

"You guessed!"

"I'm clever. Listen, why don't you bring Barry for dinner tomorrow?"

"Okay, fine. Well . . . I'll have to check with him. I'll call you if there's any hitch, okay?"

Don't, Ju-lie. Don't do it. Ju-lie.

"Yes, okay, darling, that'll be fine."

Ju-lie. Don't. Don't do it. Ju-lie. Don't make me.

"Ma? Can you hear—"

" 'Bye, darling," Margaret said, and hung up.

Why hadn't her mother heard her? Heard *him*, his voice? She looked around the room, fearfully. There was nothing, no one. Holding her breath, she cradled the receiver as though it might explode or burn her.

"Go away," she whispered. "Just go away."

It seemed that the sound she heard was in answer to her pleading. A crash. A splitting of wood. She could no longer hear Barry singing, only her own breathing. She walked as one sometimes walks in dreams, with agonizing slowness, the room stretching and shifting as if the walls and ceiling were made of rubber and some giant hand were squeezing and pulling it. Her arms outstretched instinctively to balance her against this illusion of movement, she reached the open bedroom door.

Everything steadied then. She heard distant traffic outside, an insistent knock in the old plumbing, and she saw her box, smashed and broken on the floor. Had it slipped from the bedside table, it would have come to no harm. Yet it lay on the parquet flooring, smashed and splintered irreparably. She knew it must have been hurled to the floor with ferocious strength, with the will and desire to smash and spoil. She ran to it, bent over the shattered pieces. There was no hope of mending it. How, *how* could she explain this to Barry?

Don't Ju-lie. Come away, Ju-lie.

She could not locate the source of the voice, but she glimpsed a movement by the open door, and sensed someone, something moving across the living room toward the bathroom. Her sense of threat made the air electric. As she stood up, she felt it crackle around her. She saw her coat lying across the foot of the bed and snatched it up. She ran into the living room and grabbed her purse from the arm of the scuffed leather sofa. She kept running.

In the dimly lit hall she hesitated, her hand on the lock, looking back to the bathroom. There was laughter, murmuring in the sounds of the plumbing. Her hand fumbled with the lock, turned it the wrong way. In a spasm of panic and frustration she shook the door, rattling it. Then the lock turned, clicked twice. The bathroom door opened and Barry, wearing his robe, toweling his hair, stepped out and saw her.

"Julie?"

She pulled the door open, ran out onto the landing.

"Julie? Where are you—?"

The perspective altered again. The stairs buckled and rose like the track of a demented roller coaster. Reaching blindly for the bannister, she saw its elegant wrought-iron supports shiver and coil like snakes with a black life of their own.

"Julie!"

Ju-lie.

Through a sick mist she saw him on the landing below. He was waiting for her, scowling in a way she remembered and instinctively feared. She could smell woodsmoke, hear the crackle of flames. She lurched toward him, had no choice. The stairs became firm again, still. She was able to run, her footsteps echoing and clattering. On the landing she made the terrible mistake of pausing, one hand bracing her against the wall, to look up and back.

Barry stood at the top of the flight, the white towel trailing damp and limp from his left hand. She saw the stairs shimmer and tremble like some metal-and-stone reptile gathering its force to strike.

"Julie, where the hell do you think you're going? What's wrong?" He started toward her.

"No!" she screamed. She was pressed back against the wall as though thrown and then held there by strong, relentless hands. She watched, appalled, her mind and voice frozen, as the stone steps reared up to meet Barry. She whimpered, trying to warn him, as he came on unsteadily toward her. She saw his bare toes grip the pliable stone and then, with a noise like the snapping of a high-tension wire, one black metal frond uncurled, drew back, and, like a whiplash, fastened around Barry's ankle. She saw a look of stupid surprise cross his face, and then he pitched forward, yelling. The black metal released him, sprang back unnoticed into its place. He fell, turned over, slithered toward her feet. Through her own screams she heard his head crack against the solid stone of the landing.

Below, doors opened, voices called, and as she bent to tend Barry, she saw Jo-Jo at the top of the stairs, outside the open flat door, smiling down at her. His whole presence beckoned to her.

Four

"He woke up in the hospital hours later—three, four in the morning. They let me stay with him. It was only a mild concussion but his ankle is very badly sprained. They had to strap it up for him. He's been very brave. He makes a joke of it, says that only he could manage to go skiing without breaking his ankle and then come home and fall down the stairs. Only it wasn't an accident, Mr. Dunn. It was Jo-Jo and it was partly my fault. All or partly. I don't know. That's why I had to come back."

Russell Dunn leaned back in his chair, eyes fixed on the tips of his own tented fingers. He was trying to find words to describe to himself the change in her.

"Are you angry with me?" she said into his silence but, he thought, with a hint of irritation in her voice. "I've said I'm sorry."

"No." He shook his head. "I'm not angry with you, Julie. I was trying to pinpoint how you have changed." He looked at her directly, met eyes that, he thought, saw him but did not take him in. "Do you feel you have changed, Julie?"

"I don't really know what you mean. I suppose I've changed in the sense that I've decided to come back here."

"I don't think I understand that, Julie. Can you explain?"

"I think I feel differently about . . . wanting your help."

70

"You didn't want it before, you mean?"

"Well, yes, I did, but . . . I think it's what you said about 'first aid.' I think I wanted first aid and I think, in a sense, you gave it to me. And it *did* work. Or it seemed to. Only when it wore off, things got worse."

"So how do you feel about coming here now, Julie?"

"I feel I've got to. I feel . . . this time I really want you to help me. I need it."

"I think possibly that what you're trying to say—and, please, I want you to be absolutely clear about this and to correct me if I'm wrong . . ." She nodded gravely, moistening her lips. "I think that what you're trying to say is that now you see that I can only help you to help yourself. I have no magic wand, nothing up my sleeve." He showed his empty hands, tugged down the cuffs of his jacket. "No more magic Band-Aids, Julie."

"Yes. I know."

"And that means two things. You have to be prepared to work very hard, and you have to trust me. Wait . . ." He held up his hand as she was about to speak. "That hard work will, I'm sure, often be very painful, will touch on areas that frighten and hurt you. And if I am to help you to find and become reconciled with what is troubling you, you will have to trust me even when you feel that I am your torturer rather than your helper."

"I won't run away again, Mr. Dunn. I promise you that."

He considered her choice of words. They were very spontaneous and he believed that she saw her cancellation as a flight. This was progress. He felt quietly excited.

"I'd rather you didn't make promises. There will be times, I'm sure, when you will not be able to face another session. You will be exhausted and resentful; you may even despair. I am prepared for that, but I want you to promise me only one thing: I want you, no matter how difficult it is, to speak to me. Tell me that you can't face coming. In return I promise that I won't try to persuade you to come, though I shall ask you to keep the next appointment. Will you do that for me?"

"Yes."

"Thank you."

"You make it sound very frightening."

"Let's hope that it won't be. Now, a rather mundane point, but

can you afford this? I ask because I would hate us to embark on this
. . . journey . . . only to have to break it off because you could not
afford my fees. There are ways—"

"I think I can. My great-grandmother left me some money of my
own. It was quite well invested—at least that's what Barry says—
and I never touched it until I was eighteen, so . . . I think it will be
all right."

"Good. If at some time you feel that it is not, please tell me."

"All right."

That subject closed, he wondered where next to begin. He cleared
his throat.

"You were telling me about Barry. How is he now?"

"Hobbling. Oh, he's all right, he . . . the awful thing is having to
lie to him. Well, I suppose it's not really lying, just letting him
believe what he . . . He thinks I broke the box, you see, and couldn't
face him. He thinks I'm afraid, a child," she said, her voice rising,
"and I have to let him because . . ." She shook her head, signifying
that talking about it was no good.

"It's being mistaken for a fool or a child that hurts, isn't it, Julie?
That more than the lying."

"Yes, I suppose. Not my mother, though. I *hate* that. I've never
lied to her."

"What does your mother think is happening, then, Julie?"

"Nothing. Oh, she thinks I'm afraid, upset over Barry, of course."
She could not meet his eyes.

"You haven't told her that you're seeing me?" he asked quietly,
realizing that he had assumed, until the mention of her own money,
that Julie's mother had been paying his fee and therefore approved
of his involvement.

"I couldn't tell her. I couldn't."

"I think you must."

"No."

"Julie . . . there may come a time—in fact, I'm sure there will
come a time—when I shall want to talk to your mother. And Barry,
possibly."

"No, they mustn't know. They can't—"

"Why not, Julie?"

"Just because."

"They will want to help you, too. It isn't fair to them—"

72

"None of this is fair. It's not fair to me. But it's *my* problem. I've got to deal with it. I want you to help me, not them. I'm an adult now. I don't want them . . ."

Her words, fiercely articulated, crystallized the change he had sensed in her. He realized that she had already gone further, seen more clearly than he had. He leaned forward, deliberately letting the matter of her mother and Barry drop, but noting it for a future time.

"All right, Julie. Let's begin, shall we?"

She looked at him nervously, waiting. She was doing a good job, he thought, of controlling her feelings—anger and panic, he suspected—but also saw that her hold upon herself was fragile.

"What's your first memory, Julie? The very first thing you can remember?"

"Oh, I don't know . . ."

"Please. Take your time."

She made a show of thinking, screwing up her eyes, fidgeting with her bag. After a while she said, "My childhood, I suppose."

"Can you go back further than that, to when you were a baby, perhaps?"

"No." She shook her head.

"Try, Julie. Just relax and think about it. There's plenty of time."

She wanted, he was sure, to protest at this, to tell him about Barry's accident, her present fears, and he, just as surely, wanted her to let go of these for a while, to relax. He watched, quite still. She shifted in her seat and sighed.

"It's more of a feeling, really. Not a real memory with pictures, you know?"

"That's all right, Julie."

"A feeling of great warmth and safety. A presence. Being held. No. Not a presence. A woman. Definitely a woman. Great warmth and safety. A woman. And then a face, very old, all lined and wrinkled, hanging over me. Very large. Too big. My great-gran's face. I can recognize her."

"Who is the other woman, Julie?"

"My mother, of course. I can't see her, though, but it must have been my mother."

"Did your mother leave you, Julie?"

73

"Oh, yes. She had to. She was very famous, you see. She had to go away."

"Go on, Julie. Tell me about it."

Her mummy had to go away.

It was always winter. The winter color of starched uniforms, white overalls, and stiff, large aprons that flapped like injured wings as Nanny walked briskly through the garden. They were kind enough, and times with Great-Gran were sweet, especially tea around the winter fires. Strawberry jam stayed in the mouth, a memory. She felt safe then.

The shocking red of spilled jam on a crisp white apron. A slap. Her own screams of surprise and misery, running into the garden and being marched back, slapped again. Great-Gran dressed her in her warmest clothes, with scarves and boots and mittens, and let her play out there, alone. From the great dark bushes of the drive she watched Nanny, her face as white as her apron, climb into a waiting car, its engine ticking over. Nanny was driven away. Others came and went. Their faces melted into one indifferent blur. They were differentiated only by their uniforms. The nurses wore white uniforms and were, on the whole, younger. Nannies wore tough dresses of gray or blue, always with a starched apron, which crackled and flapped as they walked.

Great-Gran taught her to read and make her letters. Great-Gran taught her how to fit the many brightly colored postcards into a series of albums. Toronto and Michigan and New York City. Paris, Lille, and Rotterdam. The names of German towns written in angular letters. From these, Great-Gran taught her geography, helped her make maps of her mother's tours. Great-Gran taught her to read so that she might decipher for herself the brief messages of love. *Hope you're being a good girl. Give Gran a big hug for me. Missing you. Love M.*

And her mummy came home, once, twice a year. Her mummy always arrived in big cars, piled high with presents. Nannies and nurses alike complained at this spoiling, the inevitable disruption of their regime. Some left. Some were dismissed. Some sulked and afterwards criticized. These events only framed the visits, over which hung a pall of gold: sunlight or firelight. Golden hair. Golden jewelry. Golden times. A companion to walk in the garden with, holding hands. Someone to take her for rides in a car, on shopping

74

trips. New clothes, the prettiest that money could buy. New toys. Games. Bedtime got later, mornings lazier. The sound of their voices. Her mother's light voice, Great-Gran's dark and frequently querulous voice, talking late into the night.

Sometimes in the morning Mummy played, great cascades of music, waterfalls of golden sound conjured out of the stubborn black and white keys.

Afterwards, the house was larger, more gloomy, silent. The garden closed tight around its walls with her mother's going. The old shawl, its once bright colors dimmed now to dust, was again draped across the closed and locked piano. She stared at it, the only thing in the house that was her mother's, with all her mother's magic locked within it. The music was locked away inside the piano and only Mummy could unlock it, with just the gentle touch of her fingers.

Outside, golden daffodils, pale sunlight, like painful leavings of her mother's visit. She explained all this to Jo-Jo and he understood.

For once he was glad to hear Denise's voice. If she had not phoned him, he would have been forced to broach the subject with her, and that was difficult for him. It made him feel vulnerable, touched upon his inadequacies.

"What's wrong with Rupert?" she asked, coming straight to the point.

"I was going to ask you exactly the same question."

"Oh, I see, it's my fault, is it?"

"I never said that, or"—he hurried on over her instantly ready argument—"or meant to imply any fault."

"Well, he was perfectly all right when he left here this morning."

"I don't agree."

"Well, of course, if you're not going to take any responsibility . . ."

"For what? I don't know yet what the cause is. If it is mine, I will, of course—"

"All right, Russell, you're not in your consulting room now." He did not answer this, but waited. He heard her take a deep breath, usually a signal that she was willing to start over, give a little ground. "Didn't you ask him?"

"Naturally. He said nothing was wrong."

"Well, he's been as miserable as sin all evening. I couldn't get anything out of him."

"He told me you'd explained about the computer game."

"What's that got to do with anything?"

"I thought . . . I wondered if it might have made him uneasy with me, mistrustful."

"How?" she barked.

"Well, I told him I'd get him the game, you told him I wouldn't."

"He accepted it perfectly well."

"On the surface, yes. I think he's afraid of provoking fights between us." Here Denise snorted. It was an eloquent sound. It said that he and she needed no help, could create their own conflicts unaided. "But I think you've undermined his confidence in me."

"Oh, that's a load of crap, Russell, and you know it. It's not even original. You're just trying to get back at me. You can't bear the idea of my having any autonomous authority where he's concerned. I don't want to discuss your problems. . . ."

Wearily and with just a touch of anger, Russell held the receiver away from his ear, reducing her voice to a tinny buzz. He wished he had poured himself a drink before answering the telephone. Then he heard a noise on the line, obscuring her voice, and he brought the receiver quickly back to his ear. Silence.

"Are you there? Can you hear me?" he asked.

A crossed line, he thought. Someone had cut in. Denise would tell them to get off the line.

You can hear me.

"I'm sorry, but you've got a—" he said automatically, but the flat, uninflected voice was already deadly familiar. He felt his flesh creep on his back. The hand that held the telephone with too tight a grip became slick and slippery with sweat.

I told you before. You're not to see her. She belongs to me. You tell her. I shan't warn you again. You leave her alone.

Somehow, from somewhere he managed to dredge up a rasping shadow of his own voice. The prickling in his scalp, beneath his short hair, seemed like needles, penetrating and numbing his brain.

"Who—who are you?"

You know all about me. You tell her. She belongs to me.

"Jo-Jo?"

Then the voice laughed. It was like a child's angry parody of a laugh, mocking and yet brittle, cold. Then it ceased. The line sounded dead, open.

76

"Jo-Jo?" he heard a slight burring noise, but nothing else. "Answer me, please . . ." Russell stopped. He felt the blood mount to his cheeks and burn there. How long since he had blushed? He was a grown man, for God's sake, sitting in his own home, talking to a . . . to someone who had never even existed. He put the receiver down, clenched his hands together. Someone who had never existed outside the mind of a lonely child, now a young woman. A cigarette . . .

The phone rang. He reached for it at once and then hesitated. This time he must be prepared. What should he ask? Challenge the voice, say: Is that you, Julie? Was it? The incessant ringing made thought impossible. It had not sounded like her. Had it?

"What the hell happened to that line?"

"Oh . . . Denise." A kind of weak relief flowed through him, and with it came a band of tension, squeezing his forehead.

"Who have you been talking to? I rang back immediately."

"You got a busy signal?"

"Of course I got a busy signal. You were talking to someone. Who was it?"

"I don't know," he said honestly.

"Another of your cranks, I suppose. Well, anyway, about Rupert—"

"Look, Denise, can I ring you back? I don't feel—"

"No, you cannot. We either discuss this now or—"

"I'm sorry," he said, raising his voice to subdue hers, "but I can't just now."

"Then forget it. I'm going to bed." She slammed the receiver down. He listened to the dial tone, waited for that other voice.

Russell: When did you first . . . see Jo-Jo?

Julie: Don't know. One of the bad times.

R: When your mother wasn't there?

J: Yes. Between nannies. Nanny Belling. After the trouble with the strawberry jam. Oh, by the way. I've been thinking about that. I think . . . I don't think it was an accident. I think . . . I'm sure I threw the jam at her. Maybe accidentally-on-purpose, you know?

R: Why, Julie?

77

J: Don't know. Maybe just to be naughty. It doesn't matter, does it?

R: Perhaps you felt bad about it, guilty?

J: She hit me.

R: Maybe Jo-Jo threw the jam and you—

J: No. Jo-Jo wasn't there then.

R: When did he come?

J: After. Right after. Yes.

R: That day?

J: Yes.

R: When Great-Gran put your warm clothes on and let you go to play in the garden?

J: I wanted her to go. Nanny Belling. I was glad and then I was sorry, afraid. I knew I'd made her go. . . . Then I went back through the shrubbery, around the side of the house. It was so dark in there, I thought it must be night already, but it was only the bushes. There was a fire. . . .

R: Go on, Julie.

J: We had a gardener. An old man. I don't know where he came from. He didn't come every day. Great-Gran was always complaining about the garden, the difficulty of keeping it up. He had a funny name. Mr. Crump. That's right. Crump. Only I didn't call him that. I called him Crumble.

R: There was a fire, Julie. . . .

J: Yes. Right at the bottom of the garden. Crumble'd been burning old plants, wood . . . I don't know. All day, the smell of it. Smoke. There was no wind. It just hung in the air, drifting up. Nanny said it got everywhere. That's right. Nanny was in a bad mood because . . . yes . . . she said Crumble's bonfire had ruined her washing. Black smoke, she said, on her washing. She went on and on about it. She complained to Great-Gran, but Great-Gran said Crumble had to have a fire. It was essential. And he'd waited for a windless day and it was far away from the house and . . . Nanny wouldn't let me go out. *That's* right. It's all coming back to me now. How can you forget so much, Mr. Dunn, and yet it's all there, really?

R: Just concentrate on it, Julie. Don't let it go.

J: I don't see what all this has to do with . . . all right. I'll try. She wouldn't let me go out. Not even for my afternoon walk after lunch. She said the smoke would get in my lungs and give me a cough. "And we don't want you in bed for a week, do we, miss? Or getting all covered in soot. Don't blame me. It's not my fault. Blame that stupid old gardener." She made me do copying, *all* afternoon. Just copying, out of a book. And she made me do it again because she said there were mistakes. And then we had tea....

R: Go on, Julie.

J: I was trying to remember. . . . Why didn't I have tea with Great-Gran? Great-Gran wasn't there . . . Great-Gran wasn't there. . . .

R: All right, Julie. It's all right.

J: She couldn't have been there because I had tea with Nanny. Tea in the nursery, not downstairs with Great-Gran.

R: But she came back, Julie, didn't she? She was there later?

J: Oh, yes, yes, of course. Yes, she was.

R: So it was all right, after—

J: Yes. After I'd thrown jam on Nanny's clean apron and she'd hit me and I ran out into the garden. The smell of woodsmoke. She caught me and she slapped me again and she dragged me back to the house and . . . that's right . . . Great-Gran was standing there, in her coat and hat and gloves. "What on earth happened?" she said. "I thought for a moment there was blood on your apron, Nanny. I thought the child was hurt."

R: So it was all right. She was back. Yes, Julie?

J: Yes.

R: The bonfire, Julie. Did you perhaps go to play near the fire?

J: I don't know. I'm tired. It must be time. . . .

R: Not quite yet, Julie. Try to remember the fire. You could smell the smoke. . . .

J: The sun came out. You couldn't see the flames. Only little flames. You know the way they seem to lick along a burnt stick? It was just stick and ash. The sticks were black and white, glowing red in places. Little flames running up and down them. I got a stick from Crumble's wheelbarrow and poked the fire. I wasn't allowed to poke the fire. I used to watch Great-Gran . . . it was naughty but I didn't care because Nanny Belling was gone and Great-Gran had gone out and I was cross with her and now she'd be cross with me. She was always cross when a nanny went and this time it was all my fault. All my fault. So I poked the fire and

didn't care and it blazed up again. The flames got bigger, dancing. . . . It was hot. And then . . .

R: Yes, Julie?

J: Then . . . Jo-Jo was in the flames.

R: Go on, Julie.

J: I can't.

R: He was *in* the flames . . . burning?

J: No. It only looked like that. I saw him *through* the flames, on the
other side of the bonfire. This sad little boy, just standing there,
looking at me.

R: Jo-Jo.

J: Yes.

R: What did you feel, Julie? It's important. Please try.

J: I wanted . . . so much . . . I wanted my mother. I didn't want
any strangers, old people . . . I wanted . . . I knew I couldn't
. . . My mother couldn't . . . without her we couldn't afford
anything. And besides, she had a sacred duty. Artists do, you
know. A sacred duty to her public . . . But I wanted, so much
. . . more than I'd ever wanted anything . . .

R: What did you want, Julie?

J: Someone . . . someone who was *mine*. Someone who was really
mine.

R: Jo-Jo.

J: He was *there*. He reached out to me. He put his hand into the
flames, right through the flames, and they didn't burn him. He
was magic. He wanted me to take his hand but I was scared. The
flames were so hot and dancing. . . . But that didn't stop him. Oh,
no. He walked . . . he came right on through the flames. For me.
I saw his feet breaking sticks and scattering ash . . . little puffs
of ash. . . . Right through the flames. For *me*. And . . . and he
took hold of my hand and held it.

R: And what did you feel then, Julie?

J: I . . . don't know.

R: Were you afraid?

J: No. Oh, no. I was . . . happy . . . happy . . . I felt . . . safe.

R: Well, of course you did, Julie. You had a friend, didn't you?
Someone of your very own.

J: Yes. That's it exactly.

R: You've done very well, Julie. But now it's time. . . .

J: How can you forget so much and yet remember so clearly?
R: Why don't we talk about that next time, Julie? Now ...

"Do you know, in all that time I can never remember Jo-Jo inside
the house? Isn't that weird? I mean, you'd think ... Because we were
inseparable. Like one person, really. But if I was out late or anything, I could hear him calling me. No matter where I was in the
house, I could hear him calling me. 'Ju-lie. Ju-lie. Can't find me.'
The garden was our place. Our world, really. Oh, it was such a
beautiful garden. Do you know it even ... even has a pond? I don't
mean beautiful in a formal way or anything. It was more of a wild
garden. Great-Gran could never afford to keep it up. But it was a
perfect place for children. I've been thinking and I want to tell you,
even though I know it's going to sound ... well ... odd. The thing
is ... well ... I was really happy then. Of course, I don't mean like
I was when my mother was there, but definitely happy. It was a
safe kind of happiness. I don't know if that makes any sense. When
Ma was there, everything was exciting, bright. Bright colors. Bright
lights. And I never, ever wanted her to go away. That was always
terrible, but it wasn't so bad after ... after Jo-Jo came. Did I tell you I
used to read about my mother, when I was older? Great-Gran used to
take three newspapers and the music journals, and then sometimes
Ma would send her a cutting and I would read about her. 'Margaret
Wells. The young virtuoso pianist.' I didn't understand a lot of what
I read, but it was so exciting and it brought her closer somehow
because I could share it all with Jo-Jo. He loved hearing about her and
sometimes he could make sense of things I couldn't. Really, you
know, I've been very lucky. There was really only that one time I was
unhappy—before Jo-Jo came. Because when Jo-Jo went, Ma was
there. She came back to stay for good. So, really, I've very little to
complain about. I've almost always been very happy. It's so silly. I
don't even know why I'm crying."

Annie, a glass of wine in her ringed fingers, looked around the
pink-and-black-lacquered room and said, "Have you ever thought
about going back into analysis?"

"No. Why do you ask?" Russell was relaxed enough to be amused.

"Because if this room came out of the last one, if this is your way
of coping with Denise . . ."

"I like it," Russell said with a fond grin of pleasure and appreciation. "I'll tell you something else. I like myself more in this room."

"Womb."

"Probably."

"Ah, well, as somebody said, there is no accounting for taste." She put her glass down on the floor, picked up the fat gray folder beside her, and opened it on her knees. "Have you considered that she may have split herself entirely in two?" Annie asked, with one of those abrupt changes of subject that was characteristic of her and probably, Russell thought, part of her own complicated defense mechanism. He nodded.

"And now she's done it again," Annie said. "Jo-Jo knows she shouldn't marry Barry. Julie thinks she should."

"Yes, but why?"

"Ah, that's just it. You're floundering."

"You think so?" Russell asked. "What about the possibility that she really feels guilty about being happy with Jo-Jo, when her mother wasn't there?"

"I'd agree that Jo-Jo is the seat of some deep guilt, yeah, but I still say you're floundering." Russell stared over her plump shoulder. "Isn't that what you asked me here to tell you?"

"That and the pleasure of your company, Annie."

"You do agree you're floundering?"

"I . . . thought I might be. I hoped you'd say I wasn't."

"Well, so far it's classic textbook stuff."

Russell raised an eyebrow at this statement, but Annie ignored him.

"Lonely child 'abandoned' by mother, 'abandoned' by a series of paid minders, invents companion. Companion goes away when mother returns. Why did she return, by the way?" Annie asked.

Russell shrugged.

"You see what I mean? You're not pushing things on, Russell. You ought to know by now. Why are you treading water?"

"Mostly because I thought that if I let her just play over that time, it might give me some clue, something more about Jo-Jo. Also, it's the one thing that calms her, makes her able to cope with her present anxieties. And don't you think that might be the beginnings of some form of reconciliation?"

"Between the child Jo-Jo and the present one, you mean?"

"Exactly."

"I'm not even sure there *is* a present one, Russell. And what more can you find out about him? What clues? From her, anyway. Maybe if you saw the mother . . ."

He spread his hands; he didn't know. And something—a fear probably of her scorn or concern—stopped him from telling her about the second phone call. It was because of that and Julie's simple conviction that he was sure.

"Also, talking about Jo-Jo as he *was* somehow seems to give her a measure of control over him now. You notice that he hasn't—"

"That presupposes a hell of a lot, Russell."

"Just thinking aloud, Annie."

"Well, I think it's time you changed tack. I also think we need a few facts here."

"Such as?" he asked affably, sipping his wine.

"You still haven't got around to the father. Oh, don't worry. I'm not even going to bother to ask you why. And where does the fiancé fit in? Why did Mother come back, just like that?"

"You're absolutely right, of course."

Annie's small eyes grew smaller when she narrowed them. She had expected justifications, an argument at least. Even when a case was progressing smoothly and had found its right, natural rhythm, Russell took suggestions cautiously, met them with countersuggestions and questions of his own.

"Why, Russell?" she said.

"Why? I don't understand."

"Why are you picking up so easily on my suggestions? Damn it, you know it's not like you."

"This case isn't like any other. I feel very uncertain about it. What you call 'floundering' . . . I promised myself that I would accept what you said. And I do see that it's sound advice, a more down-to-earth approach. Now, you wanted to tell me about one of your clients, didn't you?" he said smoothly, moving past her to fetch the carafe of Margaux from the table. "Clare, isn't it?"

"Clarice," she said dryly. "And I don't trust you, Russell. You're up to something or you're holding something back."

"Some more wine?" he offered, holding up the carafe.

"Julie, today I want to talk about the men in your life."

"Men?" she laughed nervously. "There are no 'men' in my life. Unless you mean Barry."

"I do mean, Barry, yes."

"But Barry has nothing to do with this."

"And isn't there someone we're forgetting, perhaps leaving out deliberately, for reasons I don't understand?"

She considered this, frowning, chewing at her bottom lip.

"Oh." Her face brightened with understanding, then clouded. "You mean Jo-Jo?"

"Perhaps him, too, yes."

"But we talk about Jo-Jo all the time."

"What about your father, Julie?" She looked genuinely surprised, as though thrown or lost. "Why do you never mention him?"

"Because I never knew him. There's nothing to say." She seemed to relax a little, as though a danger had passed. Russell felt a slight disappointment. Thinking about Annie's suggestion, he had begun to hope that the father might be important. Then he reminded himself that he should not necessarily believe Julie, neither her words nor the language of her face and body. Patients often had a formula by which they could cut off from what they most feared, even while seeming to talk about it quite rationally.

"There must be something," he said mildly.

"No." She shook her head. He saw that today she was holding her bag on her knees, both hands clasped firmly over the top of it.

"His name, for example?"

"Tom, I think."

"Tom Wells?"

"No. That's my mother's name. I'm illegitimate." She looked down, then quickly back up at him, challenging.

"I see. How do you feel about that?"

"I don't." She shrugged. "These things happen. Anyway, it's nothing to do with me. My mother says . . . My mother explained that it was nothing I need feel ashamed about or worry over. The child is innocent, no matter what some people may think about the parents. I really believe that. If it . . . if it happened to me, that's how I'd see it. Besides, nobody really cares about that sort of thing anymore, do they?"

It was a direct question to which he must make some kind of reply. He shrugged, and spread his hands.

"Do you want me to tell you about it?"

"If you want to. If you think I should—"

"No. I don't. I don't think it has anything to do with you or me or why I'm here," she said angrily, her face screwed up and flushed with tension and anger. She had difficulty controlling her breathing and voice. Russell opened his mouth to speak. "But I know you. I'm beginning to see what you do. And if we don't clear it up now, you'll just keep coming back to it and picking at it until . . . well, we just waste more time. Why don't you ask me a direct question?"

"Very well . . ."

"Oh, don't bother. You'll only wrap it up so I have to make a choice and wonder why I'm telling you. All right." Again she battled with her breathing. He saw beads of sweat on her upper lip. "Well, it was an affair my mother had, with a boy at the Conservatory. It was an accident. I mean I was. The pregnancy. She didn't even care for him. But she didn't want an abortion. They weren't as easy to get then as they are now. Or as safe. But anyway, she never considered it. She wanted *me.* She didn't want him. That's all there is to it." She sat back sighing, as though she had discharged an unpleasant duty and the subject were now closed.

"Were you never curious about him?"

"No. Why should I be?"

"Most . . . illegitimate persons are, at some stage in their lives."

"Not me."

"You never asked questions?"

"My mother explained everything when I was about twelve. She doesn't care to talk about it anymore."

"But you . . . I can see that would be a reason for not asking the questions. . . ."

"Children—people in general, for all I know, but especially children—don't miss what they don't know. I would have thought you would know that. I had Great-Gran, and Ma. I didn't need to know anything else."

He waited, impassively inviting her to fill the silence. She did not look at him, but at some point on the wall to her left. After a short while she began to tap her foot.

"Julie," he said quietly, "can you tell me why you're angry with me?"

"Because you waste time. You're supposed to be helping me and all you do is ask stupid questions about things that don't matter."

85

"It's a question of finding out what matters, Julie. Don't you see that?"

"But I know what matters. You know. *Jo-Jo* matters."

"You want to talk about Jo-Jo?"

"I don't have any choice. He's why I'm here. Or don't you believe in him?"

"I believe that you believe—"

"Oh, there you go again. Round and round in circles." She stood up abruptly, presumably to leave, but she did not. Russell waited while she opened her bag and took out a handkerchief, which she simply held in her hand.

"Shall we try again, Julie? Would you like to sit down?"

She nodded once and sat down, putting the bag down beside her. She began to play with the handkerchief, plucking at it, winding it around her fingers, her forearms resting on her slightly splayed legs.

"I would like to ask you something, Julie." She made no response. "If you say that Jo-Jo matters, does Barry not matter?"

"Of course Barry matters. You know he does. They both matter. You just twist my words. It's impossible to talk to you. When I say Jo-Jo matters, I mean *here*, as a problem. But Barry matters in a different way, because I love him. And if Jo-Jo would leave me alone, I could marry him and . . ."

"And what, Julie?"

"Stop coming here and wasting my time." She reached down and picked up her bag, thrust the handkerchief inside, and clipped the bag shut again. "I really don't feel in the mood today," she said faintly. "I'm sorry."

"That's all right, Julie. Has something happened?"

She shook her head sharply, then, as though afraid he might not believe her, she looked straight into his eyes and shook it again.

"No. Nothing."

"How is Barry's ankle? Is it progressing?"

"Yes. He gets around quite well now, with his stick."

"Good."

"Yes."

He looked at his watch.

"Can you just explain something to me? It's a question of getting things straight in my own mind."

"All right."

86

"Why did your mother come back to live with you? Presumably she gave up a career—"

"She had an accident. It damaged her left arm. It's mostly . . . I mean partially paralyzed. She couldn't play anymore."

"That must have been very hard for her."

"No. She says it's the best thing that ever happened to her."

"For you, then. Having your mother restored to you at such a cost . . ."

"No. I never wanted her to go away. I was glad she was with me all the time. I still am. I love my mother. She's a very special person. But I didn't . . . You have no idea . . . Why do you always have to . . . to make things sound bad?"

"I wasn't aware that I did."

"Well, that's how it seems."

"How did your mother's accident happen?"

"I don't really know. I think she slipped and fell, put her arm through a window. It's not something she cares to talk about."

"No. Understandably, perhaps."

"Can I go now?"

"You can go whenever you want to, Julie. You know that."

"Right." She stood up. "Well, I'll—"

"Julie, there is just one other thing, since our time isn't up yet . . ."

"You said I could go!" she almost shouted.

"Something I want to tell you. It's not anything you have to answer. I think . . ." He was not at all sure, and debated with himself even as the words formed in his mind. He hesitated. "I think it may help you." There was a flicker of interest in her eyes, but she remained wary, as though expecting some other trick to make her stay. She looked impatiently at the door. "On Sunday night, I spoke with Jo-Jo. On the telephone."

He could only see her in profile. For a moment he thought that she was going to break down. Automatically his hand moved toward the box of tissues. Her face squeezed tight, as though in pain. Finding reserves of strength that surprised him, she managed to get a precarious hold on her emotions.

"I see. Thank you for telling me. Now I—"

"Julie," he called, half rising from his seat.

Her legs seemed stiff. Jerkily she moved to the door, got it open, rushed out. He heard Val's voice, but no answer to it. He slumped back in his chair.

He wasn't sure, not at all, that he should have told her. He could already hear Annie's voice saying he was only trying to ensure that she came back, and that in a most unprofessional way. He tried to consider the charge, but was impatient with it. The important thing was his motive in telling her. Compassion? Had he wanted to reach out to her, to reassure her that she was not alone, that he believed in Jo-Jo? Or had he been asking for help, trying to bind her tighter to him by seeking her protection against Jo-Jo's threats? Deep down he had wanted her to crack, to admit that she had made the call, or at least knew of it. Had she come near to that? Was that the cause of her pain?

Angry with himself, he got up and began to pace the room. He had achieved nothing. He stopped at the open door, went to close it. Val leaned from her desk and reminded him that Mr. Potter was due any minute. He stared at her. He had miscalculated, acted without sufficient preparation. He fought an urge to run after Julie, to try to explain. . . .

"Mr. Potter . . ." Val said again.

"Yes, yes," he answered impatiently. "I'll be ready for him." And closed the door.

At first she had been in despair. She had hurried back to Covent Garden, muttering to herself, over and over, like a madwoman: *All right, Jo-Jo. All right, Jo-Jo. All right, Jo-Jo.* As soon as she got home, she had written a letter to Mr. Dunn explaining why, now, she could not go on with the treatment. But the letter had seemed like a cheat when she remembered her promise to him. So she made herself keep the next appointment, so that she could explain to him, face to face, that she could not go on.

"Why do you assume," Russell asked, when she was silent, "that Jo-Jo was hostile toward me?"

"Because you said you . . ." He shook his head slowly, and she went on, "Because that's his way. That's what he always does. Look at Barry. . . ."

"Always? When you were children, did he threaten you? Did he hurt you, perhaps? Or anybody?"

"No. No. He was nice. He never, ever—"

"But now?"

"I know he hates you. He tells me so, all the time. He hates you because you're trying to get rid of him."

"And he hates Barry because you want to marry him?"

"Yes. Yes, that's it exactly. So you see I can't . . . I must stop coming here."

"All right, Julie." He leaned back in his chair, like a man who has given up yet remains open, willing to be of service. "So what will you do now?"

"I don't know." She shook her head impatiently, then began to cry quietly, ignoring the tissues near at hand, occasionally wiping the tears away with her fingers.

"Tell me something, Julie. A simple question." She tried to say something, but he interrupted. "I know you don't feel like working today. I know you want to stop, but just tell me this. You were eight when Jo-Jo went away?" She nodded. "And also eight at the time of your mother's accident?" She swallowed, took a tissue at last, and rubbed the end of her nose with it. She nodded a second time. "So the two events were connected?"

"Yes."

"How, Julie?"

"Because Ma brought me to London. I just grew out of Jo-Jo, I suppose."

"I think you can do better than that, Julie."

She thought about it, tearing the tissue, sniffing.

"There was no room for him when Ma came back. I didn't have time, I . . . I was bored with him. I didn't . . ."

"Yes, Julie?"

"I didn't *need* him. Is that what you want me to say?"

"If that is so, then I ask myself . . . why do you need him now, Julie?"

"I don't. I don't. How can you say that? Can't you see how I . . . I only came to you because I couldn't bear him, because he frightens me and means to . . . to do something terrible."

"I know that, Julie. I understand. But I still think, in some way, some part of you needs him now."

"No!"

"You needed him then—and I *believe* you did—but you could send him away quite easily when you no longer needed him. You say you don't need him now, yet you can't send him away. Why not, Julie?"

"I don't know. I don't know."

"Then why did he come back, Julie?"

"I don't *know!*"

"I think you do, Julie."

"All right! To marry me!" She shouted it straight into his face, but the anger that he had succeeded in provoking gave her a little more strength. She did not break.

"How can you marry someone who doesn't exist, Julie?"

"But he does. You know he does. You've spoken to him."

"*Someone* spoke to me, Julie. *Someone* told me to stop seeing you."

"Jo-Jo. It was Jo-Jo."

"You know that for a fact, do you? You were there?"

"No. No. Stop it. Stop confusing me. I can't explain. . . ."

"Because perhaps there is something you haven't told me, Julie? Is there?"

"I don't know what you mean. I answer all your questions, or I try to. . . ."

"I think there's something you want to tell me, Julie. Deep down you want to, but you're afraid. I want you to stop feeling afraid, and I believe you will if you'll just tell me."

"I don't know. I can't. Oh, why don't you leave me alone?"

"All right, Julie."

She stared at him, her mouth hanging open. He looked deliberately around the room, then at his watch.

"All right *what?*"

"Enough, Julie. Let's leave it there."

"Do you . . . do you mean I should come back?"

"If you want to."

"I don't *want* to. . . ."

He stared at the wall above her head, where a picture hung. It was a simple botanical print titled *Myosotis,* and it hung a little askew.

"All right. I made him a promise," she said in a flat voice. "I didn't want to tell you because . . . oh, I don't know. So many reasons." Slowly he let his eyes return to her. "Because it makes me sound crazy, makes me feel guilty, too, I suppose. Guilty because all this is my fault and I . . . I don't want anything bad to happen to anyone. You must believe that."

90

He nodded once, still maintaining a deliberate, cool distance from her.

"The promise?" he said, prompting her.

"I didn't think anything of it at the time. Why should I? It was the only way I could make him go away, you see. I promised . . . God help me . . . I promised to marry him when I—when *we*—grew up. I promised to marry him if he would go away when Ma came back."

The torn and crumpled tissue fell from her fingers. Her chin rested on her chest so that he could barely see her face. She was not crying but trembling with a sort of exhausted tension.

"I keep thinking if I hadn't made that promise, none of this would have happened. That's why he won't go away. Because of my promise. I am at fault, you see. He knows it. He wants what I promised him."

"To marry him. Or to sleep with him, Julie?"

He watched the blood creep slowly into her face. She twisted suddenly, her arm crooked against the back of the settee, her face hidden in it. She drew her knees up, curled her legs against her stomach. He watched her for a moment, then went to his desk. He pretended to consult his diary, watching her from the corner of his eye.

"I think we should stop there, Julie. And I suggest that we take a short break. I want you to think about what I've said. I want you to think especially about my suggestion that part of you does need Jo-Jo after all. And I think you know more about the phone calls than you remember. I suggest you have more control over Jo-Jo than you like to admit." She did not move; she might have been sleeping. "Take your time. And during that time I would like to see your mother. Do you think you could arrange that for me?" He waited, looking at her pointedly. She lifted her face from her arm, and stared back at him.

"No," she said. "No, you can't."

"Julie, let me explain. It's often necessary, in cases like this, for me to talk to other people who are also involved. It helps me to build up a complete picture of you and your background. I want to do it now, while you take some time off, so as not to waste time. Your time and money."

She sat up slowly, put her head in her hands. He thought she shook her head a little.

"No. I won't ask her. I can't."

"Why not, Julie?" He waited. "Are you afraid of her?" After a moment she shook her head. "Afraid of what she might think of you, then?" At this her head came up. She faced him, but not before he had seen her wince.

"She doesn't have any time for mental things . . . illness. She says people should pull themselves together, that it's a form of self-indulgence to give way to . . . She expects people to be very strong. I want to be strong. I don't want to go running to her with my problems. I'm not a child. I have to do things for myself."

"That's very laudable, Julie, but you also acknowledge that you need help."

"Yours, not hers."

"And I want her to help me. She can tell me things that you can't. How would it be if I approached her myself?"

"No. You mustn't. Promise me?" She leaned forward, fierce and insistent. "Promise."

"Then we must do it together, Julie." He watched her searching for an argument against this alternative.

At last she said, "I don't want to."

"For my sake?"

"Your sake?" she scoffed.

"To help me," he began, knowing that she was weary of the formula.

"I know. I know. She won't help you."

"If she loves you—"

"Oh she loves me, all right. . . ."

"Yes?"

"What?"

"It seemed as though you were going to add something."

"She loves me. When she has time. When she remembers. All right?" She stood up. "And no, I don't want to talk about it."

"Very well. Will you ask her to see me, or do I have to insist?"

Julie weighed this for a minute, staring at the door.

"You have to insist," she said.

"Fine. I do. I suggest that if you can't persuade your mother to come here, you could invite me to your home—as a friend, if you like." He spoke briskly, fussing with his notes. Julie did not listen. She tried to imagine it and could not picture her mother in this situation. A thought, almost a hope, began slowly to form in her mind.

"She might . . . I suppose she just might believe you," she interrupted him.

He looked at her quickly. Her eyes did not flinch from his, even though they wanted to.

"I can be very persuasive," he said.

She continued to stare at him and he continued to wait.

Five

Margaret watched him from the long window on the second floor, a cold curl of fear in her chest that made her want to run and bolt the door against this man. He came with no good purpose, to dig over soil she had long thought to be sterile, weed-free. She felt as though things were poised, threatening to reach out from a dead time. She thought of graves and blood and pain, then shook her head impatiently. She was not a morbid woman, not fanciful. Part of her used to fear that one day something like this was bound to happen. But she had grown out of the fear, or so she had thought. In one sense she had buried it with her grandmother, the last living link with that time. She did not count Julie. Julie was only a child, a baby. . . . Now she felt that she had been tricked into a false sense of safety. This man, this *psychiatrist*—she spat the word in her mind, venomously—came to ask and plunder, wanting to dig up things that could only harm her and harm Julie. Well, she could look after herself, she thought, letting the curtain fall back across the window. And she would fight to protect Julie, as she had always fought. As she had fought Tom.

The thought of his name, unthought for years, stopped her in her tracks as she began to cross the room. She had no idea that it could still carry such power, the power to make her feel weak with fear and loathing. Instinctively, half conscious that she was doing so, she clutched her left wrist with her right hand, hearing her own rapid breathing. Her fingers encountered the metal of a heavy bangle, and impatiently pushed it up. Her fingers closed on withered flesh. Even from beyond the grave, she thought, and wanted to laugh hysterically. She did not believe such rubbish, but sometimes it was difficult to deny that some people exercised an influence, a power that, like an odor or a disease, lingered on, spread. . . .

She felt pure anger then, and with it a rush of adrenaline that brought a flush to her cheeks, a determined light to her eyes. She pulled her hand away from her useless wrist and walked quickly to the door, opening it a crack.

Damn you, Tom, she thought. You can't touch me or her.

Below she heard the warm baritone of Dunn's voice greeting her daughter with affection and concern, as though, she thought angrily, to impress upon her the established and separate nature of their relationship. She was irritated by the sound of Julie's answering voice, low and nervous. She still could not comprehend what Julie had blurted out:

"Ma, I've been going to see a psychiatrist. I want you to meet him. He says it's important. Please, Ma?"

Margaret would not blame herself for the explosion of her temper. How long was it since she had raised her voice in anger to Julie? But the young woman who claimed to be sick, who had lied to her, who had grown secretive and deceitful, was not her daughter. Julie had become a stranger, refusing to justify her behavior or discuss her reasons. All she wanted was to bring this man into the house, their lives. She blamed him, of course, him and all his breed. They hadn't been able to save her from Tom, so how dare they meddle with her daughter's mind, upset balances that she had so carefully built up and nurtured? It was not only Julie who stood in danger, but a whole way of life. Her life. Her sanity. Hearing them start to mount the stairs, Margaret left the door and went to the center of the room, forcing herself to be calm.

"Ma?"

Margaret turned around and walked quickly toward him, her right hand already moving out to take his, her smile dazzling.

Russell Dunn had expected a smaller woman, and one who at least had the appearance of being older. Above all, he had looked for a woman who would echo something of Julie's smallness and feminine neatness. The woman who took his hand, briefly but firmly, was honey-blonde and handsome, a vital and strong woman. It took him a moment to realize that the energy that seemed to make her glow was anger. Her eyes belied her smile; they had the blaze of an angry cat. He felt her energy like a shock wave that sent his mind reeling. Her eyes and the cool, firm touch of her fingers filled him with a totally unexpected and disturbing desire.

"Would you like a drink, Mr. Dunn? Or some tea, coffee?" She turned away from him, toward her own chair. He made himself concentrate, see her objectively and not through this sudden miasma of aroused, confusing feelings. Had he not known about her left arm, he doubted that he would have remarked upon its useless stiffness by her side. He sat a little to her right, on the end of the settee. Her chair, he noticed, was high, giving her the appearance of dominating others. A queen on her rightful throne. Not for the first time, he was glad of his height, even sitting.

"No, thank you," he said. "But may I smoke?"

He thought she was about to frown with disapproval, but she kept her face smooth.

"Of course. Julie, can you find an ashtray somewhere?"

The girl hurried to obey her mother as he bent to open his briefcase and extract the half-empty pack of filter cigarettes and the cheap lighter. Julie was used to obeying her, he thought. The mother dominated her, made her nervous. What Julie had told him, about her mother's attitude toward the illegitimacy and her accident, took on added zest now that he saw Margaret Wells. He could entirely believe that when she did not care to talk about something, the topic stayed closed.

"Will this do?"

The question was directed at her mother, though she held the blue, saucer-shaped porcelain dish toward Russell.

"Perfectly. Thank you, Julie," he said, taking it from her and turning to Margaret in time to see the flash of annoyance on her face. "I'm very glad to meet you at last, Mrs. Wells," he said.

"I . . . you won't mind if I'm frank, Mr. Dunn?" He sensed that Julie, just out of eye-range, made some movement of appeal, and he inclined his head quickly, lighting his cigarette. "I cannot say that the pleasure is mutual. I don't approve of your profession and I . . . yes, I resent the fact that Julie has been seeing you without my knowledge. I'm sorry, Julie," she said quickly, her speech becoming noticeably less formal, "but that's how I feel. It's best that Mr. Dunn knows that from the start. I'm sure he won't take offense," she added, turning her almost golden eyes directly on him.

"Not at all. And I agree with you. May I ask why you disapprove?"

"Oh, for God's sake, stop hovering, Julie. Either sit down or go away or something."

For a moment Russell thought Margaret was going to explode, to throw something or launch herself out of the chair and pace, animal-like, about the room. He did not think she was the crying kind. He turned to Julie, saw her face bleakly pale with shock at her mother's anger. And in the same split second, he sensed from the sharp intake of Margaret Wells's breath that she wished to take back her harshness and could not let herself. He leaned over and patted the other end of the settee.

"Please sit down, Julie."

She sat, head bowed, shoulders slumped.

"Frankly," Margaret Wells said, ignoring her daughter, "I think your profession is largely quackery. At its best, it's a most imprecise science and one that can do a great deal of harm."

"In the wrong hands, I would agree with you."

"Yours are, of course, the right ones," she sneered.

"Ma," Julie interjected miserably, shaking her head.

Russell saw that Julie's hair had grown, that it brushed the collar of her blouse as she shook her head, and that the red highlights had faded or washed out. It had also lost its shine.

"Naturally," he said, still watching the girl, "I believe in my own competence. The important thing, however, is that Julie believes I can help her. That is the acid test in these matters, as I'm sure you appreciate."

"Help my daughter how? There's nothing wrong with her."

"I'm afraid I can't agree."

"Then I fail to see how we can—"

"Oh, please, Ma, listen to him. Please. He can help me. He does help. You must . . ." Julie covered her face with her hands and cried. A look of naked pain appeared on Margaret's face and she grasped her left elbow tightly with her right hand. Russell felt himself strung between the two women as though on a wire. He looked steadily

97

at Margaret, though his hands shook, spattering ash onto his trouser leg. In any other circumstances he would have asked Margaret to comfort her daughter, but he sensed that any interruption from him would only shore up her resolve. She avoided his eyes, her lips moving soundlessly. The battle between her instincts and her chosen stance was all too clear.

"Darling, don't," she said at last. "Please don't." He caught her eye then, and risked a nod of encouragement. Margaret pushed herself up from the chair and went to her daughter. Her skirts ballooned around her as she knelt, reaching her good hand to the girl's wrist and murmuring to her. "It's all right, darling. Please, just tell me what it is. Come on, now."

Russell Dunn looked away, closing his ears as far as he could to the automatic, soothing words. He inspected the room, finished his cigarette, and carefully stubbed it out.

"Would you like to go to your room, lie down?" Evidently Julie nodded or whispered something, for they stood up together, Margaret's arm thrown awkwardly around the girl's bent and shaking shoulders. He watched them shuffle toward the door. There Julie paused and looked back at him, her face red and swollen.

"It's all right, Julie," he said quietly. She tried to say something but could not. He smiled reassuringly.

Alone, he lit another cigarette and walked the length of the room. Margaret Wells's anger was genuine, but her manner toward Julie was a pose she could not maintain under pressure. Was she afraid for Julie? Afraid of him? Was there something she did not want him to know? More likely, he thought, she just resented that Julie had turned to him for help, rather than to her. Did she want to hang on to Julie, then? How did she react to Barry? How would she react to Jo-Jo?

"I'm sorry about that," she said, coming back into the room. "I've sent Miss Tidy—my housekeeper—up to her. She'll make her a hot drink or sit with her. Well . . ." She faced him stiffly from across the room. "I suppose you're used to such scenes." He shrugged noncommittally. "Perhaps you can understand now why I find the whole thing so . . . unpleasant. I just don't see what good it can do to upset a person, make her so miserable. Oh, but I know I'm wasting my breath. It's impossible to make you people see in any but your own way."

98

"You've been in analysis yourself?" he asked, walking back to the settee, his left hand cupped under the long ash of his cigarette.

"Certainly not."

"And yet you have such strong feelings about it."

"I have strong feelings about a great many things. I don't believe it is necessary to experience torture in order to know that it is degrading and painful and morally reprehensible."

"You think I'm torturing your daughter?"

"Well, what *am* I to think? You saw how she was."

"Your manner upset Julie, Mrs. Wells. I didn't. And I suspect a great deal of her distress comes from the sheer social embarrassment of hearing her mother, whom she loves very much, speaking so frankly to someone she trusts and needs."

"You dare to criticize me?" Margaret said, her eyes blazing now. "To tell me how to behave? My God, you've got almighty nerve."

"I was not criticizing, simply pointing out—fairly accurately, I think—what happened here. Julie was nervous about my coming. It has put her under a great deal of extra pressure."

"Then why do it?" Margaret demanded. "Yes, torture isn't so bad an analogy, now I come to think about it."

"To help her. To ask you to help me to help her."

"Oh, I do have some role, then, do I? Some useful function left that you can define for me?"

"Mrs. Wells, I am not trying to take your daughter away from you."

"I'd like to see you try."

All the old clichés about lionesses at bay, their courage and resourcefulness in protecting their threatened young, flooded into his mind. The imagery suited her perfectly, with her golden eyes and hair, her natural solidity and grace. It also made her unbearably attractive.

"I'm not a foolish or suicidal man, Mrs. Wells," he said, and smiled.

She looked away, as though impatient, but he felt her anger soften a little. Margaret found herself staring at the liquor table.

"I'd like a drink," she said. "What about you?"

He turned to look at the table.

"If you have some wine . . ."

"I can get some."

"No, please, don't go to any trouble."

"You don't drink spirits? Some sherry, perhaps?"

"No, thank you."

Instinct, years of conditioning, made it impossible for Margaret to leave him empty-handed, to ignore the matter of the wine. But she wanted to. She wanted to show him, through discourtesy, how much she resented him. Exasperated with herself, she dropped a handful of ice cubes into a glass and swore under her breath.

"I won't be a moment," she said, making for the door.

Russell thought that he had made some headway, had at least enabled her to release the accumulated excess of her anger, if not its substance. Perhaps now, if he was cautious, he might be able to win a measure of her confidence—sufficient, at least, to make her answer a few questions.

"I'm afraid you'll have to open it yourself." She dangled a bottle of wine before him and he took it, glancing at the label.

"Yes, of course. Julie told me about your accident," he said casually, carrying the bottle to the liquor table and finding a corkscrew.

"Why would she do that?"

Russell drew the cork, then apologized and offered to fix her drink for her.

"Thank you, I can manage perfectly well," she replied. At the table, he saw that she was indeed quick and practiced, a person who had come to terms with her disability in a cool, no-nonsense way. He took a glass from the table and poured a little wine into it, taking the bouquet. "I asked you a question," she said.

"It's important to her."

"I don't see why. She knows nothing about it."

"It brought you back to her. Surely you can appreciate—"

"Oh, I see. It's the unhappy-childhood, absent-mother syndrome, is it? You people are so . . . hopelessly predictable."

Russell tasted the wine, fairly crude but quite pleasant, and filled his glass.

"Was Julie's childhood unhappy?" he asked, raising his glass.

"No, of course not. I don't suppose anyone, growing up, is ever entirely happy, but Julie was a lot better off than most. Not that I expect you to believe that," she said, lifting her drink and carrying it back to the high, velvet-covered chair.

"Oh, but I do. That's more or less what Julie says."

100

"Then why do you persist in saying she's ill?"

"Did I say that? I don't think—"

"Oh, don't bandy words with me. I'm not paying you, you know. You don't have to spin out the time with circumlocution."

"No. I understand Julie is paying me out of her own money."

"Yes, and I resent that, too. That money was for . . . for *her*, not to be thrown away."

"She is using it for her. In the best way she knows how."

"How can she know . . . ?"

"Would you prefer to pay yourself, Mrs. Wells? Would that make you feel . . . that you still had power over Julie?"

The gibe, cheap as it was, went home. Russell did not enjoy it, or the effect it produced on Margaret's face. He guessed that she had asked herself some version of that question many times and he recognized—how could he not?—self-doubt when he saw it.

"I'm sorry," he said. "That was . . . unprofessional."

"No doubt you think I deserved it."

"No. Not at all. I apologize."

"It doesn't matter. It really doesn't matter," she said, sounding both impatient and weary. "Let's just get this over as quickly as possible."

"Very well. If I may just ask you a few questions?"

"I want to know why you think my daughter is ill. I want to know why she came to you."

"I'll come to that, but, believe me, it will be easier if . . . Just a few questions." She sighed, gave in, drank from her gin and tonic. Her hand was quite steady, he saw, though there were lines now on her face, lines of anxiety and tiredness. The light had gone from her eyes but her attractiveness was undiminished. "When Julie was a child, say between the ages of five and eight, did she have any special friends? A little boy, perhaps?"

"No. None. She was a very solitary child."

"Why was that?"

"Why on earth should I tell you?"

"To help Julie."

"How can I help her when I . . . ?"

"I meant only was her solitude from choice, a natural predilection or . . . ?"

"No. Not really. Not that she minded. For God's sake, she was

101

a happy child, a happy young woman, until . . ." He held her eyes steadily, watched for her to get control of herself. "She lived with my grandmother until she was eight. Grandma was old; she didn't want a lot of children around. Julie was more than enough for her. They lived in the country. There just wasn't an opportunity to make friends."

"Not even at school?"

"She didn't go to school. There wasn't anywhere suitable nearby, and I wouldn't send her to boarding school. She had nannies, good nannies."

"I see."

"It sounds dreadful, doesn't it? Wrong. Saying it to you, knowing what conclusions you are bound to draw. It sounds wrong. Well, maybe it was, but it couldn't be helped. Are you saying that Julie is ill now because of that? What is it called? Lack of socialization?"

"I think Julie is a normally sociable young woman. Does the name Jo-Jo mean anything to you, Mrs. Wells?"

"What?"

"Jo-Jo. Does the—"

"No. Nothing at all. Who is this Jo-Jo?"

"You're absolutely certain? It's important."

"Of course I'm certain. I've never heard the name."

"Were you aware that Julie had an imaginary friend during those years? A little boy she invented because she was lonely? A little boy she could see and touch and talk to?"

"My grandmother . . . I think she mentioned something about it. Why?"

"That's who Jo-Jo is. And that's what's wrong with your daughter."

Margaret shook her head, a half-smile forming on her lips. "I'm sorry, I must have missed something."

"Jo-Jo is the little boy, the friend Julie invented when she was a child. Julie came to see me because she insists that Jo-Jo has come back. She says that he is 'haunting' her. In order to get rid of Jo-Jo, when she was eight and no longer needed him because you came back to live with her, she promised to marry Jo-Jo when she grew up. Now she believes that Jo-Jo has come back to make her honor that promise—and what is more, to threaten anyone who tries to prevent him from doing exactly that."

Disbelief stared at him from Margaret's face for a long moment.

102

Then she began to laugh. She laughed so hard that she had to put down her drink. She laughed so much that she had to shift on her chair and pull a handkerchief from the pocket of her skirt. She laughed until tears came, and what kept Russell tense and watchful was the fact that her laughter was neither scornful nor hysterical. She laughed with sheer, blessed relief.

"I'm sorry," she said at last. Her wet eyes shone at him. "Please . . . I'm sorry. But . . . in that case, I can explain everything. It all makes complete sense. Really, I *can* explain everything."

But not then. About that she was adamant. Her sole immediate concern was to get him out of the house, to buy time to enjoy her relief, to consolidate what she saw as her advantage. Bewildered, Russell settled for a vague appointment: Margaret would try to come to his office the following week. A little angry with himself, Russell stood on the pavement outside, staring up at the tall house while Margaret hurried up the two flights of stairs to her own room, convinced now that she could avert the danger that had threatened them.

By the time Margaret kept her appointment with Russell Dunn she felt confident that she could persuade him to drop the case, if not then and there, then perhaps after only a few more interviews with Julie, and maybe even with herself. She had considered ignoring the appointment, of course, but as her anger cleared and she was able to measure Dunn a little, she recognized him as a persistent man. He would not give up easily; he would, she was sure, be perfectly willing to make a nuisance of himself. She considered lying. She felt no shame at this; there was too much at stake for qualms.

But the first rule of any battle, Margaret knew, was not to underestimate the enemy. She was not a stupid woman; she knew that she would not feel so strongly about psychiatrists if they did not possess considerable skills. She had asked around, had listened to Russell Dunn's broadcast, and now conceded that he was an intelligent and clever man. Still, she hoped that her perfectly valid explanation of Julie's—she still did not know what to call it—"delusion," "problem," would satisfy him entirely. If not—if he demanded, out of curiosity or a sense of tidiness, other details—she would, with a natural show of reluctance, agree to give them to him. She knew that if it came to that, blatant lies would not convince.

No, she would give him the bones of the truth with just enough meat on them to invite him to sink his teeth in, but not sufficient to chew upon. To this end she had already begun to rehearse and hone her story. She had no doubt what he would ask if she was pressed into a seeming cooperation: They were so predictable. But she was determined to avoid that stage if she possibly could.

None of this determination showed on Margaret's face when, a few calculated minutes later, she entered Russell Dunn's office and politely shook his hand across the desk. She had put her hair up, thereby accentuating the strong bones of her face. Her black linen business suit and large shoulder bag presented her as a woman working on a tight schedule, with no time to waste. Forewarned, he was prepared, and so appeared composed and businesslike himself. But he had not imagined the force and effect of her attractiveness. Inwardly, he trembled. Margaret elected to sit opposite him, across the desk, a position that, he guessed, made her feel comfortable, perhaps even in charge.

"I'll come straight to the point," she said, putting her bag down. "I'm not sure how well you know my daughter, Mr. Dunn. . . ."

"Pretty well, I think."

"Then I imagine you'll agree that in some respects she is not very experienced. She's not noticeably what used to be called a worldly girl."

"I would agree with that, up to a point."

"You know that she is engaged to be married?"

"Yes. 'Unofficially,' I understand."

"Whatever that means, yes. Well, there's the cause of this present . . . difficulty. Has she told you about Barry?"

"A little. That she loves him and wants to marry him."

Margaret nodded and hurried on.

"Please understand that I have nothing against Barry. In many ways he's the sort of young man any sensible mother would welcome as a son-in-law. He's got a little money of his own, a good job, excellent prospects, and he's very ambitious. The fact that he's almost ten years older than Julie isn't necessarily a point against him, either, though I do think it has some bearing on Julie's present distress."

"How so?" Russell asked, storing the piece of information away, wondering why Julie had never mentioned it.

"Because it lends him authority, accentuates Julie's youth and

lack of experience. And Julie *is* inexperienced. My fault, I'm sure.
A woman alone, bringing up a child, perhaps especially a daughter,
is more or less bound to err on the side of caution. As you can see,
Mr. Dunn, I'm not one of your ultra-liberated ladies. I didn't put
Julie on the Pill the moment she reached puberty, and while I never
prevented her from choosing her own friends, boys as well as girls,
I certainly kept my eye on things. You would probably say I was
interfering, but I don't think I'm unduly possessive. When Barry
came along, I offered no opposition. It seems to me now that perhaps I should have, but that's spilled milk.

"What I'm trying to explain to you is that Barry is Julie's first real
boyfriend and certainly the only man she has ever slept with. I
think, at first, it was all very romantic and lovely for her. She was
very flattered by Barry. He could give her more, show her more
than a boy of her own age. And remember, marriage was in the cards
virtually from the beginning. I think, again because of her upbringing, the fact that marriage was always a possibility—an intention, in
fact—made it easier for her to be bolder. It was a safe situation, do
you see?"

He nodded and thought, not for the first time, how frequently the
word *safe* occurred in Julie's conversation, and here it was again.

"And until her eighteenth birthday it was even safer because her
youth was a protection in itself. She could always invoke me as a
brake if things went too fast for her."

"I'm sorry, I don't quite follow," Russell said. "Use you as a
brake?"

"Barry would have married her six months after she met him if
she'd been willing. I am suggesting to you that it was easier for her
to stall, delay—call it what you will—when she was underage and
needed my consent."

"You withheld your consent?"

Margaret shook her head impatiently.

"The question never arose."

"Would you have done so?"

"I honestly don't know. If the situation were the same now,
certainly, but then, had she wanted to go ahead, I think I would not
have stood in her way, provided I felt she was really happy and
convinced in her own mind." Russell nodded again. "As it was, on
her birthday, I made it clear to both of them that Julie was a free

agent. It was her decision and I did not intend to influence it one way or the other. I now think that was a mistake. I should have been firmer."

"Why?"

"Because, Mr. Dunn, what's wrong with my daughter is that she is in a total panic. Barry has been pressuring her for months to announce the engagement, name the day. Only recently she was talking of a June wedding. But that's beside the point. The point is that Julie is having second thoughts. I'm not saying that she doesn't love Barry. Maybe she does. What she has realized is that she's not ready. A situation that was essentially vague, though flattering and romantic and exciting, has become a reality. She's eighteen and she's facing the very real prospect of tying herself to one man for the rest of her life."

"Oh, surely not, these days," Russell could not help putting in.

"As I said, Julie is inexperienced—old-fashioned, even. I am sure she sees it that way. Very few people actually marry with the possibility of divorce in mind, especially the young."

Russell thought of his own marriage, Denise in white, himself in a formal suit. Of course they'd scoffed at it, pretended they were only doing it for the families' sake, but they had meant to stay together, had trusted that life would unfurl according to an unquestioned pattern. And look at us now, he thought.

"It wouldn't surprise me if Julie weren't wishing she could play the field a bit," Margaret went on. "Well, and why not? But she's scared to back down. Scared of hurting Barry, unable and unwilling to commit herself. Afraid that if she does back out, she'll never get another opportunity. Mr. Dunn, my daughter's out of her emotional depth and she feels she's drowning. What do drowning people do? They panic. Whatever prompted her to come running to you, I don't know, but it does prove to me that her fears about the situation are much greater and deeper than I had realized."

"That, at least, is something," Russell said levelly.

"Well, I hope I've helped to clarify things for you," Margaret said briskly, picking up her bag.

"Indeed you have, in many ways. But may I ask you . . . Do you think this panic of Julie's is sufficient to make her invent a third person, a man who is hell-bent on preventing the very thing she fears, according to you?"

Margaret hesitated, reluctant to meet his eyes. "You're the psychiatrist, Mr. Dunn, not me. But I would think it possible, in extreme circumstances. Is it entirely without precedent that a young girl should seek to provide herself with an excuse, no matter how bizarre, when she feels herself to be in a situation that she is socially and emotionally unequipped to handle?"

"No, but such a girl would have to be extremely neurotic, deeply disturbed in some other crucial aspects of her life. . . ."

"Of course. That is how you are bound to see it. Look, this person, this figment of Julie's imagination—"

"Jo-Jo he's called," Russell said firmly, fixing her with his most relentless stare.

"Whatever . . ." She waved the name away with her good hand. "By your own admission he is a remnant of her childhood, her very *early* childhood," Margaret stressed. "Isn't that proof in itself of what I'm saying? She's immature, unable to cope. She's regressing. God, if we still had her old playhouse, it wouldn't surprise me if she had crawled in there and started to suck her thumb, waiting for Barry and the whole thing to go away."

"Is Barry such an ogre?"

"Of course not. But he's older, more mature. To her he must seem . . . powerful. She can't stand up to him, now that she's promised . . . Oh, don't worry, Mr. Dunn, I do blame myself. I do see that I should have played a more active part in that relationship. My only excuse is that I did not want to be an interfering, possessive mother."

"There are worse things," he said mildly.

"Really? In your book, or rather Dr. Freud's, I thought there was no more damaging and destructive a figure—"

"A common misconception, Mrs. Wells."

Margaret heard the reproof in his voice and smiled a little to acknowledge the style with which it had been delivered. The interview, from her point of view, had gone well and she felt that she could almost like the man. Quickly she corrected herself. She had nothing against the man except his profession and his interference in Julie's life.

"Well, I'm very glad we had this talk, Mr. Dunn. . . ."

"Just a moment more, please. . . ."

"I'm very busy," Margaret announced, as though this could in no way be denied or avoided. "In fact, I have a lunch appointment."

"This won't take a moment. I feel much better about Julie's present state of mind, now that you are fully aware of it. As she's probably told you, we've reached a point in our . . . journey together . . . where I feel that Julie needs a break, time to reflect. . . . She may be blocked. I'm not sure. Certainly there is a hiatus. Sometimes these things are natural, inevitable, a part of the whole process." Margaret looked at her watch, frowning. "Mrs. Wells, you do want to help Julie, don't you?"

"Of course," she said. And I shall, she thought. Don't you worry.

"Then I would like to propose that we stick to the original plan. But I shall require two things of you." Margaret's eyebrows rose and Russell knew exactly, almost to the precise words that hung on the tip of her tongue, what she would say. "I want you to promise me that you will call me if she becomes upset in any way. And I want you to keep her next appointment."

"I surely don't have to remind you that I am *not* your patient, Mr. Dunn, and never will be."

"I am fully aware of that, Mrs. Wells. It's precisely because I know who my patient is and have her best interests at heart that I am asking you, please, to help me. Will you do that?"

"Put like that," Margaret said, almost teasing him, "how can I refuse? However—"

"Look, Mrs. Wells. I need your cooperation. I accept your dislike of my profession. That does not concern me. But your daughter has placed herself in my hands. Until she removes herself, I am responsible to and for her. Now, either you help me or you don't. Let us be quite clear about which it is to be, for I, too, am very busy."

"I really don't see how I can help. I've told you—"

"There are questions about Julie's childhood, about her birth, that I have to ask. You will not be 'on the couch' as you would doubtless put it, Mrs. Wells. I'm not looking for new patients. I need some background information, another perspective on Julie's life. You can give that to me, if you will."

"All right," Margaret said, standing up. Awkwardly she hitched the strap of her bag onto her left shoulder. "When is Julie's next appointment?"

"On Friday at eleven."

"I'll see if I can manage that."

"Please call my receptionist if you can't," he said, dismissing her.

In spite of her protestations about her limited time, Margaret was half an hour early for her lunch appointment and had, besides, taken the day off. Summer was coming to the city, bringing its attendant tourists and travelers, causing the pigeons to strut and bask with new confidence. Margaret crossed the piazza near St. Paul's Cathedral, deliberately scattering a pool of cooing birds into a flurry of feather and wind. She waited on the stone steps at the entrance to the tall and fashionably curt building, glancing at her watch. She felt pleased with the interview; it had gone more or less according to plan. She thought that when Dunn had taken time to examine her explanation, he would find it quite plausible. He would come to see the next appointment as no more than a tidying-up session. If not . . . well, Margaret had contingency plans, which was why she was waiting, with mounting impatience, for Barry Irving. Only one thing slightly bothered her. Perhaps she should have put up a greater show of resistance to the idea of visiting Dunn again, been less quickly willing to tell him about Julie's background. Could it be that now that he had lost the advantage of surprise—now that she saw him as a containable threat—he had been able to charm her a little? The thought should have been followed automatically by a smile of dismissal, but none came to her lips. The thought, preposterous as it was, lodged uncomfortably in Margaret's mind. It didn't matter anyway, she reminded herself. With Barry's help she would soon be able to remove Julie, at least physically, from Russell Dunn's influence. She smiled then. Margaret enjoyed a battle.

Barry walked pretty well with his stick now, the ankle supported by an elastic brace. His face was still tanned, but that could not conceal his diffidence and nervousness at being summoned to this secret, unexplained meeting. He greeted Margaret—they had never resolved whether they should kiss or hug or shake hands, and so did not touch each other but stood close, smiling too broadly—and remained on the steps for a moment, discussing where they should go. Margaret wanted somewhere reasonably quiet, Barry a place unlikely to be thronged with his colleagues. They settled on a wine bar in a narrow, time-untouched street behind the cathedral, which had half a dozen more or less private booths at the back. Barry sat in the corner of a high-backed banquette, his left leg stretched along and supported by the seat. A mauve candle in an old wine bottle stood between them, its neck and shoulders festooned with stalactites of wax, white, pink, lilac, yellow. A blond waiter held a light to the candle and Barry instinctively moved it to one side. Margaret consulted the waiter about the wine, and ordered paté and salad for herself.

"You must be wondering why I asked you to meet me," she began, after tasting the light, dry Rhine wine he had selected.

"Well, I did wonder a bit when you said not to mention it to Julie."

"You must, of course, if you feel uncomfortable. But obviously it's about Julie. Anyway, you might decide that it's best she doesn't know." Barry turned his glass by the stem, staring into it. Margaret gave him plenty of time to speak, then went on, quelling a feeling of impatience at his slowness. "Then I can count on your help?"

"If you're going to ask me to stop pressing her about the wedding, it's already done. I decided that in France. I told her as soon as I got back. But she said she wanted to go ahead. We'd both been thinking, you know, being apart. But then I had this blasted accident." He looked ruefully at his ankle. "Since then we've hardly discussed it at all."

"Then don't. Not just yet. Look, Barry, the truth of the matter is that Julie's got herself into a state about it all. More seriously and deeply than either of us realized. It came as a shock to me, I can tell you."

"You mean she's got cold feet?"

"Barry, I don't think she knows from one moment to the next what she wants. Today, perhaps, she'd marry you by special license. Tomorrow she might have a fit of hysterics at the very thought."

"But why? She says she loves me and she knows—"

"Because she's young, Barry, and scared. Of course she loves you. But she needs time. I don't believe she's ready for marriage, for the commitment."

"Well, I've never made any secret that the sooner the better for me, but I can wait. I will."

"Good. That's what I'd hoped you'd say. Because I want to take her away for a while. I don't think she'll be too keen on the idea, which is why I need your support."

Barry groaned, hunched his shoulders. Margaret feared he was becoming stubborn.

"Away from me, you mean?"

"Only incidentally, Barry. You obviously don't know that she's been seeing a psychiatrist."

"A psychiatrist? A shrink? Julie? Oh, come off it!" He wanted to laugh, but Margaret's stern expression made him suppress the impulse.

"That was more or less my reaction," she said.

"But why?"

"Because she feels . . . confused."

"Why didn't she talk to me, then?"

"Or to me?"

"I must say I think that's a bit strange, going to a shrink behind my back."

"And mine."

"But why?"

"I've told you as much as I can, as much as I know. She's scared herself into a corner, Barry."

"There's nothing wrong with her, is there? Nothing I don't know?"

Margaret saw his anxiety and confusion. He was an orderly young man; he wanted an ordered life and the right girl. The faintest taint of something . . .

"Not that it would make any difference," he said quickly, as though picking up on Margaret's thoughts. "I just think I have a right to know, that's all."

"Of course you do. That's why I'm telling you. I think perhaps you should try to regard it as a nervous condition, a minor one, brought on by pressure, worry about her own abilities as a wife, your wife. It's really nothing to worry about."

"*You* look worried."

"I'm her mother."

"Of course. Sorry. It's just such a shock. Why didn't she tell me?"

Margaret shook her head. Who can guess, reliably, at the motives of those who feel unable to cope, even to trust those who care most about them?

"It makes a kind of sense," Barry went on. "She's been very nervous. Especially when you were away. Before, even. And then breaking that box I brought her. I never could fathom that."

"You mustn't blame her. I'm sure she feels terrible about it. In fact, I know she does. It wasn't meant to hurt you, I'm sure. She loved the box. Truly she did. She told me so on the phone, minutes after you gave it to her."

"And minutes after that she smashed it to smithereens."

"It was a symbol Barry, symptomatic. My guess is she suddenly felt very frightened. You came back and she felt she had to make a commitment."

"But I told her—"

"People don't always hear what they are told. Especially not when they're upset. I suspect she smashed the box because she was afraid to commit herself. Try to look at it this way—better the box than you."

His hand, stretched toward the wine bottle, suddenly froze, hovered in the air a moment, then withdrew. Margaret frowned, looking at him. In the dim light at the back of the bar, he looked shocked, even frightened. "Barry, what is it?"

"I . . . don't know, really. I just suddenly had a thought."

"What? Please tell me. You know you can trust me. Together we can help Julie get over this."

He leaned back against the banquette, digging into his inside jacket pocket. He pulled out a piece of paper, half a sheet of lined notebook paper, roughly torn. It was folded once, imperfectly. He slid the paper across the table, toward Margaret.

"You'll probably think I'm nuts, but, well . . . do you reckon this could have anything to do with it?"

Something suddenly made Margaret afraid. She looked at the paper, not touching it, not wanting to touch it.

"What is it?"

"Read it, go on."

He obviously felt better. He filled their glasses. The waiter appeared, balancing two plates of food, with cutlery wrapped in bright yellow napkins. Margaret picked up the sheet of paper to make room for her plate. She opened it.

$$\text{J}{\scriptsize\text{ULIE}}\ \text{L}{\small\text{O}}^{\text{VES}}\ _{\text{ME}}$$
$$\text{N}{\small\text{OT}}\ _{\text{YOU}}$$
$$\text{C}{\small\text{LEAR}}\ _{\text{OFF}}\ \text{OR}\ _{\text{ELSE}}$$
$$\text{J}{\small\text{O-J}}{\small\text{O}}$$

112

The block letters were crude and uneven, scored heavily into the paper, ignoring the lines. Margaret folded it quickly.

"Where did you get this?" she demanded, thrusting the paper across the table at him, as though even touching it sullied her. Her mind screamed: It had not gone this far. It could not have.

"In with my mail this morning. Hand-delivered. And what's more, it's not the first."

"No?"

"That's right," Barry said, spreading paté thickly on a wedge of French bread. "Some weeks back. Before I went skiing, anyhow. I thought nothing of it. Well, to be honest, I thought it was a joke. One of the chaps I live with, you know. They're always ragging me about Julie, and they're great ones for practical jokes."

"What did it say? What did you do with it?"

"I threw it away. They wouldn't admit anything, of course."

"What did it say, Barry?"

"Oh . . . 'Leave Julie alone.' Something like that."

"You threw it away?"

"Right. Why? Do you think it's important or something?"

"No," Margaret said quickly. "No, of course not. It's nonsense. . . ."

"Well, yes, but . . . Anyway, I hung on to this one. I was going to ask Julie—"

"Please don't," Margaret said urgently, wishing now that she had kept the note herself. "Promise me you won't?"

"All right. If you say so. But I don't like it. It's gone beyond a joke, and—well, a chap can't help wondering." He chewed for a moment, reflectively. "I thought some old flame, you know? A blast from the past. Some chap who still fancies Julie, carries a bit of a torch for her . . ." He ate greedily as he spoke. The food on Margaret's plate suddenly filled her with revulsion. Yet she envied his composure and realized that she could—she *must*—use it.

"No. Nothing like that. I know. I promise you. There's no one but you, Barry. Never has been. Which is perhaps why Julie has got herself into such a state."

"Okay. Right. I believe you," Barry said, munching, "but some joker wrote it."

"Yes."

"Well, I'm bound to wonder, aren't I?"

"Maybe it's like the box, Barry. You understand about that, about how she could—"

"Well, sort of. I'm not much good at symbols and stuff. It's all a bit deep for me. Still . . . hey, wait a minute, you mean . . . ?"

"Julie wrote it. That's just how she used to write to me, when she was about five. I was traveling a lot then. That's just how she formed her letters. We had terrible trouble . . . getting her to follow the lines."

"I didn't mean to upset you," he said, seeing Margaret's anxious frown.

"No. Of course not. I'm glad—really—that you showed it to me. It's just that it shows how far it's gone. Do you see?"

Barry made a visible effort to force his mind to comprehend. "You mean she's breaking my presents and writing those notes and yet she still loves me?"

"I don't expect she knows she's doing any of these things. They're only symptoms, Barry, like spots are a symptom of chicken pox. They only show how deeply confused she is."

Very slowly, taking a sip of wine, Barry nodded. "It's not really my sort of scene, but yes, I do see, I think."

"It's very important, Barry," Margaret said, making her tone brisker, "that you don't mention any of this to Julie. It will only upset her. God knows what it would do to her," she added to herself, her voice cracking. "Trust me. Help me," she pleaded.

"Sure. Anything. But hang on a minute . . . I mean, if it's as bad as all this, well, maybe she *should* see a shrink?"

"No." Margaret, without knowing she was going to do so, banged the table with her fist. Barry started, drew back in his seat, alarmed. "They only make things worse. Believe me. All Julie needs is time—time and care and understanding. Oh, please, Barry, because you love her, be generous . . . please. . . ."

"Well, I must say, I don't like the idea of anyone messing with a person's mind, least of all Julie's. Okay," he said, reaching a decision. "You're her mother. You know best. All *I* want is for Julie to be all right. What do you want me to do?"

"Thank you. You'll never know how much I appreciate—"

"Oh, rubbish. We both want the same thing, don't we?"

"Yes, of course."

"Well, then," he said, wiping the last smear of paté from his plate with a crust of bread, "you just tell me what to do and it's as good as done."

It was more difficult than Margaret had imagined to turn her mind back to the time of Julie's birth and before. Perhaps she was inhibited by Russell Dunn and his watchful, listening presence, but she allowed that he had made every effort to dispel the unavoidable sense that she was in a psychiatrist's office. Coffee was served, she was not tape-recorded, and his questions and interruptions were so few that when she became absorbed in her story, he seemed no more than an abstract, listening ear. The difficulty lay within herself; it began with years of determined effort not to dwell upon these events and ended with accretions, built up like layers of mist, with which she hoped to blind him to the truth. Margaret had difficulty not in recollecting, but rather in controlling and monitoring her feelings for Russell Dunn's use.

He began by asking her to confirm Julie's illegitimacy, and that she did in a matter-of-fact, even offhand way. It was an accident, she said, foolish and avoidable even then, but she was young and inexperienced; such things happened to other girls, never to oneself. She had gone straight from school, a minor public school with an excellent musical tradition, to the London Conservatory, where she had specialized in the piano, her first instrument. She loved the life: a bed-sitting room, freedom, concerts, her own studies. For the first time in her life she had glimpsed the possibility of a solo career in music, and that became, immediately, a goal for which she was prepared to work with complete dedication. She questioned now whether ambition, prompted by the hope of travel and an outwardly glamorous career, had not caused her to lose touch with some essential part of herself: the simple love of making music. Later she became somewhat mechanistic in her approach, and perhaps the process toward that had begun then. But Mr. Dunn wasn't interested in that, was he?

He was, but he did not say so. He was increasingly interested in everything about her. Perhaps more than other students, Margaret's life revolved around the Conservatory and, in common with everyone else there, she soon became aware of Tom Rudzinski. He was handsome, flamboyant, mercurially temperamental, at once the joy and despair of the staff. His rebellion was legendary. He questioned everything he was taught, worshiped the avant-garde, and went out of his way to stir up the calm waters of musical academe. The students were polarized by him, one faction believing him to be an attention-seeking nuisance, more concerned with personal image than music, while others regarded him as a genius, in embryo at least. This latter group, to whom Margaret was drawn, confidently predicted that he would become a major composer, or an idiosyncratic but brilliant conductor at the very least. He was unlike anyone Margaret had ever met. She admired and found herself infected by his energy. Predictably, when his manner toward her became more personal, confiding, and romantic, Margaret was deeply flattered.

Rudzinski was a vociferous proponent of "free love." Margaret knew that he had had affairs with other students, even the wife of one of his tutors according to whispered rumor. In common, probably, with those other women, she felt that he showed her alone another side of himself: the tortured, the doubting, the vulnerable, the gentle. She became his lover with a sense of inevitability, even of predestination. Together they would forge a new, radical musical and artistic future.

It was in her final year—at the point when Margaret had begun to suspect that Rudzinski's interest in her was beginning to wane, and that his feet were made of clay—that the eminent Viennese conductor, Maestro Willi Dekker, heard her play. He was complimentary, made one or two incisive suggestions about her interpretation of Bartók, and presented her with two complimentary tickets for one of his London concerts. She would never forget that concert as long as she lived. During it, during the *Lulu* Suite of Alban Berg, to be precise, she realized that her period was three days late. The seat beside her was ominously empty: Tom Rudzinski had clearly stood her up.

Her abiding memory of the ensuing weeks was less precise. They were reduced to a blur of rush and anxiety. She had her finals to contend with, the graduation concert to prepare. Rudzinski was paying open court to another bedazzled girl and subjected Margaret to long, self-justifying perorations designed to explain why they were no longer "good" together. Margaret, tired and miserable and afraid, soon ceased to care what he did or said. She immersed herself in her work and slept every minute she was away from it. She was simply too busy and too numb emotionally to think about the baby at all. In the moments before she fell into a deep, exhausted sleep, she used to pray that it was a false alarm, that her periods would return.

She graduated, she won the gold medal, and she was confirmed to be three months pregnant. She told no one, least of all Rudzinski. She knew, from the moment her condition was confirmed, that she would have the baby. Abortion was not impossible. She did not lack sympathetic and knowledgeable friends. She could have found the money, but abortion never existed as a true possibility for her. She thought about it and dismissed it. In retrospect she saw that that decision had been the easiest part of the whole procedure. She would have the baby, but she did not know how or where. On the strength of her graduation performance, she had been offered a few engagements and she wondered how long it would be before she was unable to fulfill them. Wondered, but did nothing. Furthermore, she lacked the energy and resolve to apply herself to the really important business of auditioning for agents and beginning to build a career. She could not see beyond the moment. Pregnancy made her lethargic.

"Then Willi Dekker rescued me," she told Russell Dunn with a bright and grateful smile. He had read of her graduation success, made enquiries. Through his London agent, who swiftly became Margaret's, he made her the sort of offer all young musicians dreamed about. The following spring he was making a major tour of America, featuring the music of Bartók. He invited Margaret to play the piano concerti with him. Always the publicist, he saw the advantage to himself—his career had always been controversial in America—of launching a new young protégée on an ensured but unpredictable public. Margaret saw that this was an opportunity that would never—*could* never—come her way again. More important, it roused her, set the adrenaline flowing again. With a speed and decisiveness that surprised her even now, Margaret accepted, canceled all her existing engagements, and announced that she was withdrawing from musical life to prepare for the tour. Then she boarded the first available train for her grandmother's home in the country, on a one-way ticket.

Why there? Why had she not turned to her parents or friends, Russell Dunn asked. Margaret saw, or thought she saw, the suspected trap in such a question, but it held no dangers for her. She answered simply and truthfully. Her parents were divorced, had been since she was six. Her mother had "got religion" and, at the time of Margaret's pregnancy, was heavily engaged in missionary work in Africa somewhere. They were not close. Her mother's God had come between them. As for her father, whom she saw on his rare and brief visits to London, he had remarried and was working in the Middle East. He had a second family to consider. Besides, her maternal grandmother, Helen Dunbar, had been a mother to her—had been all her family, in fact. It was with her that she had spent most of her school holidays; it was she who had encouraged Margaret's talent. She was herself a gifted amateur musician and she understood what an offer such as that of Maestro Dekker meant to a young artist. She was also not overly prone to make moral judgments. Margaret felt—and rightly, as it turned out—that she would accept the pregnancy as well as the career.

Of course, in the long autumn evenings when Margaret had finished working on the Bartóks she and her grandmother considered adoption, too, but as time passed and Margaret grew larger, they realized that there was only one solution for both of them. The tour would make Margaret financially independent. The expected spinoffs, such as recording contracts and other engagements, would make her comparatively rich. She would be well able to support a child, to pay for nurses and nannies, and she would be spared the anxiety of knowing that her child was in the care of paid strangers, if Helen acted *in loco parentis*. "I had never thought to be a great-grandmother until I was too old to enjoy it," she had said, and the bargain was sealed. Julie was born and named but never christened, "perhaps out of defiance of my mother," Margaret added slyly, to tease Russell, who smiled in return.

It had been hard leaving her baby, of course. But easier then, with so much before her. In fact, it had become harder as Julie grew and became a person in her own right, but she forced herself to do it. The child was happy and well cared for, and Margaret's career seemed to be self-perpetuating, like a great roll of carpet that uncurled before her and that she had to tread. She worked, and incidentally became Dekker's mistress for a while. He helped her career enormously, especially in America and on the Continent. She made records; she was famous, acclaimed. The work never ceased; it was almost all-consuming.

Probably she would have gone on forever if she hadn't begun to run foul of the younger critics, even some of those who had once lauded her. Words like "mechanical," and "cold," "under-inter-preted," "ready-made and colorless" began to appear too often in her notices for even the most confident and self-absorbed artist not to notice them. She realized that she was becoming bored. She was relying on technique when something more, much more, was needed. Bookings began to taper off. She was in danger of slipping into the second or third rank. She realized, too, that she was tired of traveling, that she thought more and more of her daughter grow-ing up without her. Decisions had to be made about a school, a home base.

"But I couldn't just walk away from it," she said. "I couldn't. I don't think anyone can. So I rethought things, gave myself a year to prepare, to build. . . ."

She had neglected the solo repertoire, had given perhaps no more than half a dozen solo recitals in as many years, and those without conspicuous success. She settled in Vienna, accepted the absolute minimum of concert engagements, and studied the solo repertoire with the very best teachers she could find. The goal—there always had to be a goal, she reflected—was a series of recitals in London, the launching of what virtually amounted to a new career. And this time it would be a career based in England. She was going to find a flat and a housekeeper, and bring Julie to live with her. Julie would go to school. She began to make inquiries as soon as she arrived in London for the first crucial series of recitals.

"As it happened, of course, I only gave one. Though that was well received. I think, if things had fallen out differently, I could have made a success of it. I was more mature. I'd rediscovered the emo-tional aspect of playing. I wasn't confident, but I was hopeful. I think, for the first time in my life, I'd got it together, as they say. But it wasn't to be." She sat for a minute, looking at her left hand, which lay immobile in her lap, a thick gold bracelet like a manacle around the wrist.

"The accident," Russell said quietly. "It must have been very hard for you."

"Oh . . . well, yes, of course. But I could handle it," she said with a note of pride. "I did."

"Evidently. May I ask . . . ?"

119

"How it happened? It's strange, that's what everyone wants to know. It's *all* they want to know. And so very few dare to ask. One is glad of that, of course, encourages it even, but the really interesting thing is that how it happened is the least important part of it."

It was stupid, like all accidents. She had been exhausted after the first recital, keyed up and nervous. She was tired, but she could not sleep. She got some sleeping pills. She had used them maybe twice before in her life. Normally she slept well and easily. She was staying in a friend's flat, borrowed until she had time to find somewhere permanent of her own. She had taken the pills and gone to bed. It was very hot that summer. She had awakened, feeling fuzzy from the pills; she had taken a couple of drinks as well. She had awakened with a raging thirst, only to find that she had forgotten to put her usual glass of water beside the bed. Drowsy, annoyed, she had dragged herself to the kitchen and drunk some water. The flat was unbearably hot, airless. It seemed a matter of urgency, as the most trivial things do when one is only half awake, feeling bad, that she open the kitchen window. She thought that it would create a through draft into the bedroom. But the window was stuck, probably had not been opened in years, and, though she did not know this, the frame was warped, the putty dried up and loose. To make matters worse, she had to lean across the drain board in order to reach the window. She must have spilled some water in her haste to quench her thirst. The floor was wet and slippery. She lost her footing. Her left hand crashed through the window, but, unfortunately, all the glass did not fall out. Her wrist was impaled on a jagged piece, and instead of simply pulling it clear with one clean movement, as, of course, she would have done if it had not been for the pills, she twisted and turned, panicked. . . .

"There really wasn't that much damage," she concluded, "but I'd severed some of the nerves."

"You were in the hospital?"

"Oh, yes. They did everything they could, but I think I knew it was useless from the moment I became aware of what had happened. In a curious way, I think I adjusted better and more quickly than other people did. They could only see the 'tragedy,' the headlines. Oh, I'm not trying to make light of it or present myself as incredibly brave or anything. If it had happened a year or two before, I think I would have gone to pieces. Completely. But there was an element of relief in it. All the work I still had to put in to build what amounted to a new career was suddenly unnecessary. I felt free. I used my time to think how I could earn a decent living, what I was fit for. I felt, and I still do feel, that the accident forced my hand—if you'll forgive a rather unfortunate expression. I saw that there was nothing to take me away from Julie ever again. It was only a question of finding the right job and applying myself. And even that wasn't urgent. I had enough money. I was comparatively well off. There were royalties still coming in. If it hadn't been for Julie, I might have caved in. I would have felt it more keenly, I'm sure. But I had the best consolation possible. I had my daughter. It seems to me now that everything before that was a false start. I sometimes wonder still how things would have been if Dekker hadn't made that offer. Perhaps I would have been a good and contented mother from the very start. But then again, I might have hated her for preventing me from having the career I wanted. I've been incredibly lucky, you see, to have had both. And this"—she raised her left arm a little, awkwardly, stiffly—"is a very small price to pay."

That evening, Russell Dunn stopped off at his local library and borrowed the only two recordings he could find by Margaret Wells. He sat in the dusk of his special room, listening to her play, and thought that he admired her dignity and the courage she had displayed in the face of crisis. The question was, did he believe her? But then, why should she lie? He did not doubt the essence of her story. In outline, at least, it matched the little that Julie had been able to tell him. It was, he decided, the neatness that nagged at him. There was no spillage from one crisis to the next, no sense of the abiding muddle of life, any life. Scars had healed too well and perhaps too quickly. For a woman who disdained psychology, she asked him to believe that she had remarkable powers of self-analysis—the ability, in fact, to solve and tidy away each trauma as it occurred. In this respect she reminded him of Julie. Many times he had noticed a similar tendency to package and store away emotion, and in that respect, Margaret had helped him to see Julie more clearly. There was a deep conflict, intuitive or learned from her mother, between her wish to keep her emotional house in order and her feelings about how life really was. Even something so normally spontaneous and "untidy" as love was, for her, experienced and viewed only in the safe context of an inevitable marriage. That word again, he thought: *safe*. Safe from what?

He had gained, too, a keener appreciation of how frightening the eruption of something so irrational and uncontrollable as Jo-Jo must be to such a girl. Which brought him to a simple question: What was it both women feared so much that their only defense against it was structure and order carried to such a calm excess that it was seductive—that it seemed admirable, even normal? What he did not believe, even for one moment, was that she accepted, without rancor or even regret, the sudden and violent end to that career of which she still spoke with pride and passion—though this was admittedly controlled. Her line about its being a small price to pay for Julie was exactly that: a line. It made him angry because he thought it unworthy of her. And once he had grasped the essence of that lie, so sweetly told, even with dignity, the whole story seemed wrong, false in its tone if not in its facts. It was the way she told it that jarred.

As he got up to switch on the lights, he knew he was close to treating Margaret Wells as his patient. That was inevitable, but still something he must guard against. That temptation, like others, must be resisted. He had no right, he reminded himself, to question Margaret about her story. She would resist anyway. But he must know why she felt it necessary to conceal her justifiable anger from him, to go to such lengths to conceal it that he had almost been taken in.

Did she blame Julie for her accident? That seemed too obvious, even though it was both likely and understandable. He recalled how Julie, under pressure and perhaps led by him a little, had said that Margaret loved her when she had the time, when she remembered. Of course, that was how a child would perceive her mother's enforced absences, but Julie was no longer a child, even though others—Margaret to some extent and, he suspected, possibly Barry Irving—persisted in regarding her as one. So if Julie still felt that her mother's love was undependable, uncertain, then was this because Margaret's true and abiding love was music, her career? Or Tom Rudzinski? Even Willi Dekker, whose distinguished, still handsome features stared mockingly up at him from the back of the record sleeve he held in his hand? How casually she said she had become his mistress—how *baldly,* as though she almost intended to hurt him. . . .

Russell's throat contracted painfully. He had difficulty swallowing as he made himself stop there, to acknowledge and examine what he had just thought. He put the sleeve down, not trusting his unsteady fingers to handle the disc safely. He needed a drink, a cigarette. He fetched both and did not feel any better. Was he *jealous* of men who, once, long ago, she had maybe loved, certainly slept with? Was he sexually jealous of a dead man, of another who might well be? This was the sort of preposterous situation a trained psychiatrist was supposed to laugh himself out of, with ease. But he'd never felt less like laughing in his life.

And yet what he thought—or, to be scrupulously honest, felt, and felt intensely—was irrational and, worse, totally untenable. It was unprofessional. What would Annie, his conscience, say if she could read his darting thoughts? If there was one thing worse than a psychiatrist becoming too closely involved with his client, it must surely be to become involved with her mother. It amused him, for a moment or two, to imagine what Annie would likely say about the incestuous implications of such a situation. Automatically he began to answer back, to defend himself. If the patient sought in him a father-substitute, then what could be more healing and natural than that the "father" and the mother should come together and mend the broken circle?

He managed a weak smile at that, at Annie's outraged hoot of laughter. But he did not feel any better. In fact, as he drained his glass, he felt almost desolate because he knew that whatever happened, he had to stay away from Margaret Wells, had to exorcise her from his life. In other circumstances, his mind teased. . . . But there were no other circumstances. Julie was his patient and needed him. Margaret Wells would always be beyond his reach, no more substantial or available than the disembodied woman whose fingers filled the room with music as, in an act of almost acknowledged masochism, he started the record again.

Six

Lise, dressed in her outdoor clothes, brought him the copies of newspaper stories he had asked for. His last patient had left ten minutes earlier and he had, as it happened, been brooding on his theory, feeling slightly at odds with himself. He knew there was some part of what he was doing that was a subterfuge. The theory was a fairly transparent way of staying mentally in touch with Margaret Wells while enabling him to stick to his vow that he would exclude her from his life. The photocopies that Lise placed in his hands related to her accident. The truth about the accident would help him to heal Julie. Therefore his conscience was clear—almost. Lise's clothing presumably meant that she wanted to go home. He began to read the cuttings. Well, another few minutes wouldn't matter, surely? He asked her to sit down for a moment, thinking as he did so that she was an oddly ill-assorted girl.

"You don't mind, do you? Please sit."

She had a nice nose, good eyes, a pleasant mouth. The trouble was that they did not fit together, somehow. She was like a sort of composite photo of a person, crude and ill-matched. She could not hold a candle to Margaret Wells.

"Is something wrong?" she asked, making him aware that he had been staring at her.

"No. Sorry."

The cuttings told him little. They varied from the restrained,

124

factual account in the *Times*, headed PIANIST INJURED, to the more sensational CAREER RUINED—BRILLIANT PIANIST LOSES USE OF ARM in the tabloids. Her agent had made the sort of pre-prepared statement that agents always make on these occasions. The neurologist who had attended her had made one, too. The patient was remarkably brave, he had said. Russell could believe it. He took a pen and circled the man's name. Roland Curteis.

"I want you to trace this man for me, Lise, if you would. He might be retired by now, but the Royal Society of Neurologists should be able to help." He slid the cutting across the desk toward her. "The morning will do, of course."

Lise gave him a tight smile that did no justice to her pleasant mouth and never reached her eyes at all. He wondered sometimes if the women who worked with him really liked him. He must ask Annie. . . .

"Good night, Lise."

His theory was that Margaret, for reasons that were still vague to him, had injured herself—that she had, in fact, attempted suicide. She had reached such a pitch that her beloved career had seemed actually to prevent her from being the loving, full-time mother that her conscience nagged her to be. *If thine eye offend thee,* he thought. She had literally cut it out of her life. Or was it because some man, Tom Rudzinski . . . He remembered, with increasing bile, how she had described his good looks, his ebullient personality. Anyway, he had a theory. He would get to the bottom of Margaret's lies, not—really not—out of any personal interest, but to add another piece to the jigsaw puzzle of her daughter's problem. In any case, it was quite ridiculous, he told himself, tidying his desk almost compulsively, that a man of his age, experience, and training should be obsessed with a woman he hardly knew and who had never even been polite to him. He paused, pulled a notepad toward him, and wrote quickly.

Annie: Am I an emotional masochist?

He stared at the note, then tore it impatiently from the pad and crumpled it. Just at the moment of dropping it into the wastebasket, he changed his mind, screwed it into an even tighter ball, and put it safely into his jacket pocket.

Elinor Tidy had a very strong sense of what was right and what was wrong, and it was definitely wrong in her book for Julie to behave deceitfully behind her mother's back. Miss Tidy knew her place,

125

knew she wasn't family, but when Mrs. Wells had to travel, she counted on her to keep an eye on things, see that things were right. Therefore, Julie wasn't being fair to her, either. Consequently, she felt she had a right to speak out, and she fully intended to do so at the first opportunity.

She had not thought anything of it when Mrs. Wells explained, that first time, that Julie had had some boy from work in. Details did not much interest her, once she received confirmation of the evidence of her nose. Not that she flattered herself that Mrs. Wells believed that, but that made no never-mind. She knew. And now she knew, as sure as eggs were eggs, that he'd been back again. No sooner was her mother off on this latest Italian trip than Julie was up to her tricks. Now, if it had been that nice Mr. Irving, Elinor Tidy would have been willing to turn a blind eye. He was a steady sort of chap and they were sort of engaged. But Julie was playing fast and loose. It stood to reason. If it had been innocent, a friend calling in for a chat and a cup of coffee, then Julie would have mentioned it to her. But no. She must have sneaked him in the house after Miss Tidy had retired to her flat for the night, and that wasn't exactly aboveboard, now was it? She didn't approve of girls carrying on like that, and Julie knew it. Apart from anything else, he could do with a bath, whoever he was. Miss Tidy wrinkled her nose in disgust. It was a sour sort of smell, like old soil, newly turned.

Mind you, she'd never have thought it of Julie. It pained her to think of her becoming crafty and getting up to what was best not thought about, especially when she was planning to go to the altar with another man. And all this worry was too much for Miss Tidy. Lately she always seemed to be tired and a little short of breath. She was getting old, too old for this sort of unpleasantness. It took her longer to do her work now. Most afternoons she just had to have a little sit-down, and as often as not she nodded off. And then there was the indigestion. Nothing seemed to shift it. Sometimes it felt like a big icy hand was squeezing her heart. When she woke up from one of her involuntary little naps, her left arm felt all numb and sleepy, like there was something wrong with her circulation. No, she didn't need a lot of worry on top of all that. Not at her age.

Miss Tidy lifted up her gray felt hat and held it in front of her, inspecting it for dust. She felt so out of sorts that she had been sorely tempted to miss her Bible class. That showed how bad it was. She grimaced as she raised her arms to place the hat squarely on her head. It seemed as though the pain tightened into a band right across her chest. She bent over, pressing her hand to her heart, her hat all askew and silly-looking. Her heart beat fast and strong. She waited until the pain eased, her breathing settled. Bible class would do her good —calm her down and take her mind off this unpleasantness. When she got back, she vowed, straightening herself and her hat, she'd have it out with Julie once and for all. She'd feel better then.

"Actually, Ma badly wanted me to go to Venice with her, and I must admit I was tempted. But then I remembered what you'd said, you know, about speaking to you first if I decided not to come here." She spoke with a bright smile, almost as though she expected to be given a reward for good behavior.

Fatalistically, Russell contemplated the hitherto unknown fact of Margaret's absence. It was, of course, the best thing that could have happened. In time he would be grateful to her, or to her job or whatever had caused her to leave the country. But he would never forgive her for trying to take Julie with her, to disrupt his work.

"Actually," Julie went on when he offered neither reward nor praise, "Ma was furious with me. We had quite a row about it."

She was playing with him, transparently currying favor. He was depressingly sorry for Margaret Wells; he knew that Julie's decision must have hurt her. On the other hand it showed that Julie was serious when she said she wanted to be an autonomous, adult person. It was her motives, in this instance, that made him a little uncomfortable. He cleared his throat.

"I felt that if I went, it really would be like running away, and after all, I had promised you, hadn't I?"

"Do you want to run away?"

"No. Of course not. I wouldn't be here now if I did, would I? Though I must say," she added, "you don't seem very pleased to see me."

"I'm pleased."

"Would you have preferred my mother to come?"

He felt a sharp stab of guilt, and had difficulty controlling his features. What had made her suspect that? Or was he, from guilt and

127

his own preoccupation, reading too much into it? Either way, he did not like her very much for saying it. He uncrossed his legs and brushed a bit of lint from his trousers.

"Why do you think that?"

"Oh, no reason. I just thought perhaps you had more you wanted to talk to her about. I thought perhaps you might have been expecting her rather than me."

He shook his head. "Did you decide not to go in order to make your mother angry?"

"No. Of course not. What a horrible thing to say. Why should I—?" She seemed, almost literally, to bite her tongue. "No. Definitely not. I just wanted to keep my word to you."

"Thank you." Her look told him she felt she need not have bothered, that he had disappointed her, and if he did not do something quickly, she would very likely sulk away the rest of the hour. He decided, though, not to change tack. Not yet.

"But you did say that your mother loved you only when she had time or remembered. I thought you might be angry. . . ."

"That was a load of rot. You *know* that. I was angry, scared. Scared of you and her. And don't ask me why, because you know perfectly well. Scared of telling her about you, scared of you insisting. . . . I would have said anything then. I've always been like that, when I'm in a temper. I just say things I don't mean."

"You want to hurt the person who is hurting you?"

"Doesn't everyone?"

"In this case, your mother."

"No. After all, she wanted to take me with her. She almost begged me. Even you can't pretend that I see that as a desertion."

"You don't mind being by yourself?"

"Oh, no. I'm used to it. Ma goes away a lot. Well, she'll have told you about her job and everything." Now she was fishing, afraid that he and Margaret had formed some sort of coalition against her, perhaps. When he did not take the bait, she went on, "Anyway, I'm not alone. I've got Miss Tidy. She's always there."

"And Barry," he suggested.

"Oh, yes. And Barry, of course."

"You don't sound very enthusiastic. Or do I mean 'sure'?"

Her eyes slid away from his, and remained lowered as she turned away from him.

128

"Actually, I shan't be seeing very much of Barry. He's going home to Yorkshire for the weekend. He thought I was going to Venice, you see. He was very keen on my going. So he arranged to see—"

"Couldn't you go with him? Wouldn't that be nice?"

"Oh, no, I couldn't."

"Why is that?"

"Because . . ." Her mouth trembled. She shook her head.

"Perhaps you don't get along with his family?"

"Of course I do. Why on earth shouldn't I? They're very fond of me," she said defensively, looking at him.

"Good. Then why—?"

"I would have thought you'd know. I thought you were the one person who . . . I can't. I'm afraid. I'm afraid that Jo-Jo might do something to him." She took a deep breath, and faced him squarely. "Look, one of the things I decided while I've not been coming here, since you talked to my mother, is that I have to stay away from Barry as much as possible. If I don't, I'm afraid something terrible will happen to him."

"You make it sound as though you feel you bring bad luck," Russell said mildly.

"I bring Jo-Jo!" she shouted. "Have you forgotten everything?"

"No. Very well. Tell me about Jo-Jo."

When Miss Tidy got back from her Bible class, Julie was already in her room and the prospect of climbing all those stairs was too much for her. She would feel fresher in the morning, anyhow, clearer in her mind and with her words. But she spent a miserable night, tossing and turning. She blamed those scones that Miss Scho-field had brought along for their coffee break. They lay heavy. It was light before she got off to sleep properly, which meant that she was late and everything was in a rush. Julie, of course, was always in a rush in the mornings. She flew out of the house without their having exchanged more than half a dozen words.

Her arm felt all numb again, as though she'd been lying on it, and those scones lay so heavy still that she just had to sit down for a few minutes. She poured herself a second cup of tea.

The smell of him seemed to drift into the kitchen like an actual, physical presence. He could have been standing not two yards from her, or behind her. Stiffly, Elinor Tidy twisted to look over her shoulder. There was something else, too. The smell was warm, somehow, as though fresh from his body. She wrinkled her nose. Now she bitterly regretted having given way to her aches and pains. She had to put a stop to this, once and for all.

First she opened the glass doors into the garden and wedged them. She would not have him stinking up her kitchen. Then she collected her cleaning box—it felt as though it had rocks in it—and started up the stairs. If she had not known better, Miss Tidy would have said he had just passed up the stairs ahead of her. Each frequent pause on tread or landing, as she fought her own recalcitrant breath, brought her nostrils a fresh and stronger scent of him. It occurred to her, during one of these enforced pauses, while her heart hammered at her ribs, that he might still be there, in Julie's room. This made her angry, brought a flush of color to her otherwise gray face, and spurred her on.

All things considered, it might be better so. After all, she always found it difficult to stay cross with Julie; the little minx had ways of getting around old Elli. She felt, despite the cramping pain in her side and the breathlessness, more than a match for some unwashed boy. How Julie could bear that smell near her, she would never know.

A low cry escaped Miss Tidy as she crossed the first-floor landing. Her box slipped from her numb fingers. She bent over, clutching herself. It was silly, so silly. . . . If she hadn't considered such things sinful, she would have cursed Miss Schofield's scones. Mind you, it was punishment for her own greed. One would have been sufficient, but she'd given way to temptation. As the pain passed, and the fist that squeezed her heart relaxed in mercy, the smell came to her again, stronger than ever.

Supporting herself against the wall, she turned her eyes up the stairs to the shadowy top landing. There was something wrong with her eyes. Everything was swimming, blurred. Miss Tidy staggered. The fist closed again on her heart, forcing the breath out of her in a gasp of pain. Her blurred vision made her dizzy. She hit the bannister with her right hand, bruising her knuckles. She failed to grip it. The stairs, rocking, rose up to meet her. Silly old fool, she thought, lying on the stairs. Whatever will Mrs. Wells say? Her legs refused to work. Somehow her left arm was trapped under her, and her right arm was not strong enough to lift her up. Her legs seemed to have become useless jelly. She did manage to raise her head, to look up to the landing, to Julie's door. She was more certain than ever that he was there, hiding. Well, the Lord moved in mysterious ways. Perhaps some good would come of it. He would have to help her up. The call that Miss Tidy wanted to make came out as a grunt as the fist expanded and seemed to squeeze her whole chest into a single knot of pain. Her head flopped down onto the thickly carpeted stair and remained there. Elinor Tidy was mortified to find that she was dribbling and could not stop.

The shop had been busy all day, keeping Julie occupied. She had even had to cut Barry short when he rang, because a new influx of customers made Belle frantically signal that she could not cope. Barry wanted her to change her mind, to go to Yorkshire with him, or he would change his plans, not go after all. She felt a renewal of panic from which the customers rescued her. She promised to call him at his parents' house, wished him a safe journey. It was the tourist season. It seemed to start earlier each year. Julie served a Japanese couple, then two Swedish girls. Belle was jubilant. Rik brought up some new pieces from the safe and Julie replenished the displays, slipping rings on polystyrene fingers, making patterns of necklaces and brooches on velvet-covered boards. They were all tired when, at last, Rik put up the shutters. Belle was overjoyed at the day's receipts and insisted that they all go to Berrie's Wine Bar, across the piazza, to celebrate.

Julie felt relaxed and began to enjoy herself for the first time in ages. This surprised her and she realized that she no longer took such natural things for granted. Russell Dunn, she supposed, had taught her to question everything. She withdrew a little from the chatter and noise around her. It was because everything was safe. Barry was safe, out of reach. Ma was safe, overseas. For once there was nothing to worry about, nothing *he* could do. She was, in a sense, alone with him. . . . A cloud crossed her face. Rik noticed and poured her another glass of wine, made her laugh with some outrageous tale.

They walked together, arms linked, to the Strand, and kissed and hugged each other goodbye, still celebrating, before they split and went their several ways. Julie's bus came along almost at once. It seemed that nothing, nothing at all, could mar this welcome mood. When she got home she would ring Sybil, have a good long chat. Ma might ring and Julie would be nice to her, make up with her. She seemed to be home in no time at all and, because of her mood, she did not notice that the house was in darkness until she was inside. The house felt cold, too, as though someone had switched the heat off or left all the doors and windows open.

"Elli?"

In the cold kitchen she saw the propped-open glass doors. Elli was giving the place a good airing, she supposed, shivering. She remembered how once before, recently, these doors had stood unexpectedly open and her shiver had turned to a tight crawling of the flesh. She must not give way to such thoughts, not tonight. She hurried to close the doors and lock them. She would have a long, hot soak in the bath and then phone Sybil.

She went to the top of the basement stairs and called out, "Elli. I'm home. I'm going to have a bath."

Halfway up the first flight of stairs, she realized that she had not heard the drone of Miss Tidy's television set. Probably she had some new biblical text to study. On the first landing she checked the radiator; it was burning hot. She went on and almost stumbled over Miss Tidy's cleaning box. At first her mind refused to recognize what lay on the stairs ahead of her. It was a dark shadow-shape, a heap of old clothing, a dummy.

Miss Tidy lay on her side, one leg drawn up, one eye visible. The eye did not move. There was a purplish color to her lips, and her mouth hung open. There was a terrible stiffness about her legs. A hairpin lay beside her. A lock of hair unraveled from her head.

"Elli?" Fearful, she approached the body and bent over it, covering it with her own shadow. She did not want to touch it. "Elli?"

She sensed rather than saw him. Her hand hovered, afraid, over Miss Tidy's shoulder and something, some shift of the shadows at the top of the stairs, some irresistible compulsion, made her look up. He was standing there, looking down at her, looking at Miss Tidy's body. And he was smiling.

It's all right now, Ju-lie. Don't be afraid. I'm here. We're alone now. Like we used to be, remember? Remember the forget-me-nots in the garden? Remember how we used to pick them? I never forgot you, Ju-lie. Never. And now it's time, Ju-lie. Time . . .

He began to move toward her. He seemed to pass down the stairs without touching them. His arms reached for her, reached across Miss Tidy's corpse, reached for her. She could smell him, that slightly stale and fetid odor of his manhood.

"No," she said. She was going to be sick. Bile rose in her throat. She struggled up. His eyes stared into hers, burning.

Alone now, Ju-lie. Nobody can stop us now. Remember, you promised.

Her legs moved. Her hand groped behind her as she backed across the landing, found the wall, inched along it. He seemed to loom and grow, reaching over Miss Tidy's body to touch her.

Julie turned and ran, screaming.

For the third time, Russell knotted his bow tie. He had never been good at such things, even though his hands were delicate and quick for such a large man. He used to sit down, Denise pressed against his legs, her square hands deftly competent. It still was not quite straight. The telephone rang. He tweaked the right-hand side of the bow. The phone rang again. It would ring three times before the machine took over. The tie would have to do; it was the best he could do, unaided. Margaret Wells, of course, would not be able to help him in this department. At the fifth ring, he swore. He thought he had switched the machine on. He did not want to be late. He crossed his bedroom in two strides, checked his watch, and picked up the telephone. Before he could say anything, he heard the rapid chatter of mechanical pips. A public phone. For a man in his profession, this was always a bad sign. He braced himself, mentally running through the list of current patients, wondering which of them might feel so desperate. . . .

"Mr. Dunn?"

"Julie?" His heart skipped.

"Please help me."

He sat down on the bed, picked up the spiral-bound shorthand pad and the pencil he always kept beside it, in which he noted his dreams each morning.

"First, tell me where you are."

"I don't know, I—"

"Julie, give me the number. It's on the dial in front of you. You may run out of money."

"Near Waterloo Station."

"What's the number in front of you?" She read it out, stumbling. "If we get cut off, I'll call you back."

"You've got to help me."

"How?"

"I don't know, I . . . oh, God . . . it's Jo-Jo. He's . . . he's . . . killed Miss Tidy. She's dead. He killed her. I don't know what to do. I ran. It's so horrible. . . ."

Automatic pilot. Just like broadcasting. He heard his own voice, calm and slow. Even when the pips sounded again and the dial tone burred in his ear, his mind worked calmly, efficiently. He did not even consider the possibility that she would panic now and run. The phone in that distant, no doubt stale-smelling phone booth hardly rang before she picked it up, sobbed his name. He told her exactly what to do, then repeated it, and made her repeat his address.

"I haven't got any money," she wailed. "I just ran—"

"I'll be waiting for you at the entrance to the mews. I'll pay. Hang up now, Julie. I'll see you in a little while."

Even when he had pressed the receiver cradle to obtain the dial tone again, his brain continued to work smoothly. He held at the back of his mind, for later contemplation, the possibility that Jo-Jo had . . . that Julie herself had . . .

But to touch it too soon would be to disrupt the calm he needed now to get him—and Julie—through.

He spoke to his flustered hostess, apologized, and said in all truthfulness that he doubted he would be able to get along later. He put the receiver down and laced his fingers together. He would have to go to the house and check Julie's story. He could not leave her alone, and probably would not be able to take her with him. It might be a wild-goose chase, the whole scenario a ploy to get his attention. Barry away, her mother away, Miss Tidy . . . ? *She's always there.* He was jumping to conclusions; he must question Julie closely before . . . He picked up the phone and dialed quickly, from memory. Across a background of loud rock music, Annie spoke.

"Gentlemen's underwear. How may we help you?"

"Annie, I need your help."

"Hold on while I turn this down." He heard her shouting to somebody. A dog yapped. The music faded. "Not on a Friday night, Russell. You've got to be joking."

He ignored that, knowing he could rely on her to listen without interruption. When he had finished, he looked at his watch and said that he had better go and wait for the taxi.

"Okay, a compromise. When she gets there, if you need me, call. I'll be on standby."

"Thank you, Annie. I understand. I owe you."

"You bet your life."

He pulled off his bow tie, changed his jacket, and hurried out into the mews to wait for her cab.

If it had been anyone else, he would have given her two sleeping pills and tucked her in bed. But she could not stay in his house. She was adamant, insofar as she was coherent at all, that she would not go back to the house; Jo-Jo was there, waiting for her. Miss Tidy was dead. Jo-Jo had killed her. Russell gave her a tranquilizer, holding the glass of water to her lips. He wrapped a blanket around her. She trembled and wept.

"Don't leave me. Please don't leave me."

"I'm just going across the room to telephone." He spoke to Annie again, then made a snap decision. There was nothing else for it. He would face the consequences later.

"Julie, a friend and colleague of mine, Annie, is coming over. She will stay with you while I go to your house."

"No . . . don't leave me. Please . . . I can't . . ."

"I have to go to the house. Someone has to see to Miss Tidy."

"Jo-Jo . . ." she sobbed.

"If Jo-Jo is there, I'll talk to him. Just don't worry about it, Julie."

"Tell him to go away!"

"Yes, yes, Julie. All right. Now listen to me. How would you like to go to a really safe place, somewhere Jo-Jo can't find you? Just for tonight, until you feel better."

"Safe?" Her eyes rolled at him, focused, held his.

"I know such a place. Possibly I can get you a room there. Will you go?"

"Yes, oh, yes. I can't go home. . . ."

"And will you go with Annie? Will you let her take you?"

"No, you . . . you . . ."

"But don't you see, Julie, it's better for Annie to take you? If I take you, Jo-Jo might suspect something. He might try to follow.

135

But he doesn't know Annie. If Annie takes you, I can go to your house and . . . keep him busy. . . ."

She stared at him, lips trembling.

"A place," she said at last, "Jo-Jo doesn't know at all?"

"That's right. A safe place."

She swallowed, nodded.

"Good girl. Now, can I have the keys to your house?" Slowly she turned her head, looking for her bag. Russell got up and brought it to her. She opened it and handed the keys to Russell. "Thank you. Now I have to go upstairs to make a private phone call. I'll leave the door open. You'll be quite safe here, won't you?" He thought the tranquilizer was taking effect. She nodded slowly, dreamily, her eyes slightly out of focus.

He ran up the stairs. If only his luck held. If only they could take her. He was on the board, would pull rank if necessary. If only they had a vacant room. He crossed the fingers of his left hand as he reached for the telephone.

The door was not double-locked. The lights were on. It felt warm and welcoming inside, but he did not let himself think about that. He was no professional when it came to death; he experienced the same fear, revulsion, and pity as any other layman. He knew how to check, though, and how to do so without disturbing the body. He knelt on the stairs and felt for her pulse. She was cold. Perhaps rigor mortis had already set in. He stood up and stepped over her. Julie's room was empty, the bed unmade. He hesitated outside Margaret's door, feeling like a prurient intruder. So this was where she slept. He snapped off the lights and closed the door. Snapped off his thoughts, too. He went systematically through the house, peeked into the late Miss Tidy's private domain, and felt a pang of sadness.

In the kitchen, tacked to a square of cork wall-tiles, he found a neatly written list of essential telephone numbers. He called Margaret's doctor, then the police. He thought he might permit himself a cigarette while he waited, then realized he had none with him.

He watched the stiff lump that was Elinor Tidy being carried out of the house, covered in a gray blanket. The doctor had told him and the police that he was prepared to bet it was a heart attack, but of course they would have to wait for the postmortem.

"Margaret Wells will be terribly upset," he added. "And I don't think she'll be pleased that you've put young Julie in a clinic."

"She is simply staying there overnight, or until she feels able to return here or other arrangements can be made." Even as he repeated what was becoming a formula, he acknowledged the truth of what the doctor was saying. Margaret's reaction was one of the consequences he least relished. The more pressing problem right then was how to reach Margaret in the first place. It took much longer and required much more cunning to convince the police. He had to ring the clinic, let the sergeant talk to the matron. He had to pull rank, to insist that Julie could not yet be questioned.

"You see our point, sir," the sergeant said with heavy patience, a man trying to be reasonable, "if the girl's off her head . . ."

"Ms. Wells is in shock, Sergeant. She's only eighteen. She walked in here and fell over a dead body. . . ."

"Ah, yes, sir, I appreciate that, but then she was your patient before that. You do see my point, sir?"

"Not really," Russell said wearily. "If she is well enough, you can talk to her in the morning. I'll be in touch."

They left at last, Russell having explained over and over what he planned to do, where he planned to be. He felt, inevitably, he supposed, a little like a criminal himself. Whether he would be able to make Julie understand the seriousness of the situation, he had no idea. He did not care to contemplate what the police would make of her insistence that Jo-Jo killed Miss Tidy. She must not mention Jo-Jo to them. But that was all in the future. First he had to reach Margaret Wells. He could not believe that she would go away without leaving an address, at least, for just such an emergency, but it was not to be found in any of the obvious places: the bulletin board, the dresser, beside the kitchen telephone. Perhaps Julie had it in her room for safekeeping.

His stomach rumbled loudly as he climbed the stairs. He had missed his dinner. He stopped at the first floor and went into the long sitting room. Margaret's tidy desk yielded nothing. He was about to leave when he saw the printed card propped beside the dark blue telephone: HOTEL SAN PAULO. There was even a map, a sketchy drawing of the building circled in red. And a telephone number. He noticed a film of dust on the telephone as he went to pick it up, as though Miss Tidy's passing had already been marked.

Julie did not know where she was. The room came slowly into focus, blurred. Her head ached with a funny sort of drowsiness, a cotton-wool feeling. A blue blind covered the window, but glowed with daylight. She lay very still, listened, heard birdsong. The very white, starched sheets rustled as she sat up. The room was very white, too, clean and sparsely furnished. Like a nursery, she thought. There was even a little night-light glowing softly beside her. She smiled. She heard the squeak of rubber shoes on a polished floor, the rattle of something metallic. She slid down into the bed again, snuggling safe. She was tightly tucked in. She closed her eyes and pretended to be asleep. Inside, she wanted to giggle.

The door opened. She recognized the familiar swish of the starched apron, the brisk and purposeful step. The blind rattled up, clattering, the ring at the end of its cord tick-ticking against the window. The window squeaked a protest as it was opened wider and a familiar voice said, "Good morning. And how are we this morning?"

The giggle escaped her in a burst of laughter. She bounced up in bed.

"Good morning, Nanny. I wasn't asleep. I caught you." Nanny put a cup of tea on the nightstand beside her, switched off the night-light.

"Sleep well, did we?" she asked, without a smile in her voice.

"Yes, thank you, Nanny."

"Drink your tea, then. Sister will be along in a minute."

As soon as the door closed, Julie wriggled out of the tightly tucked bed. Her white cotton nightgown fell loose to her ankles. Her bare feet touched the rubbery linoleum and she wriggled her toes. Sunlight fell through the window, making a golden rectangle on the floor. She could see the tops of trees waving against a blue sky. It was going to be a beautiful day. She ran across the floor and leaned her elbows on the window ledge. The garden exploded green before her delighted eyes. Spring flowers nodded their heads at her, and there, leaning nonchalantly against the trunk of a tree, waiting for her, was her best friend, Jo-Jo. She grinned and mouthed his name, waved to him, jumping up and down. He waved back, his solemn little boy's face shining up at her. She felt so safe.

Seven

The Hartington Clinic was in Hampstead, on a tree-lined road that rose steeply to a false horizon. It was a large, semidetached Edwardian brick villa with an ornate wood and glass porch, a far cry indeed from Margaret's bleaker imaginings: turrets that menaced the sky, barred windows, long gray corridors smelling of disinfectant and sad people. Even the nursery windows, traditionally barred for safety in such houses, caught the afternoon light freely.

Margaret, it seemed, had been traveling forever. Now, standing on the porch, her suitcase and overnight bag beside her, she felt out of her element, beached by the sudden cessation of movement. She had been unable, at such short notice, to get on the first flight out of Venice, and had taken a train to Milan and just scraped onto a flight there. From Heathrow she had phoned Russell Dunn, who informed her brusquely, without explanation, that Julie was still at the clinic. He would meet her there.

Among the many, often conflicting emotions Margaret had wrestled with during the long hours of traveling were panic and anger at the mere idea of her daughter being in a clinic. She knew about clinics and what they did to people. In his first call he had promised her it was only for "safekeeping"; Julie understandably did not want to spend the night alone in the house where Miss Tidy had died. There was no medical reason for Julie to be at the clinic; he

139

had promised her that. Except shock. Yet he had kept her there.

With a start, Margaret realized that she had not rung the bell. How long had she been standing on the porch? Her cab had already driven away. She felt conspicuous, silly. She pressed the bell quickly, tugged at her crumpled jacket, smoothed her hair. The cabdriver had probably taken her for an inmate. Margaret reached impatiently for the doorbell again, just as the door opened. A woman in a white nylon uniform, a silly little nurse's cap pinned to her brown hair, smiled at her.

"My name is Wells. I've come to collect my daughter. Could you help me with my bag, please?"

Momentarily, the red-and-black-tiled hall reminded her of Venice. A wide oak staircase rose up to a gallery. There was a passable arrangement of daffodils in a brass jug on a wooden chest. Margaret caught sight of herself in a large mirror. She was not enthusiastic about what she saw. The place smelled of some kind of chemical air freshener.

"Mr. Dunn is expecting you," the woman said, setting Margaret's case down. Margaret did not snap that she had no wish to see Mr. Dunn, that she had come simply to collect her daughter. There was no point in wasting time. She would have it out with him. She followed the woman up the stairs, along the gallery, and through an ugly steel fire door. Beyond, the corridor was cool with grayish, very clean linoleum tiles on the floor. It was light and airy and functional, and uncomfortably like a hospital. The woman stopped at a door, knocked, and opened it, announcing her.

It was a medium-sized room, made ugly by a mishmash of styles. The pretty original fireplace was at odds with the gray linoleum, the black vinyl fireside chairs. The desk was old, a fine, leather-topped piece, but it looked incongruous beside red filing cabinets and a steel sink with shining mixer taps. A strip of cheap red carpet failed to add cheerfulness.

Russell Dunn rose awkwardly from one of the chairs. In his shirtsleeves, tieless, he looked as rumpled as Margaret felt. His trousers bagged at the knees. She saw as she met his bloodshot eyes that he must have been dozing. There was a shadow of stubble on his chin, and he had pouches beneath his eyes. His appearance made her soften a little. He had, after all, taken care of everything for her, like a good, dependable friend, she thought, and the thought made her uncomfortable.

140

"I got here as soon as I could," she said, not knowing what would be more appropriate to say.

"A good journey?"

She ignored the remark as irrelevant chitchat.

"Where's Julie? I can see you haven't slept much, so I'll just take her off your hands. She *is* ready?"

"Please, sit down a moment, will you?" He took her arm, which irritated her, and led her to one of the ugly chairs. "Would you like some tea?"

"No." She sat. "I want my daughter. I want to spend as little time as possible in this place." She looked around the room, her distaste showing on her face. He sat down opposite her. The chair was too low for him. He seemed to fold himself into it, his knees sticking up too high. He rested his elbows on them, brought his hands together in a pyramid, or an attitude of prayer. "You can't keep her here, you know," Margaret said, suddenly afraid.

"There has been a development. . . ."

"What do you mean?"

"Julie has regressed to childhood." Margaret stared at him. "I'm sorry, I don't know how to break it to you gently."

"I want to see her."

"And you shall. But first, I really must prepare you—"

"What have you done to her?"

"I imagine the shock of finding Miss Tidy was too much for her mind. She has retreated mentally, has no apparent memory of yesterday at all. This morning when she woke she believed that her room here was her nursery, the staff her nanny."

"This is absolutely ridiculous." Margaret jumped up and walked across the room, turned and came back. "Then she must be made to believe otherwise. I'll tell her if you won't."

"I can't allow that."

"You can't allow—?"

"The mind is a very delicate mechanism. Julie's mind is in shock. She must be handled very gently. She must be coaxed back, not forced."

Margaret turned away impatiently, searching for something with which to fight him.

"You only said you 'imagined' . . ."

Behind her, he sighed and stood up, his knees cracking.

"There is another possible reason, an allied reason."

141

"Well?" Margaret faced him.

"Julie believes that Jo-Jo killed Miss Tidy. She may well be escaping that belief. Escaping from Jo-Jo himself."

"You've done this. You've encouraged her!" Margaret accused him, her voice breaking.

"I assure you, I cannot examine your daughter's fears by denying them. For me, as for you, they *have* to exist. You might reconsider your own attitudes in that light, if you really want to help her."

His words were like a stinging slap to the face. Margaret felt herself redden. He turned away, rubbing his eyes with his knuckles.

"Let me see her," Margaret said. "Let me talk to her."

"Of course. But gently, please. You must take your cue from her."

Dumbly, Margaret nodded.

There was a little wooden table set against one bare white wall. Julie sat at it, her right leg curled under her, her left hand propping up her head. She was chewing the end of her pen. Before her, angled to the right, was a large writing pad. It was half-covered with childish capitals that sloped and swooped as though they were in flight from the orderly prison of the lines.

Margaret, standing in the doorway, a little to one side of Russell Dunn, felt as though she had stepped back in time, ten or more years. Sunlight streamed into the room, adding to the illusion. For a moment Julie's hair spilled corn-gold over her shoulders, just as it had . . .

"Julie, here's someone to see you. A surprise." He spoke with the sort of studied kindliness that some adults adopt when talking to young children. He stood aside. Julie twisted toward the door.

"Mummy! Oh, Mummy. Mummy. Mummy."

She flung herself upon Margaret, almost knocking her off balance. They swayed and rocked together, Margaret clutching her awkwardly with her right arm.

"How are you, darling?" she managed to say. The hair beneath her fingers was light brown, collar-length. The beaming face was that of a young woman, of her grown daughter.

"Why didn't Nanny tell me you were coming? Why?" She wriggled around with pleasure and excitement, tugged at Margaret's hand.

Russell closed the door, pulled the chair from the table, and placed it close to Margaret. She looked as though she might faint.

"Oh, Mummy, it's so lovely to see you. Are you staying long? Have you brought me lots and lots of presents?"

As Margaret sat, there was a painful, awkward moment when Julie seemed about to climb onto her lap. A little frown of concern crossed her face as, presumably, she realized she was too big.

"Will you get me a new desk? This one's getting too small for me," she said, looking at the table.

"Yes . . . yes, darling. Of course. I can see," Margaret said with difficulty, "how much you've grown."

"Haven't I?" She twirled around, holding out her skirts.

Margaret looked at the table and, visibly trying to conceal her pain, she asked, "What have you been doing? Will you show me?"

"Oh, just lessons. Boring lessons. Nanny won't let me go outside. She says I've got to stay in and copy out all my lessons until I get them neat and tidy. Will you take me out into the garden, Mummy? Can we go on one of our special walks? There's tadpoles in the pond and ever so much to show you."

"Mummy's had a very long journey," Russell intervened. "She's tired. Perhaps another day."

"Oh, poor Mummy." She came to Margaret, touched her, fawned upon her in a way that would have been charming in an eight-year-old but that looked gross and unpleasant in this context. Margaret felt herself draw back. "Why are you so sad, Mummy?" Julie said, nuzzling her.

"I'm not sad, darling. It's as Mr. Dunn said, I'm just tired."

"Sorry, Mummy, sorry, Mummy."

Margaret rubbed her back gently.

"Tomorrow I'll have a special present for you. When I've . . . unpacked."

"Hug me, Mummy. Hug me." Julie laced her arms around Margaret's neck.

"I am, darling."

"No . . . properly." She pulled away, her eyes searching Margaret's face, darting. "What's the matter with your arm?" She seized Margaret's left hand, lifted it. "Poor Mummy," she said softly.

"Mummy's very tired. She must rest now." Gently, Russell pulled Julie's hands from Margaret's. "Why don't you draw

Mummy a nice picture?" He led her back to the table. Julie stood biting her lip, looking down.

"I don't know what to draw."

Over her head, Russell signaled to Margaret that she should leave. To her surprise, she was relieved. She felt like an intruder.

"What would you like to draw?"

Margaret crept to the door, opened it.

"I know. I'll draw a picture of Jo-Jo."

She was leaning against the wall, tears squeezing from beneath her closed lids. Instinctively he put his arm around her shoulders, drew her against him. She let him lead her, leaned against him. He sat her in one of the black vinyl chairs, went to the telephone, and pressed a button. He asked for tea to be sent up. Margaret balanced her shoulder bag on her knees, dabbed at her eyes with a small handkerchief.

"I don't understand. There's so much I don't . . ."

He came to sit opposite her, resisting the temptation to reach out and take her hand.

"I'll try to explain, as far as I can."

"You . . . I mean, who does she think you are?"

"She simply accepts me. Because she trusts me, because I promised her last night when she was so terribly disturbed that this was a safe place."

"Safe?"

"To her it is. And *I'm* safe. She trusts me."

"Not me?"

"Of course. But she has, in a sense, taken you back with her. I am both in her fantasy and outside it."

"What about my grandmother?"

"That's very interesting. Apparently it's all rather selective. She hasn't mentioned her great-grandmother or asked for her. Not yet."

"What if she does?"

"We'll cross that bridge when we come to it."

He rose to a tap on the door. The woman in the nurse's cap and white uniform carried in a tea tray and placed it on the desk. She gave a little smile before leaving.

"Do you take sugar?" He hesitated, then asked, "May I call you Margaret?"

"Yes, if you like. No. No sugar."

"I think it might be rather good for you."

"No. Thank you."

He poured the tea and brought her cup.

"You said that she might be escaping from Jo-Jo . . . yet Jo-Jo was part of her childhood. You heard what she said about drawing him."

"Yes, but Jo-Jo was a child then, too. He was harmless, her friend. She felt safe with him . . . like . . . like a teddy bear . . . a companion when you were away." Margaret sipped her tea. "Hard as this may be for you to believe, Julie really does feel safe here. I think she is even happy . . . happier. . . ."

"Which means," Margaret said, "that you want to keep her here. You want my permission."

"Do you have a better idea? Do you think you could cope with her as she is, if you took her now? What would you do with her? Going back to the house so soon after Miss Tidy . . ." Margaret remembered Elinor with a pang of guilt and grief. "How would you cope?"

"All right, all right," she said wearily. "There's no need to rub it in." She finished her tea thirstily and put the cup and saucer down on the floor. "What do you want me to do?"

"Let her stay here for the moment. I'll work with her every day. You can see her, but perhaps not every day. We must, at least to begin with, go along with the illusion of her childhood, and you were often absent."

"I feel as though I'm being punished."

"Nonsense. I'll keep you fully informed. You have my word. And as soon as possible, you shall see her as much as you like. Please trust me."

"It seems I have no choice." She stood up. "All right, Mr. Dunn—"

"Oh, call me Russell, please."

"And I should thank you for all you've done."

"There is just one thing. I'd rather you didn't mention Jo-Jo to the police."

"The police?"

"They wanted to interview Julie. So far, I've succeeded in stalling them."

"Poor Elinor. I keep forgetting her. Yes, of course, I'll . . . I'd scarcely mention my daughter's . . . delusions to them. You can be sure of that."

"Thank you. Actually, I'm sure they'll be satisfied once the post-mortem is completed. In any case, Julie can scarcely help them as she is."

"No. Quite. Well, I'd better get on with it."

"Will you be all right? Let me drive you . . ."

"No, thank you. If someone could perhaps call a cab?"

"Of course. I'll see to it downstairs." He opened the door for her. He thought that she looked dreadful. "Are you sure you'll be all right?"

"Perfectly, thank you," she said, and swung her bag onto her shoulder, lifting her chin defiantly.

Cars were parked in a solid line right up the hill. Afraid that he was going to be late, Barry slipped his car into the first available gap and prepared to finish the journey on foot. The gateways of many of the houses he passed bore discreet brass plaques belying their ordinariness: homeopathic doctors, Jewish societies, accountants, and investment brokers. Margaret had said that the clinic was near the brow of the hill, on the right-hand side. He stopped reading the plaques, squeezed himself between two cars and, checking for traffic, crossed the road.

He did not know what he felt about the clinic, about Julie's being there. If it was for the best . . . He did not understand any of it properly; he only knew that it frightened him. In some way he felt responsible. He kept remembering what Margaret had said that day at lunch, about how young Julie was and how he had pressured her, had tried to hustle her into a marriage for which he now saw she was plainly not ready. It was ironic, he could see, that the very childlike quality he loved most about her was the cause of her illness. His instinct now was simply to take care of her. He felt that if he could just talk to her, reassure her, he would be able to put her mind at rest. The phrase struck him as unexpectedly apt. But Margaret, when she'd asked him to come to this meeting, had not promised that he would be allowed to see Julie. It all depends on how she is, Margaret had said. Whatever that meant. Shaking his head, he began to check the plaques as he passed.

A FOR SALE sign caught his attention and he looked up. Laced

146

with scaffolding, the house had a neglected and gloomy air. Its roof was stripped back to the timbers. He heard faint pop music from a workman's transistor radio, and a whistled accompaniment, out of time. He did not know why he stopped, why he stared. He stood in the gateless gateway of the house. The driveway and garden were littered with piles of rubble, tiles, and new timber. A block and tackle rattled down from the roof. The small hairs on the back of his neck bristled. He felt drawn to the place, rooted to the spot. The rope began to ascend and Barry remained where he stood, watching it rise. A heavy load of tiles swung from the end of the rope. The tiles were thick, gritty-looking. He saw them so sharply, as though his eyes were inches from them rather than several yards away.

The rope from which they swung jerked suddenly. The load seemed to swing out from the scaffolding toward him, then swing back again. Swing forward, toward him. In that split second he knew that when the load reached the apex of its swing, the rope would break. He even saw its thick cables fraying and untwisting, as though unraveled by strong, meddling fingers. He heard a shout. The load swung out toward him and the ties that held it in place parted with an imagined twanging, snapping sound. The sound released the tiles into an outward explosion, firing them into space, through the air, toward him.

Instinct or reflex made him throw himself sideways. His left shoulder collided painfully with the high brick gatepost, spinning him around, off balance. His spine jarred as he hit the pavement and threw up his arms protectively to cover his head. The tiles rained and smashed around him. One sharp, jagged piece grazed the back of his hand. There was dust and silence and the sound of running feet. The pop music sounded again, quietly undeterred.

"Jesus Christ."

"You okay, mate?"

"I don't understand it. I just don't bloody understand it."

"Hang on. Careful. You all right, mate?"

The two white-faced men seemed to be fighting over him, one trying to help him up, the other to push the would-be helper aside. Dazed, he tried to lever himself up.

"Careful. You sure you ain't broke nothing?"

He nodded sickly. Blood was running from his hand. His back

hurt. There was a dull throb in his shoulder. The men steadied him.

"I just don't understand it."

"Made a right mess of your suit, guv."

"The whole bloody thing just seemed to go berserk."

"It's all right. Not your fault," Barry said, though he did not know why he said it. "Perfectly all right. I must go. An appointment . . ."

"You sure?"

One man pulled the other aside.

"Very decent of you, guv. Very sorry and all that." His look to his mate said he did not want any complaints or trouble. Barry nodded, as though to reassure him, as though he understood.

"The Hartington Clinic, do you know it?"

"Just up there, guv. Two doors up."

"Thank you. So sorry."

He was sorry? He thought, I'm going mad. They could have killed me. Except that they didn't do anything. The block and tackle with its load of tiles had had a terrible, incredible life of its own. *It* had tried to kill him, or to injure him, at least.

Behind him as he walked away, the workmen surveyed the debris, inspected the innocent pulley. They exchanged a look but could not make sense of it. One offered the other a cigarette. Barry turned into the gateway of the Clinic, wrapping a handkerchief around his bleeding hand.

It was not until she stood, for the second time that morning, in the waiting room that Margaret saw what a fine, summery day it was. It was more than a week now since she had first come to the clinic, and in that time she had not noticed the weather. She stood at the window, looking out onto the trees, each leaf seeming to turn and shimmer in the breeze. The room itself was dark, as though it existed in another dimension than that occupied by the trees and sunlight outside. Did Julie feel, as Margaret felt suddenly, that the clinic cut her off from the good, natural world outside? Did she feel punished by her incarceration, denied her freedom? God, how Julie had loved the old garden.

Margaret gripped the velvet curtain beside her to steady herself. Her touch produced a puff of dust, an odor of staleness. The light dazzled her. The room filled her with panic. She had been banished to this room with its threadbare carpet and sullen furniture. She could still hear the note of disapproval, even rebuke, in Russell Dunn's voice when he had "suggested" that she wait there while Barry's hand was attended to. Like Jane Eyre, she thought, locked in the—was it red?—room, punished for speaking out, speaking the truth as she saw it. But Jane Eyre was only a little girl and she . . . Was she, then, following her daughter into some haunted, incomplete childhood?

Margaret shook off the thought by moving away from the window, flicking over the pages of an old, much-fingered copy of *Country Life* that lay, with other sad, unwanted magazines, on a console table of hideous ornamentation. She was guilty of snapping at Barry. All right, she would apologize. She had reason to snap. First, he had arrived late. Second, he looked as though he had been dragged through a hedge backwards and was making an absurd fuss about a little scratch. . . .

It wasn't that, she realized as she impatiently reviewed her fault —not even his babble about bricks or tiles seeming to fly at him, as though they meant to harm him. All that, even with her temper on its present short fuse, she could have ignored, laughed off. It was Russell Dunn with his quick questions, his air of barely suppressed excitement, that had angered her. Damn it, he was colluding with Barry, encouraging his zany illusion just as he indulged and encouraged Julie. He had even mentioned Jo-Jo.

And then she was angry at Barry. She had asked so little of him since her benighted return from Venice. The very least he could have done was to put up a good front, present himself well instead of behaving like a . . . Words failed her. Instead of playing straight into Russell's hands. For he was onto something now, the very thing she feared, and she no longer felt strong enough to fight him. She had thought that Barry lacked sufficient imagination ever to "see" things or "feel" something odd. She had thought that Barry, level-headed, unimaginative Barry, might be good for Julie.

She dropped the magazine, its pages hanging open and disheveled over the edge of the table, and walked across the room to the ornate, tiled fireplace. A smeared mirror, set above the mantel, reflected her face. She fussed automatically with her hair, ignoring the evidence of strain on her face, the fact that the little extra touches of compensating makeup made her look older, harder. Was it unreasonable to want progress? Nobody had any idea how lonely she was, how afraid she was of what was happening to her daughter.

She turned quickly, almost guiltily away from the mirror as the loose brass door handle rattled, announcing that someone was coming in. A nurse looked around the room as though she could not see in its dim light. Her eyes slid over Margaret. Leaving the door open, she walked briskly to the table and closed the magazine, aligning its edge with the rest of the regimented pile.

"Mrs. Wells?" she asked over her shoulder.

"Yes."

"Mr. Dunn would like you to join him now, please."

"Thank you." She marched straight out of the room, not wanting the nurse to show her the way, which she knew perfectly well. The woman hurried after her, passed her, and knocked on the solid door before opening it to let Margaret in. Peevishly, Margaret did not thank her.

Barry was seated in one of the low black chairs, his newly bandaged hand resting on the arm. He started to stand up, but Margaret waved him down again.

"I'm sorry, Barry. I really didn't mean . . ."

"Quite understand," he mumbled, embarrassed. "Terrible strain for us all." He sounded subdued, as though he knew more than she did, had received some news. . . .

She looked quickly, suspiciously toward Russell Dunn, who stood behind the desk. Instinctively she avoided his eyes. When she saw the note Barry had shown her, the note signed "Jo-Jo," lying on the desk, she knew that they were in cahoots. Beside it was another note, the clumsy, uneven letters immediately recognizable to her. She could not read it without making a show of curiosity. She sat down on a straight-backed chair. Russell Dunn, still standing, touched the edges of the notes with his finger.

"You didn't tell me about this."

"No," Margaret said, assuming the statement was directed at her. "Actually, I only knew of two. You've had another?" she asked Barry, turning a little toward him. He nodded. She had no intention of explaining her silence on the subject to Russell.

"Three in all," Barry added in the same crushed tone. "I threw the first one away," he added to Russell.

"Barry tells me you think the writing is Julie's," Russell said.

"It is similar to the way she wrote as a child. That habit of ignoring the lines—"

"Quite." He cut her off with a wave of his hand. Not for the first time, Margaret thought that he had surprisingly small and sensitive hands for such a tall man. They did not seem quite large enough for him, and looked much too gentle. "There is something I haven't told you," he said. Margaret looked up sharply, but his gaze remained general, directed at neither of them. "Early on in my treatment of Julie, I received a threatening phone call. Later, another. The voice could have been heavily disguised. I couldn't be sure. Unfortunately, the first call, which was recorded on my answering machine, was somehow erased."

"Did this voice . . . I mean, did he identify himself? Was it Jo-Jo?" Barry asked. To Margaret's surprise and annoyance, he actually sounded scared.

"He didn't identify himself by name, no, though he insisted I knew who he was."

Margaret smiled.

"I would imagine such phone calls are a hazard of your work." She held the smile, could feel Barry's disapproval, embarrassment.

"Let us suppose—for lack of any other explanation—that the calls were from Jo-Jo," Russell went on firmly, ignoring her.

"Hang on a minute," Barry interrupted. "You said the voice could have been Julie's."

"That's my point. Whatever we want to believe individually, let us accept that these"—he picked up the notes—"and the calls were *supposed* to be from Jo-Jo. What I want you both to understand is that, although Julie must, in the physical sense, have formed these letters and spoken those words on the telephone to me, Jo-Jo was acting through her. She is not responsible. She has no memory of writing these or of making the calls. I must ask you particularly, Barry, to understand that. It is possible for Julie to love you and yet be instrumental in sending these notes. You must hang on to that if you are to help her."

Barry swallowed audibly.

"I'll try," he said. "But I honestly don't know what to think. She always seemed such a normal girl, you know?" He glanced at Margaret as though seeking confirmation. She lowered her eyes. "Young, yes, and inexperienced, of course . . . but that always made

151

me feel . . . I don't know, I'm not very good with words . . . that I could protect her, I suppose—"

"Do you still want to protect her?" Russell interrupted.

Barry thought about this, looked again at Margaret, then back to Russell. He did not understand any longer what he could protect her from. The idea of protection had always been a physical one, an image of her nestling trustingly in his arms. It was not something he had ever tried to articulate or understand. He had meant to protect her from the knocks of life, he supposed, to make things smooth for her. But Jo-Jo, whatever Jo-Jo was, was not one of life's everyday ups and downs. If Jo-Jo had been real, flesh and blood, then it would have been simple: He would have knocked his block off. But Jo-Jo was, as far as he could understand, an idea in Julie's mind, an idea that she sometimes used against him. He looked at Russell, knowing suddenly what he wanted to say.

"I can't get away from the idea that maybe what you're really saying is that it's me she wants to be protected from. Not that I mean her any harm, of course. But if she's not ready for marriage, like Margaret says . . . Look, if she's writing those notes as you say, then doesn't that mean she's afraid of me, that she's telling me to . . . clear off?"

"What do you think?" Margaret prompted Russell.

"I believe that Julie loves Barry, but Jo-Jo wants her to love Jo-Jo. Similarly, she trusts me, but Jo-Jo wants to be rid of my 'interference.' I conclude that Julie made the calls and wrote the notes, since there is no other rational explanation. But I also believe that whatever it is we call Jo-Jo motivated her and that the threats to both of us are an expression of his will, not hers." He waited, looking at Margaret, but she only shook her head. The truth was that she did not want to believe. "Barry?" Russell said quietly.

"You say she does love me. That's enough for me."

"Even though you believe you may be in danger?"

"Well," he said, shrugging, "I reckon I can handle that."

Russell nodded and looked again at Margaret, but she had nothing to add.

"Well, then, I expect you'd both like to see Julie. I must warn you that she is not herself, Barry. Please don't show her that you feel upset. Behave calmly and, above all, take your cue from her. Do you understand?"

"I'm not sure, I . . ."

"She's a child, Barry," Margaret said sharply. "She thinks she's a little girl again."

"And therefore," Russell went on, "she may not know you, since she did not know you when she was a child. I hope, however, that seeing you will perhaps . . . alter that. Now, if you're both ready?"

Margaret stood up. Barry nodded. Russell went to the door, opened it, and spoke to a person outside.

"She won't be a moment," he said, turning back to face them. "Please try to be as relaxed as possible." Margaret sat down again. Russell returned to his desk, folded the notes together, and slipped them into the pocket of his jacket.

"Just sort of follow her lead, you mean?" Barry asked.

"Exactly."

"If she doesn't recognize him," Margaret said, "should I introduce him?"

"Best leave that to me, I think," Russell answered. Margaret's lips tightened into a thin line, then her whole body tensed at the tap on the door.

"Come in," Russell called.

They saw a flash of starched white uniform behind Julie before the door closed. She stood just inside the room, looking uncertainly around her. She wore a cotton robe over pajamas.

"Mummy, Mummy, you came! You came!" With a squeal of delight she dashed across the room and embraced Margaret, who held her clumsily. Margaret had to close her eyes fiercely, will herself not to cry, as she hugged the too-big little girl to her.

"How are you, darling?" she said.

"I'm fine. I've missed you, though. Nanny said if I finished all my lessons you might come today. And I did. I did."

"There's a good girl," Margaret said. "I'm so glad to see you."

"You have another visitor, Julie," Russell said.

Her eyes went instantly to him, shining with a sort of trust. Barry stood up. It hurt him to smile. He could not speak. Julie stared at him and pulled back beside her mother's chair, as though about to hide behind it. Margaret held her arm tightly.

"Darling . . ."

"You remember Barry, don't you?" Russell said quietly. "Barry's come to see you."

Margaret stared at him intently, willing him to speak.

"Hello, Julie," he said in a hollow voice. "H-how are you?"

Julie pressed against her mother's side and began to sway from side to side. Her thumb went automatically to her mouth.

"Now don't be silly, darling. You remember Barry. Say hello to Barry."

She murmured something, shaking her head. Margaret leaned closer to her. Gently she pulled the obstructing thumb from the girl's mouth.

"Don't let him take me away. Please, Mummy, don't let him." She stared wildly, pale-faced, at Barry, cringing back behind Margaret's chair. Instinctively, Margaret stared at him too, as though trying to see him with Julie's eyes. All she saw was Barry, bewildered and somewhat hangdog. He stretched out a hand to Julie. "*No!*" she screamed, and yanked free of Margaret's grip. She flung herself against the wall, her head rolling from side to side, sobbing. Margaret stood up and went to her, tried to still her. Julie knocked her hand away with unexpected violence.

"Stop it!" Margaret shouted, the tension of the past week suddenly snapping. "Stop it at once! Barry isn't going to hurt you or take you anywhere. Oh, for God's sake, stop it." Her right hand came up and cracked sharply against Julie's cheek. The silence was intense and alive. Julie stood quite still against the wall, one cheek pressed against it as though pinned there by the force of her mother's blow. The other cheek began to glow pink, deepening to red. Margaret said, "Oh, my God, Julie . . ." She took a step toward her, her hand reaching out in apology.

"No!" Julie spat, facing her, eyes blazing. "Stay away from me! You don't care! I don't want you! You don't care about me! If you go away he'll . . . he'll . . ." She could not form the words as her teeth began to chatter in terror. She stared beyond Margaret at Barry, her eyes rolling.

"I think you'd better wait outside," Russell said, moving decisively toward Barry.

Margaret heard footsteps, heard the door open and close. Julie's gaze returned to her, steadied.

"Go away," she said. "Go on, go. I don't care. I don't want you anyway. I've got Jo-Jo. Jo-Jo'll help me. Jo-Jo won't let him take me away. Jo-Jo loves me. Jo-Jo . . . Jo-Jo? I want Jo-Jo . . ."

"All right, Julie. Come along. Let's go and find Jo-Jo."

Margaret felt herself pushed aside as Russell approached the girl and held out his hand to her. Julie threw herself against him, sobbing, clinging to him. Gently he held her, patting her back. Margaret felt her heart shrivel.

Russell carried a tray holding a coffee pot and cups into the room. Margaret sat in one of the black vinyl chairs, her back to him. He did not look at her as he passed, and he kept his back turned as he poured the coffee. He heard sniffling, tissues being crumpled. She blew her nose loudly. He offered her a thick white china cup of coffee.

"Thank you," she said automatically. Her face, which she lowered almost at once, was scrubbed more or less clean of makeup. It looked naked, painfully exposed. Her eyes were red and swollen, her nose shining. She looked her age at last, he thought, and desperately appealing.

"Sugar?"

"No. Thank you." She tested the coffee, found it too hot. "Where's Barry?"

"I sent him off. Obviously he can do no good here. It was a mistake." He clipped the words off as though angry with himself for having suggested and permitted the meeting. He picked up his own cup and half-sat on the desk, his long legs stretched out and crossed at the ankles. Margaret stared at his large feet. "I've asked him not to come again. At least not until—"

"How is she?" Margaret interrupted. Her eyes, pleading with him, were frightened.

"She's calm now."

"You gave her something?"

"No. It wasn't necessary. We talked. . . ." he said vaguely. He knew that his words hurt Margaret, that she felt it should have been she who comforted her daughter, not him, a stranger. "This is only temporary," he told her, fumbling for the right words to comfort her, "this reaction. . . ."

"Please don't lie to me," Margaret said with a shadow of her old brusqueness. "You know now, don't you, you've seen . . . ? She hates me, blames me for leaving her. . . ."

"A little, yes," he agreed. "But she also loves you. What you heard

155

just now was probably no more than an understandable resentment she ought to have expressed long ago. You and she don't talk much, do you?"

"You don't know what it's like," she said, pushing his question aside, "to know your child hates you."

He thought automatically of his own son, Rupert, how distant he seemed now at their weekly meetings. Would Rupert one day see the divorce in terms of Dad going away, deserting him?

"More important," he said, quashing the thought, "why did she have such a strong reaction to Barry?"

"I haven't the faintest idea," Margaret said, sipping her coffee.

He opened his mouth to say *I don't believe you*, but shut it and waited a moment, inviting her to qualify her bald statement.

"Think about it, please," he said finally. "It's important."

"I've told you, I don't know."

"Who, in her childhood, wanted to take her away from you? Who did she fear might want to? Surely you must know—"

"Well, I don't. No one. There was no one. She was perfectly safe."

"Her father?"

"Nonsense. If you'd known him . . . Anyway, he didn't even know of her existence, as I've already told you."

"That's your last word on the subject?"

"You want me to invent something? I've told you. If you want to know what I think . . . I don't believe there was anyone. This is just another of her delusions."

"The other being . . . ?"

"This . . . Jo-Jo, of course."

"I see." He turned to put his cup down, pushed away from the desk, and walked around it. "I'd prefer it if you didn't see Julie for a while, either. In view of what happened here this morning . . ."

"You have no right to—" she began, clattering her cup into the saucer.

"Julie is eighteen. She can choose."

"But you're choosing for her."

"I am advising, as her psychiatrist. That is my duty as well as my right. You can telephone every day. I will personally see that you are kept fully informed."

"What do you propose to do for her?" Margaret demanded, shifting her ground, not agreeing to his request.

"A course of hypnotherapy," he answered at once. "Normally it would be used to take a person back to some time in his life that he cannot consciously retrieve. I hope that by reversing the process, by using it to bring her back into the present . . ."

"You don't know what else to try," Margaret said in a dead voice.

". . . I can stabilize her, then take her back, step by step, in a controlled situation."

"One step forward and two back . . ."

"I can only ask you to trust me."

"Take her back to what? She already is a child."

"And now she must become an adult who can cope with whatever fears her childhood still holds for her. This person who wanted to take her away, for one." Margaret stood up, carried her cup to the desk. "Do you agree?"

"I don't see that I have any practical choice. You won't let me see Julie. I don't see how I can forbid your proposed treatment. As you say, she's eighteen and, well, as I have demonstrated this morning, I don't seem to be of much use to her." She turned away to pick up her handbag. Holding it, not looking at him, she said, "You will keep me informed? I may call?"

"Certainly. Whenever you like."

"Thank you for that, anyway."

"Margaret . . ."

She seemed startled that he had used her first name, and jerked her head around to look at him. There was something in his tone, something almost tender. They stared at each other for a moment, tensely.

"I don't want you to think . . . I'm explaining this badly . . ." He came around the desk, trying to organize his thoughts, wanting only to touch her, to comfort her. "I think you are beginning to interpret Julie's problem and my treatment of her as a punishment of you. Please don't." Margaret continued to look at him, her eyes exploring his face as though searching for some proof of what he said, or perhaps looking for some sign of a trick. "You and I are not on different sides of the fence. We should help each other. Please . . ."

He put out his hand and then did not know what to do with it. He lacked the courage to touch her as he wanted, knew that it was quite the wrong moment. He let his arm drop to his side.

157

"I will try," Margaret said, "to be glad that Julie has someone . . . you . . . to help her as I obviously can't. I will try to cooperate with you. It's just that I'm so . . . so afraid." She moved quickly toward the door, tears starting to her eyes again.

"Won't you let me—" he began.

"Please . . . don't be kind to me. Right now I couldn't bear that." She sniffed, pressed her hand to her eyes for a moment. Russell watched, helpless, words seething, unspoken. "The best you can do for me," she said, "is to help my daughter and take good care of her. You see, she's all I've got. I'm sorry . . ." she trailed off as tears threatened again.

Russell started toward the door as it closed behind her, and then stopped himself. It was neither the time nor the place to tell her . . . What? That the worst thing possible was happening. Despite everything, he was falling in love with her.

She was several minutes late, and he, as nervous as a young man on his first really serious date, persuaded himself that she would not come. He was embarrassed to look around the restaurant expectantly. He wanted a cigarette. This was a professional meeting, so he knew she would come, because she cared about her daughter. And if his heart sank slightly at that, he had no business to be treating the daughter or dining with the mother.

It was three weeks since Margaret had seen her daughter. Russell had been in contact with her by telephone daily, sometimes twice daily, but it had taken him that long to dare to suggest dinner. He was still surprised—even a little unnerved—that she had agreed, and he tried not to flatter himself that she saw it as anything other than a chance for her to ask more questions, for him to expand on Julie's progress. But then, of course, she did not know about his little surprise.

She was coming across the room toward him, wearing pink, a dress and jacket of some softly shining material. He thought it a surprising color for her, but one that flattered her to perfection. So intent was he on his scrutiny that he almost forgot to rise to greet her. He sensed that his words were stiff and formal on his lips. She accepted a drink and settled back in her chair, regarding him.

"I'm very glad you could come," he said.

"It was nice of you to invite me." She glanced around the restaurant. He thought, from her expression, that she approved. "How is Julie?" she asked, two small lines pulling her eyebrows closer together.

"Physically well. I have no major change to report."

"But I thought . . . surely you said you had something new to discuss with me?"

"I didn't say that it was directly concerned with Julie. But we'll come to that later."

Her frown deepened. A waiter brought their drinks. Margaret touched her glass, turning it slightly, but did not drink.

"Are you trying to be kind to me?"

"Not consciously, if that's what you mean."

"Because if you are . . . well, I can cope, you know. Yes, it is very lonely without even Miss Tidy at the house, but I have friends, my job, I don't need to be 'taken out of myself' or whatever the current phrase might be."

"It never occurred to me that you did. If I gave that impression, I apologize."

She inclined her head a little, perhaps accepting his apology. He raised his glass, inviting her to join him in a toast. There were so many things he wanted to say, old formulas, clichés that seemed, even as he considered and rejected them, to be new-minted, with precise meaning.

"To Julie," Margaret said, and drank. "So you're still going on with the hypnotherapy?"

"Yes. There was some resistance at first, which, as I told you, given her apparent mental age just now, I found surprising, but we're progressing slowly. I ask her every time—this is quite usual —what age she is. She laughs and says, 'Eighteen, of course. You know that, Mr. Dunn.' But when she comes out of the trance, she's a child again."

"Well, can't you make her . . . She can't go through life in a trance."

"Exactly. The question you didn't ask is more to the point." Margaret raised her eyebrows. "Should I suggest to her that she remember her true age when she wakes up?"

"That would do it? Simple suggestion?"

"It might. The point is, would it be wise? Julie has retreated into childhood for some reason—something more, I believe, than the

159

obvious desire to escape her present difficulties. Maybe she has to work her way through that in her own time. By bringing her out of it too soon . . ." He spread his hands and shrugged.

"What do you talk about? Does she ask for me?"

"No. We talk about Jo-Jo, her fear of him, his demands. She retreats into childhood, I'm sure, because she can control him there, because then he's a little boy again, not a potentially powerful man." Margaret did not respond to this, but finished her drink quickly. "Would you like to order now?" Russell asked.

"Yes. Thank you."

Their silence as they studied the menu was awkward, each self-consciously aware that this was not solely a professional meeting but also a social one, which inevitably contained within it other possibilities. Their exchanges were consequently stilted as they agreed on the dishes, and Russell took longer than was strictly necessary to order the wine. When he turned his full attention back to her, he did not know how to proceed.

"I've been thinking," she said hurriedly, "examining my conscience, I suppose you might call it. You see . . . I am trying to cooperate with you." Russell nodded, encouraged her to go on. "What I did the other week, slapping her, that was unforgivable. It made me question whether, if I had been with her the whole time, I'd have been a good mother. The point is, there were other scenes like that, when she was a child. Oh, I never hit her, I promise you, though I think sometimes I wanted to. But it's true, she did hate my leaving her. There were always scenes, tantrums. Sometimes she did say that I didn't care, didn't love her. So maybe it wasn't such a happy childhood after all. Or not as happy as I liked to think." She paused while Russell tasted and approved the wine.

"And all this," she went on after the waiter had left, "made me wonder if my staying away from her was really the right course. I mean, since she is a child again, living in that time when I repeatedly left—rejected her, as she sees it—perhaps if now I was with her all the time, she would begin to feel better about her childhood, about our relationship."

"You can't ever give a person a new childhood," Russell said. "You can only repair the damage that is done, not erase it."

"I see that, of course, but—"

"There is another reason why I don't agree with your idea. You

160

aren't the problem. Whatever Julie is hiding from—or seeking—is not you, is not caused by you."

Margaret was silent for a moment, then she leaned forward intensely.

"I don't see how you can possibly say that. You saw . . . I've just told you . . ."

"I didn't understand," he said. "I'm sorry."

"What?"

"That you were blaming yourself so completely."

"What else could I do? She's my daughter, my responsibility."

"The problem is Jo-Jo. Not you."

"I'm not sure *that* makes me feel any better."

"You still refuse to believe in Jo-Jo?"

"Oh, I believe in him, all right. But not in the way you and Barry apparently do. Not as a fact, a malign force . . ."

"I don't think I ever said—"

"Well, whatever, I still say he is an excuse, something Julie is using in order to avoid facing up to her present situation. Beyond that I can't go."

"A psychiatrist," he said with a smile that was meant to tease her, "might be tempted to think you were jealous of him."

"Of Jo-Jo?" she snorted. "Then a psychiatrist would be off his head."

Their eyes met and held for a moment. Russell thought she was going to add something, he hoped something personal and kind, but their meal arrived and they began to eat.

"Jealous of him how, anyway?" Margaret asked, after a silence.

"You know what Jo-Jo is said to want?"

"For Julie to honor some stupid promise . . ."

"Julie—or Jo-Jo—uses the word 'marriage' as a euphemism. Jo-Jo's wants, I'm convinced, are entirely carnal."

"Are you trying to shock me? If I were going to be jealous of my daughter's sexuality, I would have been jealous of Barry Irving. I would have tried to prevent her from sleeping with him. I knew, you understand, that it was going to happen. Even *when* it happened."

"And how did you feel about that?"

"I didn't think it was any of my business. Besides, if I'm not going to be jealous of a flesh-and-blood man, I assure you I'm not likely to be seized by maternal *angst* over a ghost."

"Is he a ghost?" Russell asked her mildly.

Margaret stared at him, obviously thrown. She tried to smile, wanting him to admit that he was joking. His expression did not change, but was a mask of polite interest.

"I don't know what you're talking about. Of course he's not a ghost. *You* don't believe in ghosts," she challenged him.

"Perhaps not. Not in ectoplasmic materializations or spectral figures, no. But perhaps in another sense . . . We say, do we not, that so-and-so is 'haunted' by the past, a memory. What are the traumas and fears I work with daily but ghosts of a kind?"

"I would call them precisely that. Traumas. Fears. Those words seem to have the force of accuracy." She turned to the hovering waiter. "The spinach for me, please. No potatoes." She applied herself to the main course. He noted that she had ordered dishes that could easily be eaten with a fork alone. As she sliced into her omelette, she said, "Well, since you don't think anything of my suggestion, perhaps you'd better tell me what it was you wanted to discuss with me."

"Yes, you may be right."

"Well?" She looked at him impatiently. "Surely it can't be so very difficult?"

"No. But I'm afraid I've been rather . . . naughty."

"What an extraordinary word."

"It sounds better than 'underhanded' or 'snooping.' "

"Snooping on me?"

He sat back in his chair, sipped some wine.

"The fact of the matter is, I spoke to Roland Curteis the other day. About you."

"Why would you do that?" she said mildly, but looking with fierce concentration at her plate. He had expected her to have "forgotten" Curteis, or to be instantly angry.

"To test a theory I had. You see, I feel you didn't tell me the whole truth when you came to my office. Certainly not the whole truth about your accident." She looked up then. Her eyebrows were slightly raised to give an impression of polite interest. Her eyes, though, were guarded, watchful. "I thought perhaps it might have been a suicide attempt."

She smiled then. "I'm not the suicidal type."

162

"Indeed you are not. On the contrary, you are extremely strong and almost pathologically loyal, I suspect."

"What an extraordinary thing to say. You flatter me . . . I think."

"It's an extraordinary thing to be, and I intend no flattery."

She laid down her fork, straightened it across her plate.

"You can be an exceedingly irritating man. Even so, I'm sorry you were disappointed."

"Oh, no, far from it."

"Oh?"

"You know perfectly well what Curteis told me. Exactly what he told you he suspected ten years ago."

For a moment her eyes took on that dangerous catlike glow, and Russell braced himself, fearing that he had precipitated a scene. But when she spoke, it seemed that she had decided to brazen it out.

"That stupid theory of his, I suppose. You surely don't give any credence to that?"

"Tell me the truth, then."

"I might," she said. "But you'll have to tell me why."

"Because," he said, speaking slowly and deliberately, "whatever it is you've been living with for the last ten years, Julie has also been living with it. The effects of it, anyway." He waited, tense, almost holding his breath.

"Help you to help her, is that it?" He nodded once, gravely. "I've been expecting this, or something like it," she said, pushing her plate away. "I've had plenty of time to think these past few weeks, too much time. I still don't know why all this should matter to you or how it can help Julie. . . ."

"You must let me be the judge of that. I may be wrong. Perhaps it has nothing to do directly with Julie, but until you tell me the truth, you may be impeding my work."

"That's harsh," she said, turning her face away as though pained.

"I don't wish to be. Believe me, that is the last thing . . ." His hand ached to reach out and touch her. "Please, won't you tell me? If you like, if you could . . . regard me as a friend, someone who is interested in *you* . . ."

"All right," she said, her face suddenly drawn and strained. "But not here. This is scarcely the place. . . ."

"You're welcome to come back to my house. We could have coffee there."

"Thank you," she said, "but I prefer to be on my home ground."

"Fine. I'll drive you."

"You don't mind the kitchen?" she said, going ahead of him, putting on lights. "Since Miss Tidy . . . I really must find someone . . . the place is getting like a pigsty."

"This is fine," he said, drawing a chair out from the table and sitting down, businesslike.

"Shall I make some coffee?"

"I'd prefer wine."

She went to a rack, pulled out a bottle of red, and placed it and a corkscrew in front of him. She fetched two glasses while he opened the bottle.

"Won't you sit down?" he said, pouring the wine.

"I think perhaps I'll make some coffee. . . ." She turned away to the stove, obviously procrastinating. "What did you mean about 'pathological loyalty'?"

"Curteis told me that he did not believe you had an accident. Also, that it was highly unlikely that you could have inflicted those precise injuries on yourself. Curteis said that he believed then, and still believes today, that you were attacked. You denied it. You've always denied it."

Her back was turned to him. A sort of shudder passed up it. She gripped the edge of the stove. Her head hung down, the hair parted to show the soft, pale nape of her neck. Then, slowly, her head came up, her shoulders squared. He deliberately did not look at her face as she turned around. He saw her hand lift the glass of wine and, following it with his eyes, watched her raise it in an ironic, mocking toast before she drank.

"I don't believe this," she said at last. "I've kept my own counsel for ten years. I thought it was buried forever. As far as I'm concerned, it's done with, finished. You understand? And now you . . . I'm supposed to tell you . . . It's too ridiculous." She shook her head a little in disbelief. "But I'm going to, aren't I? You'll sit there until I do, inscrutable, expecting. . . . I don't really have any choice, do I? Or perhaps," she went on slowly, looking him full in the face, "perhaps I actually want to tell you. That's what you would say, isn't it?"

Margaret pulled out a chair and sat opposite him.

"Most of what I told you about Julie's father was true. I may have exaggerated some things—his popularity at the Conservatory, for example—and played down others, like the way I felt about him. It seems incredible now that I—that anyone—could feel so intensely and be so blind. I was young, of course, and totally inexperienced. But there was something about him that inspired passion. He made the world go round more quickly. Anyway . . .

"He graduated ahead of me, though with less glory than he felt to be his due. But he didn't lack chances. He was offered work, good work, the sort of things most young men in his position would have jumped at. But not Tom. Nothing was good enough for Tom. He lacked real confidence, I suppose. I don't really know. I don't think I ever understood him. At the time I thought it was a phase. I thought it would pass. I tried to believe that he was right to value himself and his talents so highly, but another part of me knew that no one was going to hand him one of the great orchestras on a plate without his serving some kind of apprenticeship. I had to pin my faith on the great work, the magnum opus he was supposed to be writing, and when I discovered that that was a lie—he hadn't set down a note, not a single bar—I saw, quite clearly, the trap I'd got myself into.

"He was living off me, drinking, doing nothing. It was sad, watching him try to keep the myth going. He was always hanging around the Conservatory. He talked, talked endlessly, but it all amounted to nothing. I threw myself into my work because I didn't know how to handle the situation. I owe him that, at least. That and Julie. I tried, I truly tried to help him, but he didn't want help. He wanted—oh, I don't know—for me to believe that there was some-thing on the manuscript paper, that his badgering for interviews with conductors and publishers would lead to something real and positive. He wanted me to believe in the myth. Perhaps if I'd been able to . . . but I was bewildered, scared . . . I began to get angry. He became jealous of *my* work. You've no idea how ludicrous that seemed at the time. But I was making progress. I began to believe in myself. And somehow, as I came to see how hollow all his plans were, I became more ambitious, more confident. Until then my talents, compared to his, had seemed minuscule, mediocre. I'd dreamed of being part of his success. Nothing more.

"But within one year of his leaving the Conservatory, our positions had entirely changed. And then when Willi Dekker heard me play . . . oh, that was the last straw. Tom hit me. He was drunk, of course. And I have to admit that he had reason to be jealous. Willi . . . well, it was common knowledge that all his protégées slept with him. Mind you, you had to have talent. He would never compromise on that, no matter how pretty your face. But the face had to please. Mine did. And I knew it from the very beginning. I also knew, before I knew I was pregnant or was prepared to admit to myself that I was, that Willi was going to be my way out.

"I didn't know how to leave Tom. Ordinary words, just telling him that I couldn't go on, I didn't love him, I couldn't pretend . . . it didn't mean anything to him. He raged. You cannot possibly have any idea. Even now I don't know how to explain. All the words that come into my mind are hackneyed, overemotional, loaded. . . . Devil, ogre, monster . . . he was possessed . . . I don't know by what or how, I only know that he became more and more violent and totally obsessive about me. My God, I was afraid of him . . . too afraid to tell anyone . . . too proud, perhaps, I don't know. I think I simply could not believe that this was happening to me, that a man could want to, that he *meant* to possess me, body and soul.

"He didn't love me. I don't think he even saw me clearly. He just wanted . . . I was just *his*, like a part of him or something he owned and, I suppose, in his own mad way, treasured, though it certainly didn't feel like that. But it *was* happening. It was real and all I wanted was to get away from him. Even then I think I was obscurely, instinctively afraid for my life.

"So I went after Dekker. I was a very hardheaded young woman suddenly. I was hungry for what he could give me, professionally speaking, and if that meant sleeping with him, well . . .

"That concert I told you about, the night that changed my life? Tom didn't stand me up. He wasn't with another girl. He wouldn't come because he knew, although of course I denied it, what was going to happen, what I was intending to do. Anyway, I slept with Dekker that night, of my own free will. He promised me nothing —no career, no help, no relationship. But I knew he wouldn't forget me. I made damned sure he wouldn't forget me.

"Tom beat me up, of course, and I lied. I lied about the bruises, too, when I went to the doctor and learned that I was pregnant.

That clinched it for me. Oh, and in case you should be wondering, there was no chance of Dekker's being Julie's father. I was a good two months pregnant when I slept with him. The baby was indisputably Tom's, and I knew that I couldn't have a baby with him. What possible life could there have been for any of us?

"I told you the truth when I said I never considered an abortion. Whatever the circumstances, that baby was *mine* and I was going to have it. And keep it. Somehow. I told myself then that I could solve any problem if I used my head and was sufficiently determined. It was just a matter of not being squeamish. I gambled—on winning the gold medal, on landing Dekker—and I never told Tom about the baby.

"He was obsessed with me, like a child, a dependent, spoiled child. Anything he couldn't have . . . Also, he needed me as much as I needed to get away from him. Perhaps more so. Probably. But I knew that if I told him about the baby he would use it to pressure me, to hang on to me. He wanted to marry me anyway. He used to weep and beg me . . . it was pitiful. It disgusted me. I made myself bear it, though, while I waited for Dekker to get in touch. I wrote to him. I telephoned. I besieged his agent and I . . . I even hinted that he just might be Julie's father.

"Willi had no paternal instinct. There was no risk that he would want to see or know Julie. But a scandal would not have done him any good, especially with a mere student. And I hinted that I might go that far. I wouldn't have, of course, because then Tom would have known about the baby, and he was no fool. He would never have believed that it was Dekker's. Or if he had, I think he would have killed me.

"Anyway, Dekker offered me the American tour and gave me money, which I gave straight to Tom, and off I went to my grandmother. I'd never told Tom about her. I don't know why, except that he wasn't interested. People didn't exist for Tom until they entered his life. He had no curiosity about one's background. He used to say that he *invented* me. Perhaps he did. Perhaps I never told him out of some sort of instinct for survival, a premonition . . . I don't know. The point is, I was able to disappear. I gave Tom the money, all of it, and I hid. I had the baby—all the rest you know.

"Except, of course, what you really want to know. You have a great capacity for silence, Russell Dunn. You are a good listener.

167

You're also very hard. Your silence is a deliberate vacuum, isn't it? And I've got to fill it. Well, why not?

"I was told later that Tom got involved with drugs at that time, on the money I'd given him, Dekker's money. I don't know if that is true. He did use them, he became an addict, that much I do know. I tell myself that I only hastened the inevitable, that I didn't cause his addiction. Sometimes I can even believe it.

"The other thing I didn't tell you was that Tom never completely dropped out of my life. That was another reason why I stayed away from Julie and kept so quiet about her. Tom was always there, in the background. There was always the chance that he would turn up, and if he ever found out about Julie . . . I, of course, was easy to find. My life was very public. He would phone or write. Sometimes he would turn up in person. He was always violent. He blamed me for everything. He was obsessively jealous of my success, of Dekker. . . . According to Tom, I had stifled his talents, sapped him dry. It was my fault that he could not compose, could not get work that was worthy of him. I owed him. And I paid. I gave him money to get rid of him. I couldn't afford a scandal either, then, and I was still horribly afraid of him. It was a very simple arrangement. I believed, or perhaps hoped, that if I listened patiently and if I gave him enough money to buy heroin or whatever, he would leave me in peace until he became desperate again. Usually a few months. A year, if I was lucky and rich enough. It was an obscene and degrading business arrangement, but I never flinched from it and I never pretended to myself that it was anything other than that. The worse he got, the more afraid I became—afraid for Julie, that he would somehow find out about her. And, of course, eventually and inevitably he did. You want to know how, of course. Well, it should be obvious to you."

"You told him," Russell said. His voice sounded odd, intrusive and out of place to both of them. Margaret smiled a little.

"Cat not got your tongue, then?"

"You told him because there was no way you could live openly with Julie in London without his finding out."

"Not quite. I could never have contemplated it if I hadn't been sure that Tom was out of my life forever. He'd gone to live in Amsterdam. He seemed more settled. He had friends there, plenty of drugs. Anyway, I was engaged there that year for the Holland

168

Festival. I knew he would look me up. I knew there would be a scene, that I would pay up again. Somebody had told him. By then a few friends knew that I had a child. People talk. Somebody—I never discovered who—told Tom. He was indescribably worse than I'd ever seen him before. Mad. Of course I denied it, and then I said she was Dekker's child . . . poor Willi was dead by then.

"He tried to kill me. There was no hushing it up this time. The police were involved. I was in hospital. He was charged, but I refused, still I refused to give evidence against him. I don't know why. I wanted to, and yet . . . I still couldn't hate him enough. Oh, I didn't love him, don't think that, but I . . . well, I felt guilty. I still felt that I had harmed him, and anyway, to cut a long story short, there was an alternative to prison. A clinic. A secure clinic, where he would receive treatment. It was run by doctors, psychiatrists, nice people. Of course they needed my cooperation, and of course I gave it; I really thought it would be the best thing for him, for me, for Julie. . . . They would get him off the drugs and then try to discover . . . to mend his mind, I suppose. If that was possible. And they promised me that he would be kept there for as long as it took. They even said that he might never be allowed out."

"But something went wrong," Russell said.

"Oh, yes. Very wrong. At first I thought he must have escaped. You read about such things. But no, oh, no. I found out later that they had let him out. Detoxified, no doubt Tom could be very plausible and rational. *They let him out.* Not for good, I have to admit, but as part of his 'treatment.' Oh, it still makes me so angry. . . .

"Somehow he got to London, somehow he found out where Julie was, where my grandmother lived, and he went there. He saw Julie for himself, and that was all he needed. My grandmother got rid of him by some miracle. She called me, but what could I do? I had to give my recital, my famous bloody recital. I had no choice. And when I got back to the flat that night, it was almost a relief to find Tom waiting for me. At least he wasn't near Julie . . . and I'd been expecting him all day, at the recital, outside the hall. . . .

"There was the inevitable scene. I drank. I drank a lot. I drank to get through it. I drank to numb myself, for courage and because I was so angry. All those promises . . . for the first time in years I had felt free, safe. . . . Anyway, I continued to deny that Julie was his child, but of course he didn't believe me. She was his and he wanted her. I had deprived him, apparently, of the one thing that would have made him pull himself together. Oh, yes, he actually had a kind of perspective on himself that night. He didn't want *me* any longer. He wanted *Julie.* I swear to you, he was as obsessive about her, about the *idea* of her, as ever he had been about me—worse, even. What I felt then was an entirely new kind of fear. I was physically afraid for Julie. If he ever got his hands on her . . . I saw my life clearly for the first time and I swore to myself, I vowed that she would never live as I had done or even know a man . . . a creature . . . never know that such a *thing* could ever exist.

"I told him to leave, of course. He just laughed. I went to call the police. I told him I could have him committed again, but this time he was going to prison. I would give any evidence that would keep him there. You see, I still thought he must have escaped from the clinic. . . .

"There was a struggle when I went to the phone. I fought him. I didn't know I could fight like that, physically I mean, with a will to hurt someone. But he was stronger than I, and . . . possessed. I know the word 'mad' is not supposed to mean anything, and certainly not to someone like you, but he *was* mad. There is no other word for it. He tried to throw me out of the kitchen window. I tried to save myself. My arms went through the glass. My right wrist was cut, not badly but enough to give him the idea. He said death was too good for me. He wanted me alive but unable to play. He wanted me to suffer as he had suffered, and for the rest of my life. He wanted me crippled and alive with the knowledge that he had Julie. He was going to cut off my hand. He was very calm about it. No histrionics suddenly, no shouting, not even any anger, it seemed. And I knew he meant it. It was just the sort of crazy, vicious idea that had always appealed to him. To think that when I first knew him I used to laugh him out of those wild ideas . . . but I didn't laugh then.

"There was a board in the kitchen, you see. Not, alas, for irony's sake, a proper chopping block. Just an ordinary board. A bread board, I suppose. Strange, I can see it so clearly, but . . . It doesn't matter. He dragged me over to it and forced my left arm down onto the board."

"God," Russell said, pressing his hand to his forehead.

"I'm sorry, I didn't realize you were squeamish."

"It's not that. . . ."

"I can't tell you much about it anyway. The board was just for show, drama. . . . I mean, there was no way I was going to stand there and let him . . . We struggled some more—I don't really remember much about it. Suddenly he had this knife, one of those sawtoothed things, and he was hacking and scraping away at my wrist while I fought him. I passed out. I don't really remember it. It didn't hurt much. The blood scared me when I came around. There was a very great deal of blood. Tom had gone. Scared, I suppose. I just sat there. I don't remember thinking at all clearly, thinking it out, I mean. I just knew that I would never play again. I would be with Julie. I'd work something out. I thought, if I can't play I can be with Julie and protect her. I got up and went to the phone. I can't remember much after that. I called an ambulance, apparently. The rest you know."

Russell felt cold, drained and chastened. He could not look at her. She stood up and began moving around the kitchen while he watched the light grow and strengthen. The day itself seemed unreal. He heard the kettle begin to sing, then boil. She made tea, set a cup silently in front of him. He got up and went into the hall, found his cigarettes in his briefcase and lit one, his hand trembling a little. The smoke made him cough.

"Why did you pretend it was an accident?" he asked when he had stopped coughing.

"Why? I would have thought that was perfectly obvious."

"I'm afraid it isn't."

"Imagine what the publicity would have done to Julie. 'Yes, darling, I have kept you from your father for eight years. Yes, he was a naughty daddy. He tried to cut Mummy's hand off'." Her voice was bleak with bitterness. He felt the almost tangible strength of her rage, still there unresolved within her. "Besides," she resumed almost matter-of-factly, "before I could do anything, just two days after I was transferred to the London Clinic, Tom's body was fished out from the Thames, just below Chiswick Bridge. They weren't sure whether he had died from an overdose or by drowning. It didn't seem to matter much which. There was no one left to blame. I had my daughter. I was free of Tom and knew that he could never harm Julie. Or so I thought until recently."

"What?" Russell had to stop and clear his throat. "I mean . . . I don't understand. Why have you changed your mind recently?"

"Isn't it obvious? When Julie told me she was seeing a psychia-

171

trist, I thought . . . I couldn't help thinking . . . God knows I tried not to. I fought you. I deliberately lied to you. I wanted to take her away . . . because I was terrified that . . . that maybe she . . . Madness can be inherited, can't it?"

"Opinions differ."

"Well, that's what I'm afraid of. Still. That Julie may in some way be like her father. That he . . . even now . . . can . . . reach me . . . hurt me. . . ."

She began to cry, her right arm across her chest, kneading the muscles of her left arm. She cried noisily, with great sobs, the tears streaming unheeded down her face. Russell put out his cigarette and went to her. She looked at him with alarm, as though she did not know who he was.

"Please . . ." he said, and put out his hand and touched her shoulder. "Let me . . ."

"Please," she said through her sobs, "you've got to help Julie. You've got to stop her from becoming . . . like him. Please, please, you've got to help her. . . ."

"In any way that I can. I promise you." His hand moved gently down her arm and freed her clinging fingers, and for a moment he held her hand in his.

She nodded, thanking him, accepting his promise, then turned away, walked toward the garden door. "I'll be all right now," she said. "Please . . . I'd like to be alone."

Eight

Julie leaned back in the chair. A long sigh of contentment left her slightly open lips and seemed visibly to relax her. She settled her shoulders more comfortably. Her arms were stretched along the chair arms, hands loosely dangling. She closed her lips, swallowed, and opened her eyes. She smiled at Russell.

"How are you, Julie?"

"Fine. I'm fine, thank you."

"What does that mean? Happy?"

"I like these times with you. I probably shouldn't say that. I mean, I'm not supposed to enjoy them, am I? But I do. These times."

"They certainly seem to be helping you. Why is that, do you suppose?"

"Because you're kind to me. You make me feel relaxed, safe. . . ."

"And the rest of the times? When we're not talking?"

"They're all right."

"What's wrong with them, Julie?"

"Jo-Jo. You know . . . Jo-Jo . . ."

"Where's Jo-Jo now?"

"I don't know. This is grownups' business. He can't . . . he's scared of you. He can't come in here. He knows that. If I were to stay with you all the time . . ."

"You know you can't do that, Julie, don't you?"

"Yes."

"Does that make you angry?"

"No. Scared. Make him go away, Mr. Dunn. Please, please make him go away."

"I can't make him go away, Julie."

"You could if you wanted."

"You can, Julie. Only you . . ."

"I can't. I can't. I don't know how."

"How do we make people go away, Julie? What are the ways? Think about it."

"I've told him. I've told him over and over . . ."

"All right. But he won't obey you."

"No. You see, he's not a little boy anymore. He's a man. Sometimes, that is . . ."

"Because you're not a little girl."

"Sometimes . . ."

"Yes, Julie?"

"I feel as though I am."

"When you're not here? When you're not with me?"

"I suppose. I'm tired. I want to rest."

"Not yet, Julie. In a minute. Tell me, how else do we get rid of people we don't want? Open your eyes, please, Julie. Look at me." She obeyed, but with a sort of sullen lethargy. "Well?" he asked.

"I don't know."

"What does Jo-Jo want, Julie?"

"To marry me."

"Well, then?"

"I can't."

"Why not, Julie?"

"Because I don't . . . want to. I don't like him. He frightens me."

"All right, Julie. It's all right. Think about what you want, Julie."

"For you to make Jo-Jo go away."

"I can't."

"Well, then . . . No. That's not true. You won't. You won't help me."

"That's not true. You know it isn't true. You're not being honest with yourself or me."

"I am. I always tell you. I tell you everything."

174

"What does Jo-Jo want, Julie?"

She sighed, a sigh of exasperation. Her hands knotted into fists. "To marry me."

"What does marriage mean?"

"You go to a place—a church—and wear a white dress, a pretty dress, and you say 'I do' and you promise to love and cherish and obey and you . . . you get married."

"And then, Julie?"

"You . . . have a party." She laughed, clasped her hands together suddenly, and kept them clasped together, pressed to her bosom. "You have a lovely party with champagne and cake and you get all dressed up in pretty clothes and go on holiday. It's called a honeymoon. Why is that?"

"I don't know, Julie. But after that, what do you do?"

"It's called a reception."

"After the reception, Julie, what?"

"You go away."

"And what happens?"

"You live happily ever after, of course."

"What makes that possible, Julie?"

"Love."

"Love and . . ."

"Marriage."

"What happens when you make love?"

"You feel good, you feel nice, you . . . ."

"Yes, Julie?"

"You fuck," she shouted. "The man fucks you. You're all naked and he . . . he . . . fucks you."

"And what does Jo-Jo want to do to you, Julie?"

"To . . . to . . . fuck me." She opened her hands and held them in front of her face, staring at them.

"Well, then . . . perhaps another way of getting rid of someone we don't want is to give them what they want."

"No." She shook her head, thrust her hands down into her lap.

"That's only a suggestion, Julie. If you wanted to . . ."

"No."

"Very well."

"I'm very tired. I want to go to sleep now."

"All right, Julie." She placed her arms again on the arms of the chair, sighed, and closed her eyes. "But when I tell you to wake up, Julie, I want you to remember what we've been talking about today. Do you understand? You will remember what we've said, about Jo-Jo, about what he wants."

"To fuck me," she said dreamily, her voice fading.

"Yes, Julie. And what you are going to do about that."

"All right." She yawned, let her head fall a little to the left.

"Sleep now, Julie. Rest."

His shirt was sticking to his back and under his armpits. He could smell his own sweat. He got up and walked to the desk. His hands shook as he pulled cigarettes and lighter from his open briefcase. Three times he tried to spin the wheel, and when the flame finally caught, he had to steady his right hand with his left in order to light the cigarette. He drew deeply on it, went to the window, and stood looking down into the back garden of the clinic.

What had he done?

He felt sick. He knew that he would conceal this from Annie at their next case conference. He would not enter it in the notes. He felt sick, and fought an urge to run to the bathroom, essentially an urge to hide. The cigarette made him feel sicker but, masochistically, he continued to smoke it. He had done nothing but urge her forward, prompt her to carry the fantasy to its full and total conclusion. It was her choice. He had asked her simply to confront the reality of her fantasy. It was a permissible step. If she gave herself to Jo-Jo, it would only be in her mind. And, satisfied, Jo-Jo would go. It was a perfectly reasonable line to take. So why did he feel as though he had officiated at her rape? What if something should happen to her? What if it terrified her? He longed to take it back, to undo what he had done, not without thought, not on the spur of the moment. It was too late. He looked over his shoulder at her, at the top of her head where it showed over the back of the chair. He closed his eyes tightly. He saw Margaret, her face blank with horror. Her eyes accused him. *What have you done? What?* The stub of his cigarette burned his fingers. He dropped it, snatching his hand to his mouth, sucking at the sore place. He put his foot on the cigarette, flattened it on the floor. Then, carefully, he bent and picked it up, carried it to the wastebasket beside the desk.

"Julie? Time to wake up now." His voice shook. He spoke with

176

his back to her, unable to watch. "When I count to three, Julie, you will wake up. Ready? One . . . two . . . three."

He heard her stir behind him, then bounce out of the chair.

"Mr. Dunn?" She tugged at his sleeve, her face shining, bright, innocent.

"Yes, Julie?" He thought his heart was going to break. He wanted to hug her to him, to keep her safe, safe. . . .

"Can I go and play in the garden this afternoon? Can I go and play with Jo-Jo? Can I, please?"

He pulled free of her tugging hand, straightened his back.

"Yes, Julie," he said. "Yes, I rather think you can."

After Nanny had seen her into bed, fussed with the blind and opened the window, shown her where the call-bell was and wished her good night, sweet dreams, Julie sat up in bed, her arms clasped around her knees. There was a dread at the back of her child's mind. They had had such a good time in the garden today. They always had a good time in the garden. Always except . . . No, always. She wished she could talk to Mr. Dunn, she craved the safe feeling his presence gave her. She did not understand why Jo-Jo stayed silent and apart from her. He was angry, but she had done nothing to upset him. She could feel his anger from the corner where he stood, sulking when there was no reason. Jo-Jo was strange and unlike himself. It seemed he was often that way now, and she did not understand it. She knew him always happy, except when she was sad. His moods no longer accorded with hers, and this made her feel especially lonely. Jo-Jo's strangeness frightened her. He had grown so much, become a man, almost someone different. She lay down and pulled the covers up to her chin. Perhaps she fell asleep. Perhaps she slept for a while, lightly.

The blind flapped in the night breeze. The plastic ring on the end of its cord ticked against the radiator. Outside, the same breeze made the trees talk in a murmurous rustle. In the room of shadows, Jo-Jo stood very large beside the bed. He was very large and strange. She shivered, even though it was a warm night, as he drew the covers slowly back from her body, pulled them right down and dropped them in a pile on the floor. She thought how angry Nanny would be and started to sit up, to retrieve them. His hand pushed her down. She saw his teeth, as white as moonlight, bared. His hand burned

177

through the cotton of her pajamas as, button by ceremonious button, he unfastened the jacket, his fingers singeing her cold, sweating skin. His hands burned on her breasts, kneading. She averted her face from his fetid smell. Something made her let him go on. His hands moved down, stretching the elastic of her pajama pants, drawing them like a protective husk from the chill of her limbs. His burning hands gave her body new shape and meaning. She was cold wax warmed to life, molded. Her child's mind watched her body made adult by his coaxing, squeezing hands. Liquid fire started in her, spread upward and outward. She became damp and dreadful as he bent and separated her limbs, arranged her like a jointed doll into positions that had no meaning for her, that in their openness and exposure became frightening. The bed sank with his weight. His black silhouette, slashed by the white of grinning teeth and rolling eyes, reared between her strangely splayed and lifted legs. Fingers and tongue transferred fire to her coldness, coaxed molten flame from her rigid body, *was* her body. . . . He loomed down, pressing on her. Her wax flesh melted to bruised bone. She felt him hot and heavy on her, suffocating. The smell seeped from every pore of his hot and burning body. She felt a terrible hardness prodding at her, trying to invade her with urgent nudges. The smell caused her throat to contract. A sense of something terribly wrong made her writhe and struggle beneath him. She cried out, forbidding him. Her nails sank into his flesh. She kicked with her legs and beat with her fists and still he tried to pierce her, stab her, each attempt filling her with a greater revulsion. She knew that if he succeeded, she would be damned. Her body turned to ice, to frozen terror. His breath hissed and his blood moaned in her ears. She saw a shattered box floating like so many toy boats on the surface of a pool; saw concrete steps melt and shimmer; saw a fire burning, burning and consuming a child, and smelled the smoke of burning flesh. She cried out, again and again. No. No. No . . . And then she saw her mother walking toward her, her left arm held out, the hand hanging, almost severed from the white bone of her wrist. Her mother's warm blood fell on her in great drops of red rain, and by this terrible token, this splashing on her naked flesh, she knew that Jo-Jo no longer covered her, that he was gone. She reached for her mother's arm, wanting to kiss the wound, to stanch it with her lips, but she, too, had melted into the shadows of the night.

The blind flapped in a breeze from the open window, like a great, awkward bird, flying away.

At seven, when Nurse Stackwell went off duty, she reported that Julie Wells, unlike Mrs. Costigan, had spent a quiet night, as usual. At seven-thirty, when Sister French hurried to answer Mrs. Costigan's bell, she told Tina Bungako to wake the other patients and give them their morning tea. Tina Bungako pushed the rubber-wheeled cart down the corridor, making an impatient face at Mrs. Costigan's yelled obscenities, and stopped outside Julie Wells's door. She drew tea from the urn, added milk, and tapped on the door before opening it. The room felt cold.

"Wakey-wakey, rise 'n' shine," she said, setting the cup down and bustling, her large hips swaying, to the window. A quick jerk on the cord of the navy-blue blind sent it rattling up. Tina Bungako turned, her handsome white teeth exposed in a welcoming grin. The grin faded.

Julie was splayed on the bed, naked, the covers heaped on the floor. Her skin was waxen white, her eyelids and lips tinged with blue. Tina Bungako gulped back a scream as she saw the blood. For a split second, before her mind caught up with her shocked eyes, she thought that the girl had been stabbed or wounded in some terrible way. Then, with a grimace of distaste, she realized that her period had started.

She moved as swiftly as her heavy body would permit, yelling at the top of her voice for Sister French to come help, come see.

Julie rested against extra pillows, an old woman's crocheted shawl incongruous around her shoulders. A thick, glossy magazine lay across her thighs. She looked up from it, stared at him.

Russell Dunn stood just inside the door. He had cut himself shaving and there was a little crust of dried blood, more brown than red, just below the jawline. He felt her eyes on it, felt embarrassed. Though fully briefed by Sister French, whom he knew to be a conscientious and reliable nurse, he did not know how to begin or precisely what to expect.

Julie smiled and closed the magazine.

"Hello, Mr. Dunn. Come in."

"Hello, Julie." He closed the door, put his briefcase down. "How are you?"

"Fine. How are you?"

"Oh, I'm . . . very well, thank you. It's a lovely day. Sister tells me you have a temperature."

"A slight one," she agreed, snuggling deeper into the shawl and the pillows, her hands folded neatly over her abdomen. "I managed to kick off all the bedclothes without noticing. I may have caught a chill. Why are nurses so keen on open windows? Oh, please, sit down." He fetched a chair from the little table she used as a desk and placed it beside the bed while she went on talking. "And my period's started. I often run a temperature when that happens. I'm perfectly all right. You look worried. I'll be up and about tomorrow, right as rain."

"Good. Good. I'm glad to hear it."

"So I may as well ask you now—when can I go home?"

"Oh, well, that depends . . ."

"I'm not staying here," she said with a new firmness. "Well, today, okay, but no longer. You can't keep me here, you know. I'm over eighteen."

"Yes. Yes, I know you are."

"Well, there's no need to sound so surprised about it. In fact, I'll soon be nineteen. Won't I?"

"Yesterday you . . . you didn't know you were eighteen," he said.

"What nonsense!" She reminded him of her mother in her assertiveness, but he caught a quick flicker of panic that momentarily shook her composure. But she knew that he had seen it. "The truth is I'm not sure how long I've been here. One loses track of time."

"Four weeks, almost."

"That long? Heavens. No wonder I want to go home."

"You were very unhappy."

"Well, I'm fine now."

"So I see. I'd like to talk about that. . . ."

"Not now. Not today. I don't feel up to it."

"I think we'll have to talk about it before you can go home."

"You can't keep me here," she repeated. "Really, four weeks?"

"You don't remember anything?"

"Oh, yes . . . not much. Can Ma come and see me today?"

"Yes. I'll phone her."

"She won't want me to stay here." He refused to respond to this. "Did you put me here?"

"Yes. You were very upset, not yourself. It was after you had found Miss Tidy."

"Oh, no . . . oh, my God."

"It's all right, Julie. Calmly, now."

"No, no . . . I mean . . . it's just so awful that I'd forgotten all about . . . Oh, poor Elli. What happened?"

"She died of a heart attack."

"Oh, how awful. Poor old Elli. And Ma must be absolutely devastated."

"It's been a very difficult time for her, yes."

"I should have been there to help her."

"You were not capable."

"I suppose it was the shock of finding Miss Tidy like that. . . ."

"You remember that?"

"No . . . yes. Poor old dear. How awful . . ."

"And before that?"

"Of course."

"But not the last weeks, being here?"

"Well, sort of, yes. I remember talking to you and that the food's absolutely yukky, and Ma coming and . . . and . . ."

"What, Julie?"

"I don't know. Feeling very . . . sort of lonely, I suppose. I'm sorry, my brain's really not working very well. I do feel terribly tired." She tried, unconvincingly, to yawn.

"You were a child again."

"Really?"

"You thought Sister French and the other nurses were your nanny, and yesterday you—"

"Well, I would, wouldn't I? I've never been able to see a starched apron or even a white coat without thinking of nannies, endless nannies. But you needn't worry anymore. I know they're nurses. You see, I really am quite better. I feel well." He looked at her until she said, "Stop looking at me like that. All right. Not a hundred percent better. You're right. We do have to go on talking. But I don't have to stay here."

"What happened last night, Julie?"

"Last night? I told you I—"

181

"What happened to make you know your correct age? What made you become yourself again?"

She unclasped her hands, began to pleat the turned-back edge of the sheet. She shrugged her shoulders.

"I don't know. Nothing. You ought to know better than me."

"Not always, Julie."

"I'll remind you of that." She laughed. "All right. I know what you're going to say." He looked at her quizzically, inviting her to tell him. "Work at it. Think about it. That's what you always say when I can't find the words and you think I'm being evasive."

"And are you?"

"No. I think . . . You say I was a child?"

"You certainly spoke and behaved like one."

"Well, then, perhaps that was a way for my mind to rest. You know—no responsibilities. Escape. All that sort of thing. I do feel refreshed, honestly. Like I've had a lovely long sleep and dreamed all my worries away." She smiled. "You're not convinced."

"Should I be?"

"It's the best I can do."

"For now, yes."

"Oh, you're going to go on and on about it, aren't you? Well, all right. I'll try. I'll work very hard. But not today."

"Very well."

"And you'll get Ma to come?"

"Yes. Would you . . . perhaps like to see Barry, too?"

"Oh . . ." She looked shocked, then nervous. "No. No, not today. Soon. When I go home. Not in here."

"Why not here?"

"Because he wouldn't like it. He'd feel awkward. Besides, I want to look my best."

"As you wish. Only he has been very concerned about you."

"He's very sweet." She smiled, stared at the window. "You know, I suddenly feel ever so tired. I'd really like to take a nap."

"All right." He stood up, carried the chair back to the table.

"But what?" she said.

"I don't understand."

"You always have one last question."

"Yes, I do, don't I? Well, then . . ."

"Yes?" He thought she looked almost insultingly eager to cooperate.

182

"What about Jo-Jo?"

"Oh, Jo-Jo. What about him?"

"Is he here today?"

"No. Of course not. Oh, I don't know. To tell you the truth, I'd forgotten about him as well."

"To tell me the *truth?*"

She became serious, took on a slightly lost look, and frowned in the old way she had when she was really concentrating.

"I don't honestly know. But I feel safe. Do you know what I mean?"

"Yes."

"But you want to know why."

"Yes."

"I can't tell. Just a feeling . . . Have I been going on a lot about Jo-Jo lately?"

"Yes. Yesterday you went out into the garden to play with him." She laughed, a little hysterically, he thought, but also falsely. "And yesterday," he went on, cutting through her laughter, "you told me he wanted to fuck you."

She caught her breath sharply. She blushed quite naturally and he thought he saw a shine of tears in her eyes. The blush deepened. Her hands clutched at the edge of the sheet. He thought that she wanted to slide down into the bed and hide. With difficulty she said, "I'm sure I didn't . . . put it like that."

"Yes. Exactly."

"Was it necessary for you to repeat it?" She almost shouted this, her shock turning to anger.

"I believe it was, yes."

"Well . . . you're the doctor. What do you want me to say?"

"I wish that you would tell me about last night."

"Do you see some connection, then?" she asked, challenging him. "Do you?"

"No. Definitely not. I will try to understand what you want . . . and tell you . . . but not now . . . please . . . I'm very tired."

She turned over and buried her face in the pillows, weeping quietly.

"Julie . . ." He went to her, tried to touch her shoulder. She wriggled away from him.

"Please . . . I just want to see my mother. I'm not upset. Really

183

I'm not. It's just tiredness. Please, leave me alone now. Get my mother. I want to see my mother."

"Yes I will. I'm sorry, Julie."

She shook her head, waved him away. He picked up his briefcase and opened the door. What have you done? he asked himself again, and got no answer.

Julie sat stiffly in the chair she had occupied on her very first visit to Russell Dunn's consulting rooms.

"You see, I know that if I ever let him . . . you know . . . go the whole way . . ." She looked up at him where he sat behind his familiar desk, apparently determined to prove something to him. "If he ever succeeded in penetrating me, I mean," she said rather too loudly, ignoring the flush of pink that rose to her neck and cheeks, "I feel I would be lost. I would belong to him forever, in a way I can't explain." She looked down at her hands. "Like being damned. Besides, it would be wrong, quite wrong."

"What do you mean by 'wrong,' Julie?"

"Well, I would have thought that was obvious. You do know right from wrong, don't you?" He let the question hang. She glared at him. "I can't explain. Just wrong. A sin."

"Do you believe in sin?"

"Yes. Of course. Doesn't everybody?"

"I mean in a religious sense."

"I don't understand."

"In the religious sense a sin is usually defined as a breach of some divine law or commandment. Its commission would involve some kind of expected punishment."

"So?" She sounded bored with the topic.

"Well . . . I wonder who would punish you if you, er . . . gave in to Jo-Jo."

"I don't know. Look, there's something I've really got to say to you. If we're to go on with this—I mean, if it's really important for me to talk about sex all the time—then I think I'd better see someone else. A woman."

"You don't want to talk about it?"

"Not to you."

"Why not?"

184

"Because you're a man. It's embarrassing." The silence was long. She battled with tears. Tears of temper, he wondered, or of genuine distress? "Anyway, you haven't answered my question."

"I'm sorry. Which question was that?"

"Whether it really is important for us to go on with . . . this line of questioning."

"I believe it is, yes."

"Well, I'd still prefer . . . I think I ought to see a woman."

"If you really want to, that can, of course, be arranged."

"But *you* don't think it's a good idea. I knew you wouldn't."

"I wonder if you're trying to avoid the issue, or put it off."

"Well, what if I am? That's my right, isn't it?" She got up, walked to the window, and stood there fidgeting. Quietly he asked her please to come and sit down. "No!" she shouted. "I don't have to! You can't force me! I am *not* a child!"

"Very well." He got up and moved to one of the couches so that he could see her.

"And stop looking at me. Everyone keeps on looking at me."

"It's important that I see you, Julie. We communicate with our bodies, our faces. . . ."

"Oh, yes. Bodies. Always bodies. Well, I'm sick to death of being a body."

"You're not a body to me, Julie. You're a whole person. Your body is only part of the total you."

"I don't want to talk about it."

"I'm only trying to show you that it is safe for you to sit down and look at me. Just as it has always been. Nothing's changed."

"That's not true." She walked quickly across the room, picked up her bag, and stood facing the door. He did not turn to look at her. "I don't want to leave until this is resolved," she announced.

"Let's try to resolve it, then."

She sat down in the chair she had previously occupied. He did not move.

"It's just that I don't feel comfortable anymore, now that I know what men are like."

"How do you know?"

"Because of what happened . . . Jo-Jo . . ."

"All men are not like Jo-Jo."

"They are to me."

185

"Julie," he sighed. "Let me try to explain something to you. You're afraid of your own sexuality. You are beginning to realize for the first time that there was a sexual element in your childhood relationship with Jo-Jo. It never occurred to you, did it, to wonder why it was a little *boy* you invented?" He waited for a response, but she sat rigid, staring into space. "It's perfectly healthy but, superficially, perhaps a little surprising. I think the fact that you chose to invent a boy shows a healthy curiosity about the opposite sex, from whom you were almost entirely cut off in your childhood. But you could have chosen a little girl to befriend you. I think you have become aware of this sexual element because of what happened between you and Jo-Jo at the clinic. You also know that your mind had to play a part in what Jo-Jo did, or tried to do. You feel guilty because you feel you've spoiled an idyllic part of your life, of yourself—"

"I see," she interrupted. "It all comes down to sex and it's all my fault."

He almost said, *That's your mother talking,* but stopped himself in time.

"There is no question of fault," he said. "Your sexual feelings are perfectly healthy. Sexuality, you see, isn't something that happens suddenly when you meet a nice man, like Barry. Children are sexual, too. And young women have desires, fantasies . . ."

"I don't want to hear any more."

"Well . . . I'd like you to think about it."

She stood up.

"I'd like to go now, even if the time isn't up."

"It nearly is." He rose, too. "I'll make a deal with you. We'll leave this area for a while, if you wish. There is something else I'd like to explore next time. Is that acceptable?"

"Yes. I suppose so."

"Then, if you still feel you want to see a woman . . ."

"You feel rejected, don't you? You wouldn't have brought that up otherwise."

"No, Julie. I just think you might be blocking our progress, but I can live with that for the moment. Let's leave it until you feel more comfortable."

"I suppose I should be grateful to you."

He did not comment on that, but went to his desk and drew his notepad toward him, signaling that she was free to go now.

186

She did not move. "You are very kind to me. I do know that. I do appreciate it. It's just that I'm . . ." He looked at her, inviting her to go on. She shook her head. "I'll go now."

"I'll see you next week."

"Oh, that reminds me . . . there is something else."

"Yes? We still have a minute."

"No, it's nothing like that. It's about my birthday."

"Yes, Julie?"

"It's next week."

"I know."

"I don't feel like celebrating much. Nothing big, you know? But I wondered . . . Ma and I wondered if you'd come to Sunday lunch. Just the four of us."

He felt a prickle of apprehension, and repeated the phrase. "The *four* of us?"

"Barry and me. You and Ma. Will you?"

The perfect nuclear family, he thought, everyone neatly cast in his own role. No wonder she felt awkward about discussing her sexual fantasies with him. Would his presence at the Sunday lunch table make it all right for her to relax with Barry? Was it partly Margaret's idea, or entirely hers?

"Sundays are difficult for me," he said, stalling, not knowing whether he should accept or refuse. "May I think about it?"

"Yes, of course. You didn't mind my asking, did you?"

"No. On the contrary. I'm very flattered that you should want to celebrate your birthday with me. And rather surprised, I must confess."

"I . . ." She looked at him slyly. Her smile was teasing, watchful. He looked away. "I hope you'll be able to make it," she said. "Goodbye."

"Goodbye, Julie."

In the end, of course, he accepted. His curiosity would not let him do otherwise. That and the chance to see Margaret. He would not let himself dwell on the ethics of his decision. This is not an ordinary case, he told himself. He could not deny how he felt about Margaret. This way was honest, if unprofessional, and he did not think it could harm Julie.

He explained to her at their next session that he might be a little late, that he had arranged to see his son first.

187

"You could bring him with you, if you like." She sounded unconvincing.

"No, thank you. I don't think . . . It might be a bit overwhelming for him."

"Yes, I can see that. But we would make him welcome."

"I'm sure you would. Now, then—"

"Before we begin, I want to say something. I've been thinking about what you said last time, about Jo-Jo, about my inventing a little boy and what that might mean sexually."

"Yes?"

She avoided the clear invitation to go straight on.

"And about my own sexual feelings. I don't see how I can feel guilty about them, since I've had a sexual relationship with Barry and that didn't make me feel guilty. I think you're wrong about that."

"But Jo-Jo is different, isn't he?"

"Well, of course, but I still don't think I ought to feel guilty."

"Neither do I."

"I mean . . . Oh, why are you confusing me?"

"I think it is you who are confusing yourself, Julie." Her face was set in a stubborn expression. After a while he said, "Why don't you tell me what else you thought? About Jo-Jo's being a boy."

"It doesn't seem such a good idea now."

"I'd still like to hear it."

"Okay. I thought maybe you were right about that, and that maybe, if I'd had a father, none of this would have happened." She paused, looking for some response from him. He made none. "I mean, you're right about it's being natural for a girl to want a male figure in her life. Most girls have fathers. If I'd had a father . . . Well? Would it have made a difference?"

"I can't tell, Julie. But it seems to me that now you're saying you mind not having a father. Perhaps you're even angry about that?"

"No. I was angry at you for saying . . . No, let me get the words right. You *implied* that I must have made those things up, about Jo-Jo."

"No, Julie. I said that your mind must have played a part in what happened between you and Jo-Jo. And there is nothing to be ashamed of in that."

"No. It happened *to* me. It was all him. I didn't . . . didn't *think* any of it."

188

"But you told me it was a dream, Julie, and you know enough about dreams to understand—"

"And what if I told you it wasn't a dream?"

"I'd believe you, Julie, and ask why you felt you had to lie to me about it."

"Because I was ashamed. Anyway, it was a dream. Of course it was."

"Whatever you say, Julie. But if you're confused about it, I suggest—"

"No. I don't want to talk any more about it. You promised me you wouldn't. We made a bargain . . ."

"I don't think we have time now for what I had in mind," he said, "and in any case I'd like to stay with your feelings about your father."

"I don't have any feelings about my father. I don't know anything about my father. And you're not keeping your side of the bargain."

"That's not quite true. You said that if you had known him perhaps none of this would have happened."

"I was just trying to play you at your own game."

"I'm not playing games, Julie. I'm completely serious."

"I thought it would please you. No. I just thought it made sense, what you said about my making Jo-Jo a boy instead of a girl. . . . I only meant to show you that I understood." She put her hands over her eyes like the monkey who sees no evil, her elbows resting on the arms of the chair. "And then I wished you were my father. I did. I thought everything would be all right if you were my father."

"But you know I'm not and never can be."

"Of course. I'm not stupid. It was just a . . . fantasy." She dropped her hands and glared at him. "Though it was an absurdly stupid one. Even stupider to tell you about it. Anyway, that's as far as I got."

"Well, that's some way. You don't remember your father at all?"

"No. I've told you."

"You never saw him? Not even once?"

"No. Don't keep on about it. Please," she added, to soften her commanding tone.

He wanted to push her, but knew that he must not. Perhaps he should speak to Margaret, ask her to tell Julie more about her father, the real story or part of it.

"What are you thinking?" she asked.

189

"I was wondering . . . perhaps you should talk to your mother about your father, ask her to tell you more about him."

"No. I can't do that. I told you. She doesn't care to talk about him. Anyway, don't you think she's been through enough? You can't want me to go on hurting her."

"How have you hurt her?"

"Do you think she likes having a crazy daughter? And losing Miss Tidy and the accident . . . Hasn't she suffered enough?"

"Do you feel responsible for your mother's accident, Julie?"

"No, of course not. Why should I? I wasn't even there. I was just a child."

"For Miss Tidy, then?"

"No. No. I just don't want to . . . worry my mother anymore. I don't want to make her talk about things she'd rather forget. It must be painful for her, and I don't want to give her any more pain. And if you want to twist that around to mean something else, you can, but you'll be wrong."

"You really are very angry with me today."

"Because you are not my father. Go on. Say it." She burst into tears, flinging herself back in the chair, rolling her head from side to side.

In some respects, he reminded himself, a child never ceases to be a child vis-à-vis a parent. And perhaps one of the ways this was done was through maintaining the ability to pick up on feelings that concerned the parent deeply and threatened the child's status. She had spoken about him to Margaret, had learned about his son. It was not the desire, inevitably frustrated, to have him as her father—nor was it simple transference—that made her angry now, but a sensed threat to her sole claim to her mother's affections. It took him a dizzy moment to perceive the flaw in his own reasoning. He pre-supposed that Margaret had tender feelings toward him, feelings that could, however subtly, be transmitted to Julie. He knew that he must discuss this with Annie. He reached behind him to the desk, picked up a notebook, and wrote Annie's name in bold letters.

"What are you writing?" She had stopped crying as suddenly as she had begun.

"A note to myself, about myself." Faced with her clear disbelief and its attendant confusions, he turned the pad around and showed it to her.

"Annie?" She sniffed. "The one who took me to the clinic?"

"The very one, yes."

"Why do you write her name?"

"That's my business."

"Oh, yes, of course. You can have secrets from me, but I have to tell you everything. That's just not fair."

"You don't *have* to tell me anything, Julie. You know better than that."

"Oh, yes, and I suppose you'll punish me by not coming to my birthday party. Julie's been a naughty girl."

"Party? I thought you didn't want a party?"

"Lunch, then," she conceded, sulking.

"Would you like to have a party?"

"With ice cream and balloons? No. No. I want *you* to come to lunch."

"Then I will. About one-thirty, I think we said?"

"Oh, Russell, Russell, Russell . . ." Annie said, amused, mock-pitying.

He smiled. He felt expansive, good. Something about the power of the confessional, he thought. It was late. The office building was quiet. Through the open windows the sounds of the city entered, muffled, soothing. The white wine was nicely chilled, with just a hint of sweetness. Annie had gone out to a local delicatessen and brought back spiced olives, a wedge of Brie, some crisp French bread. They had made a good picnic.

"I'm surprised you missed out on one obvious alternative," she went on. He raised an eyebrow, happy to let her take the lead. "Her reaction to my name. Could be she wants you for a daddy so much that she thought I might be a threat to her mom."

"Uh-uh." He shook his head, twisted the frosted bottle to make the little drops of condensation catch the light, make rainbows in miniature. "No. You've misunderstood me, Doctor."

"Oh, yeah? I don't mean a daddy in the way you see it, as we normally talk of it. I think she wants you as a *present* for her mom. She feels guilty. She owed her, right?" He nodded, interested. "Mom doesn't really accept Jo-Jo, right?" Again he nodded. "And Mom still resents you, or at least your involvement with Julie. Oh,

191

it's so neat, Russell. Even neater that you can't see it. Why does she want you to go to her party?"

"You tell me. I'm tired and content. This is your session."

"Bull session," she said amiably, helping herself to an olive and taking a moment or two to relish it, and transfer the pit delicately from her mouth to a napkin. "To prove she has power over you, to show you she can call the shots. That will impress Mom. To show she's growing out of you. And then, in effect, she's saying, 'Here you are, Mom. Here he is. I got him for you. Be happy.' She's discharged her debt to both of you, made you both happy—well, you, anyway—though she must think it'll work for Mom, too. But, best of all, then she's free to go her own sweet way. Have you considered that she might feel she took Mom from Dad, just by the circumstances of her birth?"

"No, no. I hadn't considered that. Some more wine?"

"Please."

"What is 'her own sweet way'?"

"Barry?"

"I don't see any opposition, if that's what she really wants."

"Jo-Jo, then. Free to indulge her exciting but fundamentally disturbing fantasies . . ."

"Wait a minute. You may have something. . . ." He lapsed into thought, the damp wine bottle still clutched in his hand.

"Thank you, kind sir," Annie said, with sarcasm.

"She perceived Jo-Jo as a threat to others. To me. To Barry. Maybe she really believes she's trying to protect us. Even her mother? Especially her mother, if she felt she was under threat."

"You used the past tense."

He sighed and refilled his glass.

"As I told you, since the last sessions at the clinic, when she told me about the 'dream,' we haven't really talked about Jo-Jo."

"Don't you think you should?"

"I don't want to push her. I pushed her once." He paused. He was still reluctant to face that, still uncertain of its outcome. Perhaps his guilt feelings got in the way, he thought.

"You want to tell me about that?" Annie asked.

"No," he said decisively. "You go on, please."

"I guess I'm through," Annie said. "I say she's manipulating you. All of you. She's going to tie a neat little knot and skip out from under."

"And?"

"I don't know what she'll do, if that's what you mean. Revert again? Marry Barry and live neurotically ever after? Live out some masochistic fantasy life with Jo-Jo, all on her own? I guess time, as they say, will tell. What I do know is that you shouldn't go there Sunday. You shouldn't tangle with the mother."

He smiled. "I don't think I can help myself."

"Maybe we should talk about that. What attracts you to her? Her hostility? Once you've worn her down or won her over, what then? Sounds like a potential rerun of the whole Denise fiasco to me."

"Oh, no, no. Margaret's—"

"Different?" Annie let out a burst of laughter. "Oh, Russell, you're too much. You might at least have the grace to look embarrassed," Annie said into his continued, imperturbable smile.

"But I don't feel embarrassed. She makes me feel . . . all those clichés you're waiting to pounce upon, my dear."

Annie sat back, regarding him with her small, clever eyes. He submitted to the scrutiny, certain that she could not shake him from his present and, he knew, temporary sense of well-being.

"You're such a romantic," she said at last. "You know how you really see this? A quest. Julie's the obstacle, the dragon in the cave. And you think when you've found and slain the dragon you'll automatically win the fair lady. Oh, boy! Here, I've got a new cliché for you. 'The way to a woman's heart is through her daughter's neuroses.' Required reading for every analyst in the western world. Wake up, Russell. Better yet, grow up."

"Oh, no. It's much too nice here."

Annie shook her head, partly in exasperation, partly in amusement. She helped herself to another olive and chewed ruminatively.

The glass doors of the breakfast room stood open to the little walled garden. Russell was shown out there, placed in a deck chair, given a glass of Pimm's, and told to talk to Barry while Margaret and Julie prepared the lunch. He admired the roses, asked the obvious questions about Barry's work. Even these were met evasively, making Russell intensely aware of his profession as a barrier between himself and other people. He had a ridiculous urge to shout that he was off duty, that they—he included the women, even though he had scarcely spoken to them—could drop their guard; they would be safe with him. It was not an unfamiliar feeling, but his usual methods of dealing with it seemed to have deserted him. Annie was right, he thought. Of course. It was because this was not a normal social occasion. There were too many crosscurrents. He was known, first and foremost to them all, as Julie's psychiatrist. He should not have come.

Not knowing what else to give her, Russell had brought Julie two dozen white roses as a birthday token. She carried them into the garden to show him how she had arranged them. He admired and approved. She seemed more confident than he had expected, yet discernibly tense.

Against the murmur of the women's voices as, indoors, they discussed where to place the roses, Barry asked, "How do you think she is?"

"How do you?" he answered automatically, and saw from Barry's face that this only cemented him in the role of sage and doctor. "I mean your perception of her is probably better than mine. You see her more, and in more usual circumstances."

"Actually, I don't," Barry said. "See much of her, I mean. She's very tied up with you, with your work. She says she still needs time to think, sort herself out."

"That's understandable, surely?"

"Oh, yes. It's just that I feel she's holding me at arm's length, if you know what I mean."

"But . . . how does she seem to you?"

Barry considered this ponderously. His expression betrayed, too late, that he realized Russell had turned the question around, had avoided answering it.

"She seems a lot steadier. I think she's grown up a lot. I don't mean like when she was pretending to be a kid—I mean generally."

"That's good, isn't it?"

"Yes. It's just that I don't feel I know her, really. What I mean is, well, is there any chance of her being like a kid again?"

Russell was deliberating his answer when Margaret came out, a drink in her hand. Barry kicked Russell's ankle lightly to indicate that he should not answer. Margaret made some remark about the weather, to which he made no reply. It was enough to look at her. She wore her hair in a slightly different way, parted in the center, and the sun or her hairdresser had lightened it a shade. The hairdresser, he decided, for her skin was pale, almost milky. She wore a blue and white sundress, her shoulders bare. The dress made her look younger. She went back into the house without his being aware of anything she had said, or of his having said anything to her.

"I suppose this is your day off?" Barry said.

"Yes."

"I know I shouldn't badger you, then, but can I ask you just one question?" Russell inclined his head a little. The sun—and Margaret's presence—made him feel dreamy, almost drowsy. Barry hunched toward him conspiratorially. "The thing is—do you think she'll ever marry me?"

"That's something you really will have to ask her," he said, before it dawned on him that the question, only slightly rephrased, could equally well have been asked of a father.

That made him recall his conversation with Annie. Of course he had brought what she had said with him, and although he had vowed not to, he found himself, when they all went inside for lunch, observing them from that point of view. He was more than ever conscious of his role and increasingly aware that this made him a silent guest at the feast. Not that anyone seemed to mind. Julie, in particular, seemed happy to ignore him. She chatted amicably with Barry, made him laugh. She was flirting. Occasionally, Russell caught her eye on him and knew that she, in her own way, was observing him, his every reaction. He smiled at her, turned to Margaret, and started a conversation about music. He assumed this wasn't tactless. Julie was evidently bored by the subject and ignored it, directing her full and considerable attention to Barry. Slowly, Russell began to relax. He felt that he had disappointed Julie. Her motive for asking him suddenly seemed quite simple: an impulse to have the three people closest to her with her on her special day. It was not uncommon for people to withdraw on their birthdays, to savor their specialness by surrounding themselves with those with whom they felt most comfortable—safest, he thought wryly. And that often led to disappointment. Julie discovered that he was just a middle-aged man with whom she had a special but obviously limited bond. As for his own disappointment—he looked at Margaret—well, he would deal with that later. He thought he should leave as soon as possible.

"You go and sit in the garden with Ma," Julie said at the end of the meal. "Barry and I will load the dishwasher and make some coffee. How do you like your coffee, Mr. Dunn?"

"Black, please," he said. "You're sure you don't want any help?"

"Can't you see," Margaret said with an easy smile, "that we are redundant, banished? Come along."

He followed her gladly into the garden, and stood for a moment watching her settle into a chair and lean her head back, closing her eyes against the bright sun.

"Sit down," she said. "This is an afternoon for being deliciously lazy."

He obeyed her, and sipped the glass of wine he had carried from the table. She seemed comfortably aware of his presence, in the sense that conversation was not necessary. He thought of several things to say—that the lunch was good, that she had not replaced Miss Tidy yet—but they all sounded gauche and silly. He should take his cue from her, her contentment. She offered herself up to the sun, a smile hovering at the corner of her lips, her eyes closed. Barry made an uncertain waiter, brought them coffee biting his bottom lip in concentration, walking as though on glass.

"Aren't you joining us?" Margaret asked, sitting up.

"In a minute."

She glanced at Russell, puzzled. She handed his coffee to him.

"It was very kind of you to invite me today," he said. It sounded like the most leaden of opening gambits.

"It was Julie's idea," she said quickly. "Besides, I owed you for dinner. Oh . . ." She stopped, a light flush on her cheeks. "I didn't mean that to sound so rude . . . I apologize. The fact is, I feel very nervous around you, but I didn't mean to be rude."

"Why should you feel nervous?" he asked, holding tightly to his coffee cup and staring at it.

"Because I feel exposed, I guess. It's difficult for me to accept that you, who I hardly know, actually know more about my life than anyone else. It makes me feel . . . I find it difficult to relax."

"I'm sorry. I won't stay long, I—"

"Oh, no, please. I don't know what's wrong with me," she said with a little laugh. "I'm making a terrible mess of this . . . I don't..."

Julie came quickly into the garden. Barry, a foolishly pleased

196

grin on his face, leaned in the open doorway.

"Ma, Barry and I thought we'd drive over to Richmond Park and stretch our legs. It's such a beautiful day. You don't mind, do you?"

"No, of course not, darling, but—"

"Mr. Dunn'll keep you company. You'll be all right, won't you, Mr. Dunn?" He thought there was something impish, even cheeky, about her grin. He reminded himself that he must leave.

"Go on. Have a nice time," Margaret said, her voice warm. Julie bent to kiss her cheek.

"And thanks for a super birthday."

"See you," Barry said, waving vaguely.

"Enjoy yourselves," Julie said as she disappeared into the house.

"There are so many ways to be made to feel one's age. Have you noticed that?" Margaret said. "I seem to be learning a new one every day. I mean, when the young people go running off to enjoy themselves, making it subtly though thoroughly clear that all one is good for is putting up one's feet in the sun." She raised her sandaled feet and looked at them, twisting her ankles in the sunlight.

"Do you mind very much?" Russell asked, thinking that he should leave right away. She leaned back in her chair, her face turned to him.

"Not really."

"I'll go as soon as I've finished this." Russell indicated his still steaming coffee. Margaret laughed a little.

"Now *you're* sounding nervous."

"Margaret, there is something—"

"No. Let me tell *you* something. I'm glad I told you . . . about Tom, about everything. Although I never thought I would hear myself say this, least of all to a psychiatrist, I do feel better for it, much."

"The power of the confessional," Russell said automatically.

"If you like to put it that way," Margaret said, offended.

"I, too, have a confession to make, one I think I must . . . " He looked at her. She was puzzled, perhaps a little afraid, but something about her mouth and eyes, a readiness to smile, did not reject him.

"Yes?" she prompted tensely.

"I think—no, damn it, I *know*—I'm in love with you."

She did not laugh or cry out, did not stand up and order him brusquely out of the house. He knew she was capable of any or all

197

of these responses. She was silent, her face averted, closed, her hands quite still in her lap.

At last she said, "I really don't see how that can be. I don't know what to say at all." Then she stood up, quickly. "You really are the most . . . extraordinary man. Excuse me, I rather think I'd like a glass of wine."

Her skirt brushed against his legs as she went into the house. His heart beat fast and painfully, and yet it felt heavy, hopeless. He finished his coffee, his mind suspended from thought. When the cup was quite empty and no longer provided him with an excuse to linger, he stood up and followed Margaret into the house. She was standing at the table, a glass of red wine before her.

"I'm sorry," he said. His cigarettes and lighter lay on the table where he had left them. He lit one with hands that shook like a nervous boy's. "This was neither the time nor the place . . . I'll leave now, of course. I won't bother you—"

"I rather think we have to talk, don't you?" Margaret said. "What you said, whether it is true or not, must surely complicate your relationship with Julie."

He wanted to say, Damn Julie. Talk to me, think about me. But, quietly, he agreed with her.

"Sit down. Have a glass of wine." Margaret put her full glass down in front of him, fetched another glass, and poured for herself. Russell pulled a chair from the table and sat. Moments stretched to minutes of silence. Margaret drank nervously, with small sips, while Russell stared at his glass, smoking. "I've never," she said at last, "known you at a loss for words."

"I'm sorry. I really don't feel able to discuss Julie with you now. I'll go—"

"For God's sake, man!" Margaret exploded. "You can't just walk in here, tell me you . . . tell me you love me, and then walk out!"

"It was a mistake, all right? I've said I'm sorry."

"A mistake that you love me, or that you told me?"

"Both."

"Well, thank you." She drained her glass and banged it down on the table.

"Look, I didn't mean . . . Margaret, you must understand . . ."

"Why? Why must I always be the one to understand? Right now

198

I don't understand anything. Stop treating me like one of your patients. I will react to this as I want, in my own way. *You* try to understand, for once. I was glad that you came here today, glad for myself when Julie wanted to ask you. I actually enjoyed dining with you that night, and afterwards, well, you made me feel comfortable enough to tell you . . . what I told you. I was nervous today because I didn't know if that feeling would last, but it has. I haven't yet got used to someone being that close to me, and I am still desperately afraid of what is going to happen to Julie. And now you tell me . . . oh, God, I'm going to cry."

He moved quickly around the table, pulled her against him, and held her tightly. She resisted for a moment, then laid her wet cheek against his chest.

"I don't want to do anything to hurt you," he said. "Please believe that."

"Julie . . ." she said, pushing against him.

"This is between us."

"But we can't just pretend she doesn't exist, can we?"

"If you want to."

"I don't know what I want. I'm afraid."

"Let me be here for you."

"How can you love me?"

"How could I not?"

"That's ridiculous, romantic . . ."

He kissed her then, pressing his mouth onto hers. At first she was still, accepting, then her right arm wound around his neck and her mouth opened responsively. When the kiss ended, she leaned against his body, trembling.

"We can't," she said. "You must see . . ."

"It will be my problem."

"She's my daughter. . . ."

"Margaret, you must understand this. Either I must go now and never see you again, or—"

"That's not fair. Don't ask me to make decisions. . . ."

"Please," he said, holding her more tightly, "let me love you, or tell me—"

"I don't know. I can't."

"Please, please," he moaned, kissing the side of her face, her neck, the smooth roundness of her shoulder.

Margaret broke away from him. She stared at him, her mouth working, seeking words.

"I must look a complete idiot to you," he said, letting his arms drop to his sides.

"No . . . oh, no . . ."

"The point is, I don't care."

"Hold me," she said suddenly, desperately. "Just hold me for a moment. Don't talk."

The shadows were lengthening. The light through the hastily closed curtains had the dusty, thick quality that signals the end of a summer afternoon, the approach of dusk. Margaret lay looking at him, playing with his short, grizzled red hair.

"Do you always look so sad afterwards?" she asked.

"What time is it?"

She lifted his left arm.

"Do you always take your watch off before?"

"Yes," he said, twisting from her, searching for his watch. "Doesn't everybody?"

Margaret looked at the cleanly differentiated bumps of his backbone and tried to remember. His presence blotted her memory. He strapped on his wristwatch. She wanted to hold back the moment, to laze, to be comfortable for another hour. So many things she did not know about him. She wanted to understand, to snuggle close to him, warm. She touched him, smiling, trying to hold him.

"I really think we ought to—"

Her hand fell from him. Her face closed. "What would Julie think if she walked in?" she said for him, in a flat voice.

"We both knew," he said, turning to her, touching her. "We knew we would have to face it."

"I don't want to. Why can't things just stop now, as they are? I hate time." She slapped at his wristwatch.

"My dear, darling Margaret," he said, leaning over her and kissing the tip of her nose before she jerked her face away. "You wouldn't last an hour without your daughter."

"And you would?" she said bitterly, staring at the window, the crack of thick light between the curtains. "You with your *special* relationship with her?"

"I'm not sure what you want me to say to that," he said, tensing.

200

"No." She sighed, pushed herself up. "Neither am I." She shook her hair back, let it fall again over her face. "You're right, of course. And you're also the first man ever to have shared this bed. I don't suppose," she went on, swinging her feet to the floor, her back to him, "that Julie thinks I have a sex life." She bent to the floor, picked up her brassiere, and began to put it on.

"I'm very flattered," he said. "Truly. Thank you."

"Does she think I have a sex life?" Margaret stood up, searching for her other clothes. "You'd know, wouldn't you?"

"We haven't discussed it," he said. "But I have to say that if we had, I wouldn't be at liberty to tell you."

"How nicely you put things. How carefully."

"You're angry with me. Believe me, that's the last thing I want." He began to dress, trying not to hurry. Margaret brushed her hair with haphazard, angry strokes. He fastened his trousers. She laid the brush down as though defeated, her hair sticking out from her head on one side, smooth and loose on the other.

"The fact is," she said, "I'm jealous of my daughter. Of my daughter and you. I didn't bargain for that."

"No," he said, standing behind her, squeezing her shoulders. He kissed the top of her head. "Frightened. A little guilty, maybe, but not jealous."

"Will you talk about me to her?"

"When and if necessary, Julie and I will discuss her mother. I made love to *you*. You must remember that crucial difference." She twisted into his arms, held him tightly with her right. "Remember," he whispered, "how strong you are. You can handle this. You can handle anything."

"And you?" she asked.

"I shall have great difficulty putting you out of my mind. A great reluctance to do so, too."

"I don't want you to," she said. "I don't want to share you at all. There, you see, I *am* possessive."

"You are a good mother. You will continue to be a good mother. And when all this is over—"

"No." She shook her head vehemently. "No promises. That I can't handle."

He kissed her. She drew away from him and tugged a comb through her hair, avoiding his eyes in the mirror.

"After all," she said, "we are grown-up people. No doubt we'll manage. Now I think we'd better go downstairs. In fact, I rather think you'd better go."

"Yes," he said meekly. "Only I rather think you'll have to throw me out. I've forgotten already how to leave you."

"You," she said, touching his face as she went toward the door, "are a dangerous man. My first instincts were right."

"What were they?"

"To keep you out of my life."

"Never act on first instincts." He caught her hand as she started to open the door. "I love you."

Margaret looked at him steadily.

"Perhaps," she said.

Sullen-faced, Barry drove Julie home. They had not gone to Richmond Park, but to his flat where, despite all his pleading and his gentleness, Julie had been unable to make love with him. She wanted to, of course she did, but she could not explain to him why her body seized up on her, became cold and sore, why her mind reeled with fear and a kind of nebulous disgust. When she closed her eyes to receive his kiss, she had seen the contours of Jo-Jo's face pressed against hers, his eyes glittering, his hands moving. . . . She had pushed Barry away roughly, feeling sick.

Of course he had been angry. She accepted that. He had a right. She had listened to his complaints, rehearsing apologies, promises she suspected were empty. He fumbled for words to express his feelings, his wounded pride. Not only did she seem cold toward him, distant, but now she even rejected his legitimate advances.

"I don't know what's happened to you," he concluded, "but you're not the darling girl I fell in love with."

She regretted losing her temper, but she could not take back the words she had flung at him.

"Try treating me like a woman, then. Make me *feel* like a woman, and then—"

"I don't understand you," he had interrupted coldly. "I'll take you home."

And as they turned into Broom Road, approaching the square, Jo-Jo suddenly spoke to her out of the purr of the engine, with such clarity that she started. She turned to Barry, sure that he must have heard the voice. He refused to look at her. His mouth was set, the corners pulled down. She opened her mouth to speak, but knew that it was useless. She slumped back in her seat, knowing that Jo-Jo was a presence behind her. She had no energy to resist him. She let him speak, listened while her stomach curdled. And it was like so many things that Jo-Jo had told her. She realized that she had known it all along, that the knowledge he so eagerly imparted had been locked in her mind, just waiting for Jo-Jo to pull it out, to articulate it into poison.

"I won't come in," Barry said, the engine idling. Jo-Jo's harsh laughter echoed in the sound.

She unbuckled her seatbelt, waited so that Barry could kiss her if he wanted. Her flesh went cold at the thought. He kept both hands on the steering wheel, and stared out into the dusky square. Again the uselessness of trying to apologize numbed her. She felt Jo-Jo waiting impatiently.

"By the way, I'm going out of town for a couple of days this week or next. Important client thinking of expanding. I have to go and look at his setup, check the lay of the land. It's a bit of a feather in my cap, actually."

"That's good. I'm pleased for you."

"Thanks. So, well, I'll call you."

She watched the car swing away and accelerate. She felt numb, and wondered if she would ever see him again. Inside the house, she stared hard at her mother's face, her hair, her dress.

"Is something wrong?" Margaret asked.

"No. It's nothing." It did not show on her face. Some things only showed inside, were too terrible and ugly to be reflected in the face. Julie knew this for herself.

"Did you have a nice time?"

"Yes. Did you?"

"Yes. It was very . . . pleasant. And useful. Russell thinks you and I ought to talk more . . . about your father. . . ."

"Bit late for that, isn't it?" Julie snapped, a hint of bitterness in her tone.

"He didn't mention it to you?" Margaret said, ignoring her outburst.

"He might have. I don't remember. He's always going on about . . . things."

"Are you all right, darling?"

"Yes. Yes, of course."

"We don't have to talk if—"

"For Christ's sake, Ma, leave me alone. I just want to go upstairs for a bit, okay?"

Upstairs, she washed her burning face in the bathroom. Jo-Jo told her in the gurgling water what she had to do. She wanted to be sick. She stood outside her mother's bedroom door, holding her breath. She thought that if she let her breath out it would sound as a scream or a cry, perhaps even laughter. She pushed the door open. Her breath left her body, hissing.

I told you . . . I told you.

She stared at the rumpled bed, covers thrown back, tumbled, the pillows dented, displaced. She closed the door.

I told you, Ju-lie . . . If they can . . . What's sauce for the goose and the gander is good for the gosling. . . .

She turned and looked at him. He was barring her way. Her body was suddenly feverish, moist. The strength of her involuntary reaction pierced her. The contrast, when Barry touched her . . .

"Go away," she whispered. "You must go away."

You want to, Ju-lie. You know you want to.

Her flesh, her autonomous body agreed with him. She watched him approach, smiling in triumph, without tenderness. She wanted to cry out at his intimate, squeezing touch, but was dumb. There was a singing in her veins, a fizzing that made her feel faint. She wanted, she needed to give in to him. . . . In his eyes she saw only greedy desire, a selfishness that negated her, reduced her to mere flesh and bone. Through the fire, she thought, on the other side of the fire, there is only ice.

"No," she said. "No, I won't." She made her feet move, willed herself to push past him, run down the stairs.

"Darling, you were very quick. You startled me."

Guilty conscience, Julie thought.

"All right, then. Go on. Tell me about my father."

Julie sat in a chair, rigid. Margaret tried to ignore her anger, to remain calm herself.

"Where to begin?" she said, playing for time. "Is there anything you want to ask me? That would probably be easier. . . ."

"You sound just like Russell Dunn," she accused. "All right, I'll ask you. What was he like in bed?"

204

Nine

He had been tense, inevitably, before she arrived, but there was nothing noticeably new in her manner, nothing he had not seen before. It was what he mentally called one of her "cool" days. She was neatly dressed in a gray and white cotton dress, buttoned to the neck, with a small white collar. Her hair was drawn back and held by a twisted elastic band. Her "cool" days were characterized by a studied, distant manner that he thought was meant to match or counteract his own professional one. On her "cool" days she invariably asserted herself, led the conversation. He prevented this by asking her to lie down on the couch. Her hand flew to her neck, the gesture striking him as an overdone parody of the outraged maiden. He saw all the associations the couch had for her, but he would not discuss them now. They had made a bargain, which she had accused him of not keeping. Any discussion might lead to last Sunday's events, of which neither had spoken. He explained that he wished to hypnotize her.

"Why do you want to put me in a trance?"

"I want to take you back to your childhood."

"I don't need a trance for that."

"To some parts we haven't encountered yet."

"Ask. Ask me questions. That's what you do, isn't it?"

"Why are you afraid of the couch?"

"I'm not."

"Of the trance, then?"

"No."

"Is it because you feel vulnerable lying down?"

"No. Not particularly."

"Then why are you afraid?"

"Oh, if you're going to make a big thing of it . . ." She jumped up and flounced to the couch, then stood looking down at it, trembling. Very slowly she forced herself to lie down. She fussed with her skirt, tucking it around and under her legs like a cocoon.

"Are you ready, Julie?"

"Yes."

"Then I want you to relax. You're going to go to sleep. . . ."

She fixed her eyes on one of the prints hanging on the wall. Tiny blue flowers on long stems. A botanical drawing, several views. The word *Myosotis* in fine, cursive black letters. Her eyes closed. Her mind began to drift from the drone of Dunn's voice. He loves me. He loves me not. He loves me. He loves me not. Forget-me-nots.

"Are you comfortable, Julie?"

"Yes."

"Open your eyes, please. How old are you, Julie?"

"Nineteen. I've just had my birthday. I'm nineteen."

"Good. Now I want you to think back, think back to when you were much younger, a little girl. You're twelve, Julie. Ten. Do you remember?"

"Going to school. Going to school with Sybil and Miss Chalmers. Miss Chalmers was nice. I liked Miss Chalmers. Miss Chalmers gave me the best part in the end-of-term play."

"All right, Julie. Now I want you to go back another year, and another. Let's go back to when you were eight, Julie."

"Everything was so strange, so new. I couldn't get used to all the traffic. I was a great help to my mother because she couldn't use her left arm anymore."

"Before that, Julie. Was it strange at your great-grandmother's? How did you feel then?"

"It was . . . just the same as always. There were lots of forget-me-nots in the garden that year." She moved, lacing her fingers together, stretching her feet. She closed her eyes.

"Open your eyes, please, Julie."

"I'm tired."

"No, you're not. Not tired yet, Julie."

"All right, then. I'm thinking."

"What are you thinking, Julie? Tell me what you remember."

She drew a deep breath, and sighed. Her body became loose, relaxed.

"No, not tired. Couldn't sleep. I heard Nanny talking. I should have been asleep. She was talking to . . . to Margery. She said it was bound to happen one day. A mystery solved, Margery said, and laughed. I didn't understand. I didn't understand. I should have been asleep. I was afraid. . . ."

"Who is Margery?"

"Oh, you know. The maid. The woman who helped."

"That's right. And she was talking to Nanny?"

"Yes. Nanny said, 'He'll take her away. Stands to reason. Then what'll we do?' They had their jobs to think about, you see. It wasn't easy. . . . I don't want to go away. I don't want to. He's going to take me away. Don't let him."

"Who is going to take you away, Julie?"

"That man."

"What man is that?"

"The shouting one. The one who came . . ."

"And how did you feel about that, Julie?"

"Scared. I couldn't sleep. No matter how hard I tried . . . I was too frightened."

"Something happened that day, Julie. Something that frightened you."

"She said . . . Margery said if there was going to be more carrying on like today, she wasn't sure she wouldn't be better off out of it. 'Poor little mite,' she said. 'She's too much for the old woman,' Nanny said. 'Much too much. And now this.' "

"What did Margery mean, Julie? What 'carrying on'?"

"I don't know. I don't remember."

"Try, Julie. It's there. You can . . ."

"Shouting. They pushed me out of the house. . . ."

"Who was shouting? Who pushed you?"

"Don't know. Voices. Nanny. 'Go out and play, miss. And stay out of sight.' Her face was as white as a sheet. She threatened to call the police."

"Who, Julie? Who?" She shook her head. Her body reflected the

207

signs of some struggle, then she became still, very still, her breathing shallow and even. "Julie? Why couldn't you go to sleep that night?"

"Sleeping. Want to sleep." She tried to turn over, to pillow her cheek against her hands.

"Julie, look at me. Look at me, Julie." Drowsily, she obeyed. "Now tell me, Julie. Before you heard Nanny talking to Margery, why couldn't you get to sleep?"

"Why?"

"Yes."

"Oh . . ." She yawned, had difficulty keeping her eyes open. "That must have been because I'd killed Jo-Jo."

Russell's knee cracked sharply in the silence. He realized how tight his body was, and made himself relax, muscle by muscle. Julie slept. He switched off the tape recorder and stared at her innocent, sleeping face.

"Now tell me, Julie. Before you heard Nanny talking to Margery, why couldn't you get to sleep?"

"Why?"

"Yes."

"Oh . . . that must have been because I'd killed Jo-Jo."

Russell switched off the tape recorder. She had shown no emotion throughout. Now she continued to sit like some gaudy monument, her eyes cast down. She was dressed, at least to Russell's eyes, like a 1940s tart: hair hidden under a turbanlike hat; wide, padded shoulders; ankle-strap shoes that looked somehow too large for her feet. The dominant color of her "costume" was electric blue, and this was echoed on her eyelids. Her makeup was a deliberate mask, as though her face had become blank, an egg onto which any features could be painted. She had little black net gloves on her hands. She crossed her black-stockinged legs and arched her ankle so that the sheen of the stocking caught the light, making her leg look like some stylized erotic drawing. Russell looked away. She raised her eyes and glanced at him, then dropped them again. Russell cleared his throat, tried not to think about the two messages Margaret had left on his machine, neither of which he had answered.

"I don't understand this heavy silence at all," Julie said flatly.

"We often sit in silence. You don't usually mind."

"Very well."

208

He took out his handkerchief, touched it to his nose, refolded it, and put it back in his pocket. He wished he could smoke a cigarette. He looked at his watch.

"Are people supposed to be more or less truthful under hypnosis?" she asked, as though making conversation.

"Neither. Just less inhibited. Sometimes the unconscious mind blocks off a memory. Waking, we literally forget. Often it is possible for us to reach, unblock, and recover that memory under hypnosis."

"It's a bit like dreaming," she said. "Things get all muddled up."

He had played her the tape because she had flatly refused to believe she had said anything about a man shouting or that she had killed Jo-Jo. Now, he thought, she did not know how to handle the proof.

"It's funny, hearing one's own voice, don't you think? I hate it. If I were a singer or something, I would never listen to my own records. Never."

"Why is that?"

"Oh, I suppose because . . . one never sounds like oneself, does one?"

"Who do you think you sound like?"

"There?" She gestured toward the tape. He nodded. "Oh, like some prissy, tale-telling kid. I always imagine my voice is very deep and sexy." She laughed. "It isn't, is it?"

"No. It's a very nice voice."

"Thank you." She fiddled with her gloves, smoothing the frivolous net down over each finger of the left hand in turn. "Because it doesn't sound like me, I find it very difficult to say anything about it at all."

"Did none of it strike a chord?"

"Oh, yes. Some of it's true. Though it didn't all happen like that. Like I said, it's all muddled up. And some of it wasn't true at all."

"Why do you think you said it, then?"

"I don't know. Why does one dream of people one's never seen or known, and yet feel convinced that they are friends or relatives? Or, you know, when you dream of someone you really do know well—like if I dreamed of Ma or Great-Gran, say—and yet they don't look at all like themselves." She sounded quite animated, as though ready to expound some theory. He froze her with a look, aware of time running out. "It simply isn't true," she said, "that I

209

killed Jo-Jo. I mean, even you must see that it's ridiculous. If I had, I wouldn't be here now, would I?"

"Wouldn't you?"

"No. All my problems would be over, wouldn't they?" He did not answer this. When she saw that he would not, she went on. "Besides, we never had a maid called Margery. Not that I can remember, anyway. You see, it's all muddled."

"Perhaps it will become clearer to you if you think about it."

"Yes. It might. Is that what you want me to do?"

"I think it would help."

"All right. I'll try. For next time."

"I have a cancellation, a free hour tomorrow. Would you like to come in then?"

"Mm. Yes. All right. Why not?"

"Good. I'll ask Valerie to book you in at five. Can you manage that?"

"Oh, yes."

"Fine. Well . . ." She stood up and smiled a little uncertainly. "Goodbye, Julie."

"You don't like my clothes, do you?" She sounded on the verge of tears.

Carefully he said, "They're very striking."

"They've proved my point."

"And what is that?"

"You don't want me to grow up. You want me to stay a little girl, just like Barry. You both hate me to look like a woman."

"Is that true of Barry?"

"It doesn't matter anyway," she said coolly. "I dress to please myself." She went to the door. He buzzed Valerie, asked her to make the extra appointment. Julie looked at him, her expression uncertain, secretive.

"Yes, Julie?" he said.

"I was just thinking . . . Oh nothing . . . ." She faced the door and in a rush said, "I bet Jo-Jo would like these clothes."

"I tried to make sense of that tape, as much as I could. Oh, and by the way, Ma says there was a woman there called Margery. I must have forgotten. So, anyway . . . it still doesn't make sense to me . . . why I said it . . . what I meant. The only thing I can think of is I must have had a bad dream, about some man trying to abduct me. I don't remember any of this, you understand. That's what woke me up, perhaps. That would fit with your sexuality theory, wouldn't it? Little girls dreaming of nasty, threatening men . . . But I don't know. It's only what I thought, my theory. You don't believe me, of course."

"I believe you, Julie."

Today she wore jeans and a checked shirt. Her face was scrubbed, her hair falling loose from a band of ribbon.

"It was just a misunderstanding."

"You discussed this with your mother?"

"Oh, no. Not really. I just asked her about this Margery person."

Margaret's hurt and confusion had been clear on the telephone when, at last, he called and explained that he could not see her, not yet. His work with Julie was moving forward rapidly, he felt, and he feared their meeting might impede that.

"But I could come to you," she had said, her keenness taking his breath away.

"I have to think of myself as well as Julie," he had said.

"Oh, yes, of course, yourself and Julie. Not me."

"Mr. Dunn? I don't want to be rude, but I don't think you're listening."

"I'm sorry, Julie. You're absolutely right. I wasn't. It's unforgivable. It won't happen again." He felt a deep need for air, fresh air.

"Is something wrong? Oh, I shouldn't ask that, should I? Would you rather I went? After all, this is an extra appointment, and since I really can't help you with the tape . . ."

"No, Julie. No. I'd like you to lie down on the couch, please."

"But why? You've seen that I just make up a lot of nonsense."

"I don't think so. Besides, we still have further to go. If you wouldn't mind?"

She stood up, and tried to sound jaunty. "All right. After all, if I don't, you'll only say I'm scared." She stretched out on the couch.

"Are you comfortable?"

"Yes, thank you."

"Then close your eyes, relax. Just listen to my voice. You're feeling very relaxed, very comfortable . . . safe. . . ."

She was in the nursery, seated at her little desk. It was almost too small for her now. She wondered if Great-Gran would get her a

211

bigger one. Nanny bustled in and she applied herself to the work in front of her. Nanny left the door open. Downstairs, the bell rang. Voices. A loud voice. A door slammed.

"On with your work, please, miss. Remember, curiosity killed the cat."

Nanny went out in a crackle of starch, not quite closing the door behind her. Footsteps on the back stairs, hurrying. Whispered voices. Voices that sounded shocked and excited. Then Nanny was back again, the door open, and there was a voice echoing from downstairs, a man's voice, loud and angry. Nanny clucked her disapproval and crept out onto the landing to listen. Nanny often did that; then, when she heard someone coming, she tiptoed back into the nursery and pretended to busy herself with some task. This time Nanny pretended to be sorting the child's clothes as Great-Gran herself came puffing up the stairs, her face as white as Nanny's apron. The stairs were too much for her.

"I'm sorry, Nanny." She drew her out of the room and spoke in a broken, breathless whisper. "Outside . . . keep her away from the house. . . . Wrapped up well, of course." Then she called to Julie, a smile that wasn't a proper smile on her face. "You'd like to go out into the garden, wouldn't you, darling? That's a good girl. Just do as Nanny says."

"Why, Nanny?" she asked as Nanny, her face animated with suppressed excitement, buttoned her into her coat.

"Ours not to reason why, Miss. Little girls should be seen and not heard. Come along now, downstairs."

But not the proper way. Down the back stairs, Nanny pushing her ahead, through the linen room and the kitchen. Margery turning, a wooden spoon in her hand, to exchange a secret look with Nanny, who shook her head sharply. Nanny did not go with her, but gave her a little push instead, out into the cobbled yard.

"Now go and play quietly down there." She pointed to the far end of the garden. "Play quietly, mind, and stay away from the house till I call you. Stay out of sight." Nanny hurried, anxious to get back to the kitchen gossip. "And I don't want to see a speck of dirt on that coat when you come in, miss."

"Yes, Nanny." No, Nanny. Three bags full, Nanny. Something Jo-Jo had taught her. She ran in her warm clothes to the bottom of the garden. It was a misty, damp morning, the sky pressing down, gray. The trees dripped. The leaves were yellowed and brown and soggy underfoot. She stood at the end of the little pond where Nanny was always telling her not to go, and looked at brown boat-leaves floating on its still, black surface. Why did they want to get rid of her? She looked back toward the gray bulk of the house, but all she could see was smoke drifting from its tall chimneys. What was going on? Jo-Jo would know. Where was Jo-Jo?

"Jo-Jo? Jo-Jo?"

It wasn't their time, of course. He would not be looking out for her. She felt afraid without him. Not so much afraid, really, as lonely, empty. It was never really safe without Jo-Jo. This strange disruption of the fixed routine made the garden seem so very empty. As though Jo-Jo had gone away, gone away forever. The terrible thought took her breath away.

Without meaning to, she had wandered toward the shrubbery, scuffing her feet through the damp grass, the leaves. What was going on in the house? In the dark cavern made by the shrubbery, she could approach the house unseen, come close to the tall lattice windows. He was crouched down by one of them, peering in. Thrilled and relieved to find him, she ran forward, calling his name. He pressed a finger to his lips, and pulled her down beside him. His eyes were wide and troubled. He pointed to the window. Together, cautiously, they raised their heads over the sill and looked in.

She saw a man, a dark man, waving his arms in the air. He strode back and forth, up and down, pausing now and again to shout something into Great-Gran's white and frightened face.

He's come to take you away, Jo-Jo said, whispering in the leaves and the dripping water.

"Why?"

He says you belong to him. He's going to take you away.

"No. He can't . . . I won't . . ."

Jo-Jo knew. He *knew.* He knew everything. Perhaps he even knew she had been thinking he had already gone away. She felt that Jo-Jo was dying before her eyes.

You want to run away, he said, *before he takes you.*

"No. He can't. Great-Gran won't let him."

She can't stop him. You belong to him.

"No. I belong to Mummy, Jo-Jo. Mummy and . . . you," she

213

added, afraid of what she said, and yet needing to comfort him in some way.

You'll go with him anyway. They'll make you. He sounded infinitely sad.

"I won't, Jo-Jo. I won't. I promise."

He squirmed away through the wet bushes. She called after him, but he just shook his head sadly.

"I'll prove it to you. I'll show you."

She had never done anything like that before. Her legs wobbled like jelly but her fear, her distress carried her on. She pushed against the heavy front door and ran across the hall into the room where the man was shouting at Great-Gran, his voice hurting her ears with its loudness and anger.

"Julie! Really, that woman . . . I told her to . . ." Great-Gran rose up from her chair. For the first time she appeared frail in Julie's eyes. Her hands shook helplessly in the air.

"Don't let him take me, Great-Gran. Don't let him. I want to stay with Jo-Jo. I've got to. Please, please . . ." She was sobbing and clinging—she did not know how—to Great-Gran's skirts, felt the old woman's hands on her back, fluttering like moths. She had to sit down again, defeated by the wails of the hysterical child. Julie screamed when his shadow reached for her.

"Who is this Jo-Jo? What does she mean?"

She could not see him, could not see anything, her wet face buried in Great-Gran's lap, but the scent of the old lady's lavender was not proof against his smell.

"No one." Great-Gran's voice rasped with something of its old authority. "An imaginary friend she made up. It's nothing. Now please, for the last time, leave my house."

"She's crying for an imaginary friend?"

"It is you . . . you . . . you're upsetting her. Leave my house at once."

"Oh, I see, I see. You have made the child mad. Shutting her up here, hiding her away . . . You'll pay for this. Both of you. You and her whore of a mother, you'll both pay."

"No," Julie sobbed. "No. No. Don't let him. Don't let him. I want Jo-Jo. I want to go to Jo-Jo."

Her sobs were real, terrible, racking. She flung out her arms, kicked her legs, twisted small, her hands covering her face. Russell waited for the violent spasms to pass and then spoke to her gently, soothing her, telling her she would wake up, telling her she would remember. . . .

"On three, Julie, all right? One . . . two . . . three."

Her sobs, remembered from childhood, continued on into the present. Coughing, she sat up and bent forward, holding her head in her hands. Silently, Russell placed a box of tissues on her knees. She nodded her thanks. He waited while she mopped her face, got her breathing under control.

"There's more," she said bleakly, wadding the damp tissues together. He pushed the wastebasket toward her with his foot. "Thanks." She dropped the soiled tissues into it. "I ran away. He tried to grab me, to stop me. I ran out into the garden. I think he followed me. There were people shouting everywhere. I went into the shrubbery. I just kept running, running. And the worst thing was . . . the worst thing . . . oh, God . . ." She began to cry again, the tears unstoppable, impeding her words. "I couldn't find Jo-Jo anywhere. I couldn't find Jo-Jo, Mr. Dunn. I couldn't find him." He waited while she sobbed her way through a new flood of tears. "I must have fallen, I don't remember. I remember Nanny picking me up. She wasn't even cross about . . . my coat. It was all muddy, all down the front. Leaves sticking to it. She never said a word. She took me back into the house. I didn't want to go in there." She did not speak for several minutes. She began to draw deep breaths. Gradually her tears became a trickle, then began to dry on her face.

"Great-Gran had a glass of brandy. There was a fire. A fire in the grate. I sat by it, in my nightdress and dressing gown. It was like being ill, because there was still light outside. Everything felt funny, wrong. Great-Gran was sort of blue around the lips and smelled of brandy, not lavender. She told me it was all right, but I knew it wasn't. I could hear the fear in her voice. I knew something was going to happen. She said the nasty man had gone away and would never come back. She said I was to forget all about him. I would go to London soon, she said, and be with Mummy. I would go to a proper school and be with Mummy. I said, 'What about Jo-Jo?' And she said I had to forget about Jo-Jo. I was too old for Jo-Jo now. It was time to forget him. I knew what she meant, even though she didn't say, couldn't bring herself to say it. It was because that man had said I was mad, that she'd made me mad. I knew that frightened her. I could feel it, smell it. . . . She said it wasn't right, a big girl like me, talking to someone no one could see . . . that I was making myself ill over someone who didn't exist. She said it was her fault, partly, for not sending me to school, not helping me to make real friends of my own age. She cried a little. But she said that couldn't be helped now, and everything was going to change. Everything. Only I had to stop pretending about Jo-Jo. She made me promise. I had to stop talking about him. I had to stop playing with him. 'After all, what will your new friends say when you go to school, if you go around talking to yourself?' "

She sat miserable, rolling a balled tissue between the damp palms of her hands. Cautiously he looked at his watch, but she saw the movement and said, "Is it time?"

"Nearly."

"Can we go on? Please?"

"Julie, I—"

"If I don't tell you now . . . I don't think I ever will. Please, Mr. Dunn. You've got to help me. I can't . . . If I stop now . . ." She twisted herself sideways, her face buried in the back of the couch, her fists bunched.

He was torn. To give way to her now . . . But then again, to reject her now . . . He tried to remember his next patient, and found his mind a buzzing blank. That made him decide. He stood up.

"Excuse me, Julie. Just a minute . . ."

"Please? You'll come back? I don't want . . ."

"I'll just be a minute, Julie. I promise."

Outside, he held the door closed behind him as Valerie looked up at him, a puzzled frown on her face.

"Can you . . . er . . . cancel my next appointment?"

She glanced at the wall clock, then looked down at the file, ready and waiting on her desk.

"He'll have left by now."

"Then ask Annie . . . No, I'll speak to her."

"She's at that conference. She did tell you."

"Oh yes . . . yes, of course." Valerie stared at him, saw the indecision, doubt. "Tell him I have an unavoidable emergency. I'm very sorry."

"But—"

216

"Please, Val ..." His voice cracked. "Do this for me." He opened the door and walked back into the room where Julie waited.

She could not sleep for thinking about Jo-Jo. Where was he? She was worried about him. And she knew she had to tell him, to make him understand. Whatever happened to her, he had to go away; they could not be friends anymore. She kept thinking about what Nanny said, what all the nannies always said: Sometimes you have to be cruel to be kind. She crept out of bed, put her coat on over her nightgown, and drew on her socks. Downstairs she found her Wellington boots on the back porch. It was very dark and frightening but she closed her mind to that. She could not call to him, of course, for fear of waking the household, of being discovered. She thought that if they found her wandering in the garden in the dead of night, they would know that she was mad. She half believed it herself. She was tempted to run back into the house, to be mad. Mummy would come and take her away and ... Then she thought of the man, the angry man, and became even more afraid. Then she saw the light and immediately began to feel better, safe. She always felt safe with Jo-Jo.

He had built a bonfire on the bank of the pond. It was a good place, screened from the house by trees. A safe place. He was sitting on a big stone. He had a stick in his hand with which he stirred the embers. She stood on the other side of the fire, watching him. He looked at her so sadly, like he was dying. She had never seen anyone die, but that was how it felt. She went to sit with him. She tried to comfort him, but she had no comfort to give. Steeling herself, she told him he had to go away, that they could not be friends anymore, not like this. Besides, she would be going away soon to live with her mother in London. She wouldn't need him then. She was crying. She told herself she was being cruel to be kind.

Tears ran down her face as she sat huddled in a corner of the couch, looking small and cold and frightened. The tape whirred softly. Muffled voices sounded beyond the door, in other parts of the building. Russell reached out slowly and put on a lamp. She winced, even in that soft light.

Jo-Jo said that he wouldn't go away, he wouldn't, wouldn't let her send him. It was all lies anyway. Her mother didn't have time for her. The man was going to take her away. There was only one way

217

she could go to her mother. Only he, Jo-Jo, could make that happen. She tried to argue with him, but he would not listen. He reminded her about the man, the terrible threat he posed. Jo-Jo said the man could do anything he wanted. The man would not let her go to her mother. Not unless Jo-Jo fixed it.

"How, Jo-Jo?"

Magic. A spell. I can make it happen.

She conjured pictures in Russell's head. He felt damp air on his skin and saw two children, kneeling on either side of the big flat stone. He saw them, as it were, through the flickering flames, imperfectly but all too clearly.

"He said I belonged to him, no one else. Not to the man, not to Mummy . . . Ma," she corrected herself with difficulty. "Only *he* could let me go. Only *he* could make Ma come and fetch me. I was so afraid, so afraid she wouldn't come. I kept thinking that Great-Gran might die and Ma would have to go away again and there'd be no one to stop the man from coming and taking me away because I was mad."

He made her promise then, repeat after him in an eerie, singsong voice.

When I grow up . . .

"When I grow up . . ."

I, Ju-lie . . .

"I, Ju-lie . . ."

Swear and promise . . .

"Swear and promise . . ."

On my mother's life . . .

"On my mother's life . . ."

That I will marry . . .

"That I will marry . . ."

Jo-Jo.

"Jo-Jo."

I belong to Jo-Jo.

"I belong to Jo-Jo."

"On my mother's life . . ." she repeated, and caught her breath. She was beyond tears. The flesh of her face was drawn tight over the bones, making her look skeletal. Her eyes burned with a fierceness, a conviction that held Russell rapt, a part of the scene she both observed and reenacted.

218

The promise was no good unless it was sealed in blood, he said. The blood would make her mother come to her. The blood would prove that she belonged to him. She had promised. She promised.

"He put his hand, his left hand, flat on the stone between us. He curled his fingers up, three fingers, tucked the thumb underneath them. Just his first finger pointing at me. Pointing, pointing at me like a curse. I couldn't take my eyes off it. Then I . . . then I saw him raise his other hand. The light, the firelight, caught on the blade. He had a knife. I didn't really see it. He . . . had brought it down. It was just a blur in the light, dazzling. . . . I can still hear the noise it made on the stone, grinding, scraping. . . . The finger . . . the finger went on wriggling and pointing at me, even after he had pulled his bleeding hand away. I thought it was going to jump into my lap. He put his hand up to his mouth and there was blood, blood running down his chin."

She began to scream then, to scream and shout. She didn't know what she shouted. He reached for her. She scrambled up. He didn't look like Jo-Jo anymore. He looked older, grown up. He reached for her with his hand, the hand with a bleeding stump where a finger should have been, and that was when she . . . when she pushed him. She pushed him with all her terrified strength, screaming. She saw him fall into the black water, making waves, splashing her. She saw the dead leaves bobbing like boats in a wild storm. Water splashed cold and stinging onto her. She saw his arms outstretched, legs splayed. She saw him trying to get up, feet slipping in the mud. She saw him fall back. She saw him sink. She saw his face lose its shape under the water. She saw him drown.

"I killed him," she said, and her head slumped forward, her chin on her chest.

It was like a presence in the room, thick and palpable, as though what she had kept within her all these years had been given substance by the breath of her talking. His nose seemed to smell dank water, woodsmoke. In the dusk beyond the lamplight were shadowy trees and a vast stillness, wisps of smoke, the glow of embers like the red eye of an animal. He stood up quickly. Her ghosts were comprehensible, not the kind to make the flesh of strong men creep. He crossed to the door in two strides and put the main light on. He stood blinking, listening to the hissing passage of traffic outside. It was raining. The window was spotted and beaded with drops of water. No ghosts, he told himself. But it wasn't finished yet. There were many knots yet to be tied. Not tonight. But there was just one thing, one loose end. He composed himself, making sure that his voice, when he spoke, would be steady, his tone quite matter-of-fact.

"And that, of course," he said, moving back to his chair as he did so, "was the night your mother had her 'accident.'" He sat down. The tape was nearly finished. "You do understand that, Julie, don't you?"

Very slowly, she raised her face to look at him.

"Was it? I don't know." Her voice was drained of all tone, all emotion except a great weariness.

"I think you do," he persisted. "And I think you understand what that means." He waited, looking at her, and he wanted, suddenly thinking of Margaret, to shake it out of her.

"No," she said at last. "Really, I—"

"You made Jo-Jo a promise, an innocent childhood promise, in order to get your mother back. But then you 'killed' Jo-Jo, and that was a sure way of breaking the promise, wasn't it, Julie? That was a lot of guilt for a little girl to handle. And you've blamed your mother, not just for leaving you, but for making you pay such a terrible price for her presence. Most of all, you've felt guilty about the price she had to pay, the 'accident,' haven't you, Julie?"

"Coincidence," she said.

"You've always known about the accident, Julie, though you've never been able to admit it, not even to yourself."

"No. She won't tell me. We never talk . . ." She got up and moved past him to the window.

"Who was the man who wanted to take you away?"

She took a deep breath that shuddered through her body.

"My father, I suppose."

"You know."

"I know," she repeated flatly.

"And you suspect, even if you don't actually know, that he caused your mother's accident. What you don't know is why." She shook her head wearily, neither denying nor confirming. "I want you to think about it, Julie," he said, giving way to his own weariness. "Next time—"

"No." She turned toward him with unexpected energy. "No, you've done your job. You've rooted out all the hidden little secrets

220

and made sense of them. That's fine. That's terrific. But you're not nearly as clever as you think you are, Mr. Dunn. You haven't even discovered what the real problem is." She crossed the room and picked up her jacket and bag.

"Do you want to tell me about it?"

His calmness surprised both of them. He got up and went to his desk, examining the neat orderliness of it. After a moment he reached out and slightly altered the position of a paper knife.

"Yes, why not, since we've finished now."

"I have to say that I don't believe we've finished."

"That's my decision. You've always said . . ."

"Is this because you know that I . . . that your mother and I . . . ?"

"My God," she said, angry and exasperated, "the size of your ego. No, Mr. Dunn, it's not because you and my mother . . ." She parodied his tone cruelly, enjoying his discomfort. "It's because deep down I want Jo-Jo. I've wanted him from the first day he came back into my life. Oh, yes, I'm afraid of him. I think maybe I'll always be afraid of him, but that's also what attracts me. That's the bottom line, Mr. Dunn. I don't want Barry with his plans and his neatly packaged life. I will not stay in a box labeled 'little girl' by my mother and Barry for the rest of my life. That's how you all treat me, see me. All except Jo-Jo." She swung her jacket over her shoulder and went to the door.

"Julie, please . . ."

"Jo-Jo makes me feel like a woman, like my father must have made my mother feel once. I like that. And if she can't handle that, if you and Barry can't . . . Listen, Jo-Jo wants me and he'll kill anyone who tries to stop him. Like you said, I've got a lot of guilt on my plate. I don't intend to add to it. So thanks for your help, Mr. Dunn. And goodbye."

"Julie . . ." he said, but it was only a defeated whisper, inadequate to reach her. "Julie . . . please . . . At least let me drive you home." How pathetic he sounded and felt. She waited for him, silently.

Ten

The car breasted the spiral of the access road at an unhealthy pace, and barely paused at the top before accelerating onto the motorway. On the other side of the median strip, the three lanes were packed with traffic, a blurred mass of lights and colors made almost monochromatic by speed, rain, and spray. Friday night, and the flow of traffic was away from London. Barry, settling into the fast lane in the opposite direction, felt that he had the road to himself.

It was a case of absence making the heart grow not fonder, but harder and clearer. His mind had been forced to rest, to cease circling the *if*s and *but*s that had threatened to obscure the simple fact that he loved Julie. For three days he had been forced to concentrate on the financial affairs and expansion plans of a client who, from small beginnings, promised to become a force in the electronics field. Barry had rediscovered a zest for his work and a pleasure in it that had lately become muffled by his personal concerns. There had never quite seemed to be time to call Julie. Subconsciously, perhaps, he had taken this time out and now, enjoying the mechanical process of driving on a good, clear road in an excellent car, he understood why. It had cleared his head.

He loved Julie. He was a simple man, used to making and acting upon simple, clear decisions. Somehow he had been diverted from this habitual path. His way was to cut through, to take what he wanted. He did not know if Julie was "cured" because he did not comprehend her "disease." He knew that she would not die of it, however, and he was convinced now that he was the best cure for Julie's ills. She was young, impressionable, scared, and under-occupied. He saw now that she had been surrounded by overly concerned people who, undoubtedly from the best of motives, en-couraged and indulged her whims and worries. It was what his mother called, with hearty disdain, "mollycoddling." The antidote was plain speaking, a sharp dash of cold verbal water, and he had his speech already prepared.

He slowed down a little as the road narrowed to two lanes and an approaching roundabout was signaled. The rain became a visible, slashing curtain rather than an abstract spray. He heard the wind and the sound of many other cars moving past him. He swung the wheel and turned the car in an easy curve around the perimeter of the circle. Just for a moment, caught in his lights, he glimpsed a figure standing, incredibly, on the grassy mound that formed the center of the circle. Poor devil, he thought, forming an impression of soaked clothing, dark hair flattened and streaming rainwater down a pale, indistinct face. It was impossible to stop. It was forbid-den, even if the man had given any indication of wanting to hitch a ride. And then he realized that he must have imagined the man. Pedestrians were not allowed on motorways. It would be impossi-ble, anyway, to reach the roundabout without a vehicle. Unless there had been an accident, he thought, and instinctively slowed and looked back, but the spray of his own passing blotted out everything to the rear. Ahead there was no sign of a smashed or stalled vehicle. The road opened out again, inviting him. He shrugged it off, put it down to a trick of the light and rain.

He would say that they did not need a fancy wedding. A registry office would do for him. Who cared if their families were disap-pointed? They could pick up a couple of witnesses off the street. She would be therapeutically occupied in finding them a nice house and decorating it and furnishing it and looking after it. He had every intention of making her pregnant as quickly as possible. Though perhaps he would not mention that, not specifically. And, of course, if she *really* wanted a full, formal wedding—he had a sudden, heart-stabbing vision of her in a mist of white lace and sheer veiling, like a doll—that would be fine, too. Only she must organize it, not cling to her mother's apron strings. It would be, as they said in his native Yorkshire, their "do." Whatever she wanted, no expense spared. That would keep her occupied, and would, he firmly believed, perform for her mind the same cleansing process the last three days had done for him. She had been indulged too long. What Julie needed was a bit of discipline.

And if she said no?

The thought made him catch his breath. He almost laughed out loud, refusing to contemplate any such possibility. Then he had the disquieting sensation that it was not his thought, had not sprung into his mind, but had been put there, as though someone had spoken from the backseat, shattering his confidence with a shaft of doubt. He almost turned his head to make sure no one was there. Then he did laugh out loud, shaking his head, telling himself not to be so bloody silly. He was getting the motorway jumps.

How many versions of that clichéd story, modern folklore, had he heard? They all began the same way. Some perfectly innocent driver gives some perfectly innocent person a lift. Usually the passenger is in some way frail or vulnerable: a heavily pregnant woman with a load of shopping, an arthritic old lady, a lost and tear-stained child. And the unsuspecting driver sets off on his errand of mercy, probably feeling pleased with himself, chatting to the woman/old lady/child in the rear seat, reassuring her that it's no trouble, all will be well. And then the hand falls upon the driver's shoulder. A hand variously covered in sores or ghostly flesh or whittled to the white bone. The pregnant woman is a she-wolf, swollen with evil, the old lady a foul-breathed hag, the child the cold and ghastly face of Death itself. And in the shock and horror of the moment, the driver loses control of the car and goes hurtling, apparently of his own volition, to his own death.

It was one way of explaining those apparently inexplicable motorway crashes that every sane person knew were due to drowsiness, boredom, careless driving. But, of course, with the driver dead, none of that could ever be proven.

Barry eased back on the accelerator, checked the traffic in the slower lanes. He was sweating. There was no safe gap in the slower lane. A car was bearing down on him from behind, its lights piercing the spray. He increased speed steadily. He was spooking himself. And all because—the thought came unbidden and unexpected—of

224

that figure glimpsed in the rain-blurred beam of his headlights, standing incongruously in the middle of a roundabout.

The trouble with spooking oneself is that it is so difficult to stop. The sensation of someone sitting behind him returned, stronger than ever. Mingled with the engine's contentment, the wind's rush, the rain's anger, he could hear labored breathing. Such breathing, he remembered with an involuntary shiver, featured in the various tales of the evil hitchhiker. The heavy breathing of desire, the desire for destruction. His rearview mirror showed him nothing. He could not laugh it off. He slowed a little and glanced over his shoulder, prepared for anything and nothing.

Of course, nothing. Nothing but the distinct shape of a young man who leaned forward to bring his pale, waxy-featured face into the light. A fine face with remarkable bones, thick, black curling hair streaming water down a face that smiled slowly and disdainfully. The eyes contained something certain and horrible.

Julie belongs to me. You'll never have her. Never.

Barry's capable hands jerked on the wheel, shearing the car dangerously across toward the slower lane. A horn sounded angry blasts and a truck roared by, too close, drenching the side of the car with a hail of spray. Barry's reflexes righted the speeding car quickly. He checked the traffic behind. He dared not slow down.

"Jo-Jo?" he said in a whisper that sounded mad to his own ears. There was no answer. Of course there was no answer. Except, in the mingled natural sounds of his journey, he thought he caught a rumbling of laughter and, despite the heater, it felt chilly in the car, as though someone had opened a window.

He must be much more tired than he had imagined. He must have given way to the monotony of motorway driving, perhaps even dozed for a few unnoticed seconds. Carefully now, biding his time, he moved over into the middle lane and then into the slow lane. Soon there must be a place where he could stop and rest, even get out and stretch his legs. The rain would be good and refreshing on his face. As soon as it was safe, he twisted around and looked at the backseat, and of course there was no one there, nothing except his own raincoat and briefcase. He put the radio on, spun the dial until he found lively music. His lane was empty up ahead now, and as he approached London, more traffic overtook him. He hated being overtaken, dawdling in the slow lane. At the first possible moment he would move over again, get going. He was all right now.

Ahead he could see the lights of a bridge, a single concrete span crossing the road. To his left a muddy bank rose where the road had been dug through a hill. The banks on either side enclosed the wide roadway, turning it into a tunnel. He passed under the bridge and the figure of the young man came from nowhere. The man stepped from nowhere onto the road, and turned to face his lights. He saw the face again, rushing toward him as though spotlit. The same face, running with water, the smile turning to a sneer of triumph.

His reflexes made him spin the wheel. He needed extra speed to make it. He pressed the accelerator right down, shot across the middle lane, and entered the fast lane. Light flooded the interior of the car. A vehicle behind veered to avoid him. Too late and with a dreadful sense of inevitability, Barry saw that he would not be able to straighten his car in time. It crashed straight through the barrier and bumped drunkenly across the median. There was nothing he could do. He threw up his arms to cover his face as the car surged on straight into the path of the oncoming traffic. His smashed and twisted car was carried three hundred yards up the road before it burst into flames. Thirty vehicles were involved in the ensuing pileup. It was one of those inexplicable accidents, a police spokesperson said later: a tragic case of motorway madness.

Margaret knew only one way to deal with personal disappointment: She buried herself in work. Not that "disappointment" was an adequate word to describe the feelings of rejection, frustration, and pain she felt when Russell failed to call her or return her calls. And when they did eventually speak, she felt that he had maneuvered her into a totally uncharacteristic role. She heard herself pleading. The memory sickened her.

All her relations with men since Willi Dekker had been casual. A few who began as temporary lovers had grown over the years into friends. What they all had in common, from the merest passing fancy to the most serious friendship, was that they had never made her feel cheap and undignified. Russell, after all, had made the overtures. Also, he had promised much more than she had ever wanted or expected. For God's sake, she raged inwardly, he had said he loved her. It was she who had doubted, held back. In Margaret's book, even if all he had wanted was one uncommitted afternoon in her bed, he should have had the courtesy at least to call her afterwards. There were ways—Margaret had practiced them and had them practiced upon her—of disabusing a person gently, of saying "Thank you, but that's it." All her initial mistrust and resentment of Russell Dunn returned, curdled and bitter. Yet true anger, that ultimate, safe defense, eluded her. Instead, she hurt.

She could make excuses for him, of course; she could, if she chose, believe what he said about Julie's progress. He had been at pains to warn her that Julie must, of necessity, stand ambiguous and immutable between them. On the other hand he had not led her to believe that Julie represented an insurmountable, perpetual barrier. The timing was off. She could accept that, but Julie would get better, get married. . . .

After all, it was about Julie that she had first called him. All right, she had wanted to hear his voice, to know when she was going to see him next, but she had needed to talk to him about Julie, his patient. If it weren't for him, she would never have tried to talk to Julie about her father. It went against all her own instincts, the carefully nurtured practice of years. Good years, she had to believe. Safe years. And what had she gotten for her trouble? A slap in the face.

"All right. I'll ask you. What was he like in bed?"

She could still hear the cracked note of bravado in Julie's voice, see the defiant, cold tilt of her head, the dislike. What the hell had Russell been doing to her that she could spit such questions into her mother's face? Margaret stared at the music manuscript, which, because of her personal preoccupations, refused to make any sense. The question itself did not shock her. Under the right circumstances Julie might need to know about Margaret's sexual feelings for Tom Rudzinski in order to comprehend their relationship as a whole. She was even willing to concede that Julie had a right to ask such questions of her—but in that way, that tone? As though accusing Margaret of something ugly and obscene. There was dirt behind her words, a wish to wound, and she had said them at a moment when Margaret felt most vulnerable.

If she had not so recently made love with Russell Dunn, she would have dismissed the insolent, ugly question with a reprimand, but it had taken her breath away, had made her feel . . . guilty. For that she could not forgive him. Because of that she needed his moral support, and he had hidden himself behind Julie's skirts. She had refused to answer Julie's question, had sat in her bedroom trembling, trying to reach him. He had created a gulf between Margaret and her daughter that she still had not bridged. She did not know how to talk to her anymore, was afraid of what she might see on her child's face. And when he had returned her call, she had been unable to tell him.

A colleague opened her office door and said he was leaving: Would Margaret lock up? She closed the score and left the building with him, hoping he would suggest a drink in the corner pub. Instead he grabbed the first taxi, explaining that he and his wife were giving a dinner party and he must dash. Margaret walked alone through the rain, giving way to self-pity. She made herself stand at a bus stop; all the taxis were taken anyway. The longer it took her to get home, the fewer hours there would be to kill, the less time to brood on his perfunctory cruelty, the tensions that now made communication with her daughter impossible.

The phone was ringing as she hauled herself up the steps. Phones always sound more urgent and insistent through a locked door, and Margaret responded with a sense of urgency, juggling with her keys, handbag, and briefcase. At any moment she expected the phone to stop ringing. She dropped the bag and briefcase, left the door open. By the light of the streetlamps she picked up the receiver and pressed it to her ear. She even thought it might be him.

"Yes? Hello?"

"Is this Mrs. Wells? Julie's mother?" The voice was young, male, worried. Margaret did not recognize it. She closed her eyes tightly against the thought that sprang into her mind: Something had happened to Julie.

"Yes. This is she." Her voice was faint, hollow-sounding.

"Oh, I'm so glad . . . I wondered if—"

"Who are you?" she demanded.

"Oh, sorry. Fred Bartlett." He paused. Margaret wanted to scream at him. "We've never met, you don't know me. I'm Barry's roommate. Barry Irving."

"Yes?"

"Look, I'm terribly sorry, Mrs. Wells, but—"

"Julie isn't here," she said, pushing away the moment she feared. "I don't know where she is. I thought—"

"That's all right, I . . . I'd really rather speak to you. You see, the thing is, I'm afraid I've got bad news. Terrible news, actually." She could not speak. She pressed the receiver tighter to her ear. "The fact is, Barry's dead. The police have just been here. An accident. He was killed . . . a car crash . . ."

She heard the young man's voice breaking up. She thought that was only right. The whole world was breaking up around her. No Julie. No Russell. Now definitely no Barry. It did not occur to her to doubt what he said. She did not even know if she asked any questions. The boy kept saying he was sorry and then she was holding a silent receiver, standing in the semidarkness, feeling cold. Barry was dead. It was not possible. Not Barry. Barry? She wished she had been . . . She took the receiver from her ear, looked at it, and put it down. Barry was an excellent driver, first-class. He had never harmed anyone in his entire life, as far as she knew. Not Barry. Barry could not just suddenly be dead. It was ridiculous, and much, much too painful.

She closed the front door, stood blinking in the light that she must have turned on. She began to walk toward the kitchen, stumbled over her bag. She picked it up and hung it over the bannister. Her light coat felt heavy and damp on her shoulders. A drink, she thought. I need a drink. She rummaged among the bottles, unable to recognize them for a moment. She had begun to pour gin with an unsteady hand when the phone rang again.

"Margaret Wells," she said.

There was a sound like a sob, and then a surprisingly calm and definite voice, saying, "Sheila Irving here. I'm so glad I caught you."

"I'm so sorry. . . ."

"You've heard, then."

"Yes . . . just a moment ago. Someone from his flat rang."

"That'd be Fred. He's been marvelous."

"I'm so terribly sorry. . . ."

"I was . . . we were worried about Julie. . . ."

"She's not here. I don't know where she is."

"She doesn't know, then. Not yet."

"No. I don't know."

"She'll take it badly."

"Yes. I . . . don't know what to say."

"It's all right. I've not taken it in yet myself."

229

"Is your husband with you?"

"Oh, yes, he's here. Harold . . ."

A man's voice came on the line. Margaret had difficulty conjuring up a picture of Barry's father.

"I hope Julie will be all right. We're very fond of her, you know."

"Yes. Thank you. I'm so sorry."

"Yes, well, thank you."

"I can't . . ."

"I know, I know."

She felt inadequate. They had lost a son and yet they were comforting her. She finished the awkward conversation somehow and then drank some gin. It tasted brackish. What had she said? How could she tell Julie? What would it do to Julie, this terrible knowledge? How could you rehearse news like that? She looked at the telephone. Russell, of course. He would know how to do it. She would have to swallow her pride and call him. She needed to hear his voice, damn it, the comfort of his voice.

She heard the key in the lock, just as she was moving to the telephone. She went instead to the front door and tried to open it, struggling against the key. Julie stared up at her, pale and tired-looking, with dark rings of exhaustion under her eyes. He, being so much taller, though standing behind and below her, looked straight into Margaret's eyes. She thought, for one dizzying moment, that she saw real tenderness there.

"I brought Julie home," he said.

She stood back and held the door for them. Julie walked past her, silent.

"I must have a word with you," she said, detaining Russell. "Thank God you're here. I was going to call you." She felt close to silly, demeaning tears. Gently he touched her shoulder.

Julie walked past her mother, into the kitchen, where she filled the kettle and put it on the range. She felt dead inside, but the house seemed to be charged with a ghastly kind of life. She could feel it crackling in the atmosphere. Suddenly she was sure that something dreadful was going to happen, was already happening. She saw her mother and Mr. Dunn framed in the doorway like the guilty lovers they were, drawing apart from an embrace. He bent his head toward Margaret's whisper. Julie looked away, shut out. The atmosphere seemed to tighten around her. She smelled something: the sharp reek of petrol mingled with something softer, sweeter, burning. . . . She looked up at the ceiling and knew that he was already upstairs, waiting for her. His voice murmured in the singing of the kettle. The other smell, growing stronger, was blood. She recoiled as from the heat of a great and deadly fire, heard its roar drowning out all other sounds. The petrol smell and the sweeter smell . . .

"Julie . . ."

They were both fussing around her, making her sit down, treating her like a child. It wasn't even a shock when they eventually told her, exchanging looks and nods as though she weren't actually present. It wasn't a shock, not really. Jo-Jo had, in his own way, already told her. Hearing it in their tight, frightened voices lightened the atmosphere a little, that was all.

"I'm so sorry, darling. I thought maybe, later on, if you felt up to it, you might ring the Irvings. They sounded so brave, but . . ."

Tea was placed in front of her. She thought that she would not be getting married now. It was all over. She had wanted coffee. Upstairs she sensed him pacing, waiting for her, waiting to claim her now that no one—she looked, startled, at Russell Dunn—stood between her and Jo-Jo's claim, her promise. Not now that Barry was dead. She didn't feel anything. Except that it was all inevitable now, fixed and unchangeable. And in a terrible way, it was what she had always wanted.

"I'd like to be alone," she heard her own voice saying. Mr. Dunn offered to give her something, but she waved him away. She was perfectly calm. She avoided her mother's solicitous hand as well. She had known, after all, that something like this must happen. She had known from the very beginning. She wanted to get it over with now, face it out.

"Should I . . . ?" Margaret began as Julie went up the stairs with slow, purposeful steps. Russell shook his head.

"Later. I don't think she's begun to take it in yet. It's best to leave her now."

"I can't believe it. He was such a good driver."

"It probably wasn't his fault."

"Is that supposed to be a comfort?"

"No. I'm sorry."

Margaret's nerves were stretched, singing, waiting to hear Julie cry out, break down.

"It was as though she didn't care at all."

"She cares. She was exhausted anyway."

"Why? What's happened?"

"It was a particularly difficult session for her, emotionally. A real breakthrough."

"What about this . . . news on top of . . . ?"

"Curiously enough, I think she'll cope. Perhaps better because of the work we did today."

"I only hope you're right. Oh, why did this have to happen now? Or ever?"

He shook his head, knowing there was no answer.

"Barry . . . dead," she said, as though by repeating it someone might deny it, put the world back on an even keel again.

"I'll stay, if you like."

Margaret looked at him. What had happened to her anger, her resentment? What had happened to the sharpness of her tongue, which normally would have armed her against this vulnerability? She could only shrug, knowing how desperately she wanted him to stay.

"I'm sorry I haven't been able to see you. I felt . . . well, the fact is, Julie knows about us," Russell said.

"How could she know?"

"I wondered if you'd said something. Anyway, today I made it clear . . ."

"I've hardly spoken to her since last Sunday. But why, why did you . . . ?"

"I felt she might be using it in order to end her treatment. I had to bring it out into the open."

"And where does that leave us? 'Just good friends'?"

"No, of course not."

"What about me? What about *my* feelings?"

"I thought you'd understand."

She opened her mouth to say that she did not, why should she, but she closed it again. Now that he was here, she did not want to fight with him. Barry's death seemed to have squeezed everything else into proportion.

"Will she ever approve of us?" Margaret asked him. "Assuming we're going to have some sort of future together?"

"You know that's what I want."

"I hoped . . . no, I don't know." He shook his head at her sadly, as though she had disappointed him. "Well, will she?"

"In time. Or perhaps not. But then it won't really matter what she feels, because she will have taken control of her own life again."

"But without Barry . . . You know, that was my first real thought when I saw her tonight. It was dreadful, shameful, but I felt trapped. I thought, Now she won't be getting married, she won't have a life of her own, and she'll stand between us forever. What's happening to me? How can I resent my own daughter, and now of all times . . . ?"

"No, no," he said. "Come here. Let me hold you. It's shock talking, not you. Just now you don't feel very strong or brave or patient. But you are all those things and soon again you'll know you are. You love Julie. Nothing will ever change that."

She leaned against him, drawing comfort from his warmth and touch. It was he who threw her off balance. For all his cleverness, she thought, he doesn't really understand that. It is he who makes me see Julie differently. For eighteen years Margaret had wanted nothing for herself, had not allowed herself to wish or dream. And now all that was changed. She had to get used to wanting so strongly. . . . She pushed him gently away.

"I think I'd like to go up and see how she is," she said. He nodded.

"I'll wait," he said.

"I feel like I'm on trial," Julie grumbled, a break sounding treacherously in her voice.

"Don't be silly, darling."

"Don't. Don't say that." She brought her two small, clenched fists down on the back of the settee in a tense, angry gesture. "That's what I mean . . . partly what I mean," she said with difficulty, forcing her voice to be steady. "I am not a child. I am not 'silly' just because I say something you don't immediately approve of."

Margaret stared at her, at her flushed, almost feverish-looking face, the angular tension of her body as she remained leaning against the back of the couch.

"I'm sorry," said Margaret. "The habits of a lifetime . . ." She walked toward the liquor table. "Perhaps today isn't a good time. . . ."

Barry had been cremated that morning. By now, she assumed, his ashes would have been scattered on the moors near his home. Julie had not wanted to go, and Margaret, embarrassed, had not dared to leave her. The Irvings, numbed, unreachable in their own grief, had seemed to understand. She feared that later they would resent their absence. She planned to write to them. . . . If only Julie would grieve, let it out. Instead she seemed preoccupied. Any attempt to reach her was treated as an intrusion, and brought forth anger that Margaret now found more tiring than stinging. She reached for the whiskey bottle.

"Don't you think you're drinking too much?"

"What if I am?" she retorted. "All right. I'm sorry. Again." She turned her back on the table. "I didn't ask you down here to fight with you. Or to shout at you . . ."

"Patronize . . ."

"Or to patronize you," Margaret added, though the charge seemed unjust. "I thought it was time you talked about Barry. Now seemed the right time. I know you must be grieving. It would help me, too. . . ." Julie would not look at her. "But, of course, if you really don't want—"

"I do. But you won't let me do it in my own way. You won't believe me or listen to me. You just say, 'Don't be silly, darling.'" Her imitation of Margaret's voice and tone was exaggerated and cruel. For a moment they faced each other, Margaret's eyes glowing dangerously, Julie's expression set in a stubborn refusal to back down or apologize. It was Margaret who turned away.

"I'm going to have that drink anyway." Her restricted movements were made clumsier by Julie's silent disapproval. She dropped the top of the whiskey bottle, clattered it against the glass.

"Here, let me," Julie said impatiently, moving toward her.

"And don't you patronize me, either," Margaret said, her voice deadly.

"Sorry." Julie retreated.

Her drink poured, Margaret walked to her special chair. "I think we'd better start over," she said. "Will you give me another chance?"

"Yes. Of course." Julie sounded tired, like one who knew she had reached the limits of her energy.

"I know . . ." Margaret began, but suddenly every statement sounded like an assertion; the simplest words were fraught with dangerous meaning. "I think I can imagine something of what you must be going through." Julie shook her head in denial, her hair swinging. It was a movement born of impatience and weariness. "Then try to tell me," Margaret pleaded. "If you can. If you want."

"The worst thing about . . . Barry's death is . . . the waste. It was so unnecessary. And I blame myself. I knew . . . I've known all along that something like this would happen. I should have been . . . I don't know . . . stronger, braver. I should have listened to what I knew." She thumped her chest with her fist and looked up at Margaret, her face distraught.

"I don't understand," was all Margaret felt she could risk saying.

"No. No, I know you don't. And if I tell you, you'll . . ." She gestured imprecisely, indicating her hopelessness.

"You said you'd give me another chance."

"It's not your fault. I do know that."

"Please . . ."

"It wasn't an accident. Not really. Not at bottom. Jo-Jo killed him. I know that. I've always known that he would. I could have prevented it, but I . . . I thought I could beat him with Mr. Dunn's help. I never wanted anything bad to happen to Barry. . . . That time he fell down the stairs and hurt his ankle . . . and that burn . . . I knew it. Damn it, I *saw* . . . but I did nothing. And now he's dead and I don't know where it will end. Sometimes I think it's all over now. Everything's finished. . . ."

Margaret sat very still, silent. Julie's hopelessness seemed to fill the room like an infectious, seeping mist.

"You see?" Julie resumed, a hint of challenge in her voice. "You can't say anything if you don't contradict me. There's nothing you can say, except that you think I'm crazy."

Margaret ignored this, and reached for the only straw she could see.

"Have you told Russell this? What does he say?"

"You know I haven't seen him. Anyway, he'd only say, 'I believe you, Julie,' or 'Why do you think that is, Julie?' or some other bland prod to make me go on and on. . . ."

"Well, how *can* it be, Julie? For God's sake . . . it stands to reason . . . Help us, Julie. Help *me* to understand."

"You see? There you go again. You can't understand. I can't make you understand. So there's no point in discussing it."

"I'll try. Truly I will. I want to believe you."

"If we go on like this, I'll just end up feeling mad again, and I know I'm not. I know that now," she said, dropping her voice to a private whisper. "And then I'll end up feeling even more guilty. You always make me feel guilty."

"I? Oh, no, no, Julie, that's not fair."

"All my life. Ask Russell, as you so intimately call him. He'll tell you. All my life I've felt guilty about your accident. All my life I've known, deep down, that it was my fault. My pact with the devil, I suppose you'd call it."

"He said this?" Margaret asked, unable to believe that such a betrayal was possible. How many times had he told her she was a good mother—loving, caring? "He told you that I . . . ?"

"Not in so many words," Julie said, weary again. "But I know how it works now, psychotherapy, analysis . . . I can make the connections myself. I don't know what good it does me. It changes nothing, Ma. None of it makes me free of him, even for a moment."

"You blame me," Margaret said, bewildered, hurt.

"No. Yes. I blame you for not telling me that was my father . . . the man who came to the house that day, the man who wanted to take me away, who said I was mad. The one who scared Great-Gran so that she made me . . . made me send Jo-Jo away, made me promise . . . so that you had your accident. . . ."

"Stop. Wait . . . I don't understand. I didn't tell you because, darling, you were ill, feverish afterwards. Nobody understood why. . . . We thought—the doctor said—you'd been frightened into a state of shock. Our only concern was to make you well again. As you got better, we were afraid to tell you anything. We hoped you'd forgotten. The doctor said that was likely. We didn't want to remind you, we just wanted you to be happy, safe. . . . Oh, God, I can hear how pathetic that sounds. . . ."

"No . . . no . . . only maybe, if you had told me . . . maybe it wouldn't have gone on festering away inside me until . . . until I can't control it any longer."

"Julie, listen to me." Margaret leaned forward in her chair, her mind focused now, her tone firm, decisive. "Whatever you think, you did not cause my 'accident.' It had nothing whatever to do with you."

"You don't know. Jo-Jo cut off his finger—"

"Your father did it. It wasn't an accident. He wanted to hurt me, not because of you, not just because of you—"

"There, you see?"

"I'm not telling it right. It's not like that—"

"It's too late."

"I want to tell you about it. I want to tell you about him. I'll tell you anything, even that he was good in bed, if that really matters to you—"

"As good as Russell, would you say?"

Margaret could hear the words echoing, bouncing, amplified in the cage of the room, but she was unable to absorb them. She could not breathe.

"Don't look at me like that," Julie said calmly. "Jo-Jo told me. I didn't want to believe him. I thought it was just one of his nasty ideas. But then I saw your room . . . after, that Sunday. I don't know why it matters. It shouldn't. It just makes me feel—"

"He said it might hurt you. We were both afraid of that. It should never have happened. Apart from anything else, it was completely unethical on his part. It's just that Russell cared too much about you to send you off to another doctor once he realized how he felt about me. I know I was also wrong. But I never *planned* for this to happen. I want you to believe that."

"It doesn't matter," Julie said wearily. "I know you can sleep with anyone you want. You both can, as far as I'm concerned."

"It won't happen again. I give you my word. And when you see Russell, I'm sure he'll—"

"I'm not going to see him again. He can't help me anymore. I'm on my own now. I have to help myself. And you, you must do whatever you want. I don't want to feel that I've messed up another relationship for you."

"That's nonsense. And I don't care if it does sound patronizing. Julie, you can blame me all you like for the things I've really done, but I won't have you torturing yourself with something that is untrue. I left your father before you were born. I kept you from him because he was mad, a drug addict. I did not behave well with him, Russell has made me see that now. But what happened to my arm . . . that was entirely between us."

"You should have had an abortion!" Julie yelled.

"And I wish to God he'd killed me, not just maimed me. And

where the hell does that leave either of us?" Margaret shouted back. Julie turned her head away. "You want to grow up? Oh, yes, Julie, it's time you did." She stood up and went to her little desk. She opened the main drawer and rummaged awkwardly at the back of it, seeking a little knob that released a secret spring. "He killed himself, you know. Perhaps because of what he'd done to me. Perhaps through an accidental overdose. If you're going to blame anybody, blame him or me. . . . Ah," she said as the spring clicked and a small drawer, disguised as part of the solid molding of the desk, slid open.

"What are you doing?" Julie asked, twisting her head to look at her.

"I want to show you something. I want you to know the whole story."

"Did he really kill himself?"

Margaret nodded. From beneath a pile of papers she took a faded newspaper clipping and an old but still clear photograph.

"And it really wasn't an accident, your arm?"

"No. He did it. To punish me. To stop me from playing. Oh, I don't know why he did it, really. Probably he didn't know either. He was mad—"

"But did you love him?" Julie said, cutting across Margaret's fumbling search for the right words. She looked at Julie, whose face blazed with the need to know, to understand, and for a moment, Margaret despised herself for the readiness with which the familiar lies came to her lips.

"Yes," she said, sounding defeated, almost ashamed. She lowered her head, avoiding Julie's gaze.

"But that's good, that's—"

"No. He was a . . . monster. I know that. I knew that much sooner than I've ever admitted it, even to myself. In a way I can't explain, I never really let him go. I couldn't. God knows I had enough chances, every reason. He was violent, obsessive . . . but I didn't let him go. Not until that night, the night of the 'accident,'" she said bitterly, her voice breaking on the all-too-familiar word.

"Why, Ma?" Julie asked gently. "Please . . ."

Margaret shook her head as though to dismiss the question. "I suppose because . . . the very things I hated and despised about him also . . . in some obscene way you couldn't possibly under-

238

stand . . . attracted me, excited me. That's why I never told you about him," she said, facing Julie again. "Because I was . . . I am . . . ashamed of my own . . . passion. I don't know what the word is, for being so weak, so enthralled. You couldn't understand. I don't want you to. It was like a virus. . . ."

"But I do understand, Ma. I know exactly—"

"No!" Margaret shouted, walking quickly across the room. "You could not possibly know. Don't ever say that. Look!" Margaret stood over her, and let the clipping fall, fluttering, into Julie's lap. "That's the report I read in hospital, after he'd attacked me."

Julie picked up the delicate scrap of paper and began to read. Margaret looked at the photograph she held. It showed Tom Rudzinski at his best, as she had first known and loved him. On the steps of the Conservatory, leaning insouciantly against the balustrade. His thick black curls caught the light. Painfully she recalled how they had always had a glossy, bluish tinge in bright light. His handsome, undeniably handsome face was open and laughing. He looked proud and young and full of possibilities. For a moment her body ached, stirred, then her mind showed her the sunken, pallid mask that face eventually became, how it had been the last time she had seen him.

"What's that?" Julie asked, breaking into her thoughts.

"A photograph of him. Look at it. That's your father. Then I'll tell you the whole story, so that . . . at least the slate will be clean between us."

Julie reached up and took the photograph from Margaret's fingers, turned it around, looked at it. Margaret drew a deep breath and went back to her seat, trying to marshal her thoughts.

"Where did you get this?" Julie's voice was steely, her face sickly white.

"I've always had it. I took it, my first year at the Conservatory. What on earth's the matter with you?"

"You liar!" Julie shouted. She jumped up, flinging the photograph from her as though it had burned her. Margaret stared, openmouthed, saw the photograph fall face-downward on the carpet. "What are you trying to do to me?" Julie screamed, her voice terrible.

"I just wanted you to—"

"That's not my father!"

"Julie—"

"That's *Jo-Jo!* You must know . . . For God's sake, mother, what are you trying to do to me?"

She watched him grow and flow in a corner of her room, his flesh white, incandescent, the black of his hair pitiless and dreadful. He came toward her, opening his arms, opening, opening them until they seemed to embrace the whole room and she felt herself slipping away, down, down, into the vortex they enclosed. She put up her arms to ward him off. His hand touched her forearm, feeling like slime, making her recoil.

Ju-lie?

"I want . . ." She was seeing him anew, with a kind of double vision. The words stuck in her throat. His troubled, puzzled expression hung before her. She felt the impatience of his body like an electric charge, even though they did not touch. "Who are you, Jo-Jo?"

Your friend. You know. And your lover. There's nothing to stop us now, Ju-lie. You promised. . . .

His voice curled and hissed like a vapor in her ears, her mind. She forced herself to resist its honey, its oil.

"You mean because Barry's dead."

He doesn't matter. He never mattered. You promised me. You belong to me. I've waited too long . . . Ju-lie. . . .

"I know, Jo-Jo, I know." She spoke to distract him, tried to step around him. He blocked her way. The room seemed very small, claustrophobic. "Who are you, Jo-Jo? Tell me who you really are."

Your friend, Ju-lie. Your best friend ever. You belong to me. He reached for her again, his hand grazing her flesh.

"Not my father?" The word seemed to rake the flesh in her throat. She watched him intently, saw his fixed, yearning expression waver. He no longer looked kind, puzzled. She sensed another person, another creature, behind the mask of his face. Something in his eyes . . . His teeth bared in something no longer a smile.

Time, Ju-lie . . . time to keep your promise . . .

"Answer me first."

Your friend and lover. You belong to me. Nothing in the way now. Remember?

He held out his left hand with his strong fingers pointing at her. She felt sick with guilt and pity and fear. It couldn't be. It could not be. *He had all five fingers.*

"Julie? Julie?" Her mother's sharp tapping at the door broke the spell of his pointing fingers, her weakness. Julie saw his face melt and re-form, pass through shifts of intense emotion. Then he turned slowly, purposefully toward the door. She saw him ugly, evil. A light in his dark, sad eyes, making them no longer beautiful. She saw the length and sharpness of his cruel teeth.

No one in the way . . .

He moved toward the door, his arm outstretched. Julie flung her arms around him, startling him. She held him from behind, her arms encircling him, her body pressed fast but trembling against his. She moved her hands deliberately, attentively.

"Julie?"

"I'm all right, Ma. Really. I just want to be left alone."

Julie felt his body clench. She felt his anger, sulfurous and bitter. She held him tighter, moved her hands down his body, down. He sighed. She felt him turn, breaking the circle of her arms. She wanted to call out, to scream. The space between herself and the door lengthened into an endless corridor, stretching away from her, the door progressively shrinking and then vanishing. There was only Jo-Jo, filling all the space, stifling her.

"This is Russell Dunn. I'm sorry, but I can't take your calls just now. Please leave your name and number and I will get back to you as soon as possible. Please speak clearly, after the tone. Thank you." There was a click, then, instead of the expected high-pitched signal, his voice spoke again. "Since I am broadcasting tonight, it is unlikely that I will be able to return your calls until tomorrow. Please leave your message now."

Margaret gulped back tears of frustration and slammed the receiver back into its cradle. She ran back up the stairs. There was a portable radio in her room. What good would that do? part of her mind mocked her. She stopped on the landing, looked uneasily at Julie's locked door. She knew it was pointless to knock again, to call. . . . She went into her own room and switched on the radio. When she had tuned it, Bernice O'Hara's voice sounded, then his, prattling about his new, additional program, scheduled to start next month. Margaret half-heard him mouthing platitudes about women who needed help, who were alone in the house all day, often with small children.

"*I* bloody need help," she said aloud, "now." She killed his voice with a flick of the switch. Think, Margaret, *think*, she told herself. The office number, of course. Citycomm must have another number. She could reach him that way. Then, downstairs, striking fear into her, she heard a sound. She ran out onto the landing. Julie's door stood open and she knew that she had heard the front door close gently but with absolute finality.

Margaret had taken a cab to Citycomm, where she now spoke to a security guard who reluctantly put aside the girlie magazine he was studying intently. He telephoned through to the studio, sucking air through his teeth, his eyes fixed on the open magazine.

"He'll be down in a minute, if you want to wait," he said offhandedly, not looking at her.

"Thank you."

She huddled in the doorway, feeling a chill that was belied by the warm night. She ought to go back. Julie might have returned. Margaret had run out into the square, looking for her, but there was no sign. She had just kept on running until, breathless, she saw the cab coming and hailed it. What could Russell do, anyway? Julie would have gone for a walk, to cool off. She would return to the empty house, needing her mother. . . . Suddenly Margaret realized she was afraid to go back into the house alone, afraid of what she might find there. She had seen Tom's sunken, haggard, crazed face superimposed on his young and better self, had touched for a moment the horror of that night. She had never allowed herself to relive it, to come fully to terms with it. What had Julie said about Jo-Jo cutting his finger off? Madness. Her daughter was mad, she needed help. . . .

Her body stiffened. She felt a new kind of cold, as though the lifeblood were draining out of her. For the first time it had occurred to her that Julie might do something to harm herself. . . .

"Margaret? Margaret, what on earth?"

He loomed over her, holding her, became for a moment a part of her terror. Then she recognized him and clung to him, grateful for his height and solidity, the special smell of him so quickly learned, so intensely recalled. God, how she wanted him, wanted to be with him, even now.

"Julie," she said, shame blotting out her involuntary thoughts. "She's gone, run off. I had to find you. Oh, please, you must help me. Come with me."

He sorted out her babble. His simple presence calmed her, enabled her to be coherent.

"Julie is not the least bit suicidal. You must believe that. I know." He turned away from her. She thought he was dismissing her. She grabbed at him. "It's all right," he said. She saw that he was unlocking the door of his car. He opened it for her. Shaking, feeling utterly foolish, she got in. He forbade her to talk any more about it. She wept quietly with relief and anxiety as he drove. She even heard a little of what he said.

"You see?" he said as he parked the car in a corner of Broom Square, "you feel better already. Didn't I tell you you would?"

She nodded and tried to smile, but a fresh flood of anxiety prevented her.

"Would you . . . I'm afraid to go in." She held out her keys to him. He took them from her, then took her arm firmly.

"We'll go in together. There's nothing to be afraid of, you'll see."

"If anything has happened to her . . ."

"Nothing has happened to her," he said as he ushered her inside. "I'll check her room, just in case."

"She isn't there. I know it."

"Come." He held her hand, led her up the stairs.

Her door was open. Margaret gripped his hand in alarm.

"Julie? May we come in? Julie?"

She broke free of him, ran into the empty room. Russell pressed the light switch, flooding the room with light. The light hurt her because it made the room's emptiness absolute. She turned to him with a little cry, a scream brimming inside her.

"Look in your room. I'll check downstairs."

His voice, his calm worked on her again. She heard him running down the stairs calling Julie's name. The comforting sound of him faded, grew faint, leaving her empty. Her own door stood open and she pushed it wider. She had not drawn the curtains, and the soft glow of the streetlamps filled the room with shadows—huddled, rustling human shadows.

"Julie? Darling?"

She went in and turned on the light.

"Margaret?"

"Yes?"

"How do I get into the basement? It seems to be locked."

"I locked it, after Miss Tidy . . . She wouldn't be in there." She hurried down the stairs to meet him.

"Where's the key?"

"In the kitchen."

She did not want to go into Elinor Tidy's flat. She still thought of it as belonging to the housekeeper. She saw her suddenly, imagined her slumped awkwardly on the stairs. . . . He came up again, shaking his head.

"She's not here. Definitely." He looked at her sharply. "You did look in your room?"

"Yes, of course. She's not there."

"Come on, you need a drink."

"Where can she be?"

"You must think calmly. Where would she go? Friends? Barry's flat, perhaps? Don't try to rush it. Try to relax. Think calmly." He propelled her into the sitting room, and went to fix her a drink.

"What if she . . . ?"

"Why should you think that? Why should she?"

"We must ring the police."

"Not until we are certain *we* can't find her."

"But that might be too late."

He put a glass in her hand, and said, "Julie is not suicidal. She will not harm herself. Why can't you believe that? I am trained in these things. I would know. Besides, she is her mother's daughter."

"You're not God!" Margaret shouted at him.

"No," he said, "but neither are you, to decide her fate on no evidence. Now drink that and start thinking. Where would she go?" He walked around the settee where Julie had been sitting earlier, and bent to pick up something from the floor.

"Is this it?" he asked. Margaret could only glance at the photograph. It seemed horrible to her now, frightening. She nodded. He held it at arm's length, studying it, then brought it closer, peering at it. "Jo-Jo?" he said, as though talking to it, as though expecting it to answer or make some visible sign. Margaret felt sick, and watched with a kind of fascinated dread. He said it again, softly, but without the questioning inflection. "Jo-Jo."

Eleven

"So sorry to have disturbed you, Angela. Yes, yes . . . if you would. No, no, I'll be all right. Thank you so much, Angela."

Margaret sat at her desk, staring at the exhausted telephone. She had lost count of how many calls she had made, and still there was no breath of news of Julie. Nothing. Of course, the phone had been tied up so long that Julie would not have been able to get through even if she had wanted to. It was a no-win situation, Margaret thought.

"I can't think of anyone else," she said, and closed her address book, pushing it away from her.

He was stretched out on the sofa, his legs hanging over one arm. He did not answer. Margaret looked at him incredulously.

"Are you asleep?" she demanded, going to him. She bent to shake his shoulder. He caught her hand.

"No. Just thinking. Come here." He pulled on her hand. She snatched it away impatiently.

"Russell, for God's sake!" She walked up and down. "Did you hear me? There's nobody left to call. What do we do now? The police?"

He sat up slowly, stretching.

"I suppose we could report her missing, but what can they do? She's of age."

246

"You could tell them she's not well, she doesn't know what she's doing."

"But I think she does, and anyway, between us, we *know* where she is."

"You're mad. Completely mad." Margaret walked quickly to the telephone.

"Listen. She's gone because of Jo-Jo. I'm sure of that. She knows, now, who Jo-Jo really is. She knows he's dangerous. I don't think she's run away at all."

"If you're trying to tell me there really *is* a Jo-Jo, I don't want to hear it." Margaret lifted the receiver.

"Yes. And I think she's gone somewhere to protect us, to throw Jo-Jo off the scent. Now, where would she go to be with Jo-Jo? Somewhere safe. You must know, Margaret. *Think.*"

Slowly she put the receiver down again.

"You're the expert on Jo-Jo. How should I know? As far as I'm concerned, he's just a fantasy, an imaginary friend she used to play with in the garden. She always used to say, when we walked around the garden together, 'That's where Jo-Jo did so-and-so. . . .' What's the matter with you?"

He was stuttering with excitement, unable to get the words out.

"Don't . . . don't you see? That's it. The garden. Your grand-mother's house. Does it still exist?"

"Of course."

"Where?"

"We've never done anything with it. . . ."

"You mean you still . . . own it?"

"Julie does. Now. Russell, what has all this got to—?"

"Tell me, quickly. It's important."

Margaret sighed, rolled her eyes.

"Grandma left the house to me, in trust for Julie. When she came of age, it went to her."

"Do you use it? Is it occupied?"

She shook her head. "At first, when Grandma was still alive. Afterwards, Julie seemed to grow out of it. Frankly, it's something of a white elephant. I tried to rent it out a few times, but it's not really suitable. The last people left it in such a state that I swore never again . . . I just couldn't face the bother of it. So it's just sitting there. I advised Julie to sell it, but . . ." She shrugged. "Barry was supposed to be looking into it, advising her, but I don't think they ever decided anything."

"Where is it?"

"You don't seriously expect me to believe—?"

"I'm going there. Tell me where it is, quickly."

"Stoketon Claverley. It's straight up the A-1."

"You must come with me. You can direct me—"

"Don't be ridiculous. How could she get there, even if she—?"

"There must be transport. She can drive."

"Why should she—?"

"I've told you. I'll tell you again as we go." He started for the door.

"*I'm* going to ring the police."

"You're only wasting time."

"You're not doing anything," she accused.

"Look . . . I *know* she's there. It's so obvious. I should have thought . . . Margaret, trust me, believe me. I'll make you understand, I promise, only we have to hurry. I think she may be in danger."

In one terrible sense, Margaret had been waiting to hear this, to have her own certainty confirmed. She felt cold, hunched over as though to make herself small—small enough to hide from this knowledge.

"Wait. Just wait there." He ran out of the room, down the stairs. She heard him open the front door. She shouted, tried to call him back, then went to the telephone, knowing she should call the police, not knowing whether she should. The front door slammed, his feet pounded the stairs. He ran back into the room, carrying a fluttering sheet of white paper.

"Come here. Quickly." He picked up the photograph of Tom Rudzinski and laid it beside the piece of paper on the coffee table. Slowly, as though mesmerized, Margaret went to him. He took her arm, squeezed it tight. "Look. Here's my evidence, okay? That's the picture of Rudzinski, the one you showed her, right? And this . . ." Still holding her, he flipped the white sheet over. "This is the drawing Julie made that day at the clinic, the day you got back from Venice." Roughly, he pulled her a little closer to the table and she looked down at the two images, side by side. . . .

Julie was no artist; she had never shown any exceptional skill with pencil or brush, but she had had that facility with line, that instinctive eye for the telling stroke, the particular, that so many children have and lose. The crude drawing, at first glance, could easily be dismissed as a child's flat representation of the human face, but if studied, and especially in juxtaposition with the photograph, it became a likeness. It was not Tom that stared up at her, but unmistakably the child he must have been.

Margaret swayed, closed her eyes, leaning weakly against him. "How—?"

"I don't know. But you see now? We must take these with us." He released her, picked up the pictures. "Will you need a map? You can navigate. You'll need a coat. Hurry, Margaret, please."

It was easier to obey him than to argue.

The furniture loomed in ghostly shapes, dust-sheeted. Someone had rolled up the carpet. Thick dust now carpeted the floor. A broken windowpane showed a jagged shape against the close darkness of the shrubbery pressing outside. The piano looked like a crouching animal. There was no sign of the faded but beautiful shawl. She lifted one corner of the dust sheet and threw it back, uncovering the instrument. A cloud of dust rose, something small and scared scuttled away. The wood was still silky under her fingers, the lid locked fast.

Into the hall and up the stairs, her footfalls sounding hollow, puffing up little spurts of dust. Past bedroom doors scarcely remembered, a separate domain from that of the child. The old baize door into the nursery wing. It squeaked now on its sprung hinges, resisted, plopped back into its frame as though tired, where once it had swung and swung and swung. The bathroom. Nanny's pantry, stripped now of its sink and stove. Bare boards stained with the damp spillage of years. Nanny's room, chaste and forbidden, the sanctum sanctorum. For a moment, standing there, she caught the whisper of remembered voices: Nanny and Margery gossiping over mugs of hot cocoa. The back stairs. The nursery. The cotlike bed, dismantled and stacked. The little desk with the fixed seat, pushed into a corner. The fire-guard, still clipped safely over the grate with its tiles of forget-me-nots. Boxes of books piled in the middle of the room. Scraping her toe through the accretion of dust, she exposed a patch of the familiar marbled linoleum. It was so easy to keep

249

clean. "Little girls are such messy creatures. Nanny can't forever be mopping up after you, miss." No, Nanny. Yes, Nanny. Three bags full, Nanny. The window uncurtained, fastened shut. The garden a jungle now, a mesh of black, twisted shapes, curled in darkness. The pale moon of her own face reflected in the glass, against the night garden.

She knew now why she had never been able to give herself to him. That had been the obvious solution all along. Even before Mr. Dunn had spelled it out, she had wanted to. But she could not. She had known by the smell of him that something was wrong. Worse than wrong, much worse. She brought her face to her own reflection, felt the grittiness of dirt and the coldness of glass against her forehead. She knew now what Jo-Jo had become, how he had been used, perverted, resurrected to haunt her for an obscene and terrible purpose. Oh, yes, she belonged to him. Jo-Jo, before he had grown into evil, had always known that. It was the simple truth. He would not rest until he had her—*could* not, perhaps—and she almost felt a kind of pity for him. For the creature who had maimed her mother. She hardened her heart. Who had somehow frightened Miss Tidy and cajoled Barry into premature graves, who would stop at nothing until he had claimed what was his. Funny, she could weep for them now, for Miss Tidy and Barry, weep slow, consoling tears. Weep for herself, for the inevitability of it. Like a doomed bride she watched her tears drop, puffing in the black dust on the white windowsill. She let them fall, feeling that she needed them. Her life had almost begun in this room. She felt now that it would probably end there. But not quietly, not in submission. This thought stemmed her tears. She wiped them with dirty fingers, leaving black smudges on her cheeks. She pulled away from the window, sighed. She was ready. It was only a matter of time now.

She watched her reflection reappear in the black window, waver, seem to glow. Catching her breath, she looked behind her, but saw only the trail of her own footprints across the dusty floor, the scuffed place where she had paused to uncover a patch of the linoleum. She turned again to the window and saw, through the tangle of the black garden, the unmistakable yellow glow of a bonfire. Her heart began to hammer. The flames rose, settled, beckoned. She saw a rain of red sparks dying, then turned away from the window and walked slowly toward the back stairs.

"Exorcism?" Margaret laughed. "Now I *know* you're mad. I suppose years of treating the insane . . . it's bound to get to you in the end."

"Don't be cheap, Margaret," he flared. "It doesn't suit you. And never, ever about my patients."

She turned her hot face away, ashamed of herself. The open map crackled on her lap. Road signs, hedges, an occasional unlit house flashed by, fell behind. Ahead, the car's lights illuminated the road. It seemed to her that the road was alive, drawing them on, not that the car was traveling it.

"It doesn't matter what you think or choose to believe," he resumed, his voice quiet and steady again. "It's what Julie believes that matters. And we—or at any rate I—have to react to those beliefs as concrete facts. She believes in Jo-Jo. Therefore Jo-Jo exists. Jo-Jo has a physical presence in her eyes and an avowed purpose: to sleep with her. To possess her, I suppose. Perhaps the whole thing is a metaphor."

"Don't make it any more complicated," Margaret said.

"I'm sorry I shouted at you."

"I deserved it." She touched his forearm gently. He took his left hand from the steering wheel and held her hand for a moment, pressing it. "I'm afraid," she said.

"You're strong and brave. Remember that."

"You make me less so. I rely on you."

It was his turn to laugh.

"Like hell you do. You fight me every inch of the way. Which is one reason I love you. I should have told you; I always see a relationship as a battle."

Margaret smiled. "Come wrestle me and be my love?" she teased. "Original, anyway."

"Something like that. But you're strong enough for that, too."

"Go on," she said, "you're straying from the point."

"Where was I?"

"Something about metaphor."

"Oh, yes. Forget that. An aside. Jo-Jo is. Jo-Jo wants to possess her. . . ."

"It's such a damn silly name," Margaret burst out. "If only he'd been called . . . I don't know . . ."

"Tom?" he suggested, watching from the corner of his eye. She flinched.

"I wouldn't put it past him," she said, low and bitter. "Perhaps that's what I was always afraid of, instinctively, knowing him."

"What?"

"Incest. That is what we're talking about, isn't it?"

"If you like. Or an extraordinarily obsessive Elektra complex. You takes your pick. . . ."

"Don't. It's not funny."

"It's just nomenclature, playing with words. What I'm trying to say to you is that explanations don't matter."

"I can't accept that. Maybe I'm just stubborn, but I can't get away from the fact that Tom is dead. She never knew him. Why, of all the people in the world, should she choose him?"

"Try it the other way around. Who in the world would have more reason to choose her?"

"If he were in the world . . ."

"Wait. You said . . . you said something about him and passion, that he inspired it . . . something like that. The man you described to me was obsessive—maniacally so, possibly. Fixated. You can see for yourself how such a man would react when he discovered he had a child, that that child had been kept from him, was ignorant of his very existence. . . ."

"I did see for myself. He damn near killed me."

"I have a friend," he went on, slowing as they approached a roundabout, ignoring her hurt outburst, "a psychic, a man who is regarded as eminent in his field. That's beside the point. Anyway, he's a man who believes absolutely in all that you find irrational mumbo-jumbo."

"You mean you believe it?" Margaret asked, looking at the strong silhouette of his head against the passing grassy mound of the roundabout. The car swung left, straightened again.

"After years in practice I've learned never to be surprised by the human mind. I've learned to keep an open mind myself. Damn it, I've had to. Anyway, my friend would say that a man such as you describe Tom Rudzinski to have been, would be bound—would be *certain*—to come back." Margaret snorted in disbelief, dismissing the idea. "No, hang on, please. Not in any corporeal form, but through the sheer force of his emotions, his obsessions, his passion, his anger, his frustration. . . . God, can't you just imagine how such a man might feel? Like a bomb . . . a . . . I don't know . . . a capped well . . ."

"You almost sound as though you admire him."

"I pity him. As you do, my love."

"I still don't see—"

"Sometimes, when I'm working hard and well and closely with a particularly disturbed client, I find it hard to believe that all that emotion can just disappear. That, anyway, is what my friend would say about Tom."

"You said not physical, not corporeal . . . but you say that Julie . . ."

"Perhaps Julie gave him shape. Perhaps when she felt the force of all that emotion, she gave it a form, and the form her unconscious mind offered her was that of her father, the bogeyman of her childhood, who frightened her so much. She never dealt with that fear, you know. It's been locked up inside her—"

"She could only have seen him for a minute," Margaret protested.

"That's what skeptics say when people claim to have fallen in love at first sight."

"Then I'm glad I'm a skeptic."

"But you wouldn't deny the fact of love. How it comes about, when and how long it takes, remains one of the great mysteries. Personally, I think it always will be, precisely because the explanation is less important than the fact."

He rested his case. Margaret was silent. She consulted the map.

"The turnoff is about another ten miles, I'd guess."

"Fine."

"But you can't explain—nor, I bet, can your 'psychic' friend—how Jo-Jo came to have such a resemblance to Tom *before* Julie had even glimpsed him."

"Oh, yes I can. Easily," he said, letting a note of smugness creep into his voice. "Julie made the drawing long after she'd seen Tom and the returned, grown-up Jo-Jo. She drew—no doubt quite unconsciously—what she imagined the adult Jo-Jo would have looked like as a boy, because she thought herself a child at the time. I would be prepared to bet that if we could find a contemporary drawing of Jo-Jo, he would look completely different. Did she make any, do you know?"

253

"I've no idea. You really do have an answer for everything, don't you?"

"No. A few. Mostly hypotheses. Though I would stake my reputation on that last one. It's a fairly common phenomenon in acute cases of regression. The two worlds get muddled, as it were. A sort of mental trick photography, double exposure, whatever they call it."

Margaret watched for the turnoff sign. The closer they came, the greater was her sense of dread. That mattered more than the half-answered questions, the explanations that buzzed in her head. In a sense he was right. Her fear—for Julie, of the whole situation—was more important than any rationale.

"So what are we going to do," she asked, "when we get there?"

"Whatever is necessary," he said, changing lanes, anticipating the sign. "You see, I don't really have any answers at all. In my job you simply have to react to the situation, to whatever terror is offered you."

The gate, green now with moss and neglect, hung lopsided from broken hinges. Russell got out of the car, tried to lift it free of the gravel. It creaked, cracked, swung, and settled. He got back into the car, wiped his hands on a rag.

"What's wrong?"

"Gate's stuck. We'd better park here." He backed the car, turned it, and eased it up onto the damp grass verge beside the garden hedge. Margaret sat still, unwilling to leave the sudden safety of the car. Russell handed her a blanket. "Here, take this. It might be cold." He carried his briefcase and a large, powerful flashlight.

"You think of everything, don't you?" Margaret said, unclipping her seatbelt.

"I was not a Boy Scout for nothing. You all right?"

"Of course." She opened the door and climbed out. The air was cold and damp, ripe with the smell of old vegetation, a hint of woodsmoke. He played the flashlight beam over her, startling her. She followed him through the gate. The beam showed the weeds and moss growing through the gravel. They followed the dense, dark curve of the shrubbery. Ahead of them the house rose, bulky, square. Julie would be wise to sell it, he thought. It must be worth a small fortune. And for other, more important reasons. Margaret shivered beside him.

254

"Are you sure you're all right?"

"Yes. It's just so strange, coming back here like this. I haven't prepared for it as one normally would. For me it was always a happy house, a refuge." She walked ahead of him to show that she was not afraid, but stopped suddenly. He caught up with her, shone the beam ahead. The heavy door was ajar. Margaret felt the big, solid key in her pocket.

"You see?" he said. "Come on."

The door opened easily, silently. He shone the light around the big, chilly hall, up the stairs.

"Julie? Julie?" Her voice echoed, faded, seemed scarcely to dent the silence.

"Gently," he told her. "We'll find her. We mustn't startle her."

Margaret moved away from him, felt along the wall. A light switch clicked, but no light came on. She swore.

"Look," he said, holding the beam steady on the newly disturbed dust. It showed a clear path of footprints into the sitting room and another coming out, leading to the stairs. Margaret pushed him forward. The piano gleamed blackly at them, reflecting the light, which was otherwise absorbed by the shadowy, shrouded furniture. "Yours?" he asked. Margaret nodded, her throat tight. She started toward the stairs. "Wait. Just a moment." He put down his briefcase, squatted over it. "Hold this for me, please." She took the flashlight and held it. The locks on the briefcase snapped open with the force of rifle shots. He took out the drawing and the photograph and slipped them into his jacket pocket.

"What do you want those for?" Margaret said.

Russell paused, realizing that he had acted blindly, on instinct.

"I don't know. Maybe I don't . . . I just thought . . ." But he had not *thought*, only reacted. He did not know what to tell her. He stood the briefcase against the wall. "Come on. Hold my hand," he said, taking the flashlight from her and starting up the stairs.

"Grandma's room, mine," she said as the light floated across the doors and settled on the green baize one at the end of the wide corridor. "The nursery's through there." He tugged at her hand. She wanted to hold back, did not want him to know how afraid she was. The door squeaked a protest, stood open behind them once they had passed through. The nursery door was open. He felt he knew it already as he searched it with his light, lingering on the desk.

255

He felt Margaret trembling, heard her breathing.

"Why did you do that?" she said, frightened, as they were plunged into complete, enveloping darkness.

"Stay there."

"No . . ." she started after him. He bumped into something and cursed. "Russell?"

"Just stay there." Briefly the light flared. He stepped around the stacked boxes, killed the light again, and became a dark silhouette against the black window. Its edges seemed to glow. He made a sound, low in his throat. "Come here," he said. "I think we've found her." He turned the flashlight on. Margaret hurried to him. She stared through the window. Beyond the tangled screen of trees was a distant glow, the intermittent flicker of flames.

"A bonfire?" she said. "Why?"

He reached for her hand again and held it tightly.

The fire was close to the edge of the pond, a crackle of branches enclosing a red heart, flames leaping, dancing, licking. The breeze carried a pall of smoke toward her, stinging her eyes, clogging her throat. When it cleared, she saw him, sitting on the big, flat stone embedded in the bank of the pond. The flames veiled him as she moved forward. Her name sang in the hot splitting of wood.

Ju-lie. Ju-lie. Can't find me.

The breeze, changing direction, obscured him in smoke. For a moment she thought that she had imagined him, conjured him, but when the smoke drifted away, he was standing beyond the flames, looking straight at her. His skin was ruddy from the heat. The stone, on which he stood, made him taller. As though controlled by him, the flames leaped higher, making him shimmer and melt. Only his face hung above the flames, his black hair tangled, his eyes compelling.

As she went slowly to him, moving around the fire, she knew that he was not Jo-Jo, never had been, and as though he read or heard her thoughts, she heard his soft, crackling laughter and something made her look away. Some movement caught in the corner of her eye made her look down into the pond. What she saw froze her. Terror was an icy itching in the flesh. She tried to look away but could not. Nor could she move. Her stomach knotted, her breathing became a series of staccato sobs.

He hung just below the black surface of the water, arms spread, legs splayed, his straight brown hair floating like water weeds around the bloated, innocent face. The blank blue eyes of a doll stared up at her, accusing.

Killed him. Jo-Jo drowned. Ju-lie.

The insidious clutch of his voice freed her. She saw Jo-Jo sink below the surface of the water as she stumbled on along the bank, the fire scorching her. He stood before her, naked, leering, his flesh pink and amber in the firelight. He showed his teeth foul-white in a smile, and held out his arms to her.

Ju-lie. Ju-lie. Come to me.

Her feet shuffled through the grass. A branch, burned through, crashed into the fire. Sparks, flung into the air like scattered sequins, danced and dazzled, settled on his flesh, flowered and died. He stepped down from his stone perch and drew her into his arms, against his flesh.

Margaret screamed. Russell pulled her back against him, his arms folded tightly around her, imprisoning her. He dropped the flash-light, saw it roll away and glow uselessly in the scrub. For some reason he had time to notice a dead leaf caught in Margaret's hair, the snag that a briar had made on the sleeve of her coat. He wanted, out of some instinct of self-preservation, to go on looking at these things, to study them, to absorb himself in them. He wanted to smell her flesh, the perfume she wore, to feel the softness of her hair against his cheek. Anything, anything rather than look up and see . . .

It seemed that Margaret's cry had awakened Julie from some deep trance. She moved now not like an automaton but with all the strength and force of a young and terrified woman. It seemed to Russell that she wrestled with a pillar of smoke, with flames and burning branches, with the very essence of fire itself. The bonfire that stood between them obscured the struggle, showed it all in flashes, glimpses, in the disjointed moments of a dream.

Margaret, struggling, twisting against his arms, her voice thick with obscenities, cries, saw the flame and smoke made flesh, saw with appalling clarity what her daughter struggled with. She lashed

257

out with her heel, kicking Russell's shinbone. His cry of surprise and pain was drowned by her terrible shout.

"Tom!"

His arms faltered around her. She broke free of him, ran toward the fire.

His slow and dreadful face swung toward Margaret, his stale breath hissing. Julie hurled her weight at him, knocking him off balance. He spun around, staggered, seemed about to fall into the pond.

Margaret knew then, with an instinct she would never, for the rest of her life, be able to explain or rationalize, that he must not be allowed to drown. She seized him, screaming, seized him with both her hands fastened to his cold, slippery flesh, and pulled him toward the fire. Her wild eyes locked with Julie's, and she saw that her daughter understood.

Russell, clutching his shin where Margaret had kicked it, started from the trees. All his life he had denied madness; he knew it to be a superstition, an imprecise term. All his working life he had studied the human mind's analyzable disorders. He was a rational man, trained to see what was there, what was actual fact, and yet he found himself looking on madness, powerless to stop it.

Julie danced around the flames, a dervish, beckoning lewdly, tempting. She touched her body, tore at her clothes, offered herself. Margaret, it seemed, her face distorted by the flames, cheered her daughter on. He turned away, disgusted, unable to watch. He bent to rub his leg and felt the folded drawing and the photograph in his pocket. He felt them beneath his fingers. Somehow they connected him with this ritual, with the writhing, obscenely dancing girl, her harpy-mother, who fought flames and almost solid smoke. He would never know why he did what he did then. He would always remember the feeling of loathing, of contamination that possession of the images gave him. He snatched them from his pocket and flung them into the heart of the fire. Heat and smoke exploded outward, driving him back, driving him away.

Something fell, crashing into the fire. Sparks and charred bits of wood, half-burned twigs and embers rose in the air and fell back into the fire. The flames leaped up. The women, working as a team, piled more and more wood on, tore branches from trees to feed the blaze. The flames rose until they threatened to burn the sky.

Margaret stared down into the fire, her heart cold and pitiless. He was not dead. She could tell that from his eyes, which rolled and pleaded with her, yet still threatened. The black, mad eyes of the man who had hacked at her wrist, his teeth bared in loathing. But his body, the body she had once delighted to touch and caress, to receive into hers, that same body which had grown foul and putrescent with desire for his own offspring, began to blacken and burn. Under her relentless gaze his flesh melted like tallow, his bones charred like wood, beaded with ruby embers. She saw the shape of his body burned into the ground, arms outstretched, legs splayed. At last the fire collapsed under its own blazing weight, obscuring even his blackened, skeletal face.

Julie stared down into the fire. Her flesh burned in sympathy with his. He rose up, reaching for her with blackened arms, flames spurting from his flesh, his fingers turned to candles, licking toward her. Only with the entire force of her will could she drive him back, back into the flames. They seemed to welcome him, to draw him down. Time and again he rose in a nightmare cycle, each time more skeletal, burned, glowing. The smoke in her nostrils was sweet with the smell of his roasting flesh, sickly sweet. Her knees buckled. She knelt beside the fire. He was almost gone, almost burned to cinder and ash. The fire would die, she knew, and a wind would rise to scatter the ash about the garden. . . .

She felt a cold, damp breath of air on her face.

Ju-lie. Ju-lie.

She lifted her head, stared through the dying flames. She had no strength left to prevent him. Some strong, healthy part of herself knew that it was necessary, essential, even though it was horrible to observe. And she had to observe it.

He rose, small and frail, from the black pond, water streaming from him. He looked so small and lonely, looked at her with such gentle, pleading eyes, that she felt her heart must surely break. Groping with her hand on the ground, she found a stick and stirred the fire so that new flames leaped up, dancing, and became yellow-transparent. She thought his name, breathed it, and little Jo-Jo, her

259

childhood friend, passed into the flames. They leaped up, held him prisoner. She hoped that they would warm and dry him. He shimmered, seemed to reach out to her, and then was gone. In the sighing and settling of the fire, she heard her name for the last time in a boy's piping treble.

"Oh, my poor, poor Jo-Jo," she whispered, and covered her face with her blackened hands, weeping.

Russell searched his pockets for cigarettes, and remembered that he had left them in his briefcase. His bones ached as he pushed away from the tree against which he had been leaning. It was like waking from one dream into another. Lifting his head to the cool air, he saw morning streaking the sky. A gray, uncertain daylight fell across the scene in front of him. The black circle of the fire smoldered sullenly, but gave out no heat. A dead leaf moved across the black surface of the pond as though propelled by a child's steady breath. Russell did not know what he had experienced. He only knew that he felt like an intruder, and was uncertain whether he dared approach the women huddled together by the remains of the fire.

Margaret's back was to him. She was kneeling, cradling Julie to her breast. He saw with certainty, now, what had previously seemed a trick of the light: She held her daughter with both arms, the left rubbing her back. Margaret held her safe, he thought, and had no wish to stop the smile that spread easily to his lips. At last he thought he understood about "safe."

Of course, he knew that paralysis could be the result of a trauma. It would be interesting to explore the possibility of a child's trauma so affecting a parent that they developed some sympathetic dysfunction. When the child was "healed," the parent's "miracle" could occur. But this child and her mother, he recognized as he moved nervously toward them, would never be a case history to him.

His tall shadow fell over them. A bird began to sing, rousing others to a chorus. The last embers died and blackened. Margaret looked up at him. Her hazel eyes were steady, searching his. In her arms, Julie stirred. Margaret bent her head at once toward her, her lips automatically forming the reassuring words and sounds of childhood. Julie sat up, pushing her mother away. Margaret reached for her, tried to restrain her. Russell put his hand on Margaret's shoulder, squeezing it tight.

Julie knelt, then stood, brushing at her clothes, straightening them. She stared briefly at the black, dead fire, then moved away, standing separate from them. Margaret continued to watch her, then slowly held out her left hand to Russell.

"Help me, please?"

He pulled her up and embraced her. She hugged him, seeking his warmth. Julie turned to look at them, then slowly walked past them and on across the gray garden, making her own way.